CW00525345

FROM THE OG LOGS
ANGUS OG

by *Bain*   Compiled by Sheila Bain   Introduced by Jack McLean

ZIPO

Copyright © Sheila Bain, 1999
Introduction Copyright © Jack McLean, 1999
All rights reserved
The moral right of the author has been asserted

First published in Great Britain in 1999 by
ZIPO PUBLISHING LIMITED
Suite 550, 355 Byres Road, Glasgow G12 8QZ
Fax: 0141 357 6862 email: zipo@014.mbe.uk.com

ISBN 1 901984 04 4

Other ZIPO titles available:

Bud Neill's Magic!	ISBN 1 901984 01 X
Lobey Dosser - Further Adventures of the Wee Boy!	ISBN 1 901984 00 1
Shuggie & Duggie in Scotsmen Behaving Badly	ISBN 1 901984 06 0
We'll Support You Evermore - A Life in the Tartan Army	ISBN 1 901984 02 8

No part of this book may be reproduced or transmitted in any form or by any other means without the permission in writing from the publisher, except by a reviewer who wishes to quote brief passages in connection with a review written for insertion in a magazine, newspaper or broadcast.

A catalogue for this book is available from the British Library

www.scotoons.co.uk

The publisher wishes to thank all those involved in the publication of this book, particularly:
Sheila Bain, Jack McLean, The Daily Record, Andrew, Debbie and Emma from Office World and Hoss.

Printed and bound in Great Britain by The Cromwell Press, Wiltshire

CONTENTS

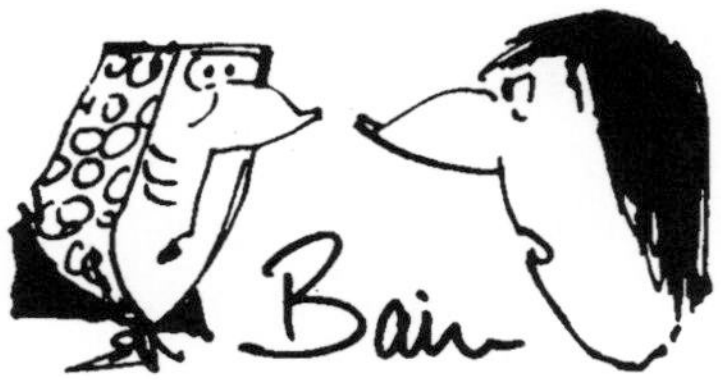

Bain

The Og Logs was the name given by Ewen to the set of notebooks in which he jotted down a memo of each cartoon strip which appeared in the *Daily Record*. Interspersed throughout are sketches to remind him of the appearance of the characters who appeared in the stories. I now find The Og Logs a very useful source of information when cataloguing or compiling cartoons for a book or an exhibition.

Sheila Bain, 1999

INTRODUCTION

In the Gaelic Og means young. Not so oddly Ewen means young as well. Angus means unique, a one-off if you like. I am not sure if Ewen Bain was conscious of any of that when he came up with the name of his hero, if hero Angus Og can be called. He was certainly conscious of the Gaelic even if he was actually born in Maryhill in Glasgow. It is ever a delight to myself that most Gaelic speakers, in Europe anyway, were born and brought up in my own native city and always nice to be able to taunt them with that fact. I speak the language not at all though my father, a second generation Mulloch from Dervaig in Mull did. My taunts are a way of getting back for the fact that my father scolded me in English but smacked me in the old tongue, (he lost his temper in Gaelic). But this is an aside which has no relevance to Ewen at all for you never met a more even-tempered man. I know better than most for I first met Ewen Bain when he was a schoolteacher back in the 'Fifties when dominies enjoyed a savagery which would have landed large numbers of them in the jail today. For Ewen was one of my Art teachers at a very famous Glasgow school, Allan Glen's.

He taught a good many years too and I don't know what he was thinking of. He lasted in that dreariest of professions until 1969 when he went into full-time cartooning. Come to think of it I did much the same thing, teaching Art while working for some years as a journalist. Ewen should have taught me better. Actually one thing I do remember that he did teach me, or at least he infected me with. I had no discipline with a class either. Ewen certainly had none. About the worst discipline I ever saw he had. He was not out to become the terror of the school.

What I did find out years later was that he enjoyed Allan Glen's Art department a lot mainly because the school, a hotbed of science which had as alumni such figures as Lord Kelvin, Alexander Fleming, John Logie Baird, and incidentally Charles Rennie Mackintosh, had in his years a magnificent variety of eccentrics such as Ralph Cowan who in the 1950s sported shoulder length hair, and the splendidly splenetic James McGill. The sort of boys who specialised in Art in this technological hothouse of a school were pretty eccentric too. Ewen flourished in the place.

He was already becoming famous as a cartoonist and one of his tricks when we boys in his class became a little over exuberant was to draw caricatures of the locals on the blackboard. He drew other teachers, (he was especially satirical about the headmaster, a bully who thought Art impossibly effete), and the boys in the class. I wish he'd given me the sketch he did of me, to the howls of my fellow pupils, on paper. I had affected the best "*bop*" hairstyle in the school, all quiff and Trugel and Duck's Arse. He had me portrayed as some eighteenth century Macaroni with several other boys assisting in holding me up, my coiffeur being that heavy. He'd drawn a crane with a comb in its maw. The strange thing was - well not so strange when you got to know Ewen - was that it wasn't cruel or anything, even if it was marvellously satirical. In fact, being selected for his sketches was definitely a kudos. But this was something I knew long before most of the populace of Scotland and beyond did, when he was delighting us all with his Angus Og strips. Ewen drew himself on that blackboard, often. And he drew himself as what was to become the infamous, the nefarious, Angus Og.

Sheila, his wife of nearly forty years spoke of the Ewen she knew better than anybody else - talking to her of her extraordinary husband, you get the impression that Ewen was so unique that even she couldn't get to the hidden depths of this highland loch of a personality. Sure he was born in Skye and like many first generation highlanders spent his summer holidays on that idyllic, (then more than now), island. Thus he inherited that slow, dry, humour which is characteristic of the Highlander. But Western Isles and Hebridean are different from main-landers. For a start they leave their islands: they don't stay. There was never much alternative. The result is a bittersweetness about the island's men and women. And it shows in their humour. Ewen inherited that sense of cool irony, that slowness and sleightness of hand. Highland humour is not the quick urban slickness of the cities or the glibness of, say Ireland, but belongs to the world of Celtic magic in which the trick of story and fable is the belated surprise, as though the three card trick of the street busker was somehow a shock to the prestidigitateur himself. If this sounds dreadfully analytical I am going to get worse.

For Ewen was, after all, brought up in Glasgow, then even more than now, a big city with an improbable American feel to it; packed full of wideboys, spivs, city slickers and with a level of bibulous daftness which gladly welcomed the surrealism of foreign climes such as the Hebridean islands. Ewen went to Woodside Secondary, a good, though hardly posh, school in what is now called the West End of Glasgow. He was a good though barely diligent pupil but found himself enrolled at Glasgow School of Art. This was barely conceivable for Highland lads o'pairts and I went through the same experience myself. A spell in the Royal Navy during the war, (he was of course a coder), was followed by his graduation at the Art school and then schoolteaching which was then about the only damned thing an art school graduate could earn a living at unless it was bar-work or hawking your mutton round unsavoury districts in Earl's Court. I am sure many an art teacher thought a little of the latter as an alternative. Before Allan Glen's it was a spell at Kennedy Street, a rough junior secondary school not a kick in the bahookie from Glen's itself geographically but a million cultural miles away from the alma mater of Lord Kelvin and his ilk, and then some years in Kingsridge in Drumchapel, an unlovely establishment in which art teaching must have been like growing potatoes. It was underground and nobody dug them up. I mention the schools quite simply because there is a book waiting to be written about art teachers everywhere who suffered at the hands of school boards and the like and got to buggery out of it on the strength of talent and desperation.

At first he did little box cartoons, for the old *Glasgow Bulletin* and other publications and then started up his first Angus Og strip for the *Bulletin* itself. Later he went to the Scottish *Daily Record* and the *Sunday Mail*. Like most of us who transfer from bloody awful trades like teaching or insurance or whatever into journalism or art or music I'll bet he thought he was lucky to be earning a living without working.

This is of course nonsense because deadlines are bastards and the worst of all deadlines are for columnists like myself but even worser for cartoonists. News people always know how things are going to turn out because they deal, sort of, in realities. Columnists and cartoonists make up their own endings. But it is always a damn close run thing.

He died, following influenza, in December 1989, just before Christmas. Sadly missed isnae the phrase at all. Despite attempts by many a talented cartoonist nobody has ever replaced him. I suppose in a way Ewen did replace another humourist; wee, giant Bud Neill, both so different from each other and so similar. If that's a cliché it is a truism as well. Bud Neill I never met but he created a world which we recognised though God knows how because it was his own wee world. Ewen Bain did the same. Bud was a bit of a cartoon character himself with his Cab Calloway zoot suits and Kandinsky ties. Ewen was always immaculately dressed but in a style which made you realise a half hour later that was not only of it's own but you couldn't remember what he was wearing. He was a wonderful storyteller but afterwards you discovered that you'd done most of the talking. He was shy but garrulous, abstemious and liked a dram, gentle with a nice wee tartness when he wanted it. The most apolitical of men who lampooned politicians in a way so soft, so off-beat that it must have got to them in the way of the white rose of Scotland of Hugh MacDiarmid: *"So white, so sweet, and broke the heart"*.

This makes Ewen and indeed Angus Og seem somehow melancholy but despair and sadness is never very far away from a Gael's psyche. It is a graceful and silvery sadness lightened by idiocy and a sudden inexplicable vitality. Ewen's creation - I suspect a kind of alter ego - Angus Og, was a certain type of Highlander. A Western

Isles flyboy. He has a long history in literature, from the Ancients to recent times. Arnold Bennett's the Card could be Angus, but so could Sergeant Bilko, or Del Boy in Fools and Horses, or Lafcadio or Julian Sorel or É. The great thing about Angus was that he was ever inventive, ever enthusiastic, ever at it. Always trying to make a pound or a point or two. His greatest accolade, ever, came from Mephistopheles himself when our Angus becomes an employee of his. Looking down on earth Satan says to his executives: "*Oh, Good! Our Drambeg agent is a disgrace to Christmas*". Truth to tell Angus Og, the perpetually young, the always unique rapscallion which Ewen Bain created, was a disgrace to all of us with any sense of morality, seriousness, or a finely-tuned pomposity. In short, a role model for Scotland's - anywhere's - youth at that.

But if Ewen created Angus Og as his larger than life protagonist he created too a grand number of characters in a technicolour unknown to Hollywood at its most vulgar. There was his constant pal, his inverted Sancho Panza, Lachie Mor. Lachie I've met, many times. Often seen in double vision - for Lachie took a dram from time to time - Angus's bosom buddy never wavered in his support for the Og vision of more money and more fun. Angus's brother, Donald, was a yokel in dungarees, a nice, thick, lad ever capable of being duped by his smart brother, or indeed Rosie the cow if it came to that. (Rosie the cow became a favourite character of mine. Rosie somehow spoke to you but not as well as Granny McBrochan's cat who spoke in spades.) Granny McBrochan's cat was an often vile tempered toper who could not only speak but could do it with an aplomb which often saw off even the best of Angus's oratory. He is a very sharp cat indeed and where would Granny McBrochan be without him? A speywife without a cat would be sad indeed, and Granny was but a wifie without him. Granny herself was a foul-smelling old witch who could have the Reverend McSonachan Wee Free theology tied up in more knots than Pascal and St. Ignatious Loyola could have managed even with the help of the Almighty. You will discover the depths of the harassed Rev. McSonachan's woes at the hands and deeds of Angus. The minister's cat, Obadiah, certainly will attest to that.

But the good meenister is not the only mortal enemy to our hero. There is always the local polis, Constable McPhater. The constable has spent a heritage let alone a lifetime intent on getting his hands and the long arm of the law on Angus. To no avail, as you might expect. The other Drambeg persons who most wish to get their hands on Angus are the Laird of Drambeg and his lady wife. The Laird and spouse are probably the last humans in the world to use the epithets "*blaggard*" and "*cad*" but they do so regularly of Angus, and, one confesses, with righteousness on their sides. Above all on this island who wants a hands-on experience, so to speak, is the long suffering Mairileen, Angus's sort of girlfriend who has pursued him long and lustily for, well, the decades Ewen wrote the script. Angus may very well be persuaded to fall, temporarily, for some beauty from off the Glasgow boat, but he will never fall for Mairileen's less than feminine wiles. The poor girl is of course a dreadful slur on Highland womanhood but then she is also nearly accurate and I didn't say that. Not lastly but lastly enough for me are my favourites: Angus Og's Glasgow cousins. Neds and fall guys, spivs and sharpies, and easy on the ears, (the lassies on the eyes). There are a lot more characters in Ewen Bain's world but, don't you think that's enough to be going on with? Dear God, Angus is a sufficiency for us all.

Jack McLean, Glasgow 1999

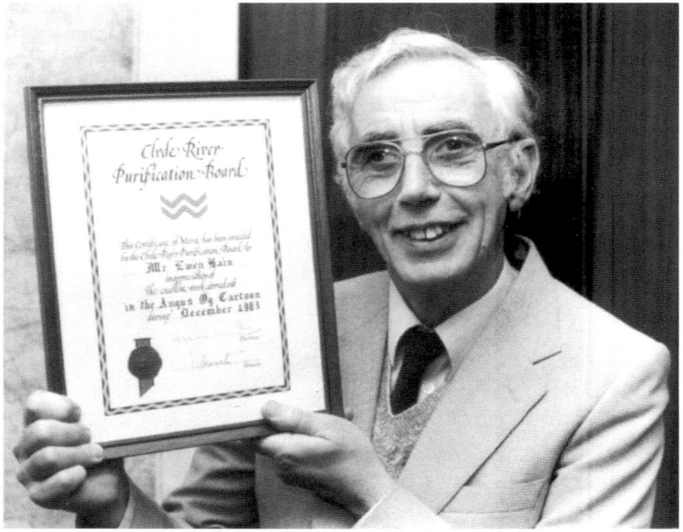
Clyde River
Purification Board
Mr Ewen Bain
in the Angus Og Cartoon
December 1983

**EWEN BAIN
AND THE CLYDE RIVER
PURIFICATION BOARD AWARD**

Ewen was presented with this certificate for his many tributes to the work of the Clyde Purification Board in his Angus Og story *The Kelpie* which appeared in the *Daily Record* between November 1983 and January 1984. I seem to remember a news item about salmon reappearing in the River Clyde after an absence of many years. This probably was Ewen's inspiration for the story and, not content with salmon, the appearance of the mythical Kelpie, a water horse, and of course - mermaids!

Sheila Bain, 1999

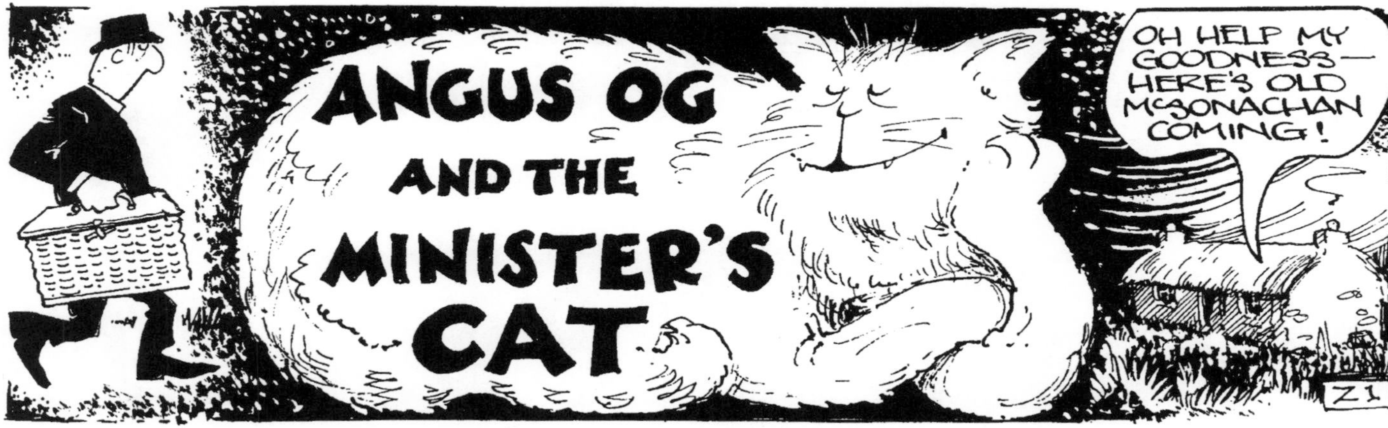
ANGUS OG AND THE MINISTER'S CAT
OH HELP MY GOODNESS— HERE'S OLD McSONACHAN COMING!

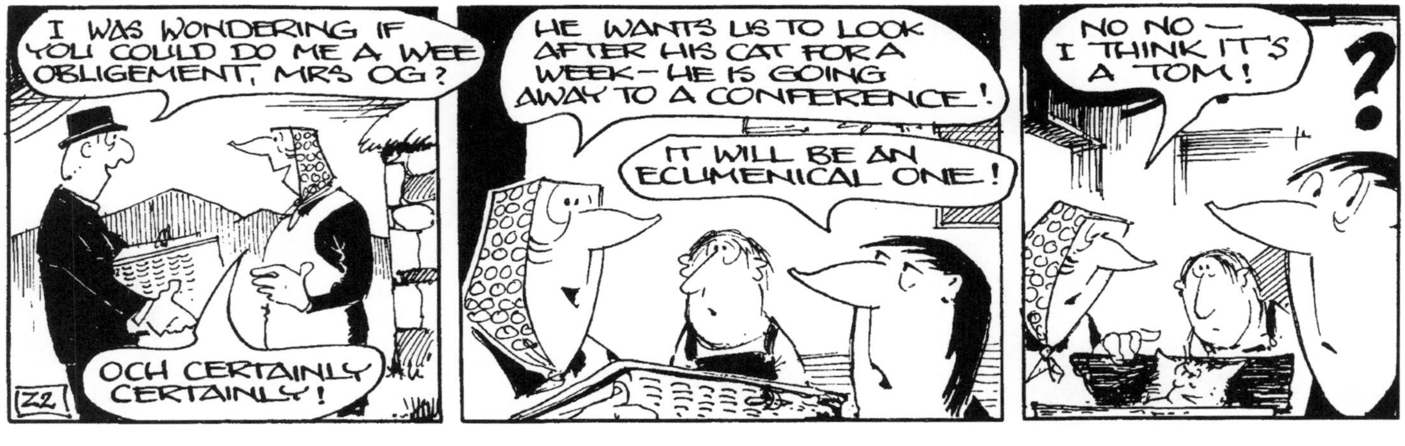
I WAS WONDERING IF YOU COULD DO ME A WEE OBLIGEMENT, MRS OG?
OCH CERTAINLY CERTAINLY!
HE WANTS US TO LOOK AFTER HIS CAT FOR A WEEK—HE IS GOING AWAY TO A CONFERENCE!
IT WILL BE AN ECUMENICAL ONE!
NO NO— I THINK IT'S A TOM!
?

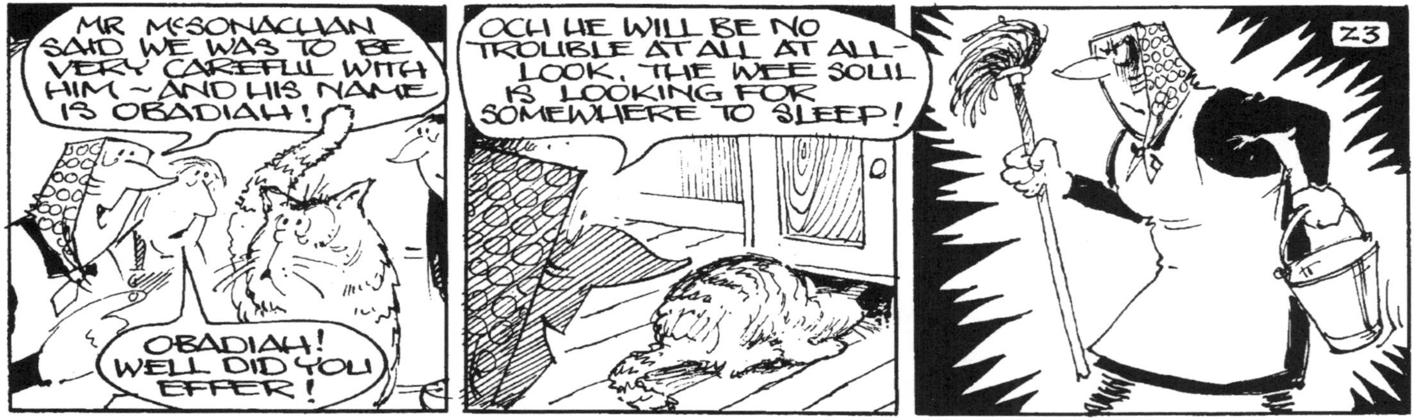
MR McSONACHAN SAID WE WAS TO BE VERY CAREFULL WITH HIM ~ AND HIS NAME IS OBADIAH!
OBADIAH! WELL DID YOU EFFER!
OCH HE WILL BE NO TROUBLE AT ALL AT ALL - LOOK, THE WEE SOUL IS LOOKING FOR SOMEWHERE TO SLEEP!
23

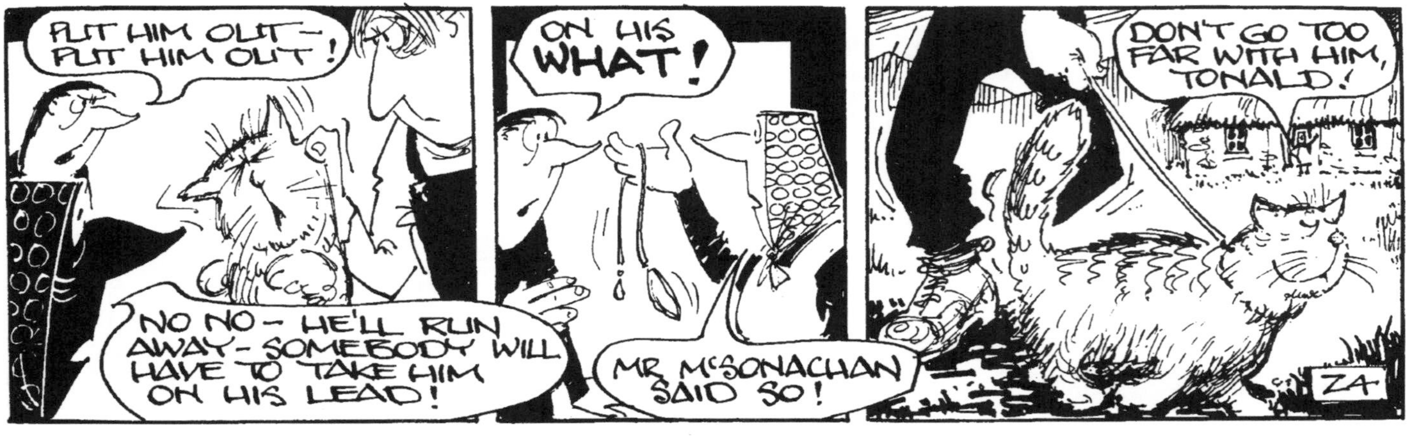
PUT HIM OUT - PUT HIM OUT!
NO NO - HE'LL RUN AWAY - SOMEBODY WILL HAVE TO TAKE HIM ON HIS LEAD!
ON HIS WHAT!
MR McSONACHAN SAID SO!
DON'T GO TOO FAR WITH HIM, TONALD!
24

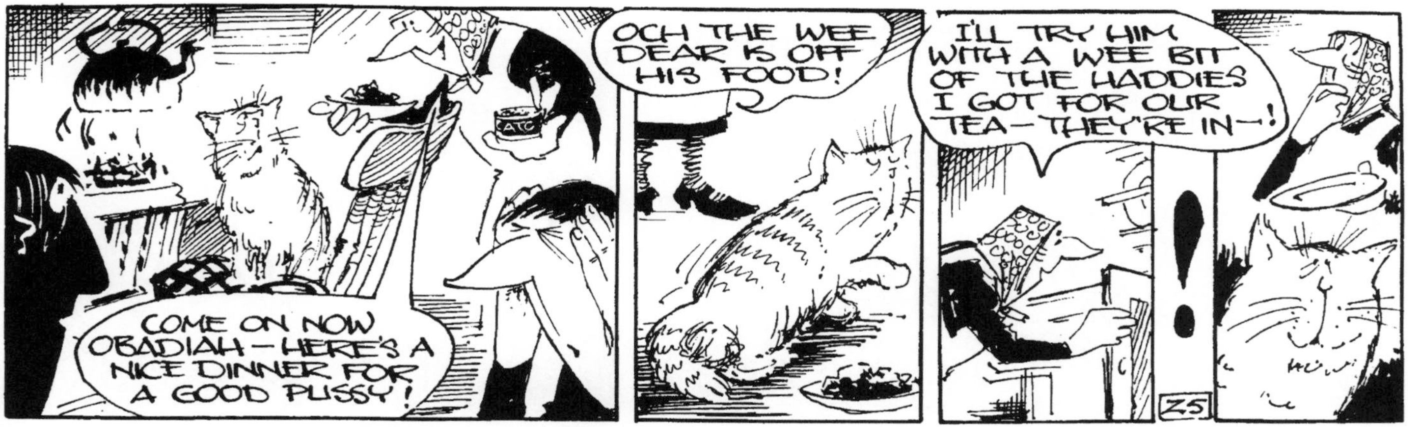
COME ON NOW OBADIAH — HERE'S A NICE DINNER FOR A GOOD PUSSY!
OCH THE WEE DEAR IS OFF HIS FOOD!
I'LL TRY HIM WITH A WEE BIT OF THE HADDIES I GOT FOR OUR TEA — THEY'RE IN —!
!
25

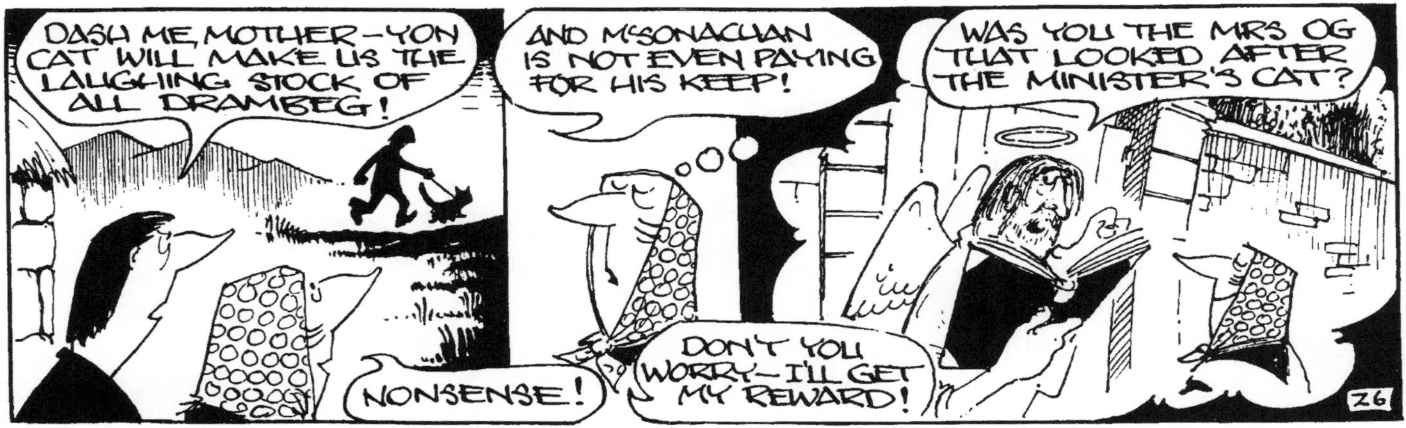
DASH ME, MOTHER — YON CAT WILL MAKE US THE LAUGHING STOCK OF ALL DRAMBEG!
NONSENSE!
AND McSONACHAN IS NOT EVEN PAYING FOR HIS KEEP!
DON'T YOU WORRY — I'LL GET MY REWARD!
WAS YOU THE MRS OG THAT LOOKED AFTER THE MINISTER'S CAT?
26

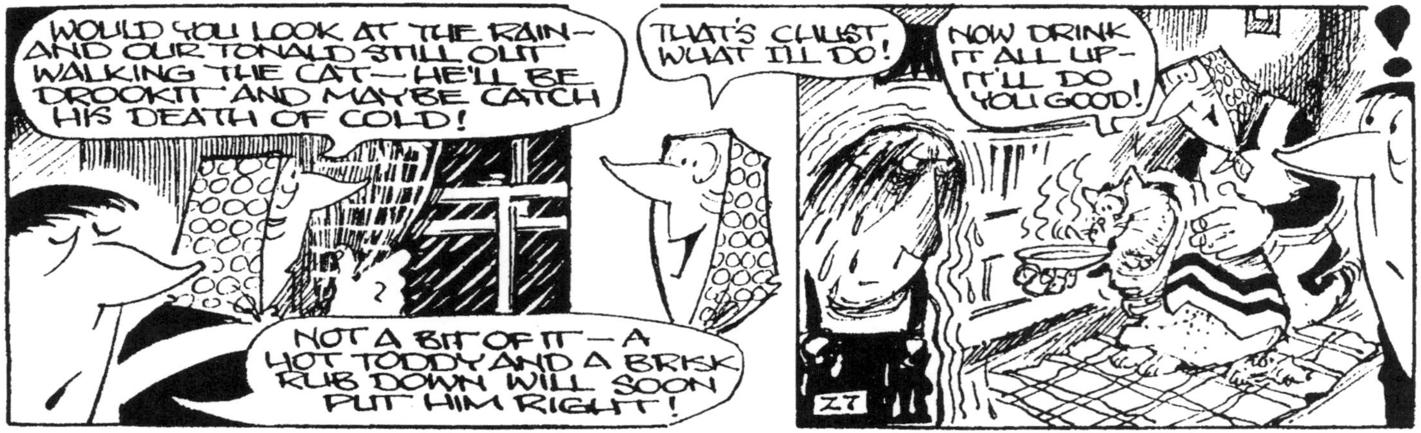
WOULD YOU LOOK AT THE RAIN-AND OUR TONALD STILL OUT WALKING THE CAT-HE'LL BE DROOKIT AND MAYBE CATCH HIS DEATH OF COLD!
NOT A BIT OF IT-A HOT TODDY AND A BRISK RUB DOWN WILL SOON PUT HIM RIGHT!
THAT'S CHUST WHAT I'LL DO!
NOW DRINK IT ALL UP-IT'LL DO YOU GOOD!
!
27

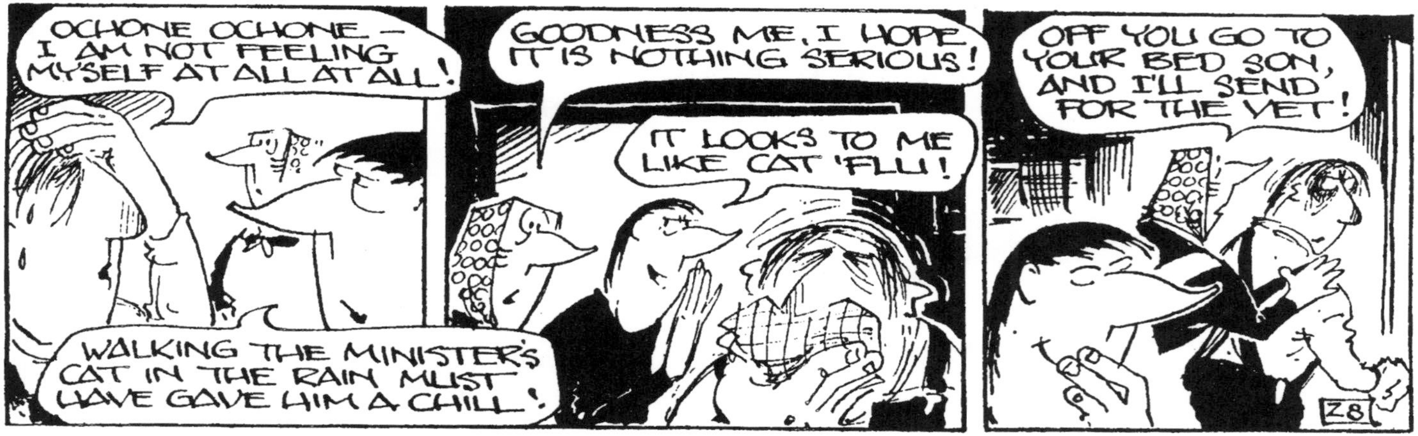
OCHONE OCHONE-I AM NOT FEELING MYSELF AT ALL AT ALL!
WALKING THE MINISTER'S CAT IN THE RAIN MUST HAVE GAVE HIM A CHILL!
GOODNESS ME, I HOPE IT IS NOTHING SERIOUS!
IT LOOKS TO ME LIKE CAT 'FLU!
OFF YOU GO TO YOUR BED SON, AND I'LL SEND FOR THE VET!
28

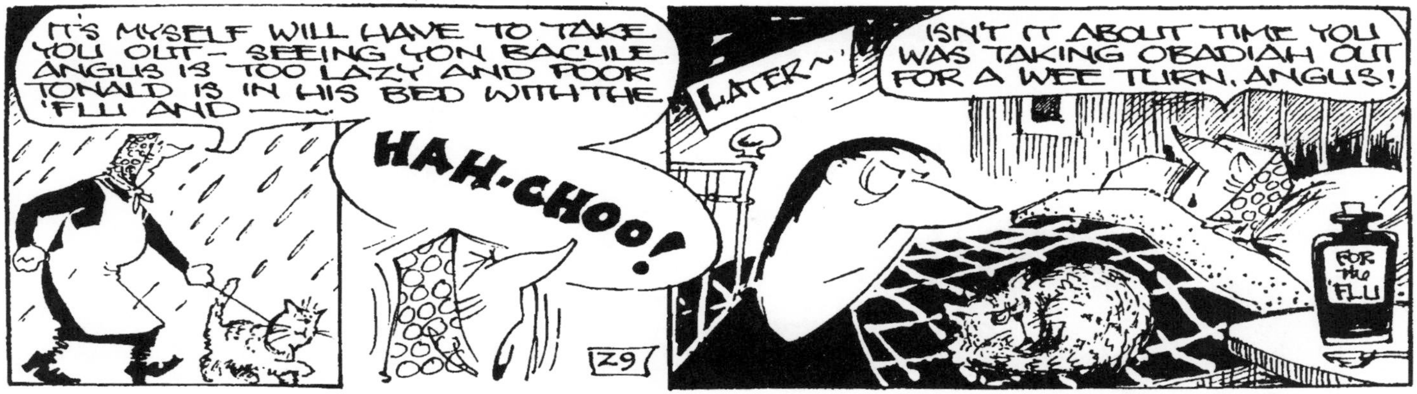
IT'S MYSELF WILL HAVE TO TAKE YOU OUT - SEEING YON BACHLE ANGUS IS TOO LAZY AND POOR TONALD IS IN HIS BED WITH THE 'FLU AND ——
HAH-CHOO!
Z9
LATER~
ISN'T IT ABOUT TIME YOU WAS TAKING OBADIAH OUT FOR A WEE TURN, ANGUS!
FOR the FLU

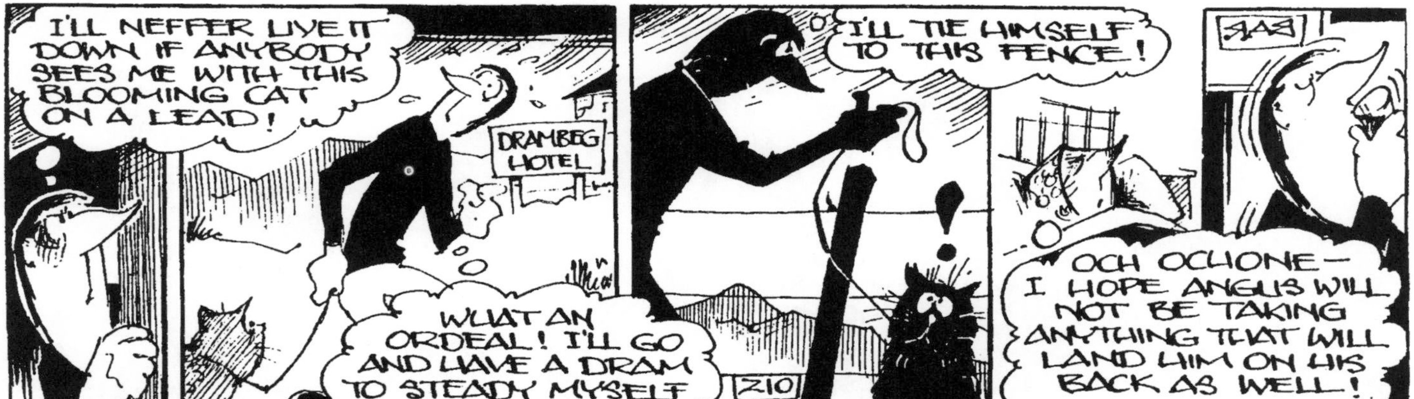
I'LL NEFFER LIVE IT DOWN IF ANYBODY SEES ME WITH THIS BLOOMING CAT ON A LEAD!
DRAMBEG HOTEL
WHAT AN ORDEAL! I'LL GO AND HAVE A DRAM TO STEADY MYSELF
I'LL TIE HIMSELF TO THIS FENCE!
Z10
BAR
OCH OCHONE — I HOPE ANGUS WILL NOT BE TAKING ANYTHING THAT WILL LAND HIM ON HIS BACK AS WELL!

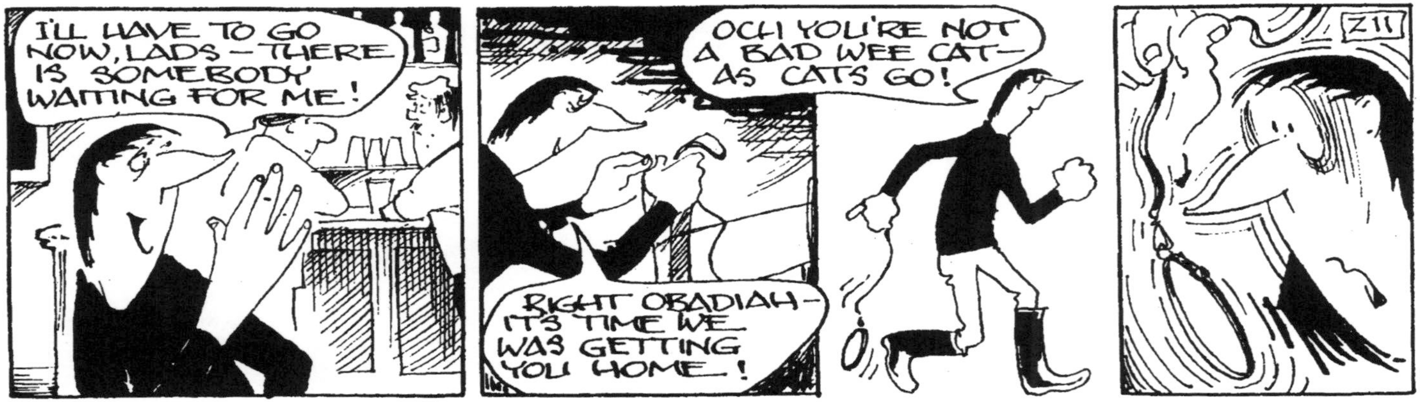
I'LL HAVE TO GO NOW, LADS – THERE IS SOMEBODY WAITING FOR ME!
RIGHT OBADIAH – IT'S TIME WE WAS GETTING YOU HOME!
OCH YOU'RE NOT A BAD WEE CAT – AS CATS GO!
211

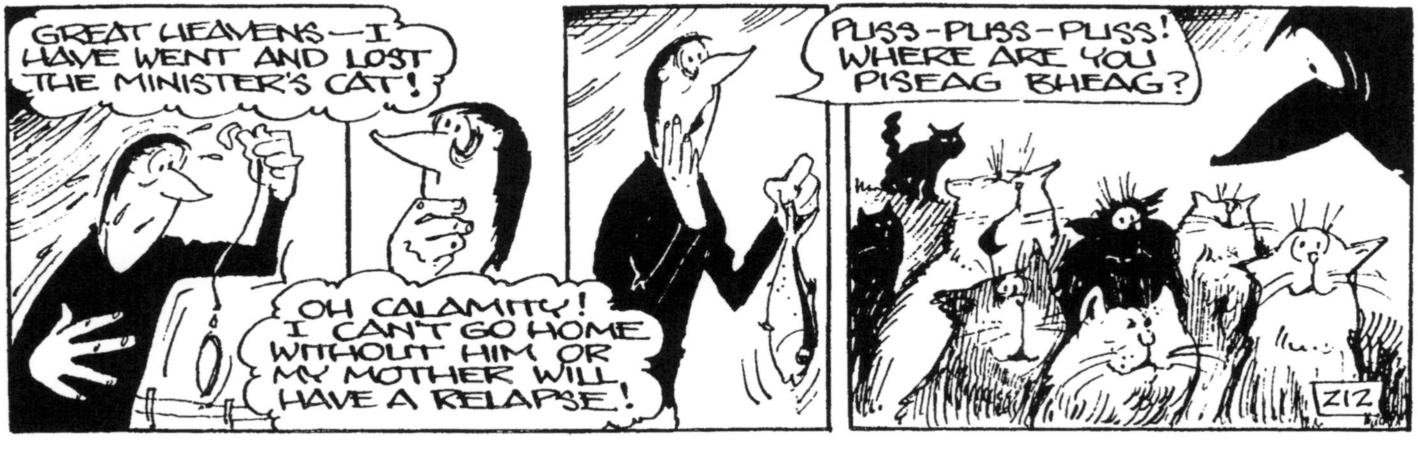
GREAT HEAVENS – I HAVE WENT AND LOST THE MINISTER'S CAT!
OH CALAMITY! I CAN'T GO HOME WITHOUT HIM OR MY MOTHER WILL HAVE A RELAPSE!
PUSS-PUSS-PUSS! WHERE ARE YOU PISEAG BHEAG?
212

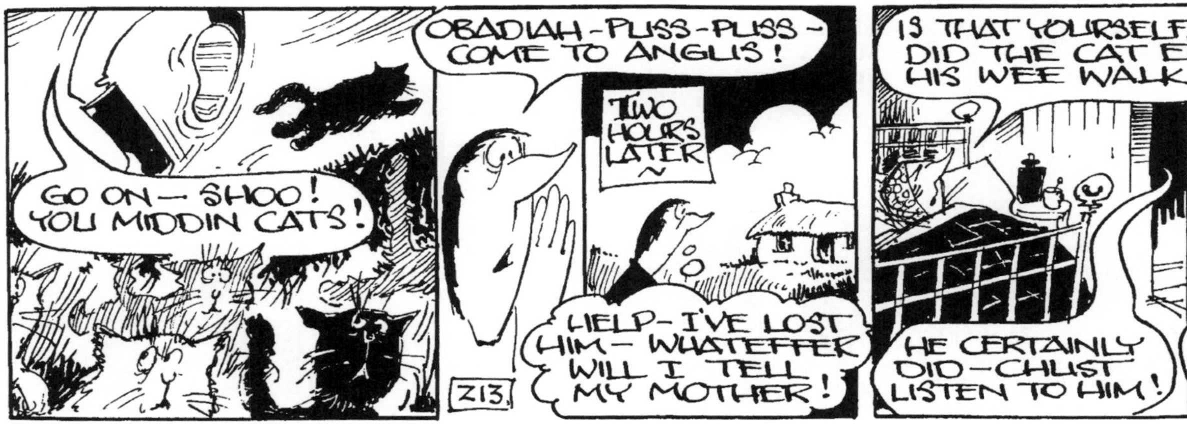
GO ON — SHOO! YOU MIDDIN CATS!
OBADIAH - PLISS - PLISS - COME TO ANGUS!
TWO HOURS LATER ~
HELP - I'VE LOST HIM - WHATEFFER WILL I TELL MY MOTHER!
213.
IS THAT YOURSELF, ANGUS? DID THE CAT ENJOY HIS WEE WALK?
HE CERTAINLY DID - CHUST LISTEN TO HIM!
MIAOW!

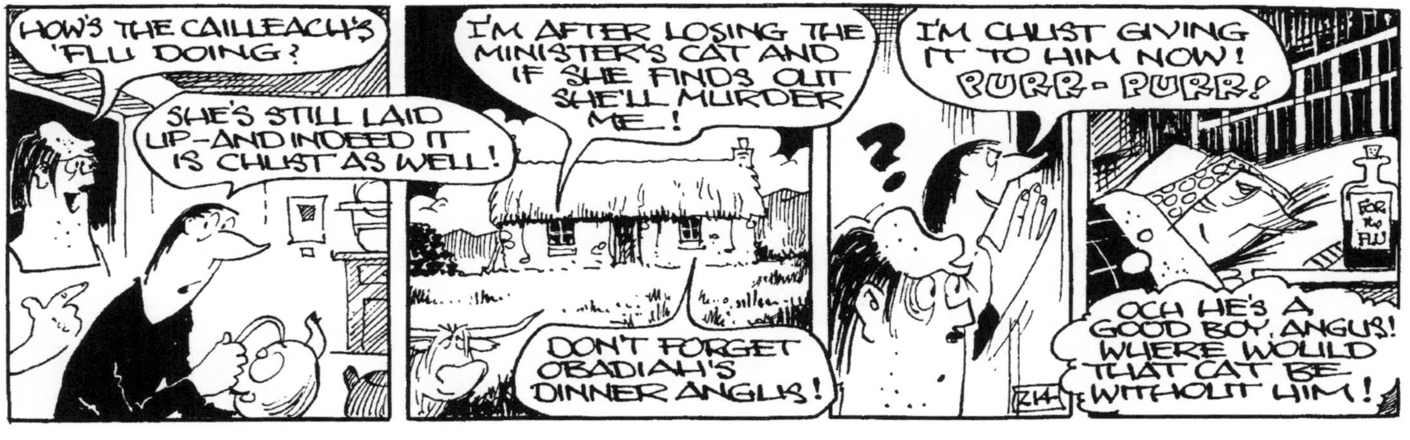
HOW'S THE CAILLEACH'S 'FLU DOING?
SHE'S STILL LAID UP - AND INDEED IT IS CHUST AS WELL!
I'M AFTER LOSING THE MINISTER'S CAT AND IF SHE FINDS OUT SHE'LL MURDER ME!
DON'T FORGET OBADIAH'S DINNER ANGUS!
I'M CHUST GIVING IT TO HIM NOW! PURR - PURR!
FOR THE FLU
OCH HE'S A GOOD BOY, ANGUS! WHERE WOULD THAT CAT BE WITHOUT HIM!
214

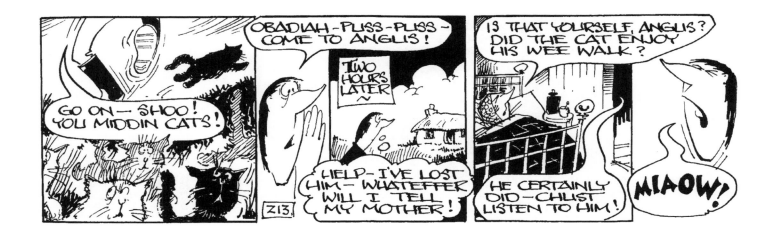

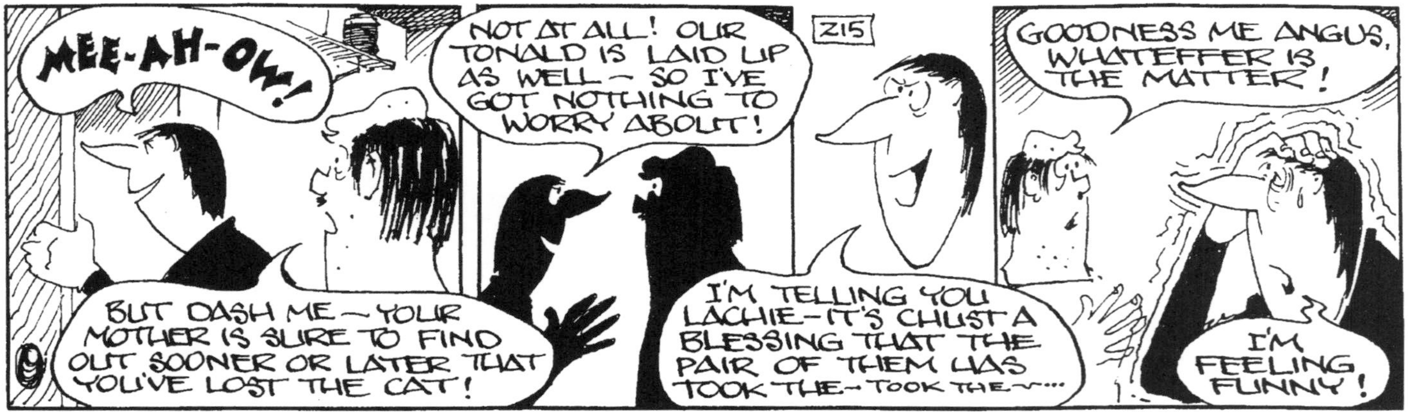
MEE-AH-OW!
BUT DASH ME — YOUR MOTHER IS SURE TO FIND OUT SOONER OR LATER THAT YOU'VE LOST THE CAT!
NOT AT ALL! OUR TONALD IS LAID UP AS WELL — SO I'VE GOT NOTHING TO WORRY ABOUT!
215
I'M TELLING YOU LACHIE — IT'S CHUST A BLESSING THAT THE PAIR OF THEM HAS TOOK THE — TOOK THE —....
GOODNESS ME ANGUS, WHATEFFER IS THE MATTER!
I'M FEELING FUNNY!

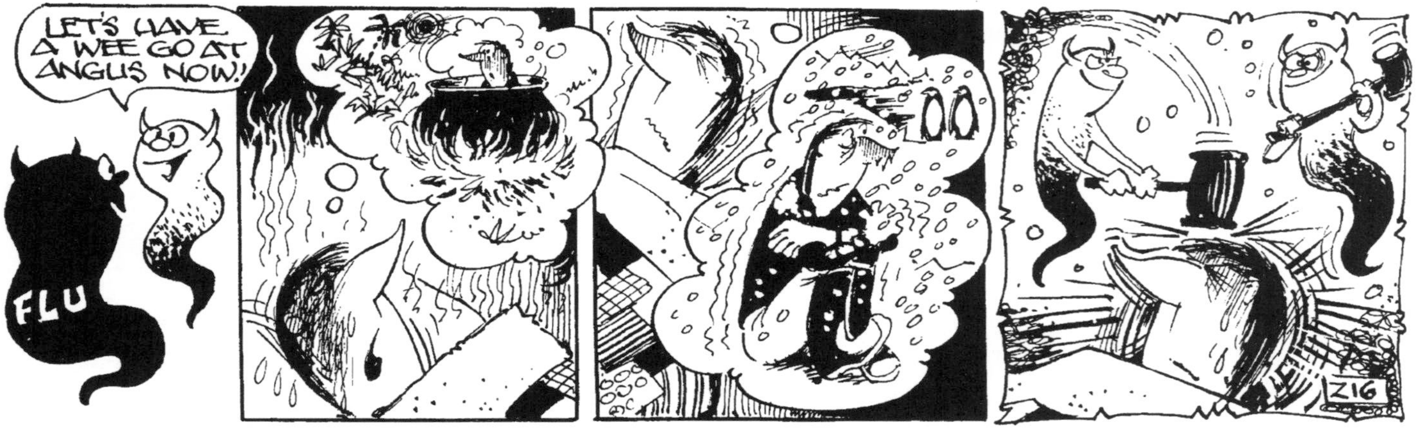
LET'S HAVE A WEE GO AT ANGUS NOW!
FLU
216

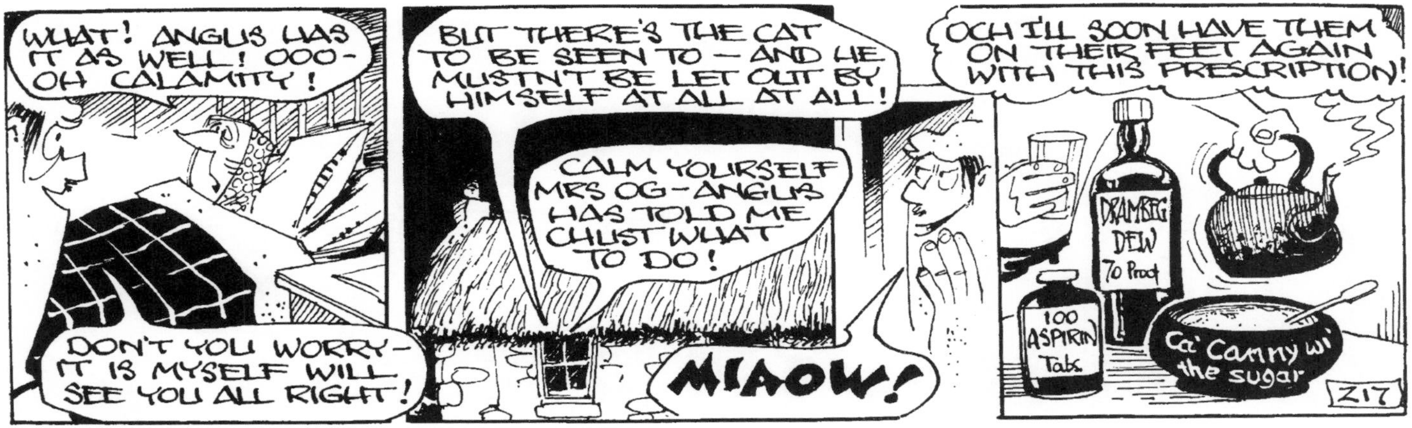
WHAT! ANGUS HAS IT AS WELL! OOO-OH CALAMITY!
DON'T YOU WORRY- IT IS MYSELF WILL SEE YOU ALL RIGHT!
BUT THERE'S THE CAT TO BE SEEN TO — AND HE MUSTN'T BE LET OUT BY HIMSELF AT ALL AT ALL!
CALM YOURSELF MRS OG - ANGUS HAS TOLD ME CHUST WHAT TO DO!
MIAOW!
OCH I'LL SOON HAVE THEM ON THEIR FEET AGAIN WITH THIS PRESCRIPTION!
DRAMBEG DEW 70 Proof
100 ASPIRIN Tabs.
Ca' Canny wi' the sugar
217

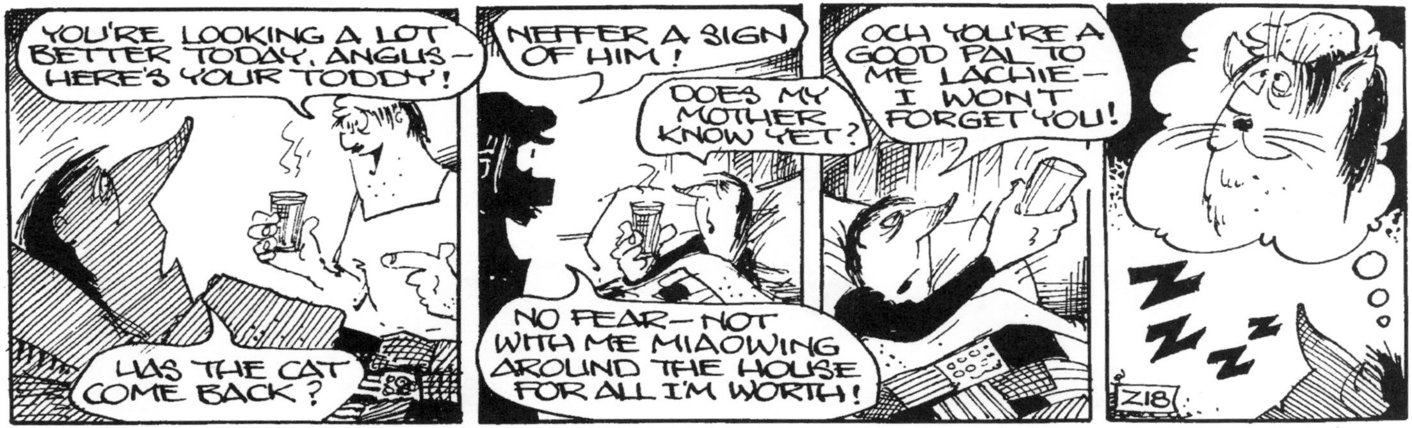
YOU'RE LOOKING A LOT BETTER TODAY, ANGUS - HERE'S YOUR TODDY!
HAS THE CAT COME BACK?
NEFFER A SIGN OF HIM!
DOES MY MOTHER KNOW YET?
NO FEAR - NOT WITH ME MIAOWING AROUND THE HOUSE FOR ALL I'M WORTH!
OCH YOU'RE A GOOD PAL TO ME LACHIE - I WON'T FORGET YOU!
Z Z Z Z
218

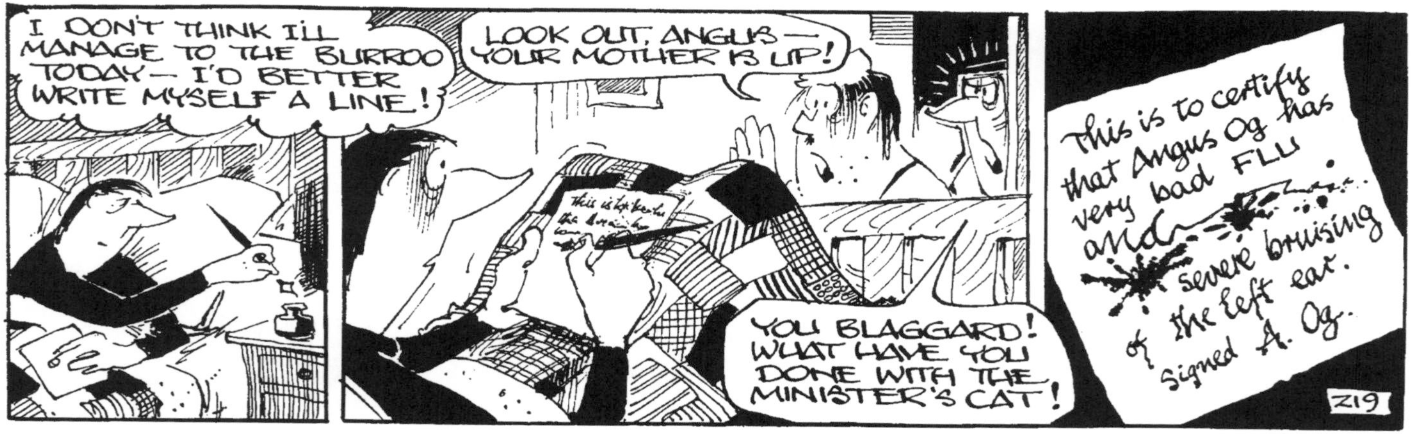
I DON'T THINK I'LL MANAGE TO THE BURROO TODAY— I'D BETTER WRITE MYSELF A LINE!
LOOK OUT, ANGUS— YOUR MOTHER IS UP!
YOU BLAGGARD! WHAT HAVE YOU DONE WITH THE MINISTER'S CAT!
This is to certify that Angus Og has very bad FLU and severe bruising of the left ear. signed A. Og.
219

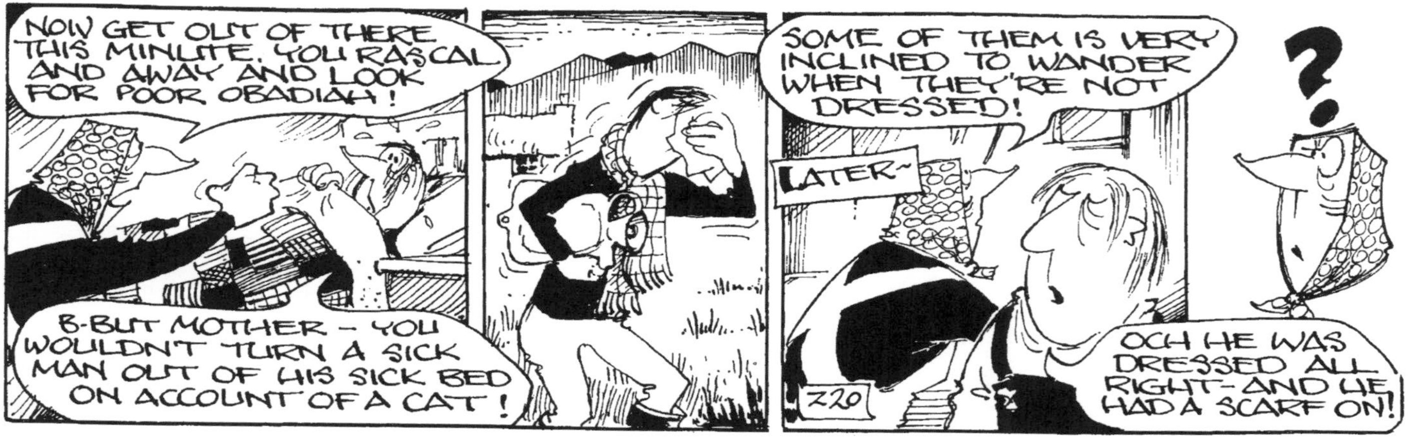
NOW GET OUT OF THERE THIS MINUTE, YOU RASCAL AND AWAY AND LOOK FOR POOR OBADIAH!
B-BUT MOTHER – YOU WOULDN'T TURN A SICK MAN OUT OF HIS SICK BED ON ACCOUNT OF A CAT!
LATER~
SOME OF THEM IS VERY INCLINED TO WANDER WHEN THEY'RE NOT DRESSED!
?
OCH HE WAS DRESSED ALL RIGHT– AND HE HAD A SCARF ON!
220

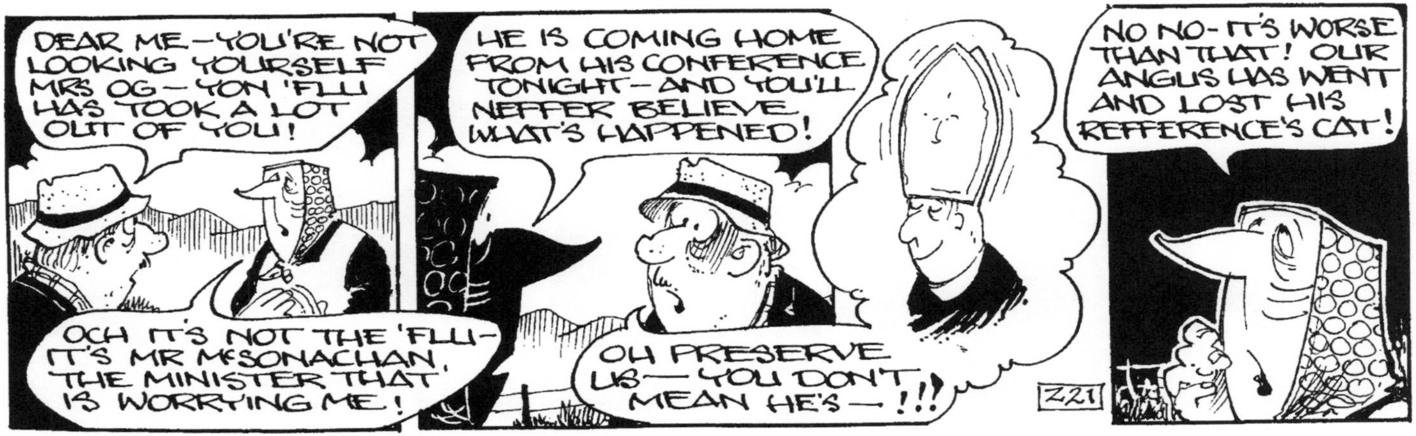
DEAR ME—YOU'RE NOT LOOKING YOURSELF MRS OG—YON 'FLU HAS TOOK A LOT OUT OF YOU!
OCH IT'S NOT THE 'FLU—IT'S MR McSONACHAN THE MINISTER THAT IS WORRYING ME!
HE IS COMING HOME FROM HIS CONFERENCE TONIGHT—AND YOU'LL NEFFER BELIEVE WHAT'S HAPPENED!
OH PRESERVE US—YOU DON'T MEAN HE'S—!!!
221
NO NO—IT'S WORSE THAN THAT! OUR ANGUS HAS WENT AND LOST HIS REFFERENCE'S CAT!

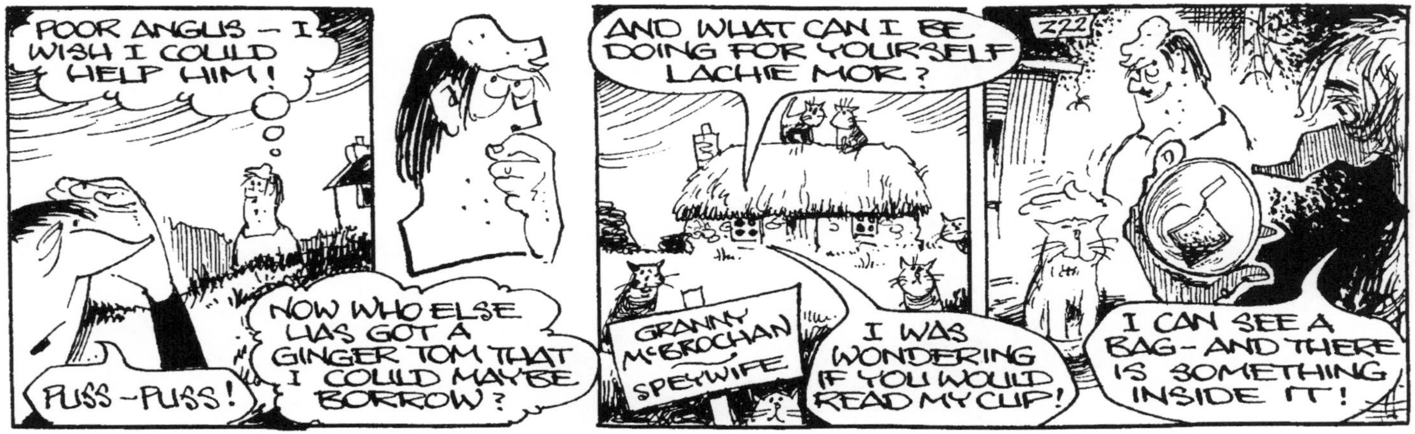
POOR ANGUS—I WISH I COULD HELP HIM!
PUSS-PUSS!
NOW WHO ELSE HAS GOT A GINGER TOM THAT I COULD MAYBE BORROW?
AND WHAT CAN I BE DOING FOR YOURSELF LACHIE MOR?
GRANNY McBROCHAN SPEYWIFE
I WAS WONDERING IF YOU WOULD READ MY CUP!
222
I CAN SEE A BAG—AND THERE IS SOMETHING INSIDE IT!

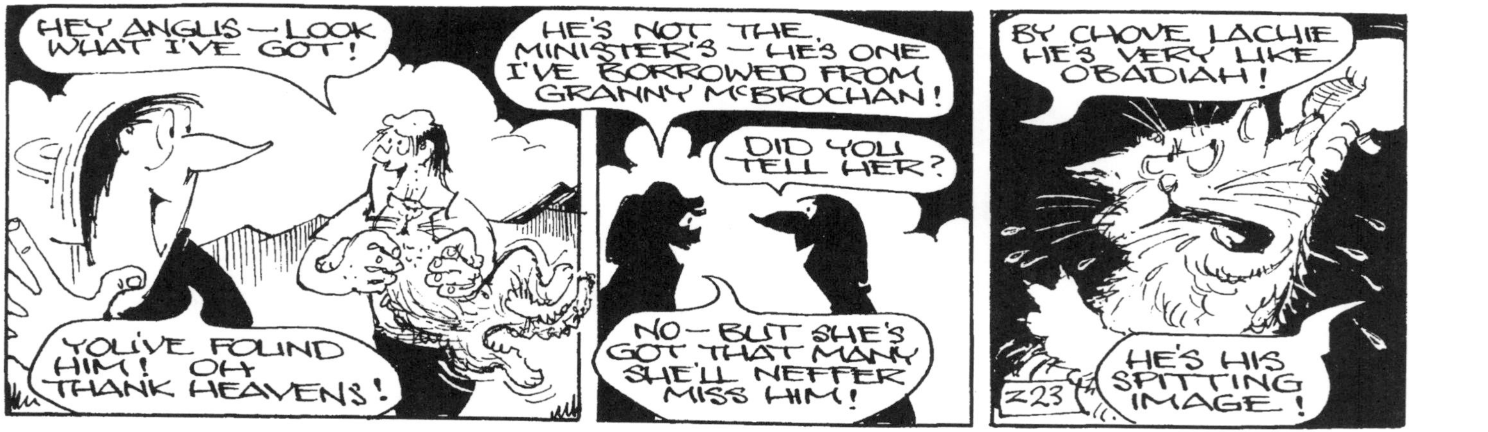
HEY ANGUS — LOOK WHAT I'VE GOT!
YOU'VE FOUND HIM! OH THANK HEAVENS!
HE'S NOT THE MINISTER'S — HE'S ONE I'VE BORROWED FROM GRANNY McBROCHAN!
DID YOU TELL HER?
NO — BUT SHE'S GOT THAT MANY SHE'LL NEFFER MISS HIM!
BY CHOVE LACHIE HE'S VERY LIKE OBADIAH!
HE'S HIS SPITTING IMAGE!
223

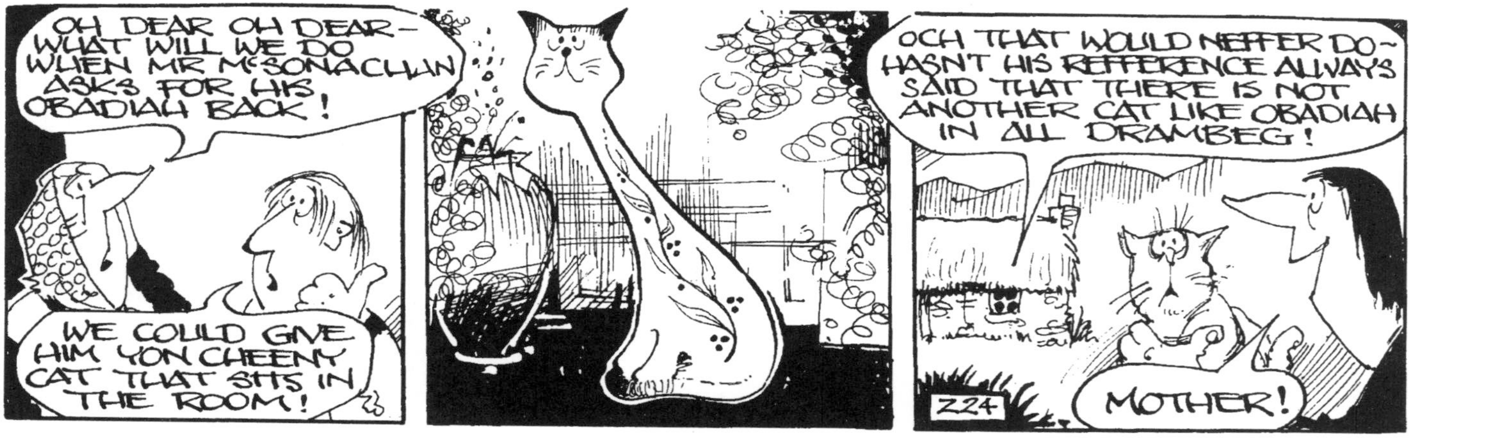
OH DEAR OH DEAR — WHAT WILL WE DO WHEN MR McSONACHAN ASKS FOR HIS OBADIAH BACK!
WE COULD GIVE HIM YON CHEENY CAT THAT SITS IN THE ROOM!
OCH THAT WOULD NEFFER DO — HASN'T HIS REFFERENCE ALWAYS SAID THAT THERE IS NOT ANOTHER CAT LIKE OBADIAH IN ALL DRAMBEG!
MOTHER!
224

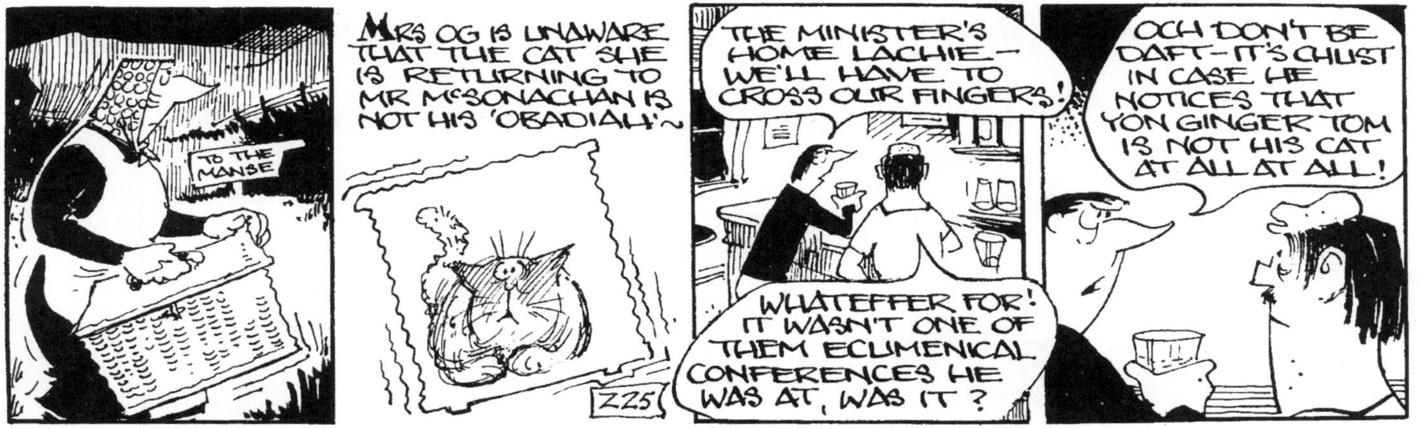
TO THE MANSE
MRS OG IS UNAWARE THAT THE CAT SHE IS RETURNING TO MR McSONACHAN IS NOT HIS 'OBADIAH'~
225
THE MINISTER'S HOME LACHIE- WE'LL HAVE TO CROSS OUR FINGERS!
WHATEFFER FOR! IT WASN'T ONE OF THEM ECUMENICAL CONFERENCES HE WAS AT, WAS IT ?
OCH DON'T BE DAFT- IT'S CHUST IN CASE HE NOTICES THAT YON GINGER TOM IS NOT HIS CAT AT ALL AT ALL!

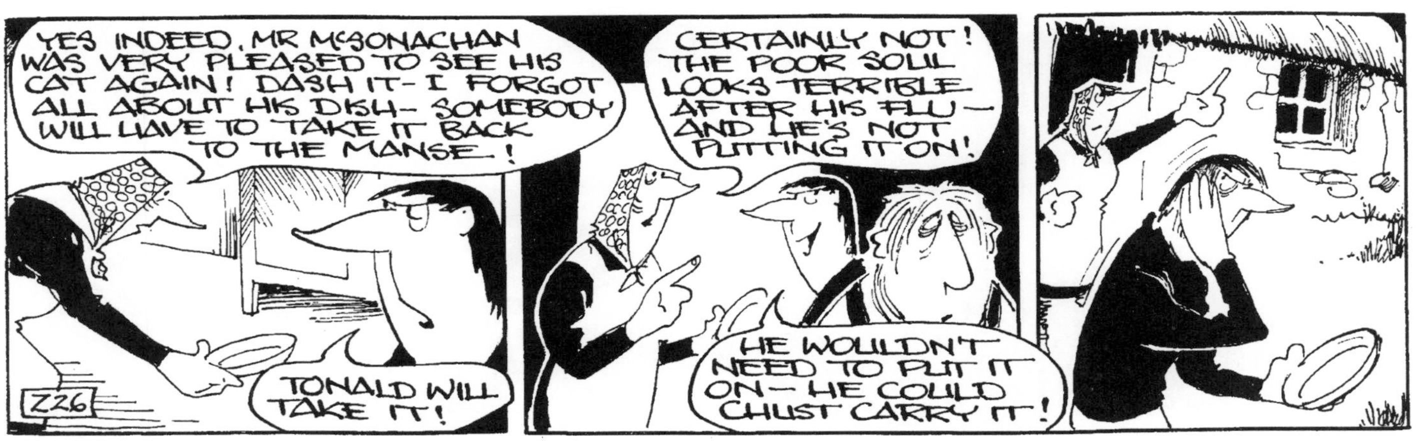
YES INDEED, MR McSONACHAN WAS VERY PLEASED TO SEE HIS CAT AGAIN! DASH IT- I FORGOT ALL ABOUT HIS DISH- SOMEBODY WILL HAVE TO TAKE IT BACK TO THE MANSE!
TONALD WILL TAKE IT!
226
CERTAINLY NOT! THE POOR SOUL LOOKS TERRIBLE AFTER HIS FLU- AND HE'S NOT PUTTING IT ON!
HE WOULDN'T NEED TO PUT IT ON- HE COULD CHUST CARRY IT!

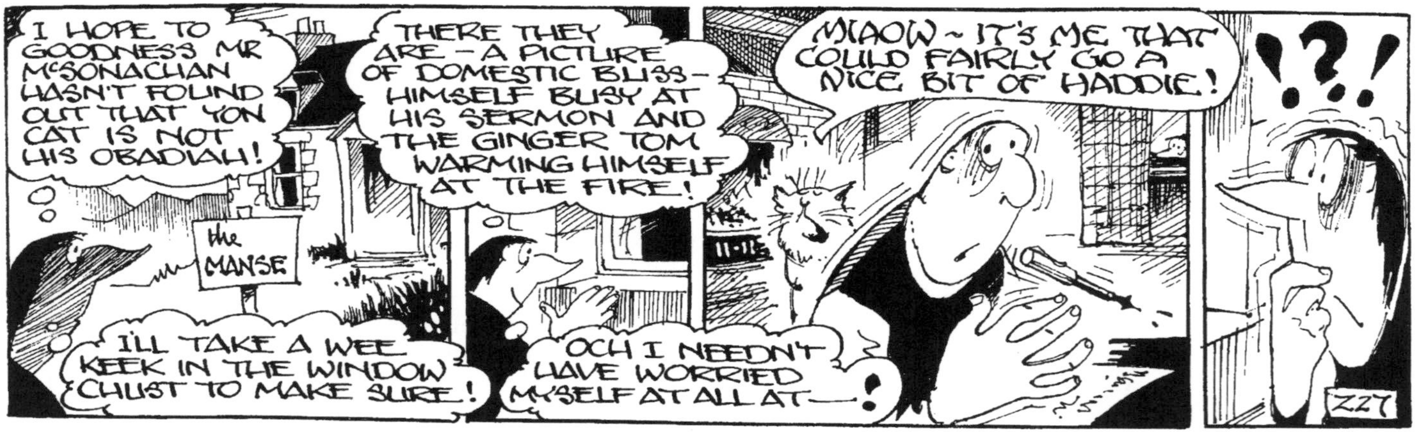
I HOPE TO GOODNESS MR McSONACHAN HASN'T FOUND OUT THAT YON CAT IS NOT HIS OBADIAH!
the MANSE
I'LL TAKE A WEE KEEK IN THE WINDOW CHUST TO MAKE SURE!
THERE THEY ARE – A PICTURE OF DOMESTIC BLISS – HIMSELF BUSY AT HIS SERMON AND THE GINGER TOM WARMING HIMSELF AT THE FIRE!
OCH I NEEDN'T HAVE WORRIED MYSELF AT ALL AT—!
MIAOW – IT'S ME THAT COULD FAIRLY GO A NICE BIT OF HADDIE!
!?!
227

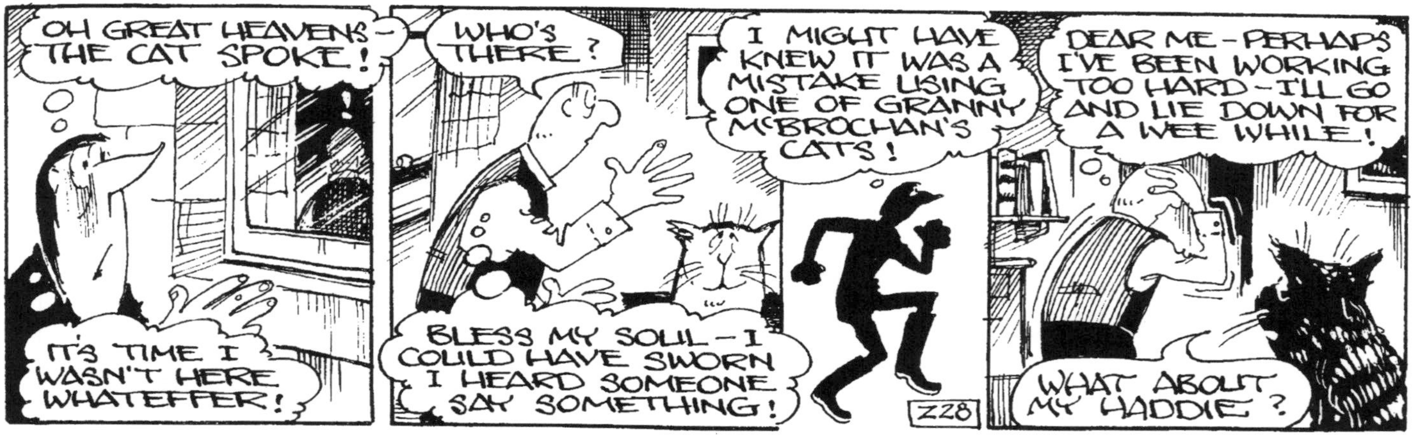
OH GREAT HEAVENS – THE CAT SPOKE!
IT'S TIME I WASN'T HERE WHATEFFER!
WHO'S THERE?
BLESS MY SOUL – I COULD HAVE SWORN I HEARD SOMEONE SAY SOMETHING!
I MIGHT HAVE KNEW IT WAS A MISTAKE USING ONE OF GRANNY McBROCHAN'S CATS!
228
DEAR ME – PERHAPS I'VE BEEN WORKING TOO HARD – I'LL GO AND LIE DOWN FOR A WEE WHILE!
WHAT ABOUT MY HADDIE?

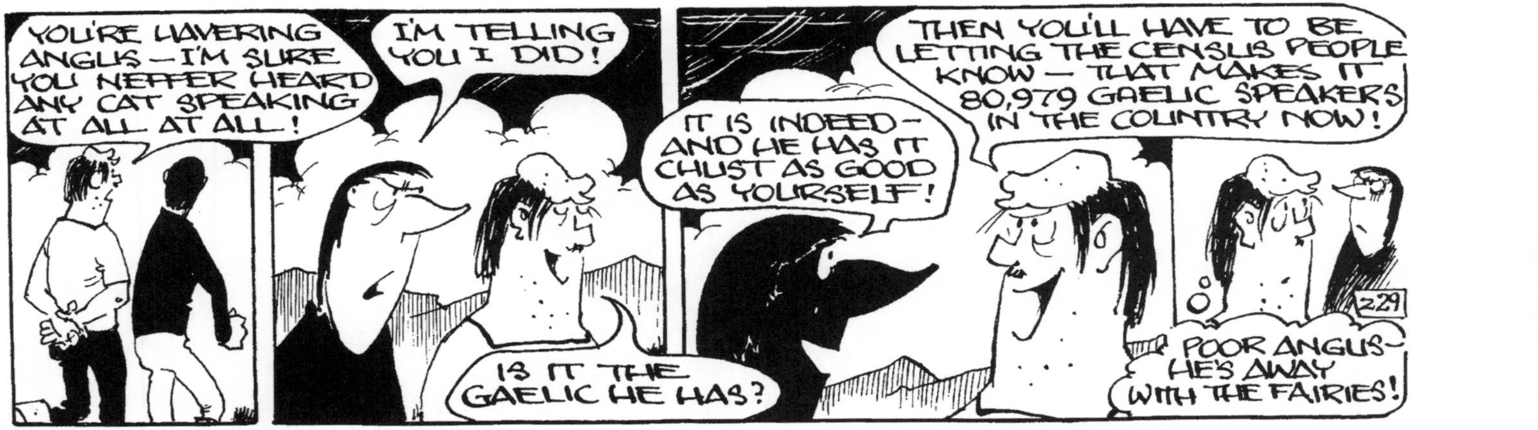
YOU'RE HAVERING ANGUS – I'M SURE YOU NEFFER HEARD ANY CAT SPEAKING AT ALL AT ALL!
I'M TELLING YOU I DID!
IS IT THE GAELIC HE HAS?
IT IS INDEED – AND HE HAS IT CHUST AS GOOD AS YOURSELF!
THEN YOU'LL HAVE TO BE LETTING THE CENSUS PEOPLE KNOW – THAT MAKES IT 80,979 GAELIC SPEAKERS IN THE COUNTRY NOW!
POOR ANGUS – HE'S AWAY WITH THE FAIRIES!
229

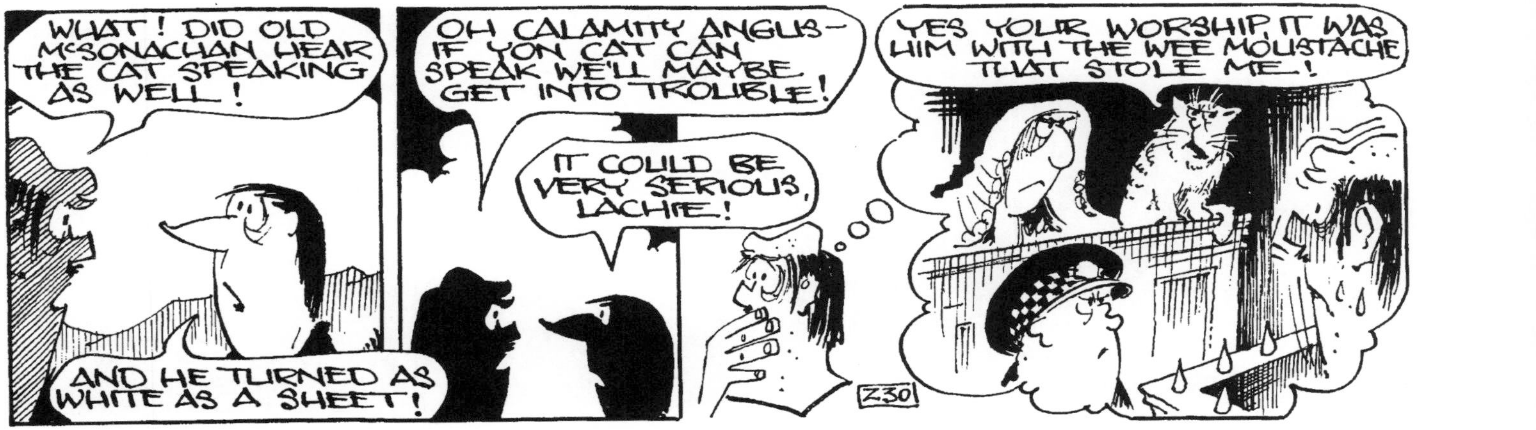
WHAT! DID OLD McSONACHAN HEAR THE CAT SPEAKING AS WELL!
AND HE TURNED AS WHITE AS A SHEET!
OH CALAMITY ANGUS – IF YON CAT CAN SPEAK WE'LL MAYBE GET INTO TROUBLE!
IT COULD BE VERY SERIOUS, LACHIE!
230
YES YOUR WORSHIP, IT WAS HIM WITH THE WEE MOUSTACHE THAT STOLE ME!

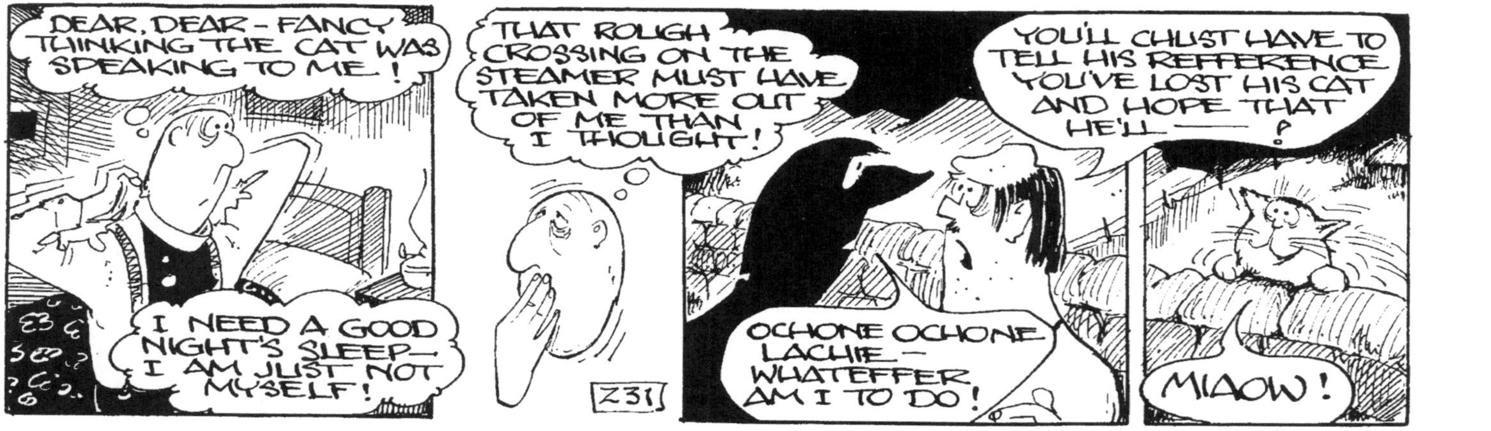
DEAR, DEAR - FANCY THINKING THE CAT WAS SPEAKING TO ME!
I NEED A GOOD NIGHT'S SLEEP - I AM JUST NOT MYSELF!
THAT ROUGH CROSSING ON THE STEAMER MUST HAVE TAKEN MORE OUT OF ME THAN I THOUGHT!
Z31
YOU'LL CHUST HAVE TO TELL HIS REFFERENCE YOU'VE LOST HIS CAT AND HOPE THAT HE'LL —— ?
OCHONE OCHONE LACHIE - WHATEFFER AM I TO DO!
MIAOW!

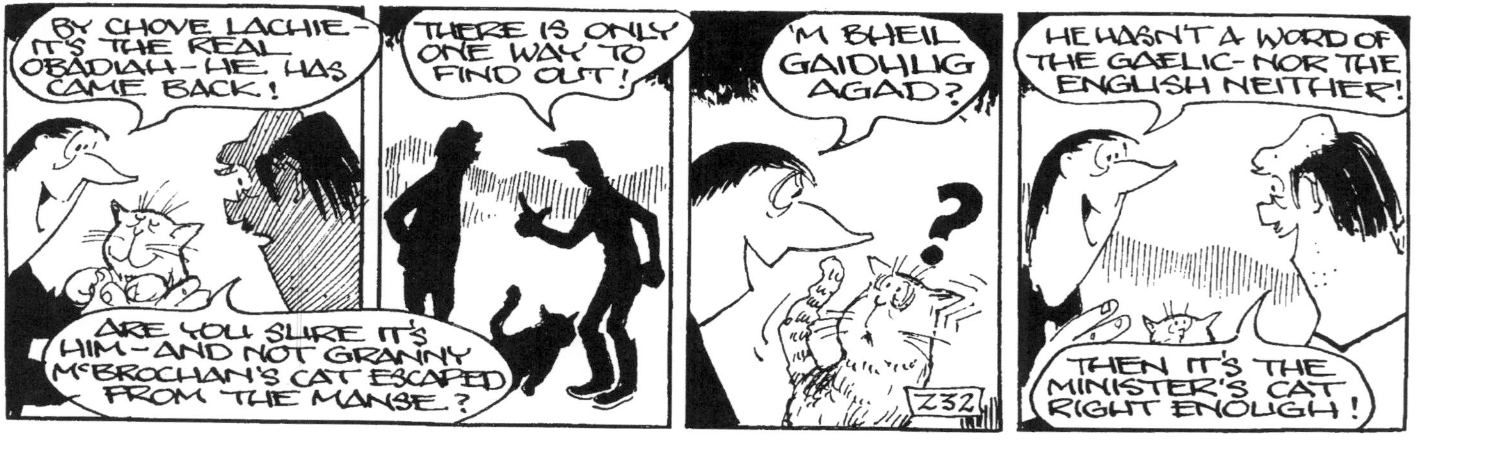
BY CHOVE LACHIE - IT'S THE REAL OBADIAH - HE HAS CAME BACK!
ARE YOU SURE IT'S HIM - AND NOT GRANNY McBROCHAN'S CAT ESCAPED FROM THE MANSE?
THERE IS ONLY ONE WAY TO FIND OUT!
'M BHEIL GAIDHLIG AGAD?
?
Z32
HE HASN'T A WORD OF THE GAELIC - NOR THE ENGLISH NEITHER!
THEN IT'S THE MINISTER'S CAT RIGHT ENOUGH!

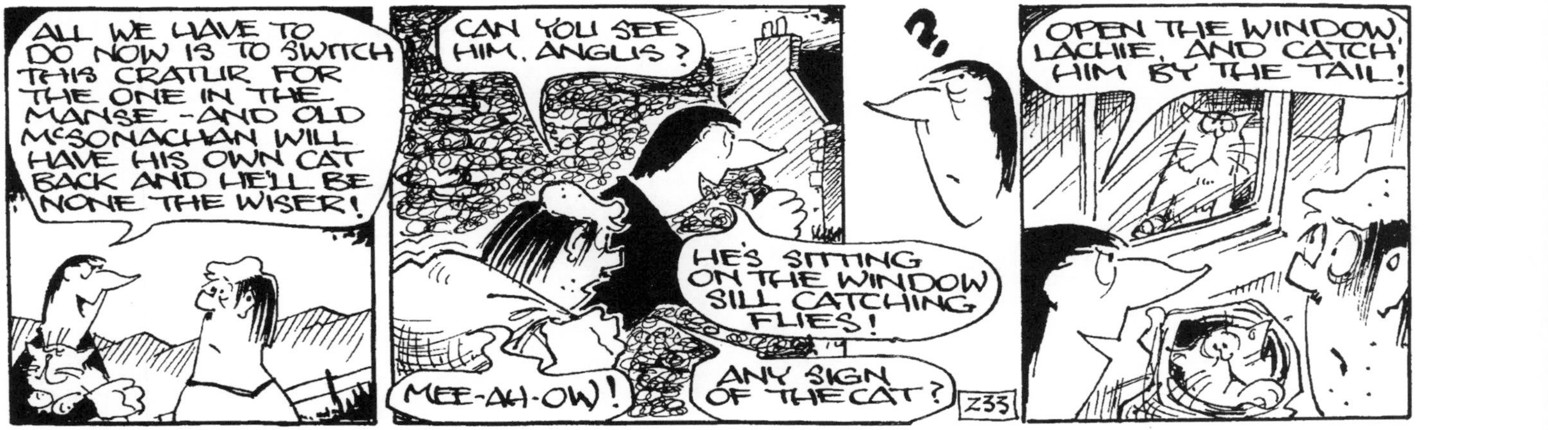
ALL WE HAVE TO DO NOW IS TO SWITCH THIS CRATUR FOR THE ONE IN THE MANSE - AND OLD McSONACHAN WILL HAVE HIS OWN CAT BACK AND HE'LL BE NONE THE WISER!
CAN YOU SEE HIM, ANGUS?
MEE-AH-OW!
HE'S SITTING ON THE WINDOW SILL CATCHING FLIES!
ANY SIGN OF THE CAT?
233
?
OPEN THE WINDOW, LACHIE, AND CATCH HIM BY THE TAIL!

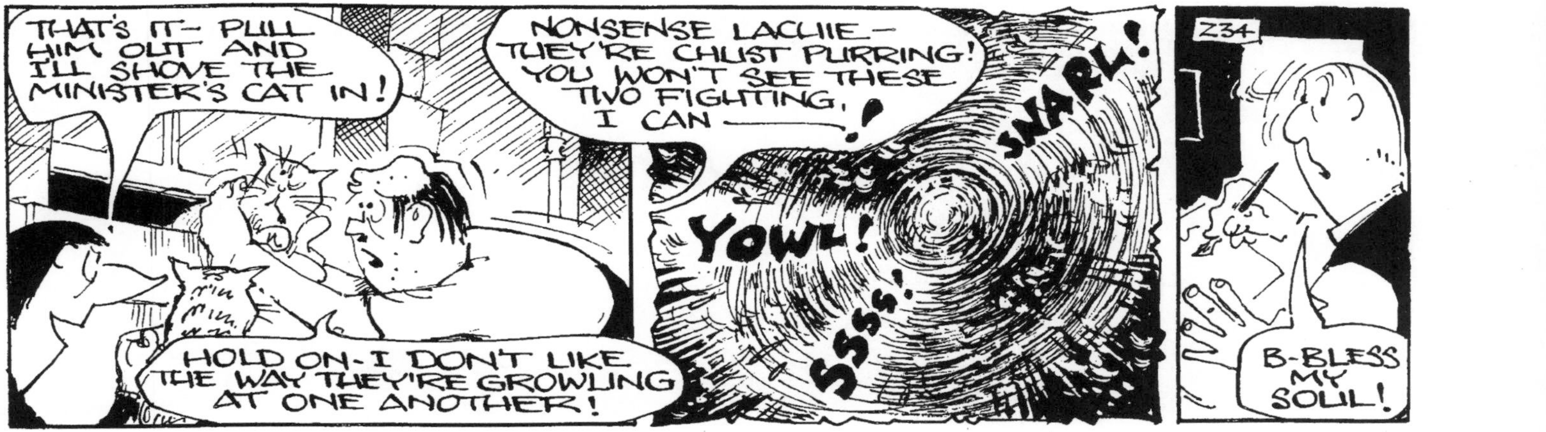
THAT'S IT- PULL HIM OUT AND I'LL SHOVE THE MINISTER'S CAT IN!
HOLD ON- I DON'T LIKE THE WAY THEY'RE GROWLING AT ONE ANOTHER!
NONSENSE LACHIE- THEY'RE CHUST PURRING! YOU WON'T SEE THESE TWO FIGHTING, I CAN ——!
SNARL!
YOWL!
SSSS!
234
B-BLESS MY SOUL!

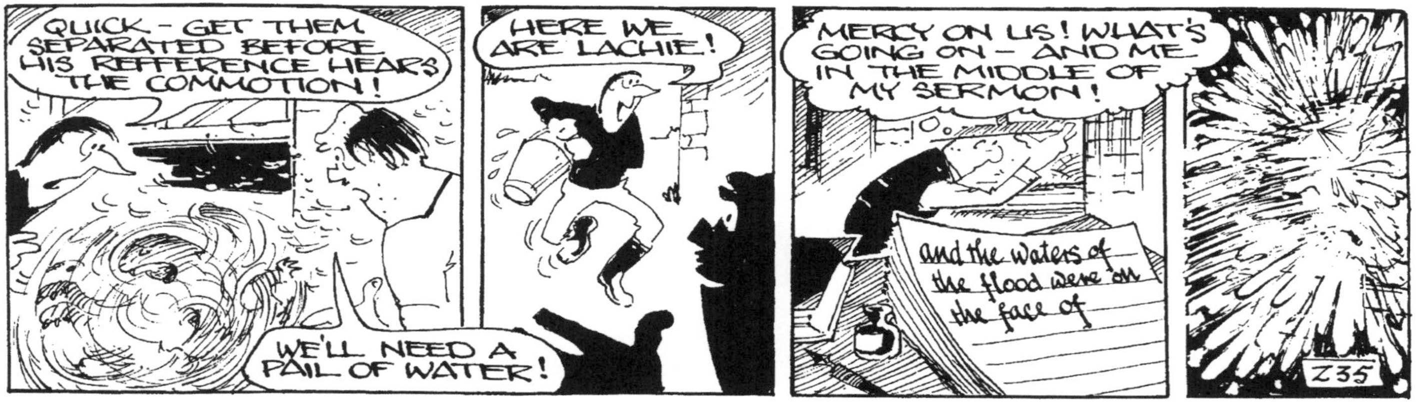
QUICK - GET THEM SEPARATED BEFORE HIS REFFERENCE HEARS THE COMMOTION!
WE'LL NEED A PAIL OF WATER!
HERE WE ARE LACHIE!
MERCY ON US! WHAT'S GOING ON - AND ME IN THE MIDDLE OF MY SERMON!
and the waters of the flood were on the face of
Z35

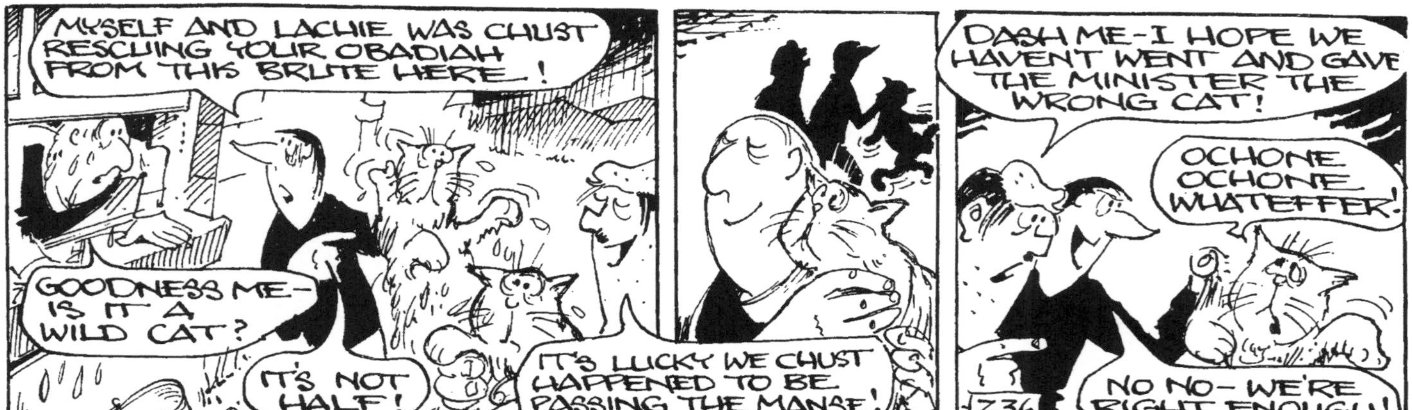
MYSELF AND LACHIE WAS CHUST RESCUING YOUR OBADIAH FROM THIS BRUTE HERE!
GOODNESS ME - IS IT A WILD CAT?
IT'S NOT HALF!
IT'S LUCKY WE CHUST HAPPENED TO BE PASSING THE MANSE!
DASH ME - I HOPE WE HAVEN'T WENT AND GAVE THE MINISTER THE WRONG CAT!
OCHONE OCHONE WHATEFFER!
NO NO - WE'RE RIGHT ENOUGH!
Z36

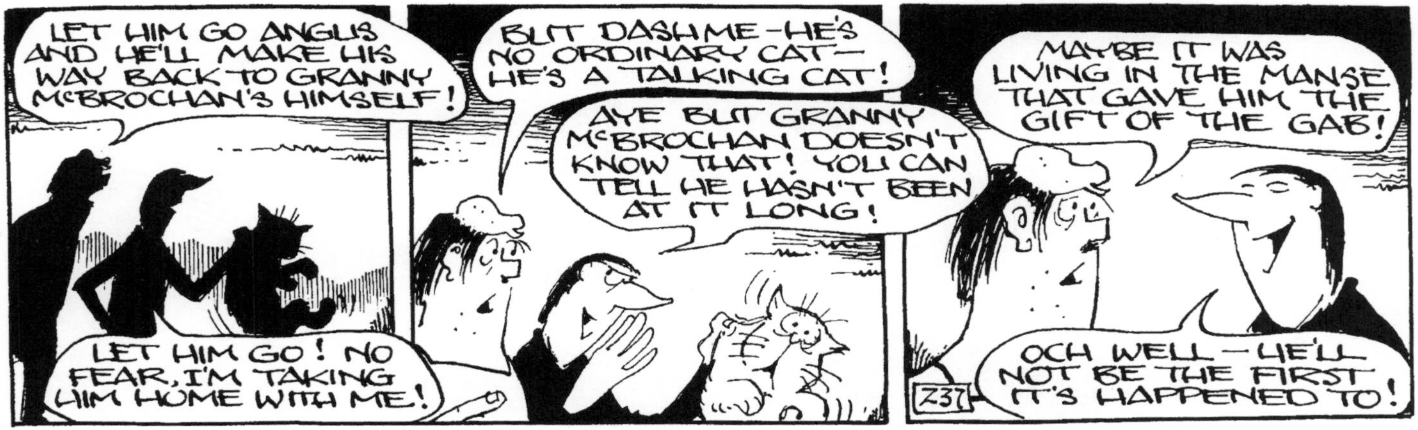
LET HIM GO ANGUS AND HE'LL MAKE HIS WAY BACK TO GRANNY McBROCHAN'S HIMSELF!
LET HIM GO! NO FEAR, I'M TAKING HIM HOME WITH ME!
BUT DASH ME - HE'S NO ORDINARY CAT - HE'S A TALKING CAT!
AYE BUT GRANNY McBROCHAN DOESN'T KNOW THAT! YOU CAN TELL HE HASN'T BEEN AT IT LONG!
MAYBE IT WAS LIVING IN THE MANSE THAT GAVE HIM THE GIFT OF THE GAB!
OCH WELL - HE'LL NOT BE THE FIRST IT'S HAPPENED TO!
237

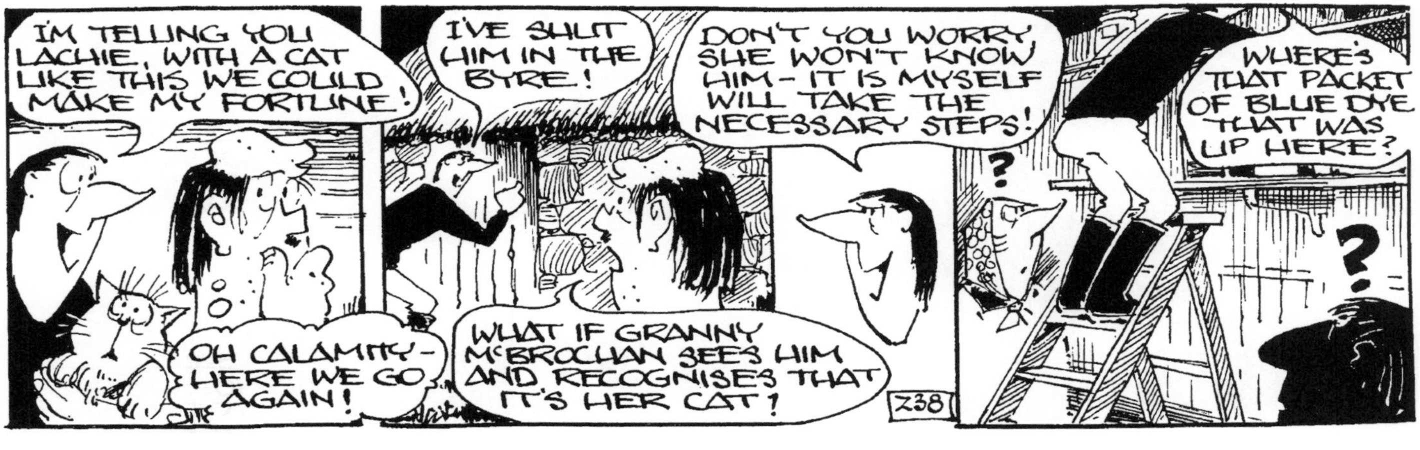
I'M TELLING YOU LACHIE, WITH A CAT LIKE THIS WE COULD MAKE MY FORTUNE!
OH CALAMITY - HERE WE GO AGAIN!
I'VE SHUT HIM IN THE BYRE!
WHAT IF GRANNY McBROCHAN SEES HIM AND RECOGNISES THAT IT'S HER CAT!
DON'T YOU WORRY, SHE WON'T KNOW HIM - IT IS MYSELF WILL TAKE THE NECESSARY STEPS!
238
?
WHERE'S THAT PACKET OF BLUE DYE THAT WAS UP HERE?
?

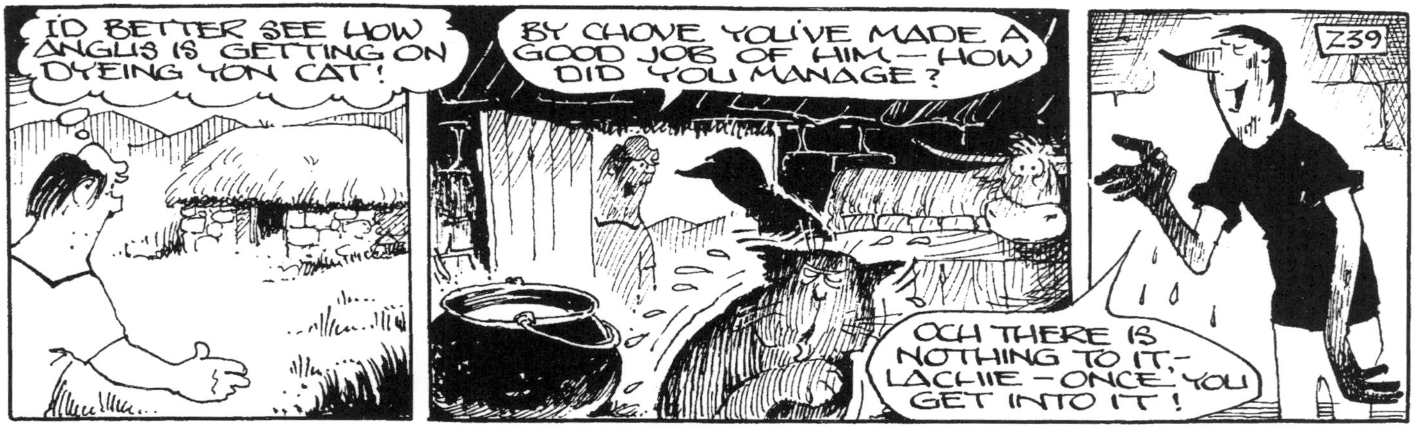
Z39
I'D BETTER SEE HOW ANGUS IS GETTING ON DYEING YON CAT!
BY CHOVE YOU'VE MADE A GOOD JOB OF HIM — HOW DID YOU MANAGE?
OCH THERE IS NOTHING TO IT, LACHIE — ONCE YOU GET INTO IT!

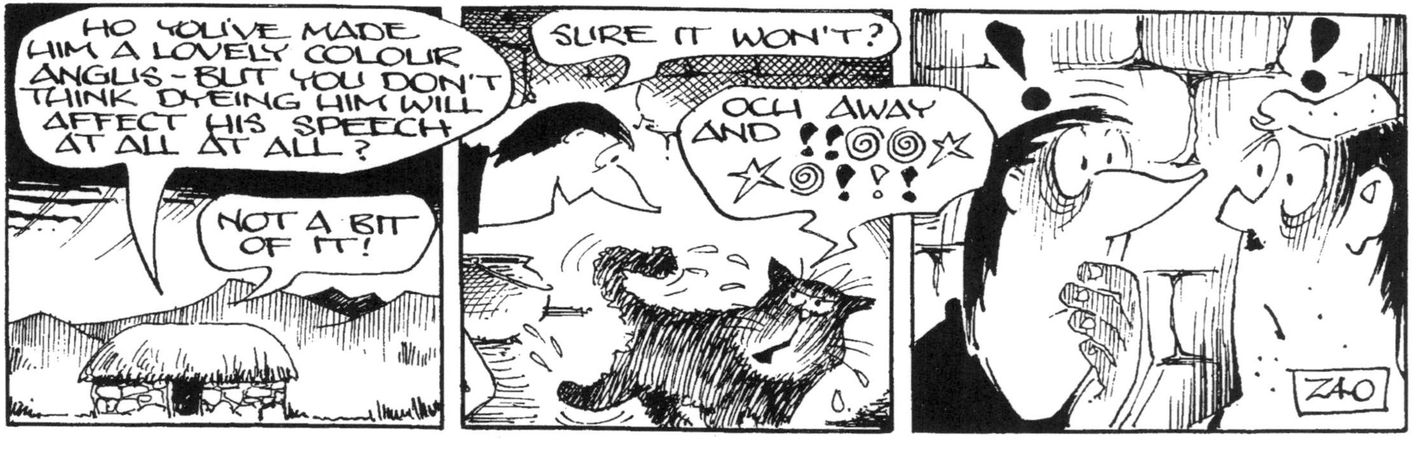
HO YOU'VE MADE HIM A LOVELY COLOUR ANGUS - BUT YOU DON'T THINK DYEING HIM WILL AFFECT HIS SPEECH AT ALL AT ALL?
NOT A BIT OF IT!
SURE IT WON'T?
OCH AWAY AND !!@@★★@!?!
Z40

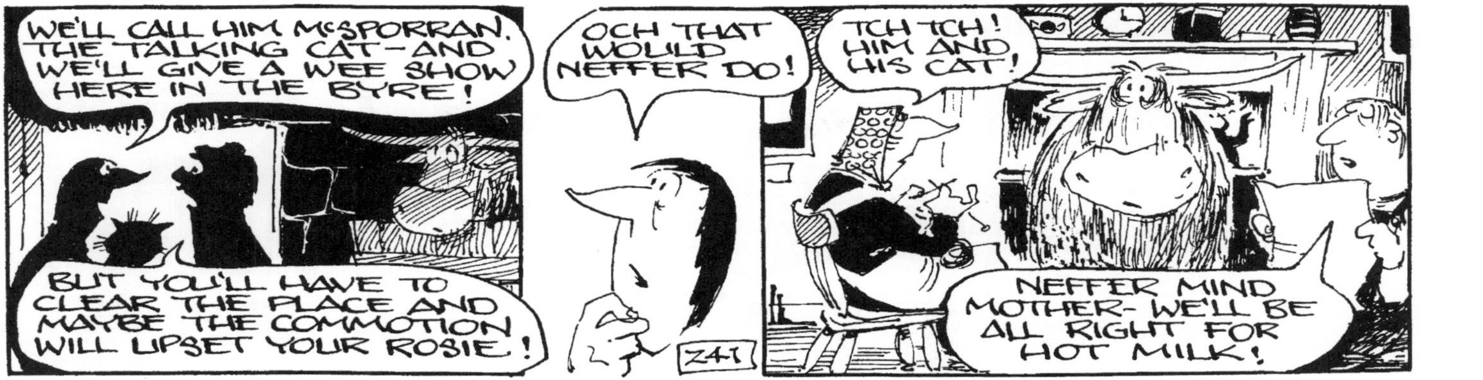
WE'LL CALL HIM McSPORRAN. THE TALKING CAT – AND WE'LL GIVE A WEE SHOW HERE IN THE BYRE!
BUT YOU'LL HAVE TO CLEAR THE PLACE AND MAYBE THE COMMOTION WILL UPSET YOUR ROSIE!
OCH THAT WOULD NEFFER DO!
241
TCH TCH! HIM AND HIS CAT!
NEFFER MIND MOTHER- WE'LL BE ALL RIGHT FOR HOT MILK!

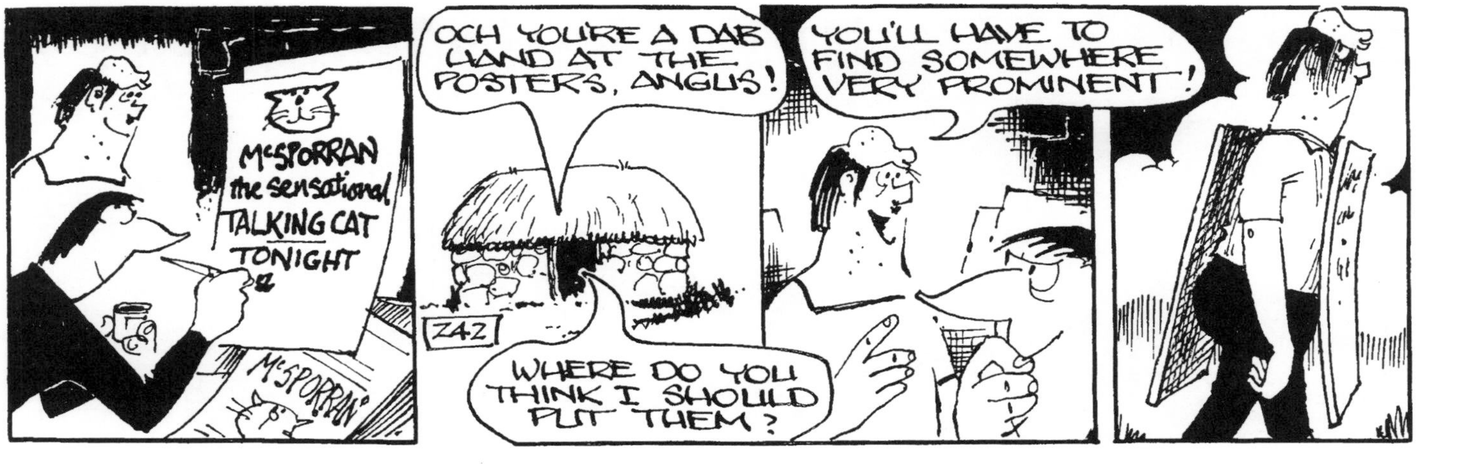
McSPORRAN
the sensational
TALKING CAT
TONIGHT
McSPORRAN
OCH YOU'RE A DAB HAND AT THE POSTERS, ANGUS!
WHERE DO YOU THINK I SHOULD PUT THEM?
242
YOU'LL HAVE TO FIND SOMEWHERE VERY PROMINENT!

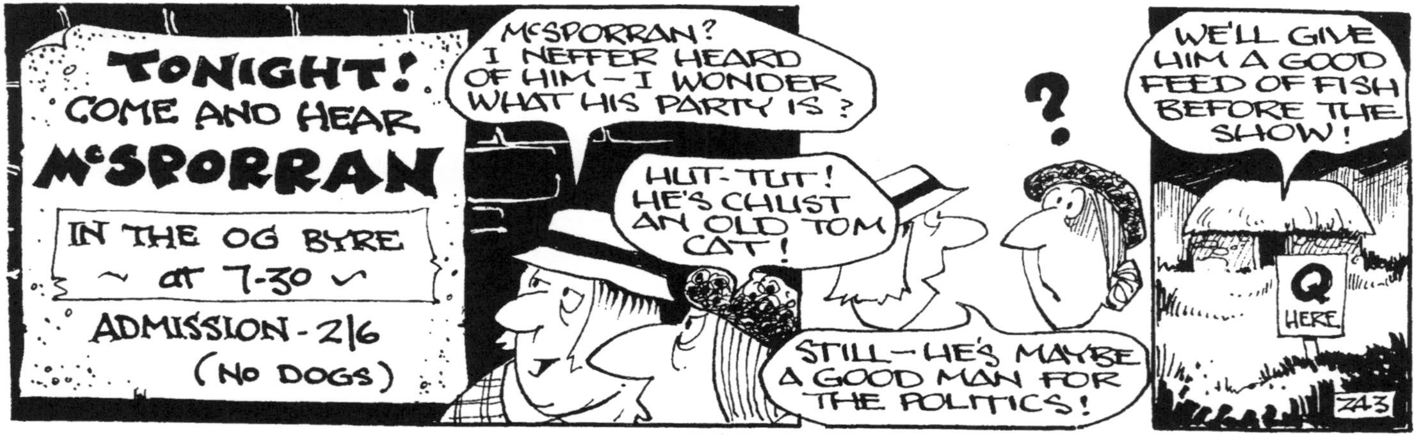
TONIGHT!
COME AND HEAR
McSPORRAN
IN THE OG BYRE
~ at 7-30 ~
ADMISSION - 2/6
(NO DOGS)
McSPORRAN? I NEFFER HEARD OF HIM - I WONDER WHAT HIS PARTY IS?
HUT-TUT! HE'S CHUST AN OLD TOM CAT!
?
STILL - HE'S MAYBE A GOOD MAN FOR THE POLITICS!
WE'LL GIVE HIM A GOOD FEED OF FISH BEFORE THE SHOW!
Q HERE
243

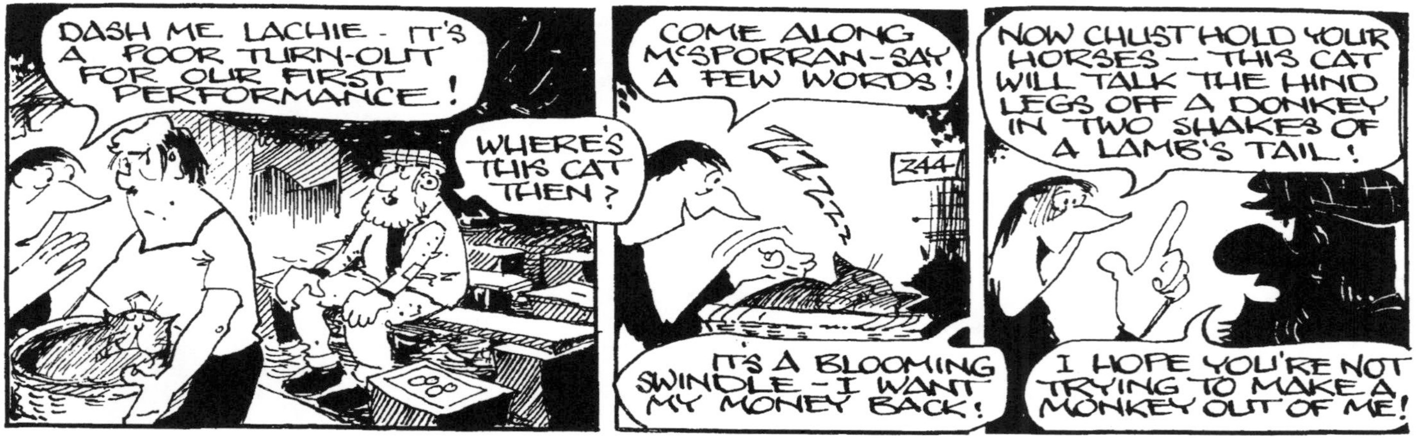
DASH ME LACHIE - IT'S A POOR TURN-OUT FOR OUR FIRST PERFORMANCE!
WHERE'S THIS CAT THEN?
COME ALONG McSPORRAN - SAY A FEW WORDS!
244
ZZZZ
IT'S A BLOOMING SWINDLE - I WANT MY MONEY BACK!
NOW CHUST HOLD YOUR HORSES - THIS CAT WILL TALK THE HIND LEGS OFF A DONKEY IN TWO SHAKES OF A LAMB'S TAIL!
I HOPE YOU'RE NOT TRYING TO MAKE A MONKEY OUT OF ME!

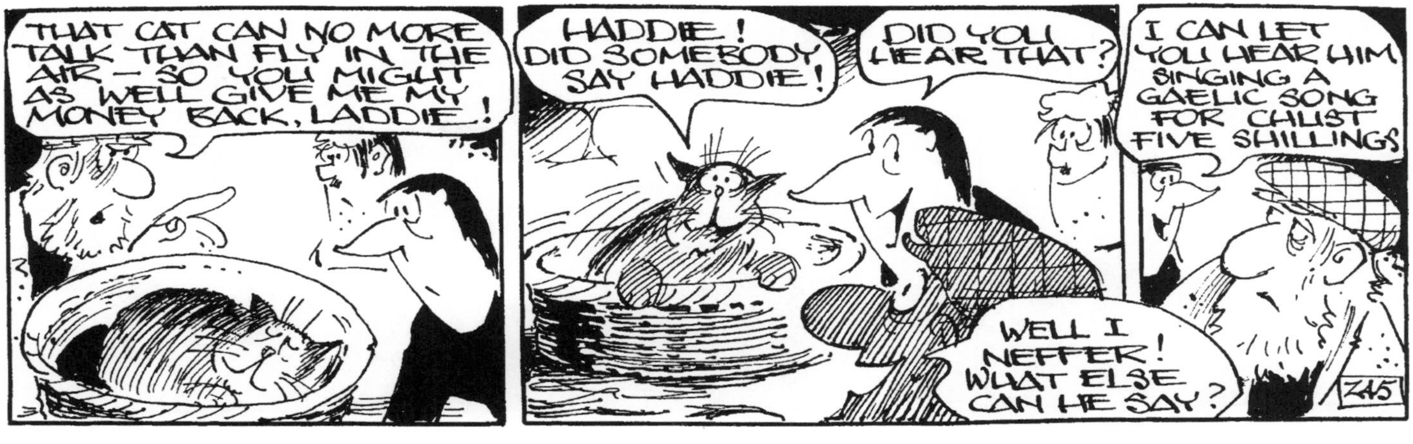
THAT CAT CAN NO MORE TALK THAN FLY IN THE AIR – SO YOU MIGHT AS WELL GIVE ME MY MONEY BACK, LADDIE!
HADDIE! DID SOMEBODY SAY HADDIE!
DID YOU HEAR THAT?
WELL I NEFFER! WHAT ELSE CAN HE SAY?
I CAN LET YOU HEAR HIM SINGING A GAELIC SONG FOR CHUST FIVE SHILLINGS
245

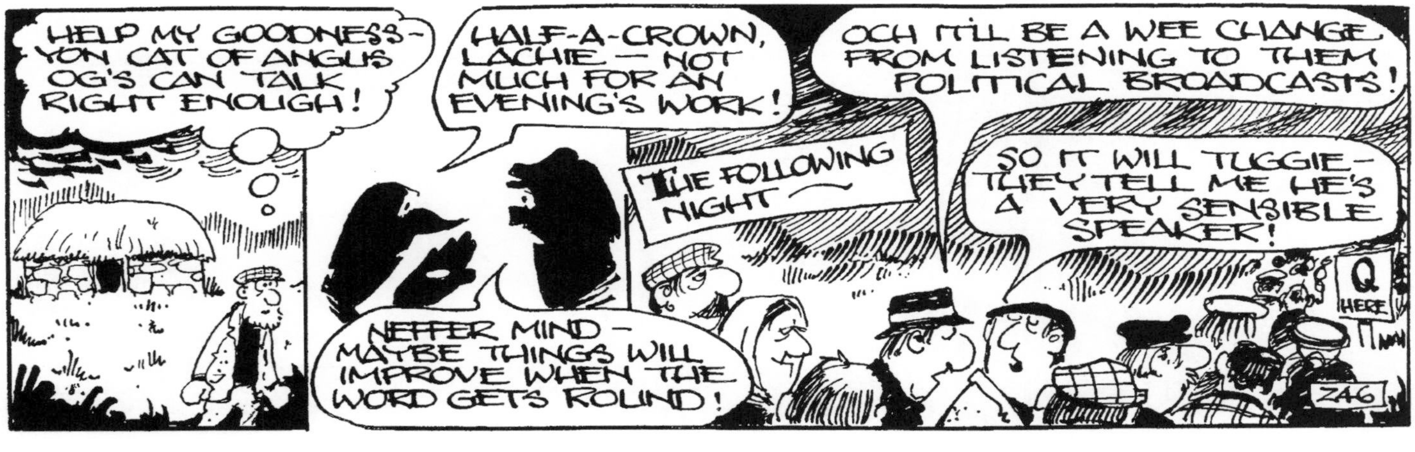
HELP MY GOODNESS – YON CAT OF ANGUS OG'S CAN TALK RIGHT ENOUGH!
HALF-A-CROWN, LACHIE – NOT MUCH FOR AN EVENING'S WORK!
NEFFER MIND – MAYBE THINGS WILL IMPROVE WHEN THE WORD GETS ROUND!
THE FOLLOWING NIGHT –
OCH IT'LL BE A WEE CHANGE FROM LISTENING TO THEM POLITICAL BROADCASTS!
SO IT WILL TUGGIE – THEY TELL ME HE'S A VERY SENSIBLE SPEAKER!
Q HERE
246

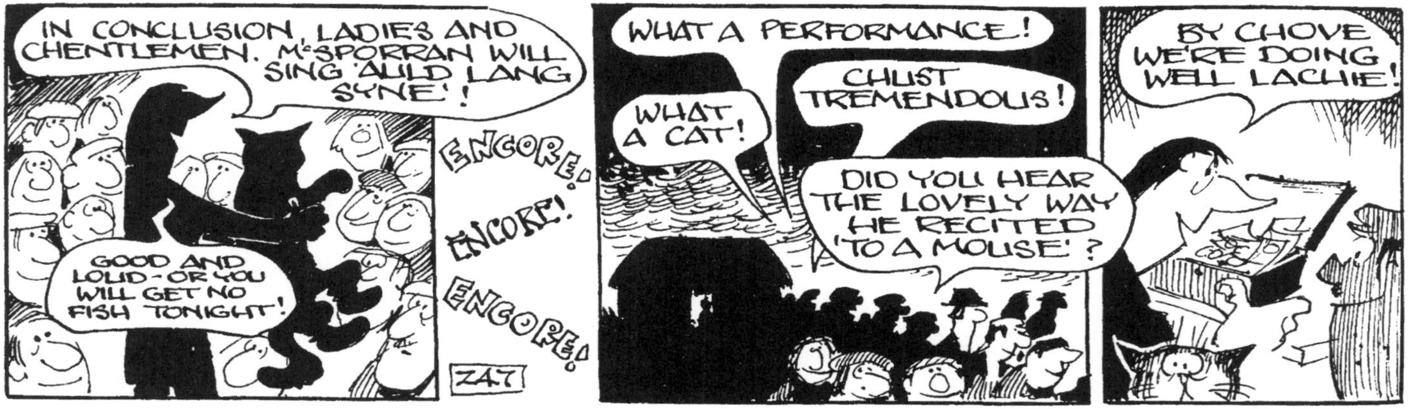
IN CONCLUSION, LADIES AND CHENTLEMEN. M^cSPORRAN WILL SING 'AULD LANG SYNE'!
GOOD AND LOUD - OR YOU WILL GET NO FISH TONIGHT!
ENCORE!
ENCORE!
ENCORE!
247
WHAT A PERFORMANCE!
WHAT A CAT!
CHUST TREMENDOUS!
DID YOU HEAR THE LOVELY WAY HE RECITED 'TO A MOUSE'?
BY CHOVE WE'RE DOING WELL LACHIE!

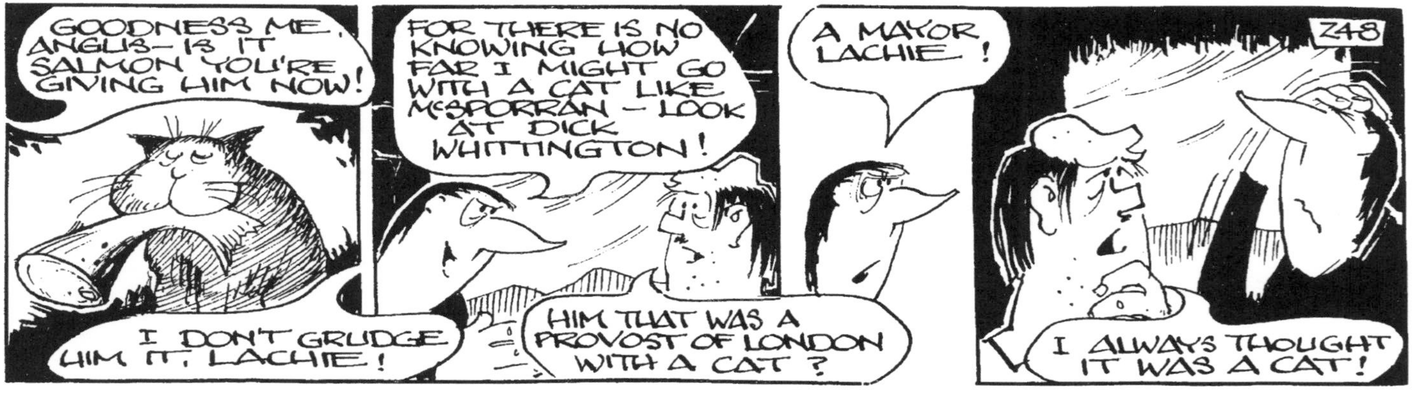
GOODNESS ME, ANGUS - IS IT SALMON YOU'RE GIVING HIM NOW!
I DON'T GRUDGE HIM IT, LACHIE!
FOR THERE IS NO KNOWING HOW FAR I MIGHT GO WITH A CAT LIKE M^cSPORRAN - LOOK AT DICK WHITTINGTON!
HIM THAT WAS A PROVOST OF LONDON WITH A CAT?
A MAYOR LACHIE!
248
I ALWAYS THOUGHT IT WAS A CAT!

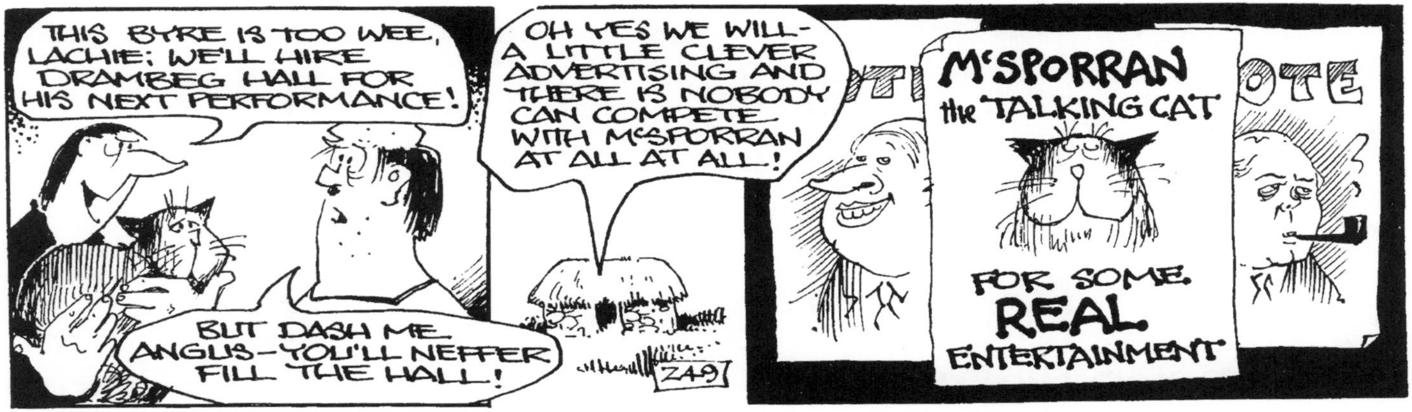
THIS BYRE IS TOO WEE, LACHIE; WE'LL HIRE DRAMBEG HALL FOR HIS NEXT PERFORMANCE!
BUT DASH ME ANGUS—YOU'LL NEFFER FILL THE HALL!
OH YES WE WILL—A LITTLE CLEVER ADVERTISING AND THERE IS NOBODY CAN COMPETE WITH McSPORRAN AT ALL AT ALL!
249
McSPORRAN
the TALKING CAT
FOR SOME
REAL
ENTERTAINMENT

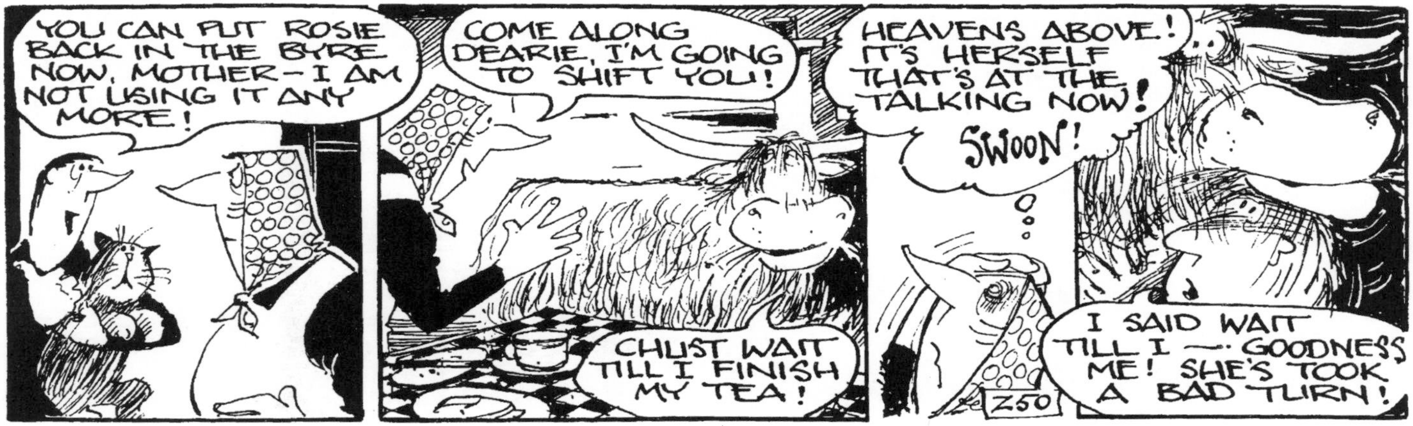
YOU CAN PUT ROSIE BACK IN THE BYRE NOW, MOTHER—I AM NOT USING IT ANY MORE!
COME ALONG DEARIE, I'M GOING TO SHIFT YOU!
CHUST WAIT TILL I FINISH MY TEA!
HEAVENS ABOVE! IT'S HERSELF THAT'S AT THE TALKING NOW!
SWOON!
250
I SAID WAIT TILL I — GOODNESS ME! SHE'S TOOK A BAD TURN!

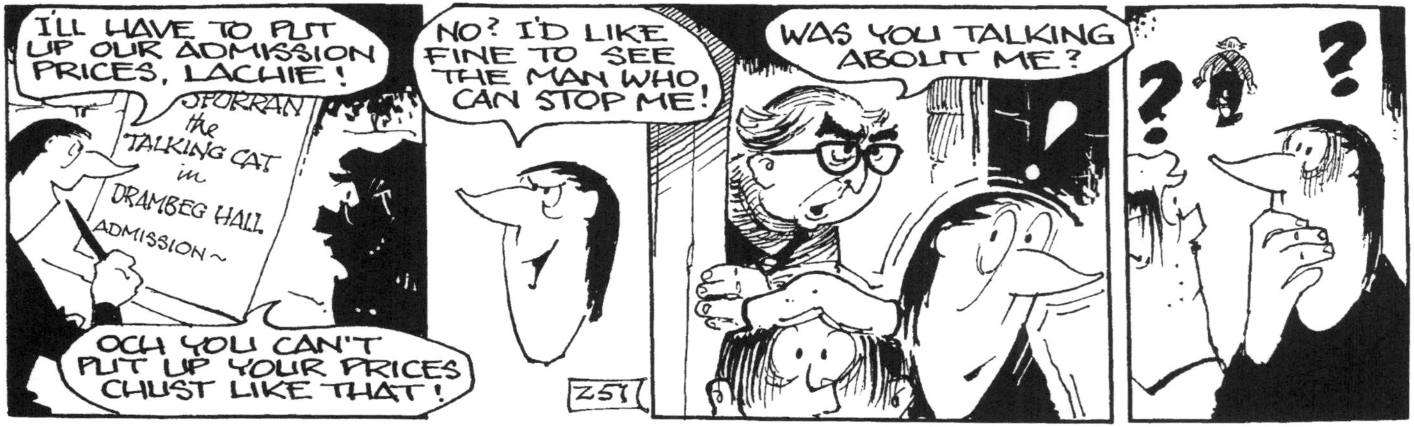
I'LL HAVE TO PUT UP OUR ADMISSION PRICES, LACHIE!
SPORRAN the TALKING CAT in DRAMBEG HALL ADMISSION ~
OCH YOU CAN'T PUT UP YOUR PRICES CHUST LIKE THAT!
NO? I'D LIKE FINE TO SEE THE MAN WHO CAN STOP ME!
Z51
WAS YOU TALKING ABOUT ME?
!
? ?

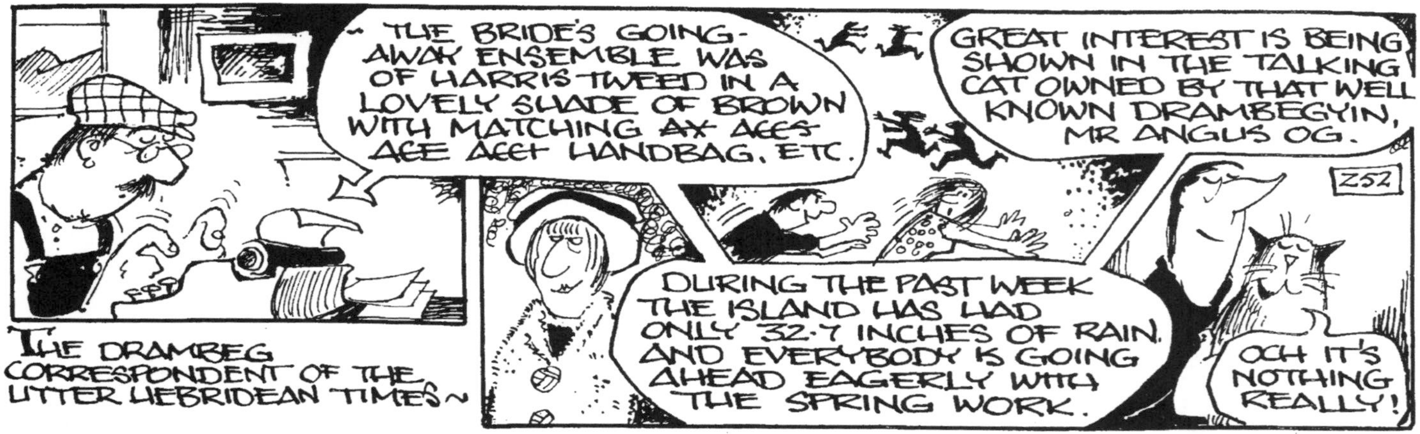
THE DRAMBEG CORRESPONDENT OF THE UTTER HEBRIDEAN TIMES ~
~ THE BRIDE'S GOING-AWAY ENSEMBLE WAS OF HARRIS TWEED IN A LOVELY SHADE OF BROWN WITH MATCHING ~~AX ACES~~ ~~ACE ACC~~ HANDBAG, ETC.
DURING THE PAST WEEK THE ISLAND HAS HAD ONLY 32·7 INCHES OF RAIN AND EVERYBODY IS GOING AHEAD EAGERLY WITH THE SPRING WORK.
GREAT INTEREST IS BEING SHOWN IN THE TALKING CAT OWNED BY THAT WELL KNOWN DRAMBEGYIN, MR ANGUS OG.
Z52
OCH IT'S NOTHING REALLY!

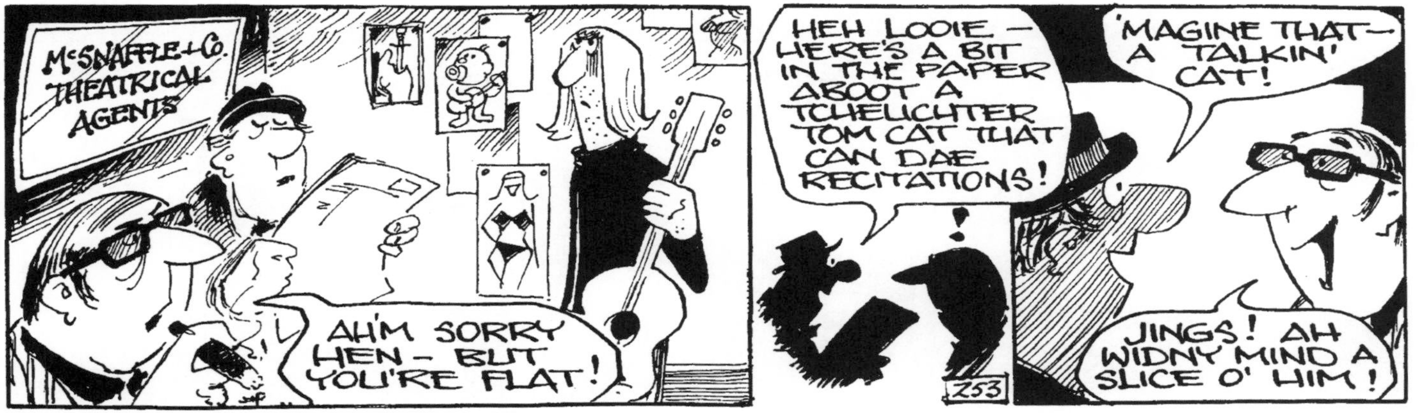
McSNAFFLE + Co.
THEATRICAL AGENTS
AH'M SORRY HEN - BUT YOU'RE FLAT!
HEH LOOIE - HERE'S A BIT IN THE PAPER ABOOT A TCHEUCHTER TOM CAT THAT CAN DAE RECITATIONS!
!
'MAGINE THAT - A TALKIN' CAT!
JINGS! AH WIDNY MIND A SLICE O' HIM!
253

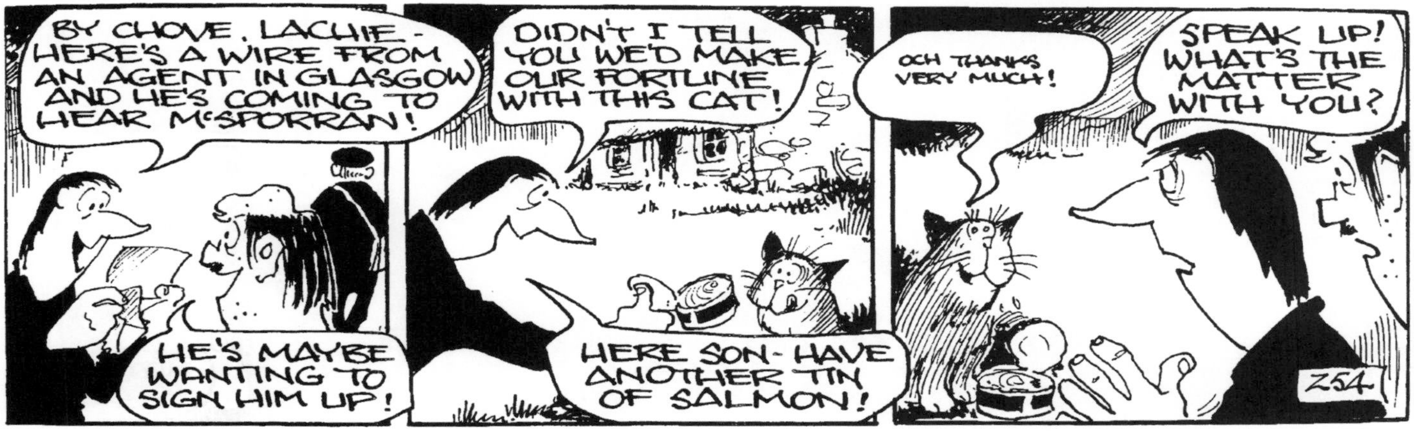
BY CHOVE, LACHIE - HERE'S A WIRE FROM AN AGENT IN GLASGOW AND HE'S COMING TO HEAR McSPORRAN!
HE'S MAYBE WANTING TO SIGN HIM UP!
DIDN'T I TELL YOU WE'D MAKE OUR FORTUNE WITH THIS CAT!
HERE SON - HAVE ANOTHER TIN OF SALMON!
OCH THANKS VERY MUCH!
SPEAK UP! WHAT'S THE MATTER WITH YOU?
254

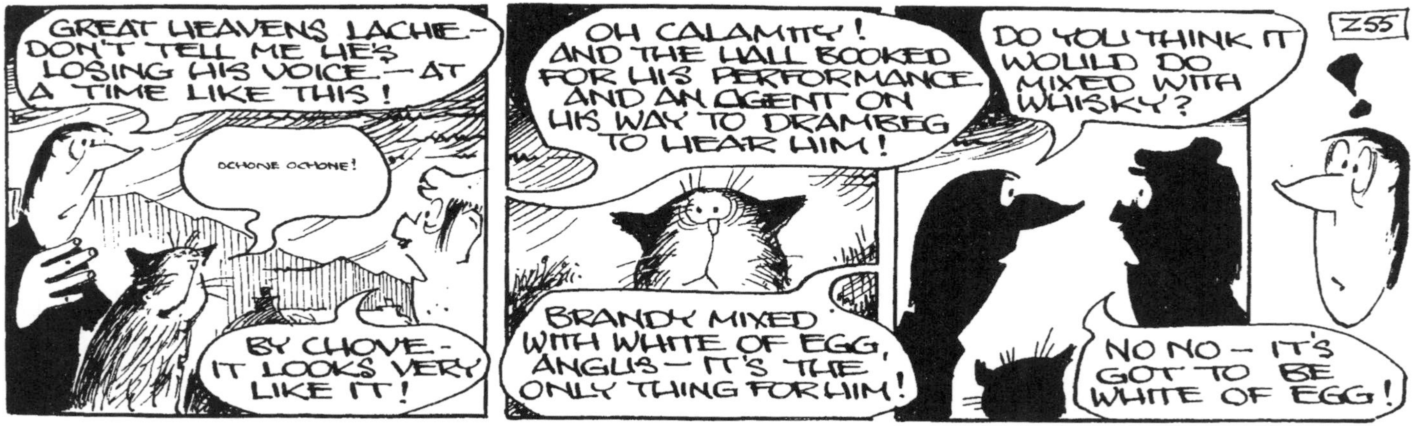
255
GREAT HEAVENS LACHIE - DON'T TELL ME HE'S LOSING HIS VOICE - AT A TIME LIKE THIS!
OCHONE OCHONE!
BY CHOVE - IT LOOKS VERY LIKE IT!
OH CALAMITY! AND THE HALL BOOKED FOR HIS PERFORMANCE AND AN AGENT ON HIS WAY TO DRAMBEG TO HEAR HIM!
BRANDY MIXED WITH WHITE OF EGG, ANGUS - IT'S THE ONLY THING FOR HIM!
DO YOU THINK IT WOULD DO MIXED WITH WHISKY?
!
NO NO - IT'S GOT TO BE WHITE OF EGG!

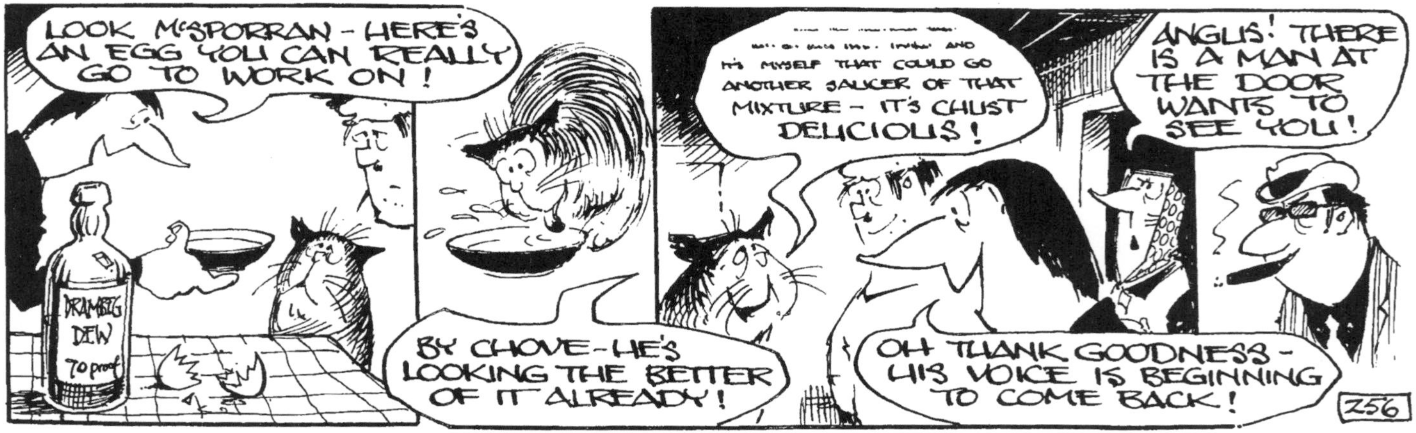
LOOK McSPORRAN - HERE'S AN EGG YOU CAN REALLY GO TO WORK ON!
DRAMBEG DEW 70 proof
BY CHOVE - HE'S LOOKING THE BETTER OF IT ALREADY!
AND IT'S MYSELF THAT COULD GO ANOTHER SAUCER OF THAT MIXTURE - IT'S CHUST DELICIOUS!
OH THANK GOODNESS - HIS VOICE IS BEGINNING TO COME BACK!
ANGUS! THERE IS A MAN AT THE DOOR WANTS TO SEE YOU!
256

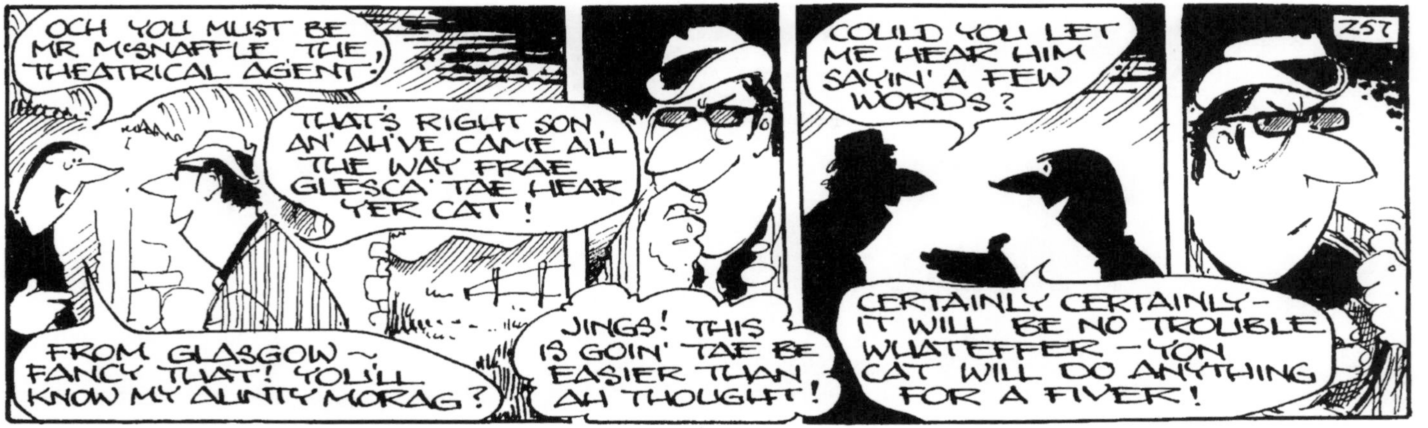
OCH YOU MUST BE MR McSNAFFLE THE THEATRICAL AGENT!
THAT'S RIGHT SON AN' AH'VE CAME ALL THE WAY FRAE GLESCA' TAE HEAR YER CAT!
FROM GLASGOW ~ FANCY THAT! YOU'LL KNOW MY AUNTY MORAG?
JINGS! THIS IS GOIN' TAE BE EASIER THAN AH THOUGHT!
COULD YOU LET ME HEAR HIM SAYIN' A FEW WORDS?
257
CERTAINLY CERTAINLY - IT WILL BE NO TROUBLE WHATEFFER - YON CAT WILL DO ANYTHING FOR A FIVER!

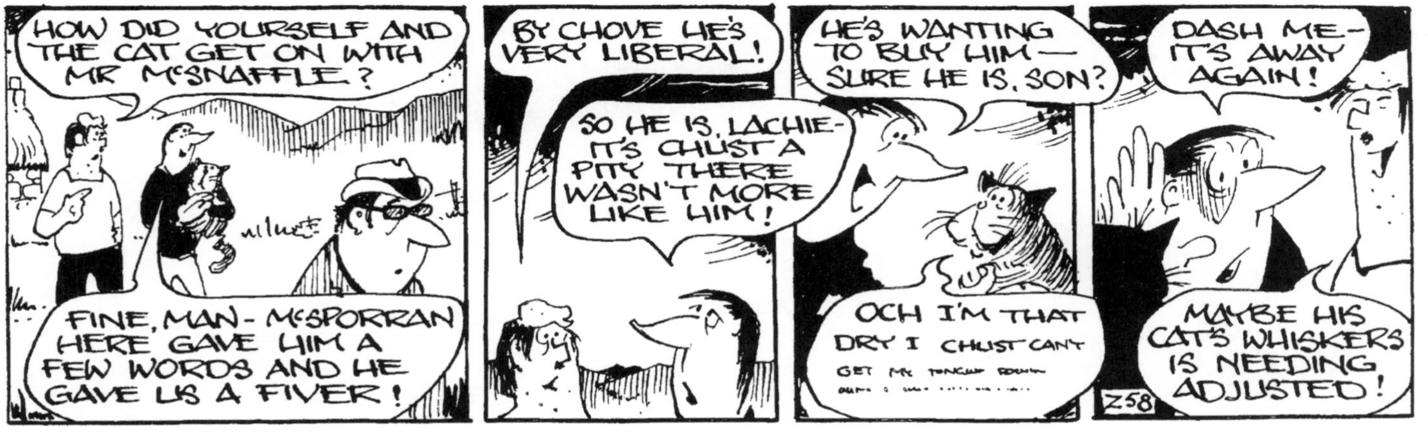
HOW DID YOURSELF AND THE CAT GET ON WITH MR McSNAFFLE?
FINE, MAN - McSPORRAN HERE GAVE HIM A FEW WORDS AND HE GAVE US A FIVER!
BY CHOVE HE'S VERY LIBERAL!
SO HE IS, LACHIE - IT'S CHUST A PITY THERE WASN'T MORE LIKE HIM!
HE'S WANTING TO BUY HIM — SURE HE IS, SON?
OCH I'M THAT DRY I CHUST CAN'T
258
DASH ME - IT'S AWAY AGAIN!
MAYBE HIS CAT'S WHISKERS IS NEEDING ADJUSTED!

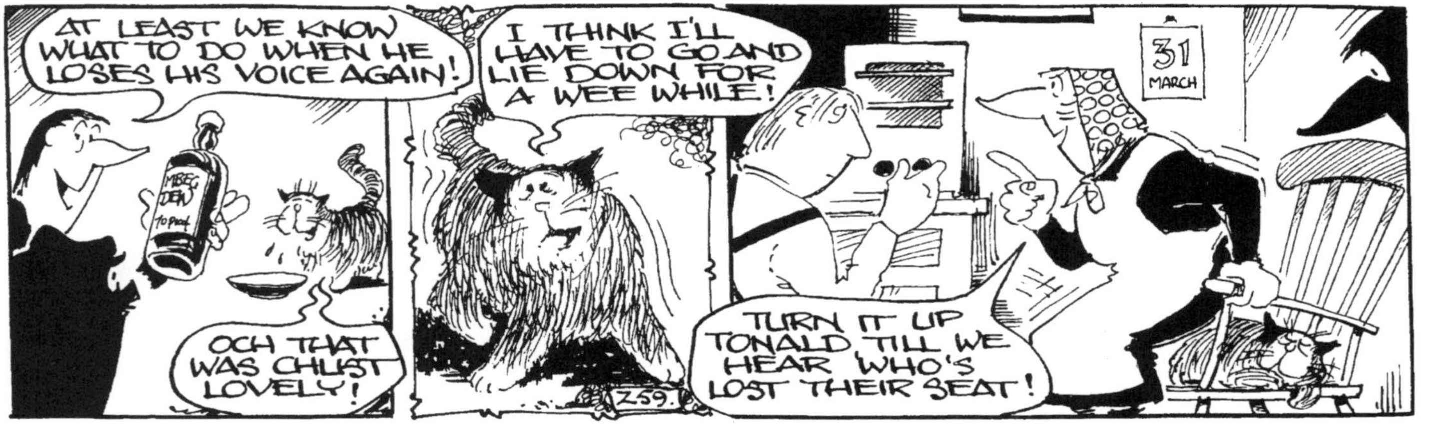

AT LEAST WE KNOW WHAT TO DO WHEN HE LOSES HIS VOICE AGAIN!
M'BEG DEW 70 proof
OCH THAT WAS CHUST LOVELY!
I THINK I'LL HAVE TO GO AND LIE DOWN FOR A WEE WHILE!
259
31 MARCH
TURN IT UP TONALD TILL WE HEAR WHO'S LOST THEIR SEAT!

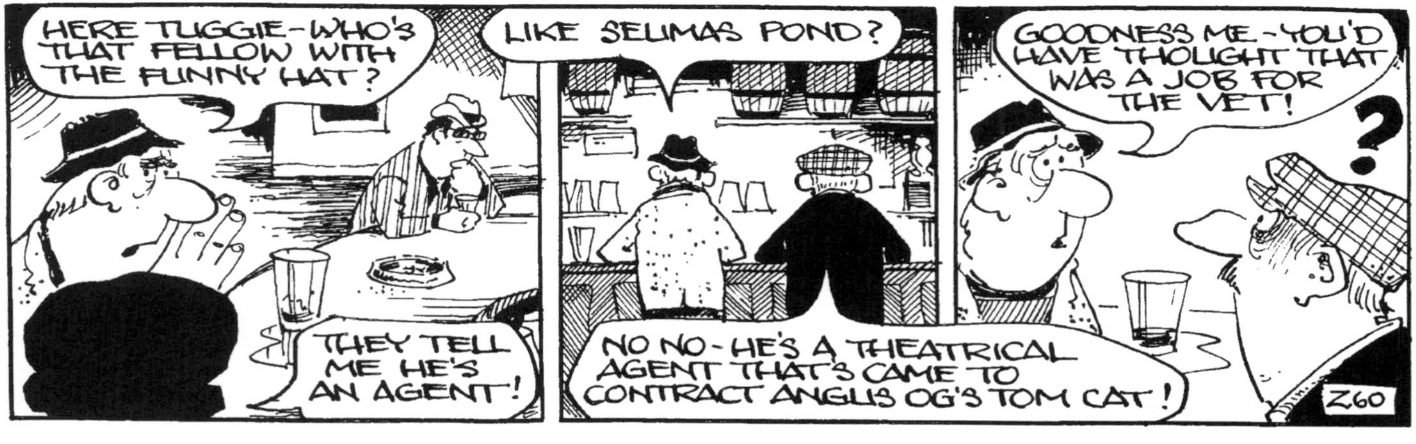

HERE TUGGIE - WHO'S THAT FELLOW WITH THE FUNNY HAT?
THEY TELL ME HE'S AN AGENT!
LIKE SELIMAS POND?
NO NO - HE'S A THEATRICAL AGENT THAT'S CAME TO CONTRACT ANGUS OG'S TOM CAT!
GOODNESS ME - YOU'D HAVE THOUGHT THAT WAS A JOB FOR THE VET!
?
260

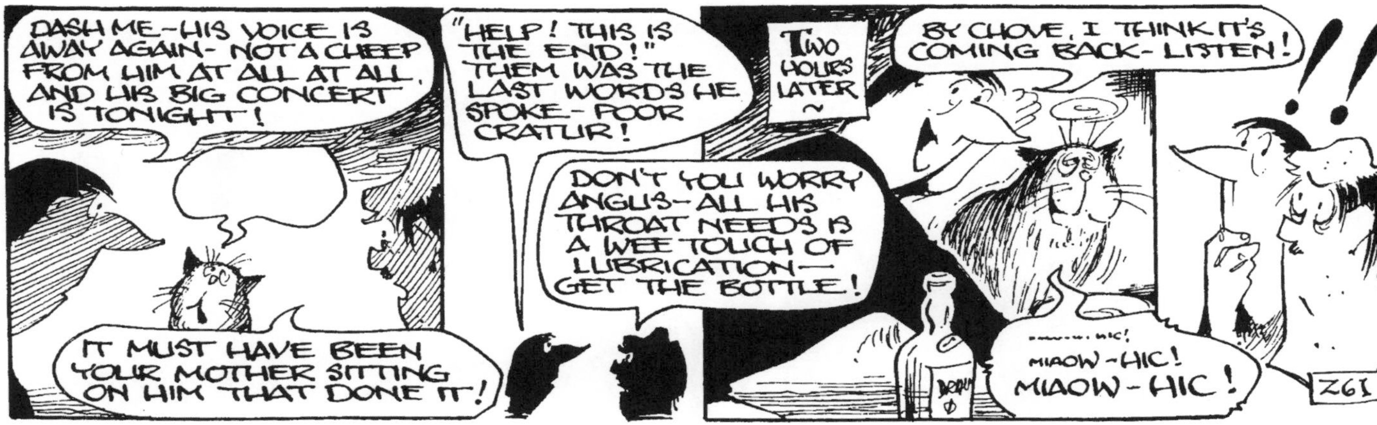
DASH ME - HIS VOICE IS AWAY AGAIN - NOT A CHEEP FROM HIM AT ALL AT ALL, AND HIS BIG CONCERT IS TONIGHT!
IT MUST HAVE BEEN YOUR MOTHER SITTING ON HIM THAT DONE IT!
"HELP! THIS IS THE END!" THEM WAS THE LAST WORDS HE SPOKE - POOR CRATUR!
DON'T YOU WORRY ANGUS - ALL HIS THROAT NEEDS IS A WEE TOUCH OF LUBRICATION - GET THE BOTTLE!
TWO HOURS LATER ~
BY CHOVE, I THINK IT'S COMING BACK - LISTEN!
MIAOW - HIC! MIAOW - HIC!
!!
261

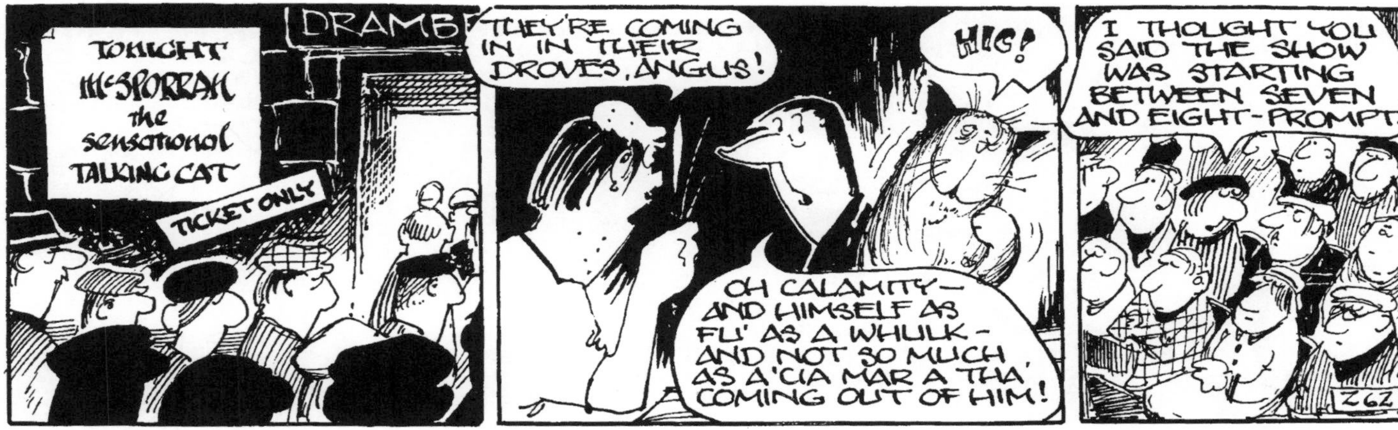
TONIGHT
MᶜSPORRAN the sensational TALKING CAT
TICKET ONLY
DRAMB
THEY'RE COMING IN IN THEIR DROVES, ANGUS!
HIC!
OH CALAMITY - AND HIMSELF AS FU' AS A WHULK - AND NOT SO MUCH AS A 'CIA MAR A THA' COMING OUT OF HIM!
I THOUGHT YOU SAID THE SHOW WAS STARTING BETWEEN SEVEN AND EIGHT - PROMPT!
262

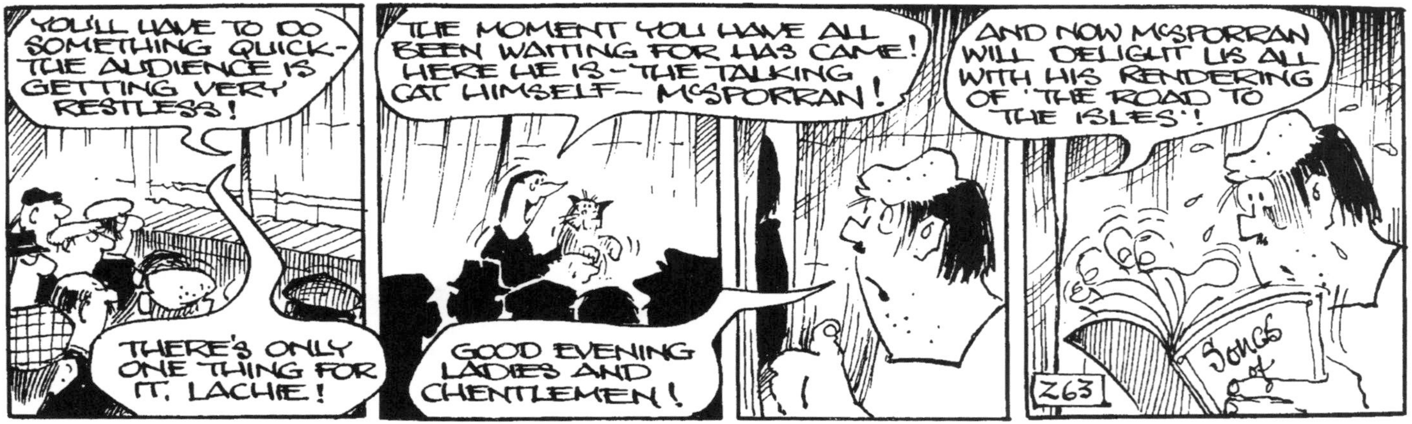

YOU'LL HAVE TO DO SOMETHING QUICK-THE AUDIENCE IS GETTING VERY RESTLESS!
THERE'S ONLY ONE THING FOR IT, LACHIE!
THE MOMENT YOU HAVE ALL BEEN WAITING FOR HAS CAME! HERE HE IS - THE TALKING CAT HIMSELF - McSPORRAN!
GOOD EVENING LADIES AND CHENTLEMEN!
AND NOW McSPORRAN WILL DELIGHT US ALL WITH HIS RENDERING OF 'THE ROAD TO THE ISLES'!
SONGS OF
263

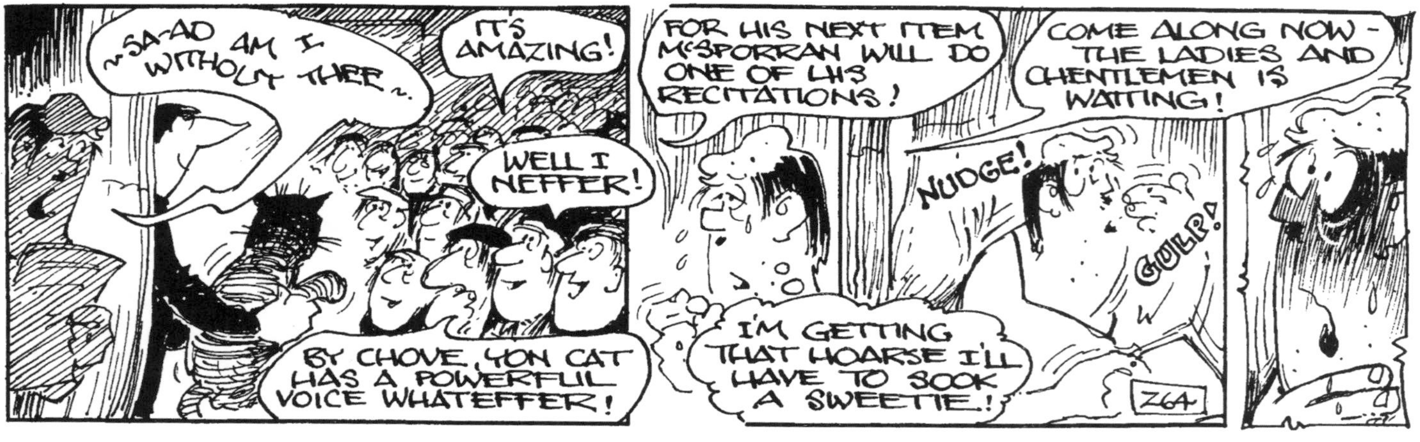

~SA-AD AM I WITHOUT THEE~
IT'S AMAZING!
WELL I NEFFER!
BY CHOVE, YON CAT HAS A POWERFUL VOICE WHATEFFER!
FOR HIS NEXT ITEM McSPORRAN WILL DO ONE OF HIS RECITATIONS!
I'M GETTING THAT HOARSE I'LL HAVE TO SOOK A SWEETIE!
COME ALONG NOW - THE LADIES AND CHENTLEMEN IS WAITING!
NUDGE!
GULP!
264

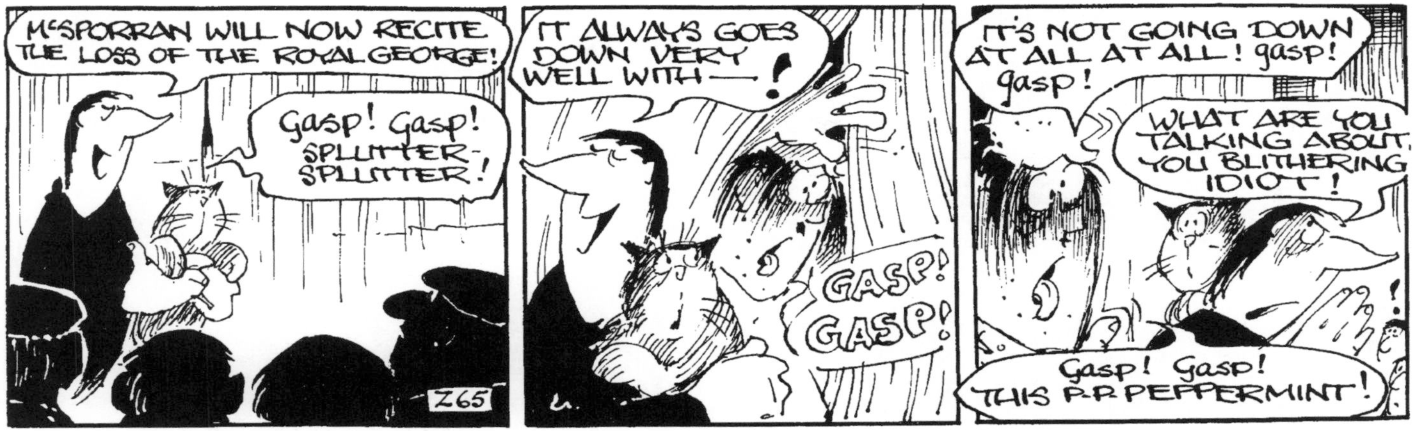
McSPORRAN WILL NOW RECITE THE LOSS OF THE ROYAL GEORGE!
Gasp! Gasp! SPLUTTER-SPLUTTER!
Z65
IT ALWAYS GOES DOWN VERY WELL WITH — !
GASP! GASP!
IT'S NOT GOING DOWN AT ALL AT ALL! gasp! gasp!
WHAT ARE YOU TALKING ABOUT, YOU BLITHERING IDIOT!
Gasp! Gasp! THIS P-P PEPPERMINT!

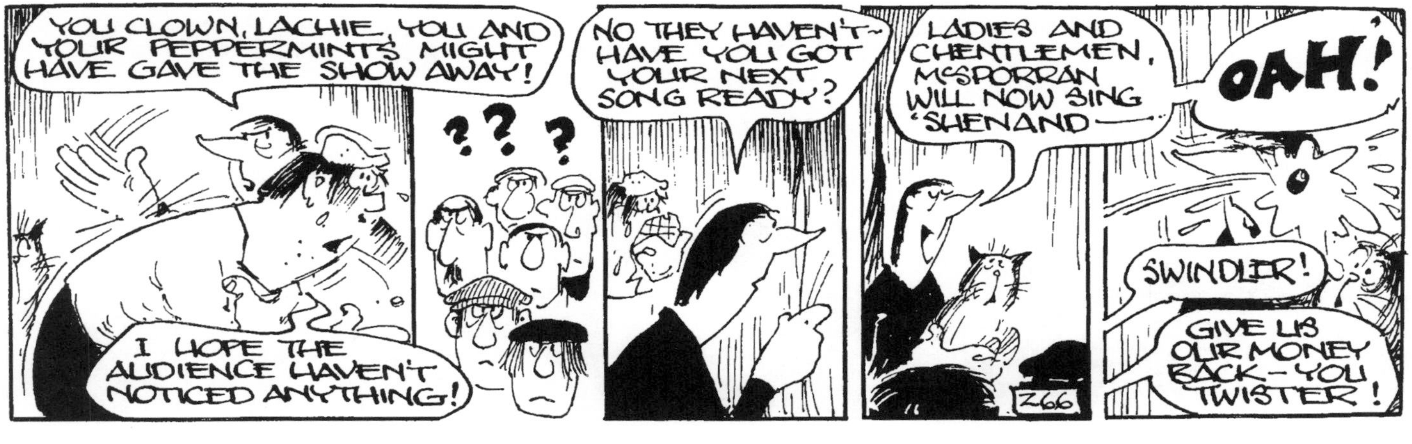
YOU CLOWN, LACHIE, YOU AND YOUR PEPPERMINTS MIGHT HAVE GAVE THE SHOW AWAY!
I HOPE THE AUDIENCE HAVEN'T NOTICED ANYTHING!
? ? ?
NO THEY HAVEN'T — HAVE YOU GOT YOUR NEXT SONG READY?
LADIES AND CHENTLEMEN, McSPORRAN WILL NOW SING 'SHENAND—
Z66
OAH!
SWINDLER!
GIVE US OUR MONEY BACK — YOU TWISTER!

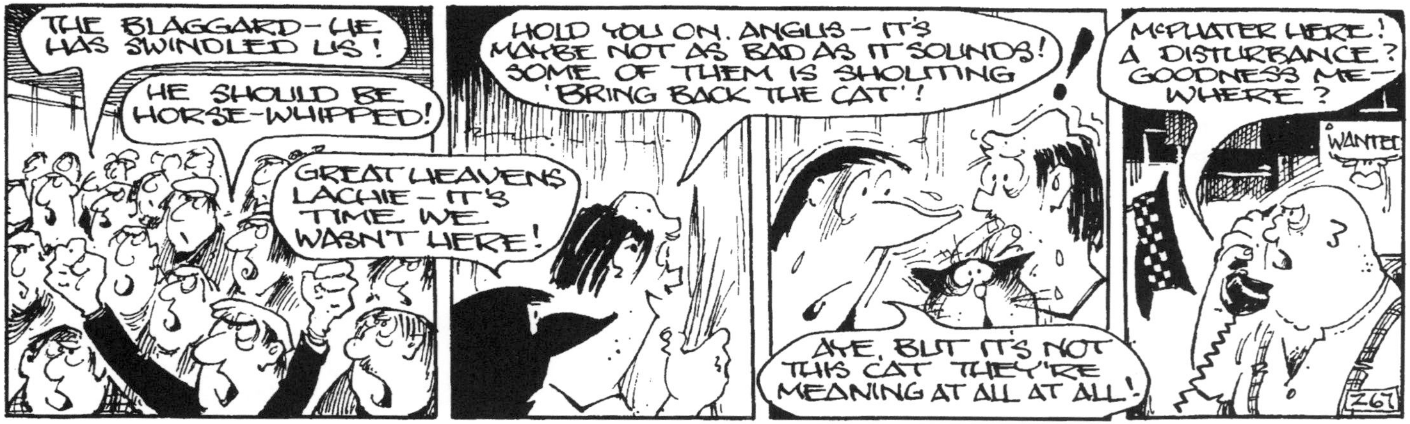
THE BLAGGARD - HE HAS SWINDLED US!
HE SHOULD BE HORSE-WHIPPED!
GREAT HEAVENS LACHIE - IT'S TIME WE WASN'T HERE!
HOLD YOU ON, ANGUS - IT'S MAYBE NOT AS BAD AS IT SOUNDS! SOME OF THEM IS SHOUTING 'BRING BACK THE CAT'!
!
AYE, BUT IT'S NOT THIS CAT THEY'RE MEANING AT ALL AT ALL!
McPHATER HERE! A DISTURBANCE? GOODNESS ME - WHERE?
WANTED
267

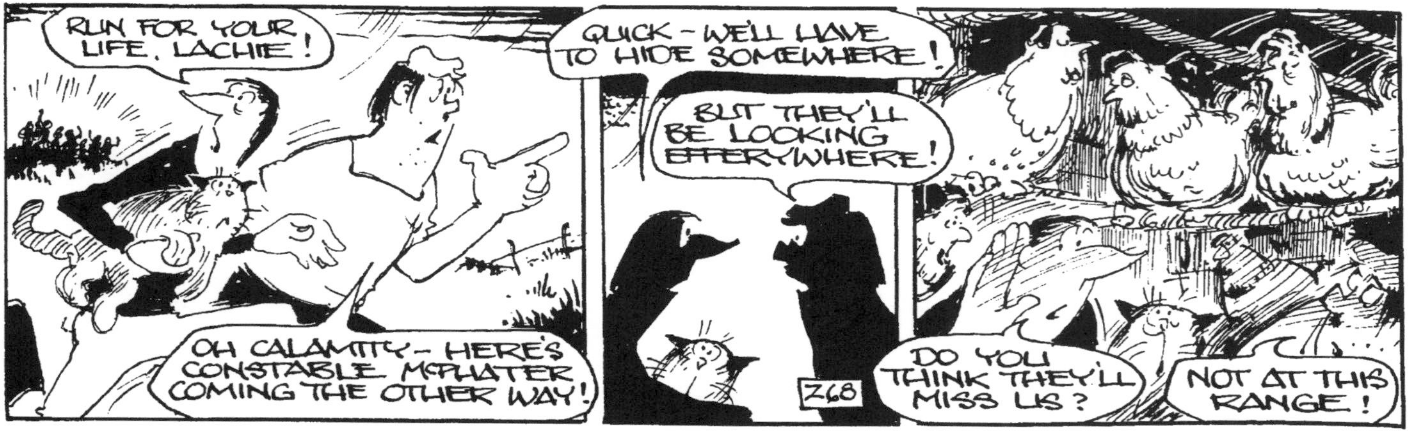
RUN FOR YOUR LIFE, LACHIE!
OH CALAMITY - HERE'S CONSTABLE McPHATER COMING THE OTHER WAY!
QUICK - WE'LL HAVE TO HIDE SOMEWHERE!
BUT THEY'LL BE LOOKING EFFERYWHERE!
268
DO YOU THINK THEY'LL MISS US?
NOT AT THIS RANGE!

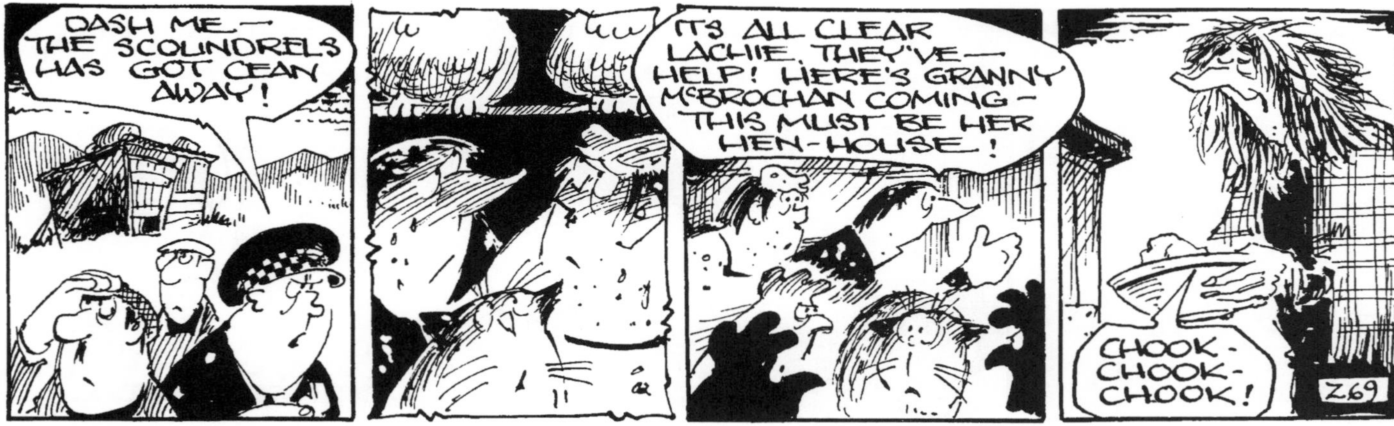
DASH ME— THE SCOUNDRELS HAS GOT CEAN AWAY!
IT'S ALL CLEAR LACHIE, THEY'VE— HELP! HERE'S GRANNY McBROCHAN COMING— THIS MUST BE HER HEN-HOUSE!
CHOOK-CHOOK-CHOOK!
269

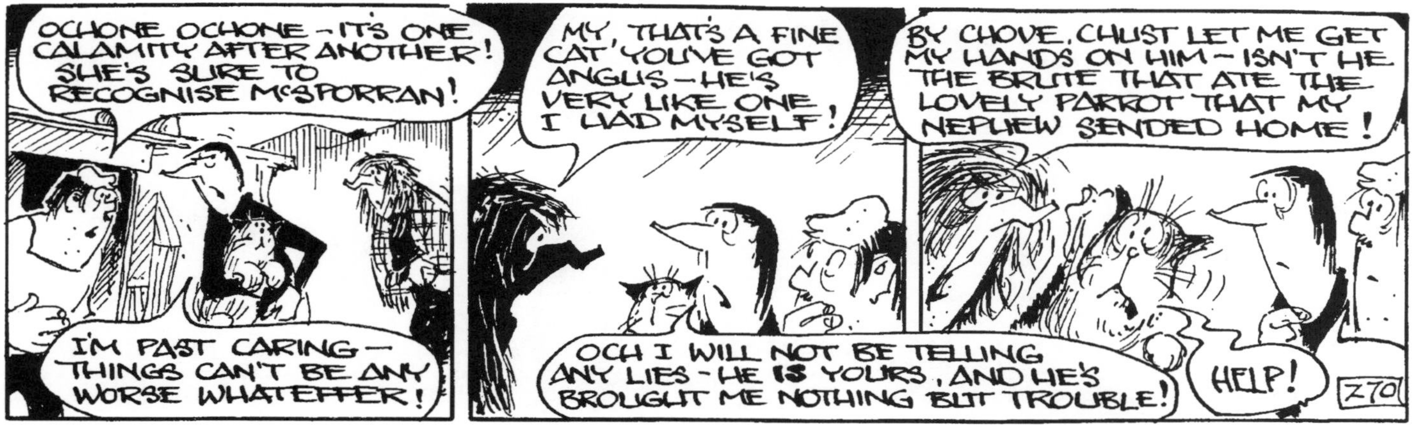
OCHONE OCHONE—IT'S ONE CALAMITY AFTER ANOTHER! SHE'S SURE TO RECOGNISE McSPORRAN!
I'M PAST CARING— THINGS CAN'T BE ANY WORSE WHATEFFER!
MY, THAT'S A FINE CAT YOU'VE GOT ANGUS—HE'S VERY LIKE ONE I HAD MYSELF!
OCH I WILL NOT BE TELLING ANY LIES—HE **IS** YOURS, AND HE'S BROUGHT ME NOTHING BUT TROUBLE!
BY CHOVE, CHUST LET ME GET MY HANDS ON HIM—ISN'T HE THE BRUTE THAT ATE THE LOVELY PARROT THAT MY NEPHEW SENDED HOME!
HELP!
270

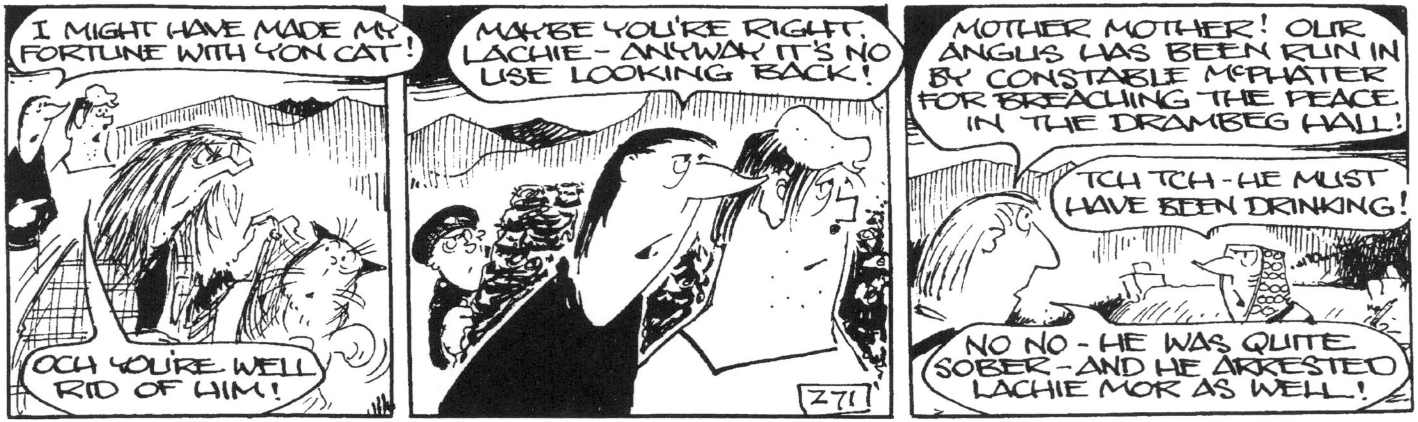
I MIGHT HAVE MADE MY FORTUNE WITH YON CAT!
OCH YOU'RE WELL RID OF HIM!
MAYBE YOU'RE RIGHT, LACHIE - ANYWAY IT'S NO USE LOOKING BACK!
271
MOTHER MOTHER! OUR ANGUS HAS BEEN RUN IN BY CONSTABLE McPHATER FOR BREACHING THE PEACE IN THE DRAMBEG HALL!
TCH TCH - HE MUST HAVE BEEN DRINKING!
NO NO - HE WAS QUITE SOBER - AND HE ARRESTED LACHIE MOR AS WELL!

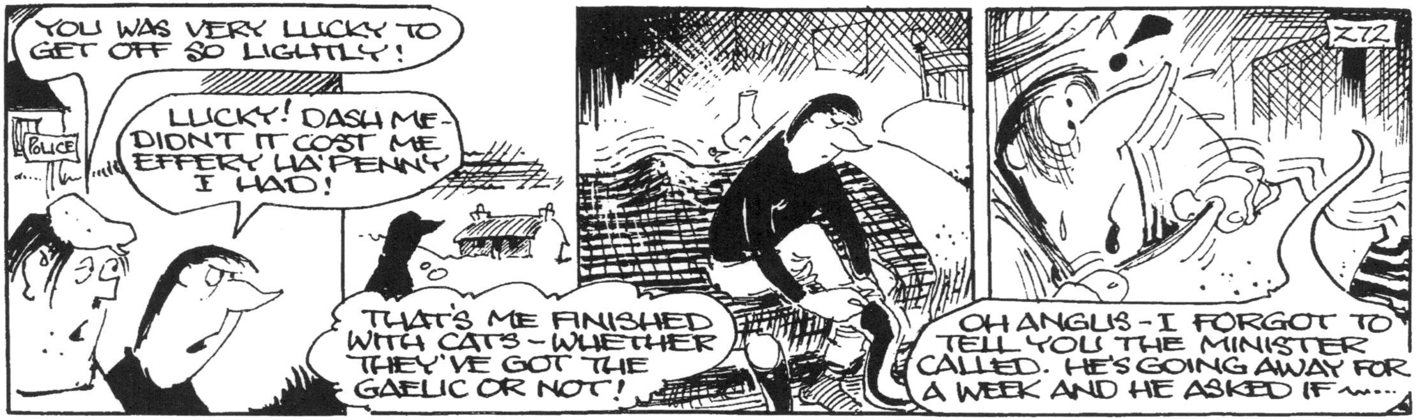
YOU WAS VERY LUCKY TO GET OFF SO LIGHTLY!
POLICE
LUCKY! DASH ME - DIDN'T IT COST ME EFFERY HA'PENNY I HAD!
THAT'S ME FINISHED WITH CATS - WHETHER THEY'VE GOT THE GAELIC OR NOT!
272
OH ANGUS - I FORGOT TO TELL YOU THE MINISTER CALLED. HE'S GOING AWAY FOR A WEEK AND HE ASKED IF ~~....

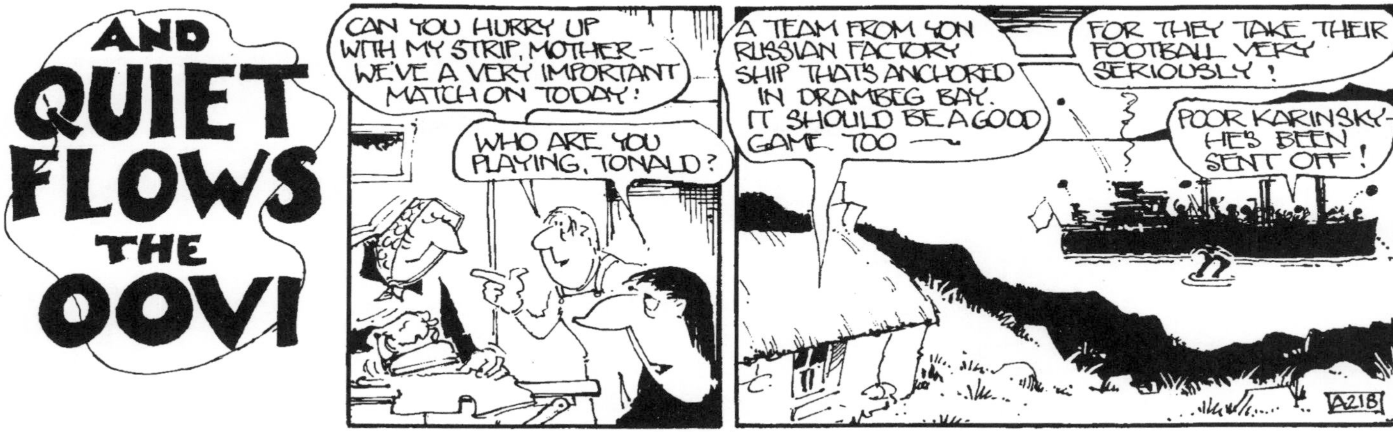
AND QUIET FLOWS THE OOVI
CAN YOU HURRY UP WITH MY STRIP, MOTHER - WE'VE A VERY IMPORTANT MATCH ON TODAY!
WHO ARE YOU PLAYING, TONALD?
A TEAM FROM YON RUSSIAN FACTORY SHIP THAT'S ANCHORED IN DRAMBEG BAY. IT SHOULD BE A GOOD GAME TOO -
FOR THEY TAKE THEIR FOOTBALL VERY SERIOUSLY!
POOR KARINSKY - HE'S BEEN SENT OFF!
A218

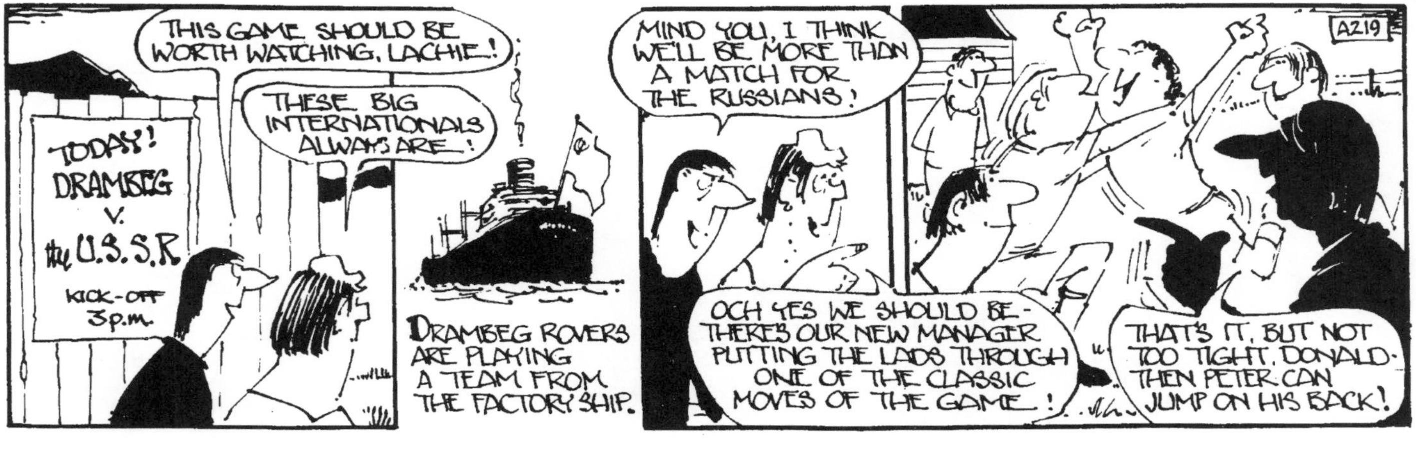
THIS GAME SHOULD BE WORTH WATCHING, LACHIE!
THESE BIG INTERNATIONALS ALWAYS ARE!
TODAY! DRAMBEG V. the U.S.S.R KICK-OFF 3p.m.
DRAMBEG ROVERS ARE PLAYING A TEAM FROM THE FACTORY SHIP.
MIND YOU, I THINK WE'LL BE MORE THAN A MATCH FOR THE RUSSIANS!
OCH YES WE SHOULD BE - THERE'S OUR NEW MANAGER PUTTING THE LADS THROUGH ONE OF THE CLASSIC MOVES OF THE GAME!
THAT'S IT, BUT NOT TOO TIGHT, DONALD - THEN PETER CAN JUMP ON HIS BACK!
A219

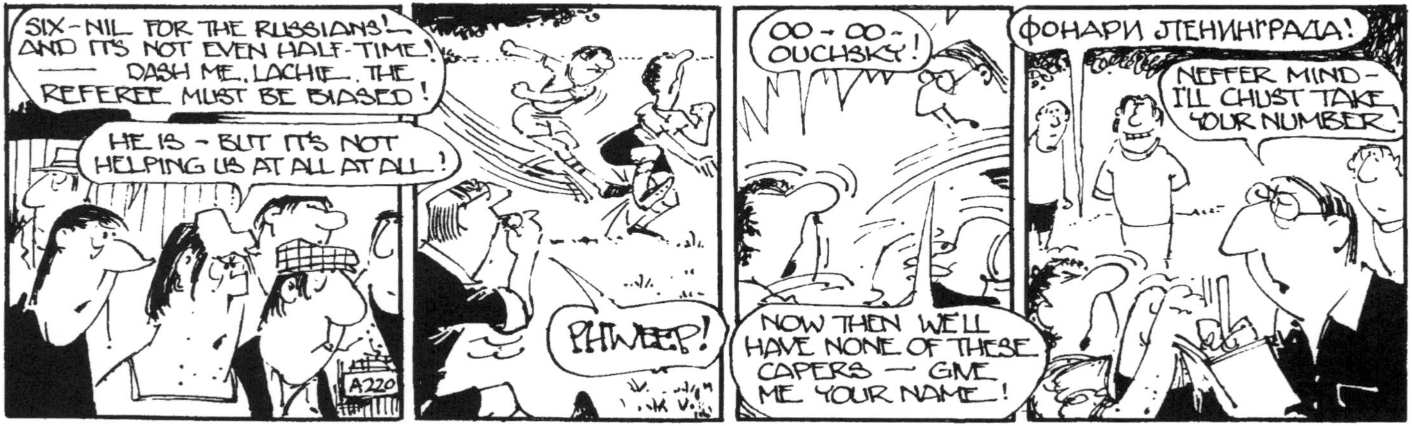
SIX-NIL FOR THE RUSSIANS! — AND IT'S NOT EVEN HALF-TIME! —— DASH ME, LACHIE, THE REFEREE MUST BE BIASED!
HE IS — BUT IT'S NOT HELPING US AT ALL AT ALL!
A220
PHWEEP!
OO — OO — OUCHSKY!
NOW THEN WE'LL HAVE NONE OF THESE CAPERS — GIVE ME YOUR NAME!
ФОНАРИ ЛЕНИНГРАДА!
NEFFER MIND — I'LL CHUST TAKE YOUR NUMBER!

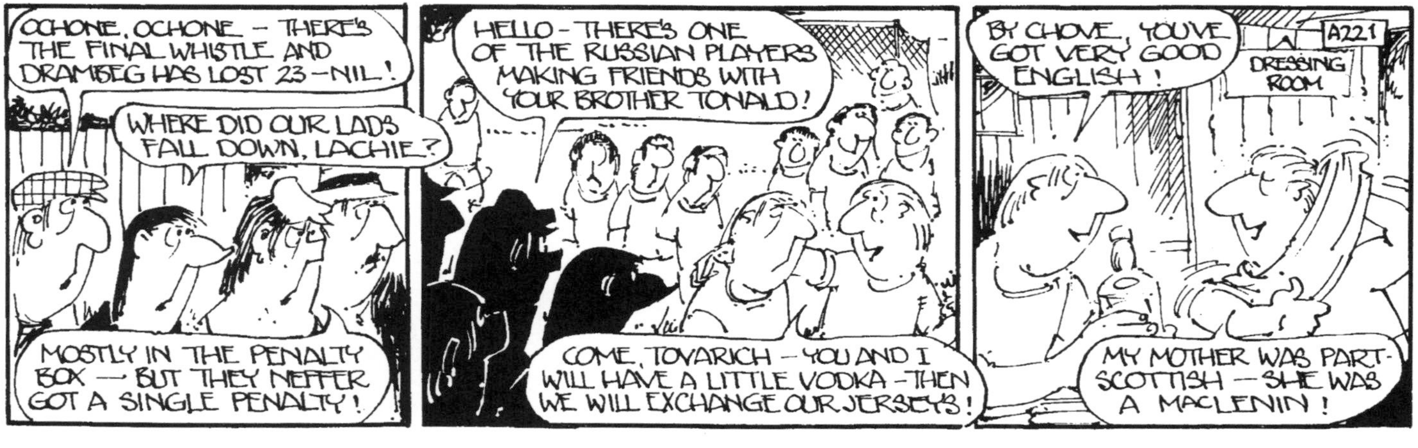
OCHONE, OCHONE — THERE'S THE FINAL WHISTLE AND DRAMBEG HAS LOST 23-NIL!
WHERE DID OUR LADS FALL DOWN, LACHIE?
MOSTLY IN THE PENALTY BOX — BUT THEY NEFFER GOT A SINGLE PENALTY!
HELLO — THERE'S ONE OF THE RUSSIAN PLAYERS MAKING FRIENDS WITH YOUR BROTHER TONALD!
COME, TOVARICH — YOU AND I WILL HAVE A LITTLE VODKA — THEN WE WILL EXCHANGE OUR JERSEYS!
A221
DRESSING ROOM
BY CHOVE, YOU'VE GOT VERY GOOD ENGLISH!
MY MOTHER WAS PART-SCOTTISH — SHE WAS A MACLENIN!

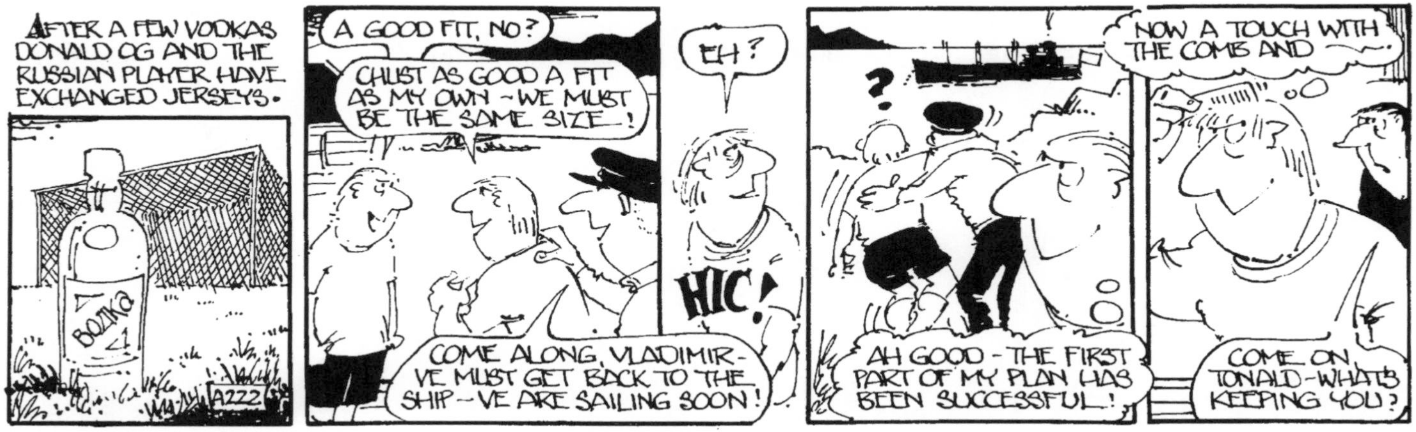
AFTER A FEW VODKAS DONALD OG AND THE RUSSIAN PLAYER HAVE EXCHANGED JERSEYS.
BOZKA
A222
A GOOD FIT, NO?
CHUST AS GOOD A FIT AS MY OWN – WE MUST BE THE SAME SIZE!
COME ALONG, VLADIMIR – VE MUST GET BACK TO THE SHIP – VE ARE SAILING SOON!
EH?
HIC!
AH GOOD – THE FIRST PART OF MY PLAN HAS BEEN SUCCESSFUL!
NOW A TOUCH WITH THE COMB AND ~~~.
COME ON TONALD – WHAT'S KEEPING YOU?

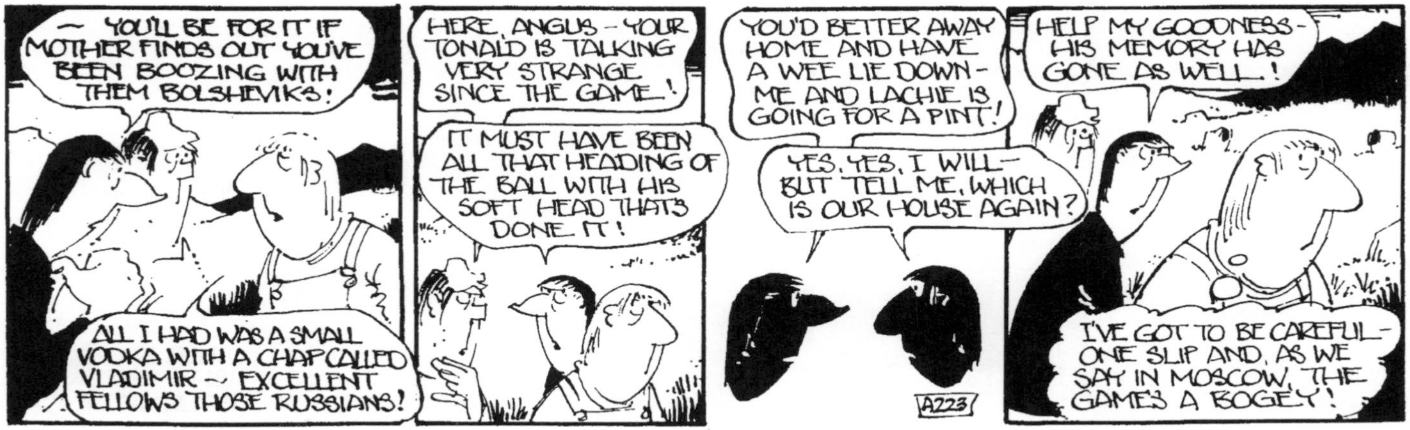
– YOU'LL BE FOR IT IF MOTHER FINDS OUT YOU'VE BEEN BOOZING WITH THEM BOLSHEVIKS!
ALL I HAD WAS A SMALL VODKA WITH A CHAP CALLED VLADIMIR – EXCELLENT FELLOWS THOSE RUSSIANS!
HERE, ANGUS – YOUR TONALD IS TALKING VERY STRANGE SINCE THE GAME!
IT MUST HAVE BEEN ALL THAT HEADING OF THE BALL WITH HIS SOFT HEAD THAT'S DONE IT!
YOU'D BETTER AWAY HOME AND HAVE A WEE LIE DOWN – ME AND LACHIE IS GOING FOR A PINT!
YES, YES, I WILL – BUT TELL ME, WHICH IS OUR HOUSE AGAIN?
A223
HELP MY GOODNESS – HIS MEMORY HAS GONE AS WELL!
I'VE GOT TO BE CAREFUL – ONE SLIP AND, AS WE SAY IN MOSCOW, THE GAME'S A BOGEY!

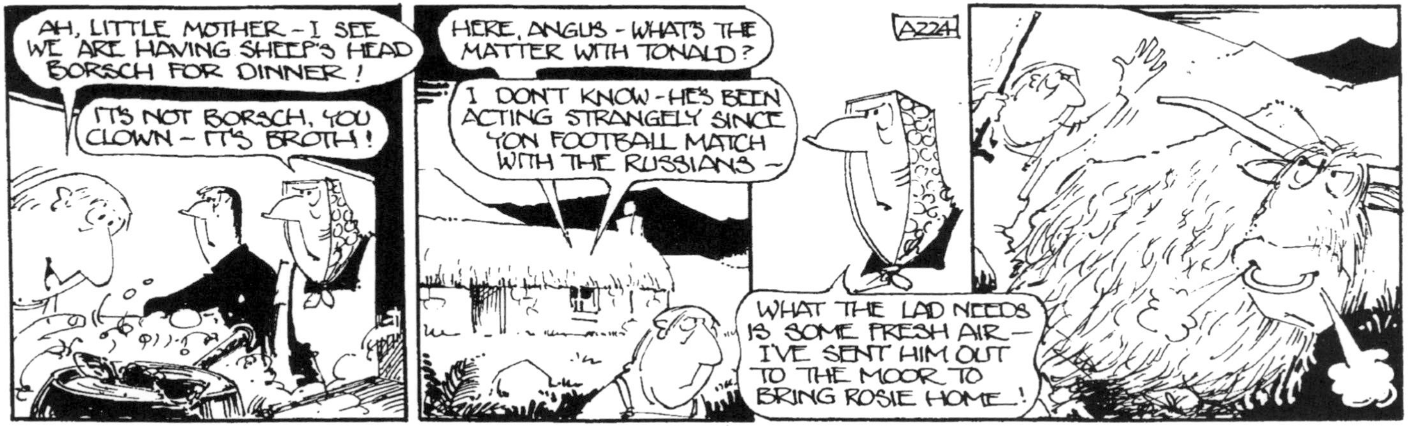
AH, LITTLE MOTHER - I SEE WE ARE HAVING SHEEP'S HEAD BORSCH FOR DINNER!
IT'S NOT BORSCH, YOU CLOWN - IT'S BROTH!
HERE, ANGUS - WHAT'S THE MATTER WITH TONALD?
I DON'T KNOW - HE'S BEEN ACTING STRANGELY SINCE YON FOOTBALL MATCH WITH THE RUSSIANS -
A224
WHAT THE LAD NEEDS IS SOME FRESH AIR - I'VE SENT HIM OUT TO THE MOOR TO BRING ROSIE HOME!

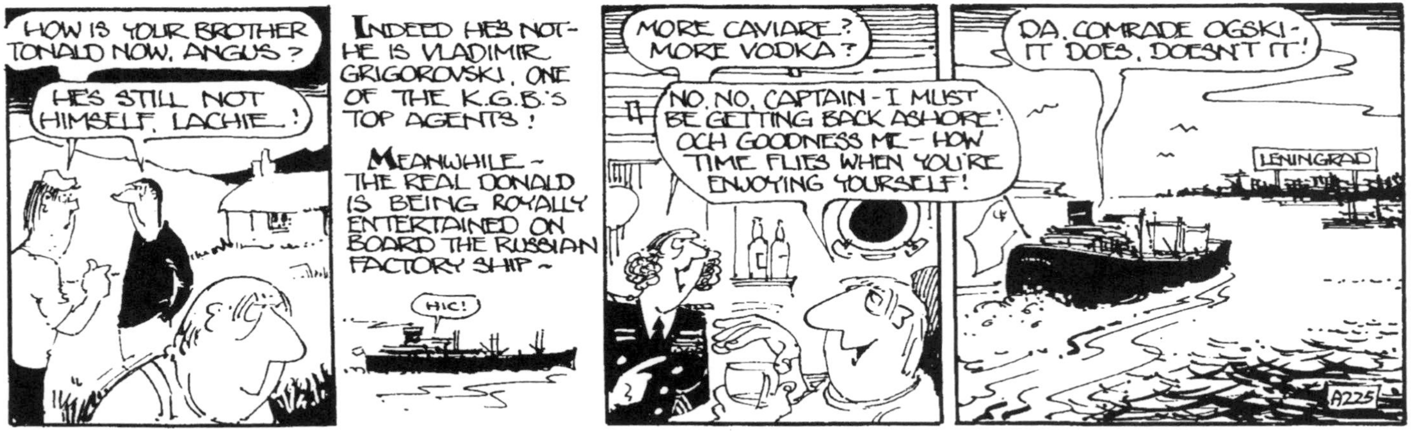
HOW IS YOUR BROTHER TONALD NOW, ANGUS?
HE'S STILL NOT HIMSELF, LACHIE!
INDEED HE'S NOT - HE IS VLADIMIR GRIGOROVSKI, ONE OF THE K.G.B.'S TOP AGENTS!
MEANWHILE - THE REAL DONALD IS BEING ROYALLY ENTERTAINED ON BOARD THE RUSSIAN FACTORY SHIP -
HIC!
MORE CAVIARE? MORE VODKA?
NO, NO, CAPTAIN - I MUST BE GETTING BACK ASHORE! OCH GOODNESS ME - HOW TIME FLIES WHEN YOU'RE ENJOYING YOURSELF!
DA, COMRADE OGSKI - IT DOES, DOESN'T IT!
LENINGRAD
A225

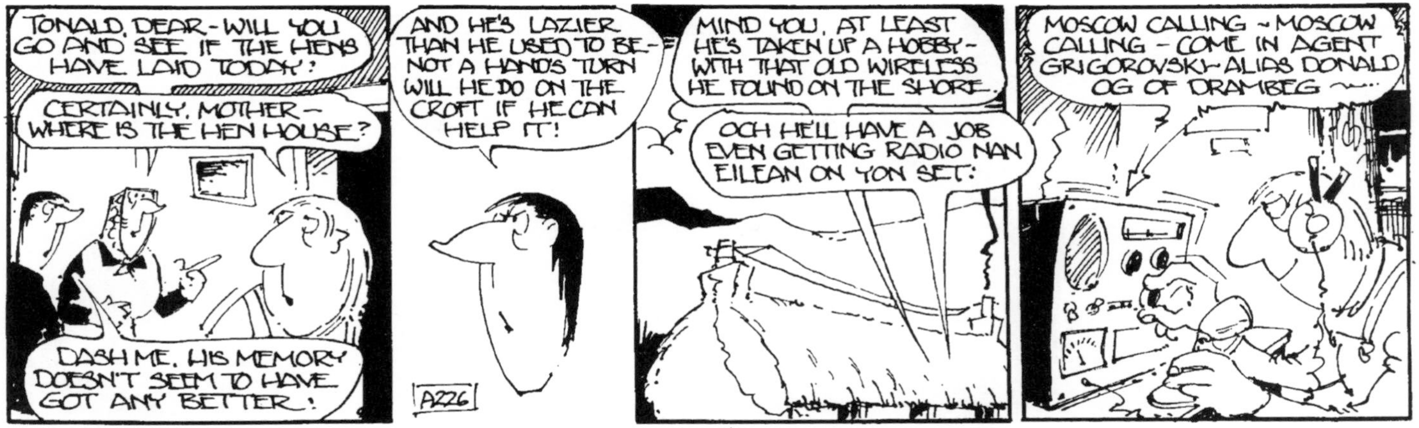
TONALD, DEAR - WILL YOU GO AND SEE IF THE HENS HAVE LAID TODAY?
CERTAINLY, MOTHER - WHERE IS THE HEN HOUSE?
DASH ME, HIS MEMORY DOESN'T SEEM TO HAVE GOT ANY BETTER!
AND HE'S LAZIER THAN HE USED TO BE - NOT A HAND'S TURN WILL HE DO ON THE CROFT IF HE CAN HELP IT!
A226
MIND YOU, AT LEAST HE'S TAKEN UP A HOBBY - WITH THAT OLD WIRELESS HE FOUND ON THE SHORE.
OCH HE'LL HAVE A JOB EVEN GETTING RADIO NAN EILEAN ON YON SET!
MOSCOW CALLING - MOSCOW CALLING - COME IN AGENT GRIGOROVSKI - ALIAS DONALD OG OF DRAMBEG ~...

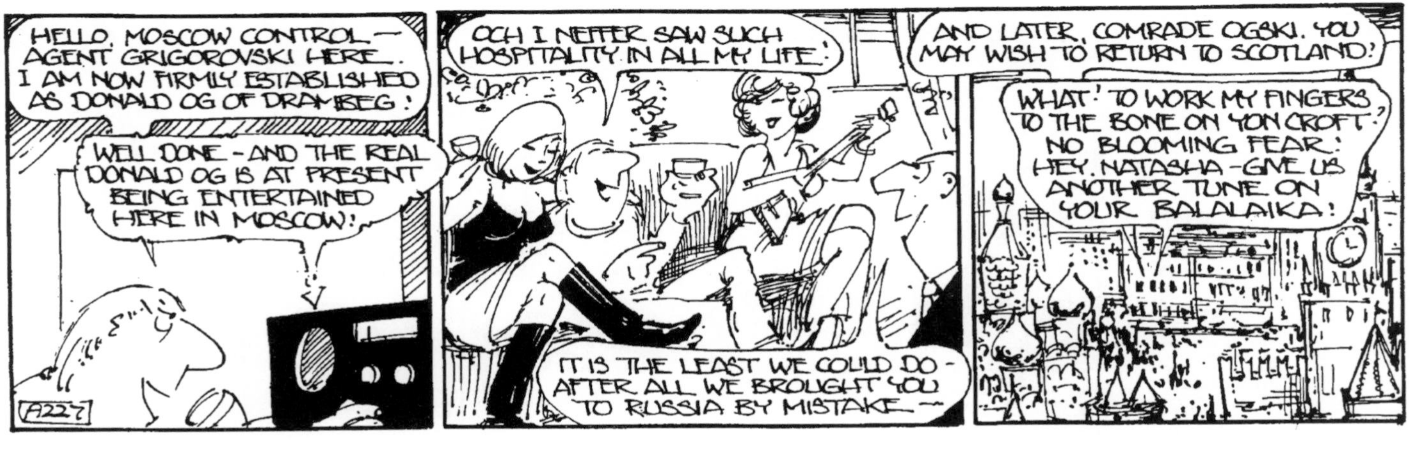
HELLO, MOSCOW CONTROL - AGENT GRIGOROVSKI HERE. I AM NOW FIRMLY ESTABLISHED AS DONALD OG OF DRAMBEG!
WELL DONE - AND THE REAL DONALD OG IS AT PRESENT BEING ENTERTAINED HERE IN MOSCOW!
A227
OCH I NEFFER SAW SUCH HOSPITALITY IN ALL MY LIFE!
IT IS THE LEAST WE COULD DO - AFTER ALL WE BROUGHT YOU TO RUSSIA BY MISTAKE --
AND LATER, COMRADE OGSKI, YOU MAY WISH TO RETURN TO SCOTLAND!
WHAT! TO WORK MY FINGERS TO THE BONE ON YON CROFT? NO BLOOMING FEAR! HEY, NATASHA - GIVE US ANOTHER TUNE ON YOUR BALALAIKA!

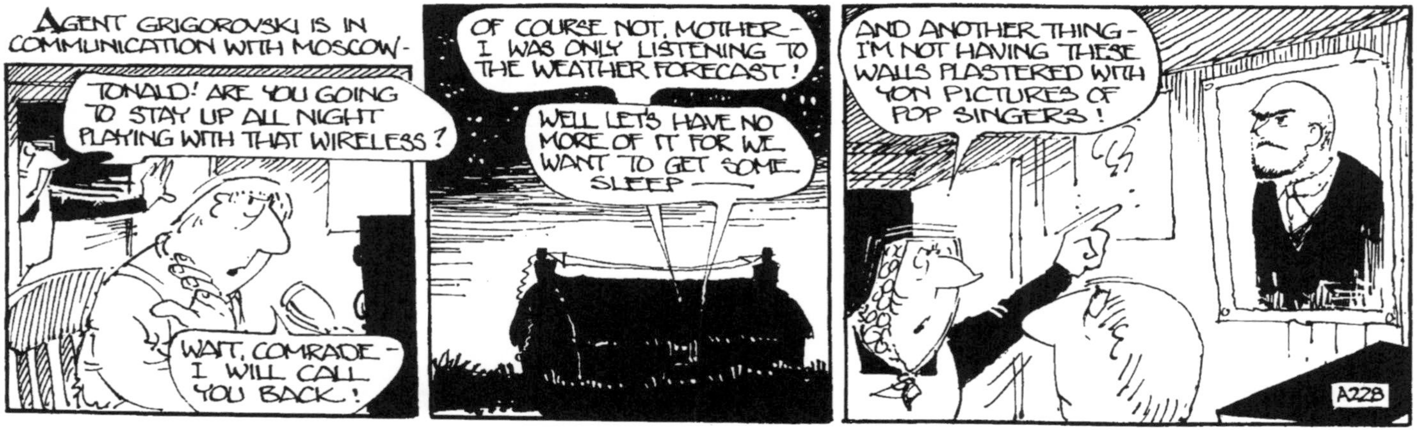
AGENT GRIGOROVSKI IS IN COMMUNICATION WITH MOSCOW-
TONALD! ARE YOU GOING TO STAY UP ALL NIGHT PLAYING WITH THAT WIRELESS?
WAIT, COMRADE - I WILL CALL YOU BACK!
OF COURSE NOT, MOTHER - I WAS ONLY LISTENING TO THE WEATHER FORECAST!
WELL LET'S HAVE NO MORE OF IT FOR WE WANT TO GET SOME SLEEP —
AND ANOTHER THING - I'M NOT HAVING THESE WALLS PLASTERED WITH YON PICTURES OF POP SINGERS!
A228

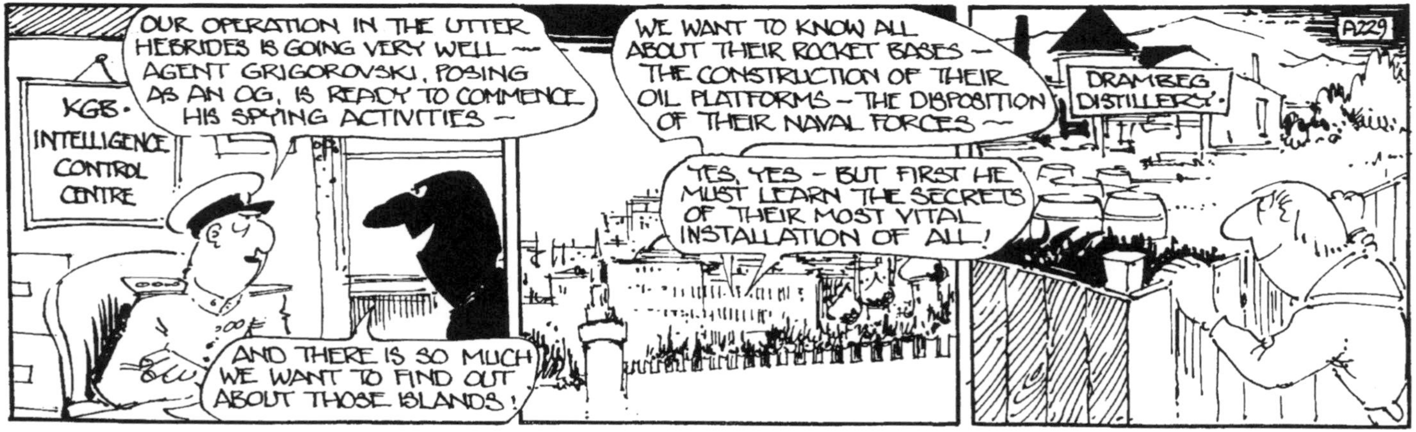
KGB. INTELLIGENCE CONTROL CENTRE
OUR OPERATION IN THE UTTER HEBRIDES IS GOING VERY WELL — AGENT GRIGOROVSKI, POSING AS AN OG, IS READY TO COMMENCE HIS SPYING ACTIVITIES —
AND THERE IS SO MUCH WE WANT TO FIND OUT ABOUT THOSE ISLANDS!
WE WANT TO KNOW ALL ABOUT THEIR ROCKET BASES — THE CONSTRUCTION OF THEIR OIL PLATFORMS — THE DISPOSITION OF THEIR NAVAL FORCES —
YES, YES - BUT FIRST HE MUST LEARN THE SECRETS OF THEIR MOST VITAL INSTALLATION OF ALL!
A229
DRAMBEG DISTILLERY.

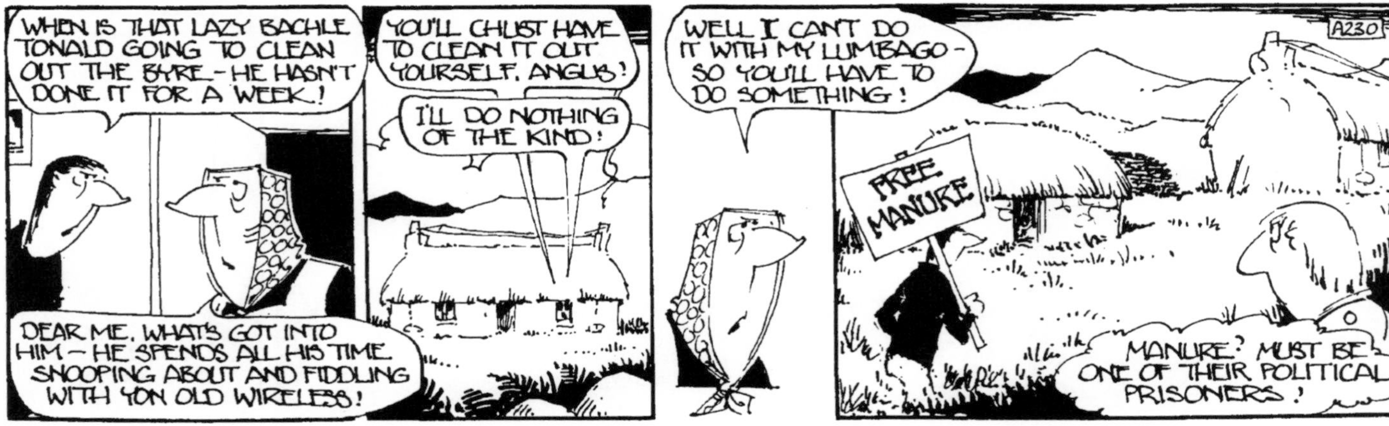
A230
WHEN IS THAT LAZY BACHLE TONALD GOING TO CLEAN OUT THE BYRE – HE HASN'T DONE IT FOR A WEEK!
DEAR ME, WHAT'S GOT INTO HIM – HE SPENDS ALL HIS TIME SNOOPING ABOUT AND FIDDLING WITH YON OLD WIRELESS!
YOU'LL CHUST HAVE TO CLEAN IT OUT YOURSELF, ANGUS!
I'LL DO NOTHING OF THE KIND!
WELL I CAN'T DO IT WITH MY LUMBAGO – SO YOU'LL HAVE TO DO SOMETHING!
FREE MANURE
MANURE? MUST BE ONE OF THEIR POLITICAL PRISONERS!

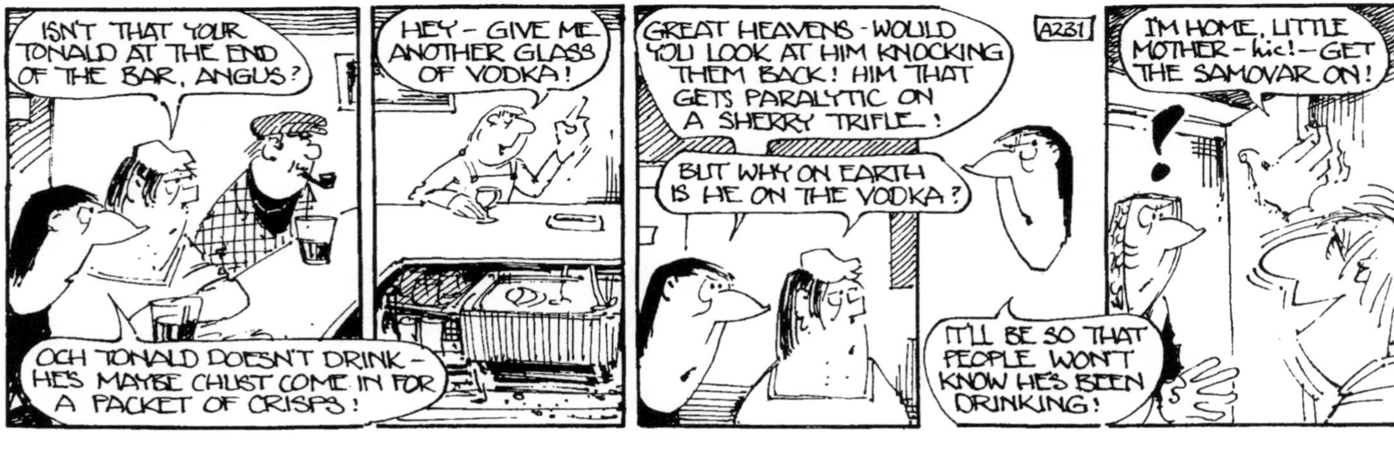
A231
ISN'T THAT YOUR TONALD AT THE END OF THE BAR, ANGUS?
OCH TONALD DOESN'T DRINK – HE'S MAYBE CHUST COME IN FOR A PACKET OF CRISPS!
HEY – GIVE ME ANOTHER GLASS OF VODKA!
GREAT HEAVENS – WOULD YOU LOOK AT HIM KNOCKING THEM BACK! HIM THAT GETS PARALYTIC ON A SHERRY TRIFLE!
BUT WHY ON EARTH IS HE ON THE VODKA?
IT'LL BE SO THAT PEOPLE WON'T KNOW HE'S BEEN DRINKING!
I'M HOME, LITTLE MOTHER – hic! – GET THE SAMOVAR ON!

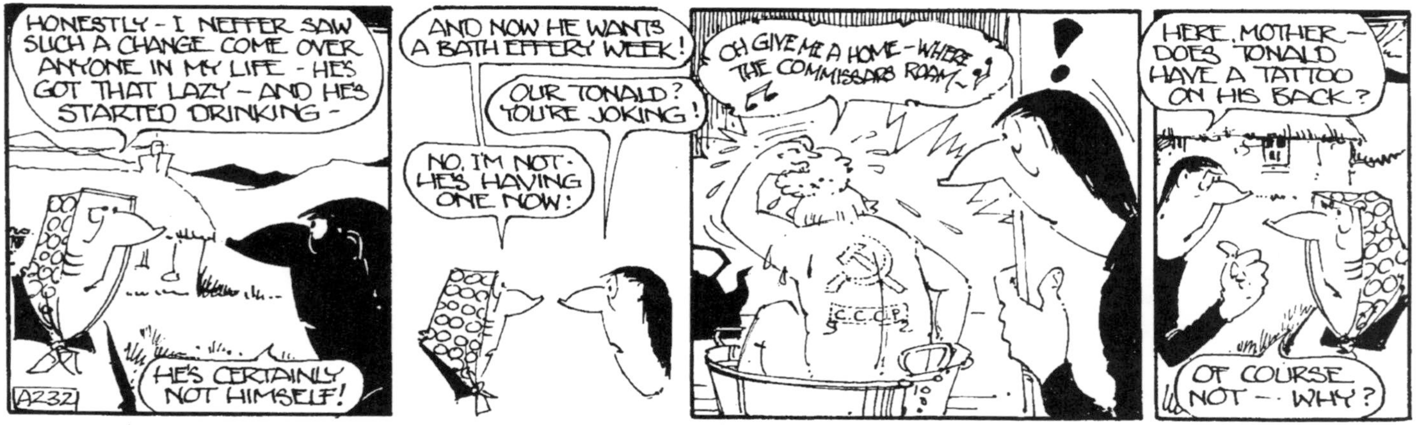
HONESTLY - I NEFFER SAW SUCH A CHANGE COME OVER ANYONE IN MY LIFE - HE'S GOT THAT LAZY - AND HE'S STARTED DRINKING -
HE'S CERTAINLY NOT HIMSELF!
A232
AND NOW HE WANTS A BATH EFFERY WEEK!
OUR TONALD? YOU'RE JOKING!
NO, I'M NOT - HE'S HAVING ONE NOW!
OH GIVE ME A HOME - WHERE THE COMMISSARS ROAM
!
C.C.C.P.
HERE, MOTHER - DOES TONALD HAVE A TATTOO ON HIS BACK?
OF COURSE NOT - WHY?

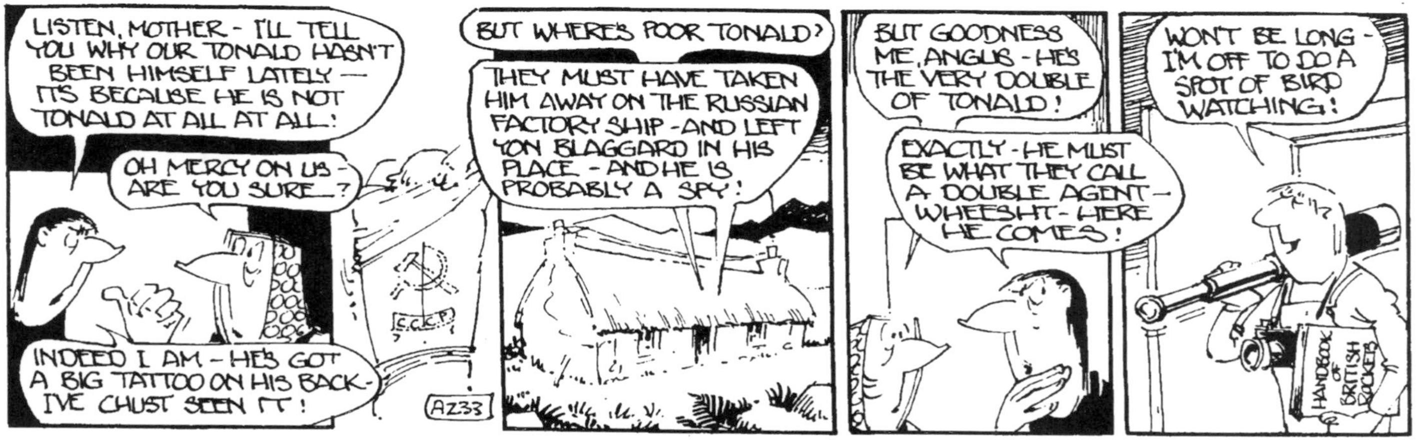
LISTEN, MOTHER - I'LL TELL YOU WHY OUR TONALD HASN'T BEEN HIMSELF LATELY — IT'S BECAUSE HE IS NOT TONALD AT ALL AT ALL!
OH MERCY ON US - ARE YOU SURE...?
INDEED I AM - HE'S GOT A BIG TATTOO ON HIS BACK - I'VE CHUST SEEN IT!
C.C.C.P.
A233
BUT WHERE'S POOR TONALD?
THEY MUST HAVE TAKEN HIM AWAY ON THE RUSSIAN FACTORY SHIP - AND LEFT YON BLAGGARD IN HIS PLACE - AND HE IS PROBABLY A SPY!
BUT GOODNESS ME, ANGUS - HE'S THE VERY DOUBLE OF TONALD!
EXACTLY - HE MUST BE WHAT THEY CALL A DOUBLE AGENT - WHEESHT - HERE HE COMES!
WON'T BE LONG - I'M OFF TO DO A SPOT OF BIRD WATCHING!
HANDBOOK OF BRITISH ROCKETS

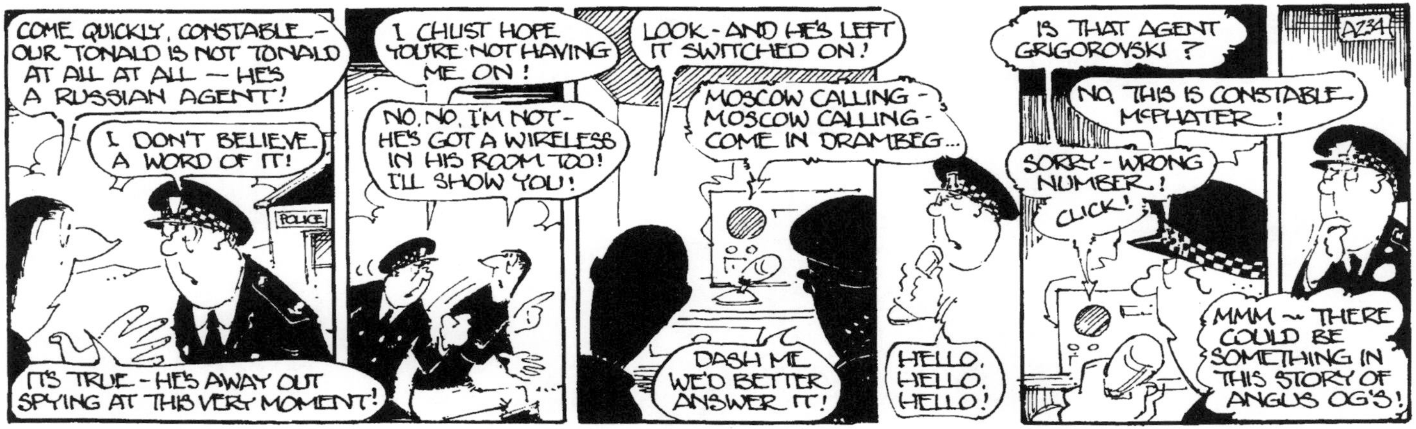
COME QUICKLY, CONSTABLE - OUR TONALD IS NOT TONALD AT ALL AT ALL — HE'S A RUSSIAN AGENT!
I DON'T BELIEVE A WORD OF IT!
POLICE
IT'S TRUE - HE'S AWAY OUT SPYING AT THIS VERY MOMENT!
I CHUST HOPE YOU'RE NOT HAVING ME ON!
NO, NO, I'M NOT - HE'S GOT A WIRELESS IN HIS ROOM TOO! I'LL SHOW YOU!
LOOK - AND HE'S LEFT IT SWITCHED ON!
MOSCOW CALLING - MOSCOW CALLING - COME IN DRAMBEG...
DASH ME WE'D BETTER ANSWER IT!
HELLO, HELLO, HELLO!
IS THAT AGENT GRIGOROVSKI ?
NO, THIS IS CONSTABLE McPHATER!
SORRY - WRONG NUMBER!
CLICK!
A234
MMM ~ THERE COULD BE SOMETHING IN THIS STORY OF ANGUS OG'S!

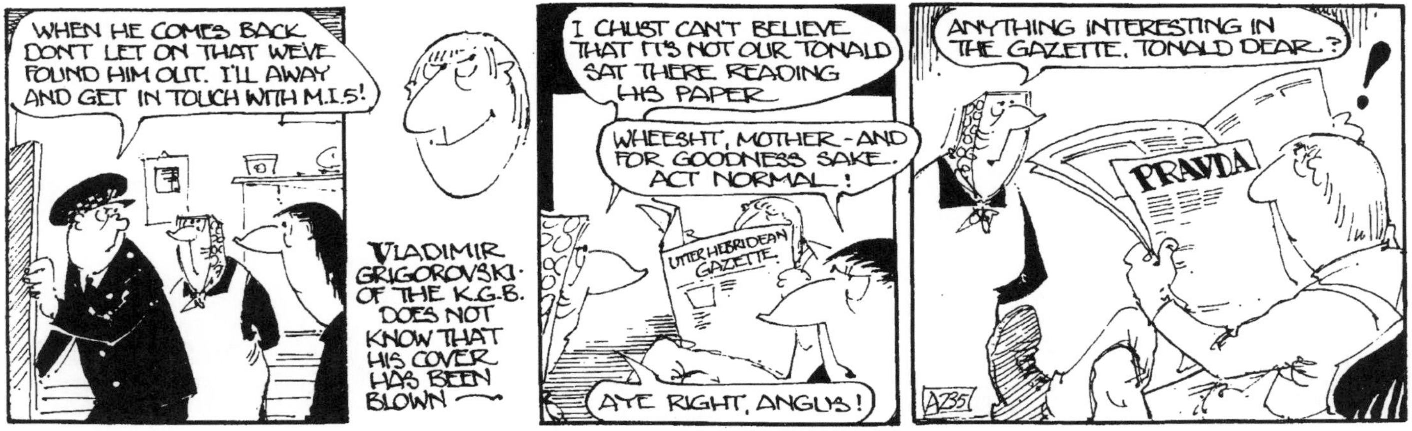
WHEN HE COMES BACK DON'T LET ON THAT WE'VE FOUND HIM OUT. I'LL AWAY AND GET IN TOUCH WITH M.I.5!
VLADIMIR GRIGOROVSKI OF THE K.G.B. DOES NOT KNOW THAT HIS COVER HAS BEEN BLOWN —
I CHUST CAN'T BELIEVE THAT IT'S NOT OUR TONALD SAT THERE READING HIS PAPER
WHEESHT, MOTHER - AND FOR GOODNESS SAKE ACT NORMAL!
UTTER HEBRIDEAN GAZETTE
AYE RIGHT, ANGUS!
ANYTHING INTERESTING IN THE GAZETTE, TONALD DEAR ?
!
PRAVDA
A235

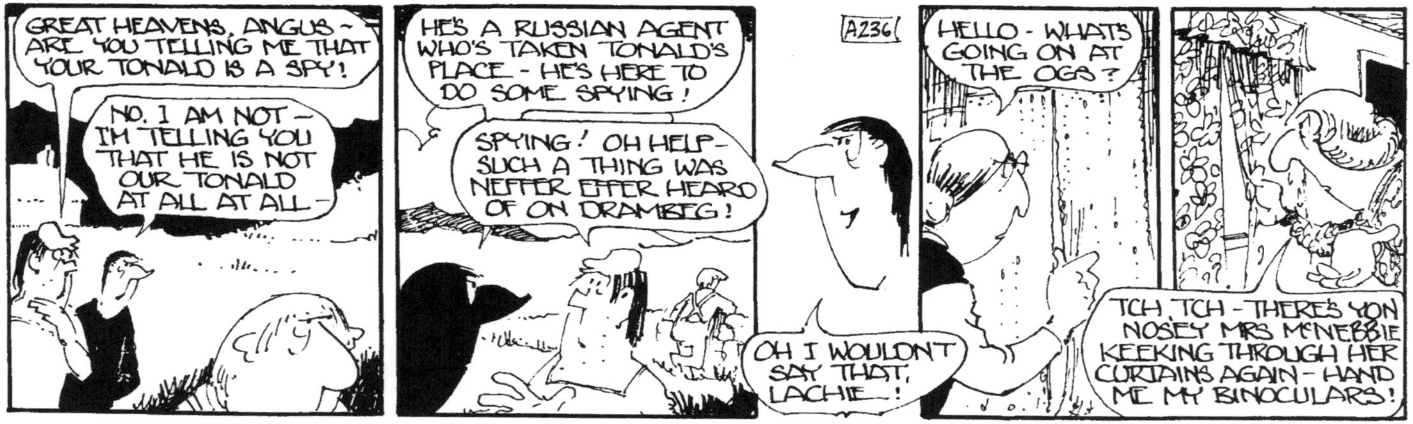
GREAT HEAVENS, ANGUS - ARE YOU TELLING ME THAT YOUR TONALD IS A SPY!
NO. I AM NOT - I'M TELLING YOU THAT HE IS NOT OUR TONALD AT ALL AT ALL -
HE'S A RUSSIAN AGENT WHO'S TAKEN TONALD'S PLACE - HE'S HERE TO DO SOME SPYING!
SPYING! OH HELP - SUCH A THING WAS NEFFER EFFER HEARD OF ON DRAMBEG!
A236
OH I WOULDN'T SAY THAT, LACHIE!
HELLO - WHAT'S GOING ON AT THE OGS?
TCH, TCH - THERE'S YON NOSEY MRS McNEBBIE KEEKING THROUGH HER CURTAINS AGAIN - HAND ME MY BINOCULARS!

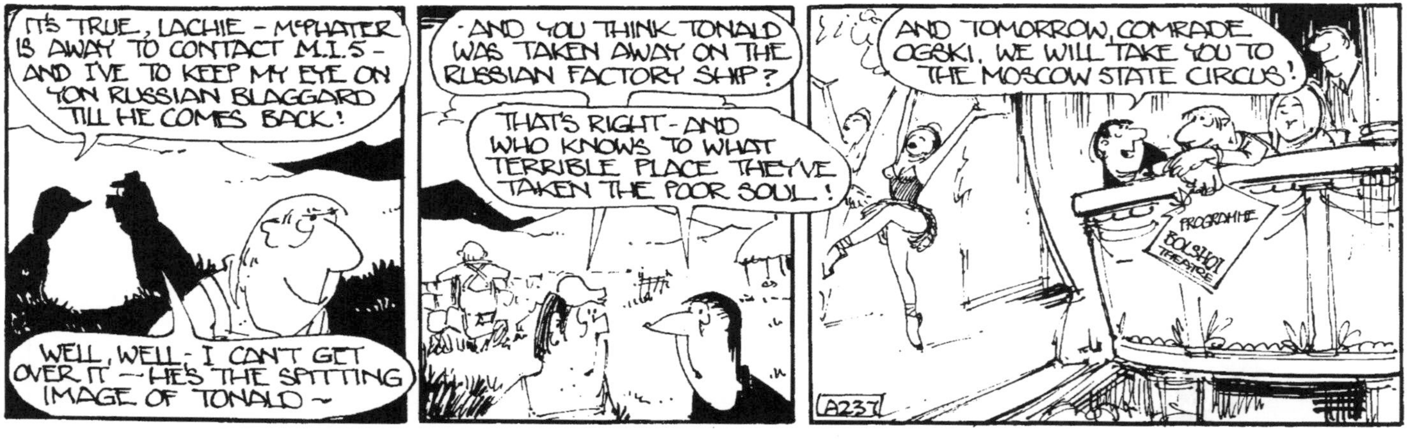
IT'S TRUE, LACHIE - McPHATER IS AWAY TO CONTACT M.I.5 - AND I'VE TO KEEP MY EYE ON YON RUSSIAN BLAGGARD TILL HE COMES BACK!
WELL, WELL - I CAN'T GET OVER IT - HE'S THE SPITTING IMAGE OF TONALD -
- AND YOU THINK TONALD WAS TAKEN AWAY ON THE RUSSIAN FACTORY SHIP?
THAT'S RIGHT - AND WHO KNOWS TO WHAT TERRIBLE PLACE THEY'VE TAKEN THE POOR SOUL!
AND TOMORROW, COMRADE OGSKI, WE WILL TAKE YOU TO THE MOSCOW STATE CIRCUS!
PROGRAMME
BOLSHOI THEATRE
A237

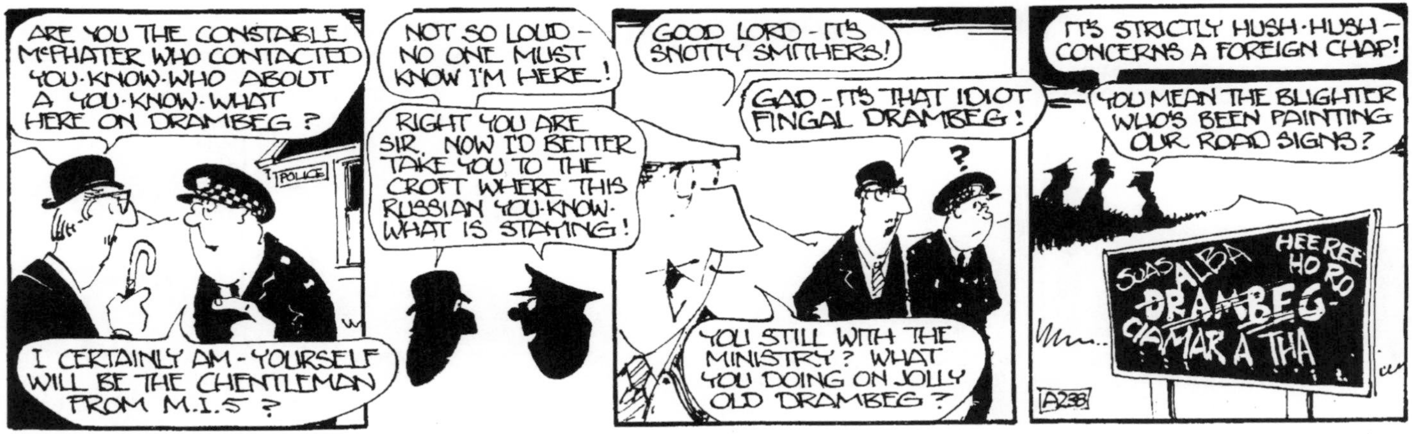
ARE YOU THE CONSTABLE McPHATER WHO CONTACTED YOU·KNOW·WHO ABOUT A YOU·KNOW·WHAT HERE ON DRAMBEG ?
POLICE
I CERTAINLY AM - YOURSELF WILL BE THE CHENTLEMAN FROM M.I.5 ?
NOT SO LOUD - NO ONE MUST KNOW I'M HERE !
RIGHT YOU ARE SIR. NOW I'D BETTER TAKE YOU TO THE CROFT WHERE THIS RUSSIAN YOU·KNOW·WHAT IS STAYING !
GOOD LORD - IT'S SNOTTY SMITHERS!
GAD - IT'S THAT IDIOT FINGAL DRAMBEG !
?
YOU STILL WITH THE MINISTRY ? WHAT YOU DOING ON JOLLY OLD DRAMBEG ?
IT'S STRICTLY HUSH·HUSH - CONCERNS A FOREIGN CHAP!
YOU MEAN THE BLIGHTER WHO'S BEEN PAINTING OUR ROAD SIGNS ?
SUAS ALBA HEE REE HO RO
DRAMBEG
CIAMAR A THA
A238

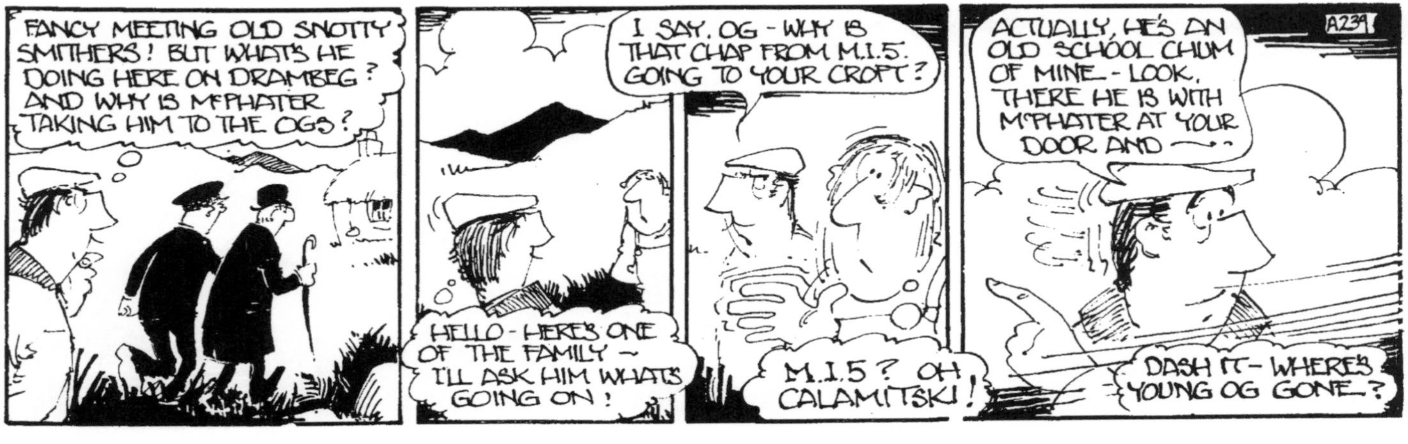
FANCY MEETING OLD SNOTTY SMITHERS ! BUT WHAT'S HE DOING HERE ON DRAMBEG ? AND WHY IS McPHATER TAKING HIM TO THE OGS ?
HELLO - HERE'S ONE OF THE FAMILY - I'LL ASK HIM WHAT'S GOING ON !
I SAY, OG - WHY IS THAT CHAP FROM M.I.5. GOING TO YOUR CROFT ?
M.I.5 ? OH CALAMITSKI !
A239
ACTUALLY, HE'S AN OLD SCHOOL CHUM OF MINE - LOOK, THERE HE IS WITH McPHATER AT YOUR DOOR AND —
DASH IT - WHERE'S YOUNG OG GONE ?

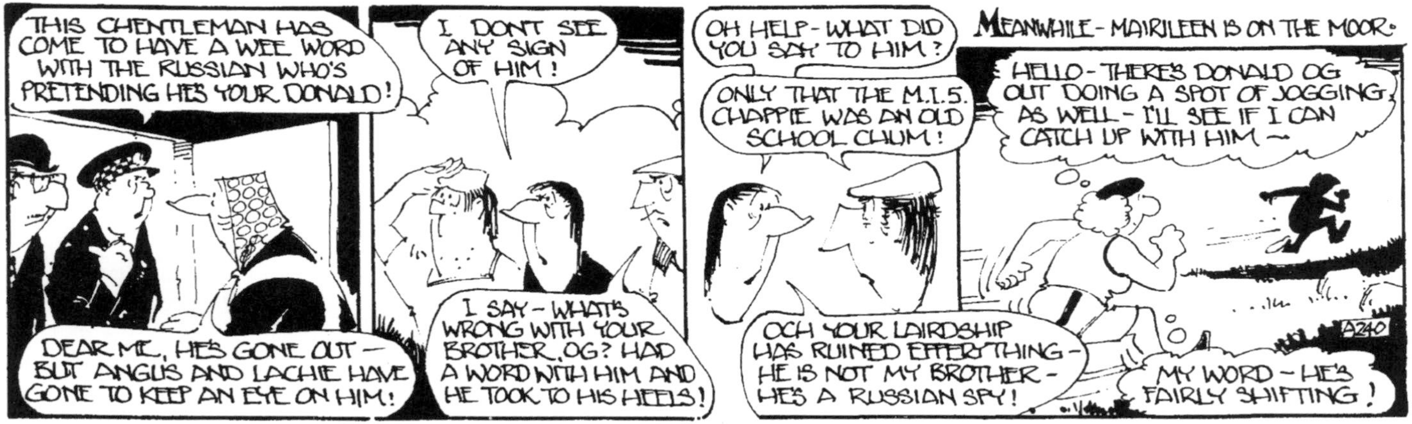
THIS CHENTLEMAN HAS COME TO HAVE A WEE WORD WITH THE RUSSIAN WHO'S PRETENDING HE'S YOUR DONALD!
DEAR ME, HE'S GONE OUT — BUT ANGUS AND LACHIE HAVE GONE TO KEEP AN EYE ON HIM!
I DONT SEE ANY SIGN OF HIM!
I SAY — WHAT'S WRONG WITH YOUR BROTHER, OG? HAD A WORD WITH HIM AND HE TOOK TO HIS HEELS!
OH HELP — WHAT DID YOU SAY TO HIM?
ONLY THAT THE M.I.5. CHAPPIE WAS AN OLD SCHOOL CHUM!
OCH YOUR LAIRDSHIP HAS RUINED EFFERYTHING — HE IS NOT MY BROTHER — HE'S A RUSSIAN SPY!
MEANWHILE — MAIRILEEN IS ON THE MOOR.
HELLO — THERE'S DONALD OG OUT DOING A SPOT OF JOGGING AS WELL — I'LL SEE IF I CAN CATCH UP WITH HIM —
MY WORD — HE'S FAIRLY SHIFTING!
A240

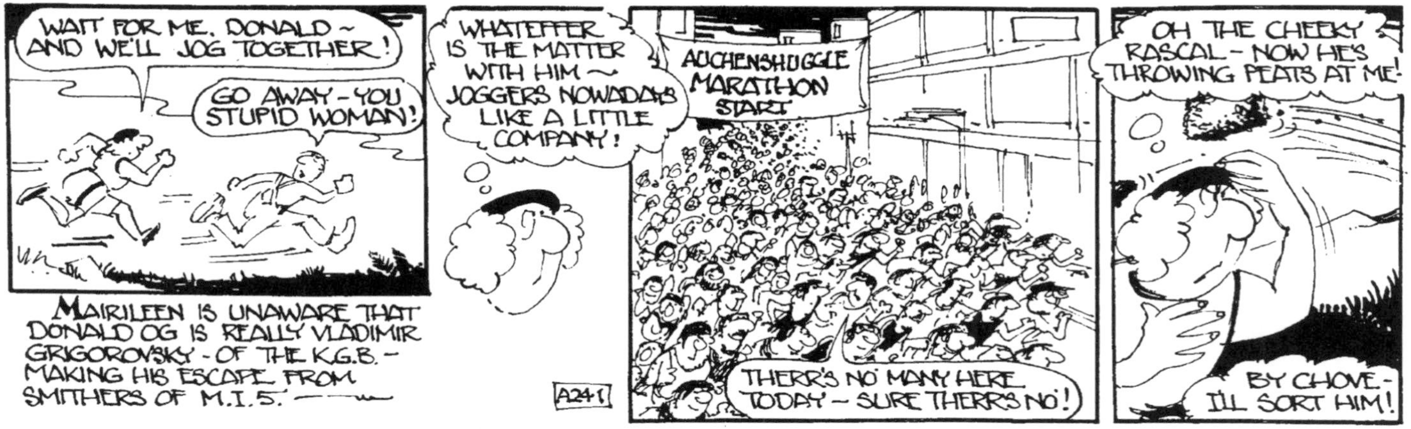
WAIT FOR ME, DONALD — AND WE'LL JOG TOGETHER!
GO AWAY — YOU STUPID WOMAN!
MAIRILEEN IS UNAWARE THAT DONALD OG IS REALLY VLADIMIR GRIGOROVSKY — OF THE K.G.B. — MAKING HIS ESCAPE FROM SMITHERS OF M.I.5.
WHATEFFER IS THE MATTER WITH HIM — JOGGERS NOWADAYS LIKE A LITTLE COMPANY!
A241
AUCHENSHUGGLE MARATHON START
THERR'S NO' MANY HERE TODAY — SURE THERR'S NO'!
OH THE CHEEKY RASCAL — NOW HE'S THROWING PEATS AT ME!
BY CHOVE — I'LL SORT HIM!

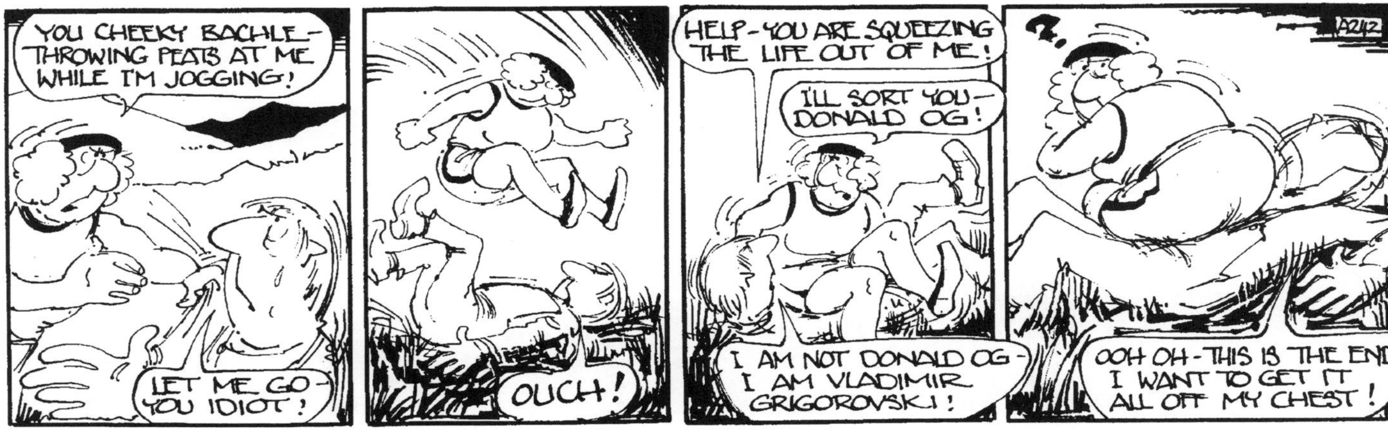
A242
YOU CHEEKY BACHLE - THROWING PEATS AT ME WHILE I'M JOGGING!
LET ME GO - YOU IDIOT!
OUCH!
HELP - YOU ARE SQUEEZING THE LIFE OUT OF ME!
I'LL SORT YOU - DONALD OG!
I AM NOT DONALD OG - I AM VLADIMIR GRIGOROVSKI!
?
OOH OH - THIS IS THE END! I WANT TO GET IT ALL OFF MY CHEST!

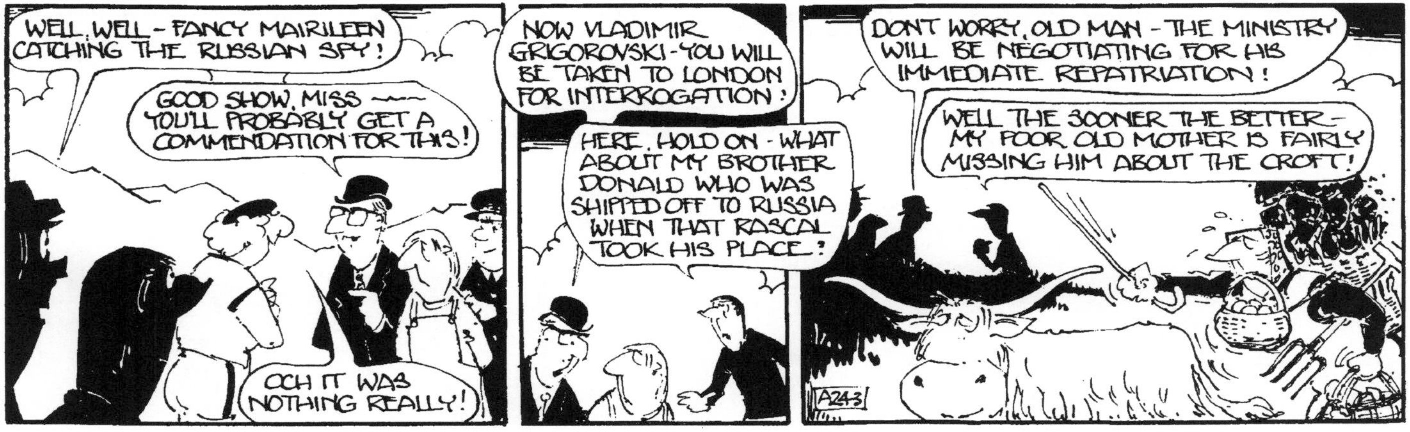
WELL, WELL - FANCY MAIRILEEN CATCHING THE RUSSIAN SPY!
GOOD SHOW, MISS — YOU'LL PROBABLY GET A COMMENDATION FOR THIS!
OCH IT WAS NOTHING REALLY!
NOW VLADIMIR GRIGOROVSKI - YOU WILL BE TAKEN TO LONDON FOR INTERROGATION!
HERE, HOLD ON - WHAT ABOUT MY BROTHER DONALD WHO WAS SHIPPED OFF TO RUSSIA WHEN THAT RASCAL TOOK HIS PLACE?
A243
DON'T WORRY, OLD MAN - THE MINISTRY WILL BE NEGOTIATING FOR HIS IMMEDIATE REPATRIATION!
WELL THE SOONER THE BETTER - MY POOR OLD MOTHER IS FAIRLY MISSING HIM ABOUT THE CROFT!

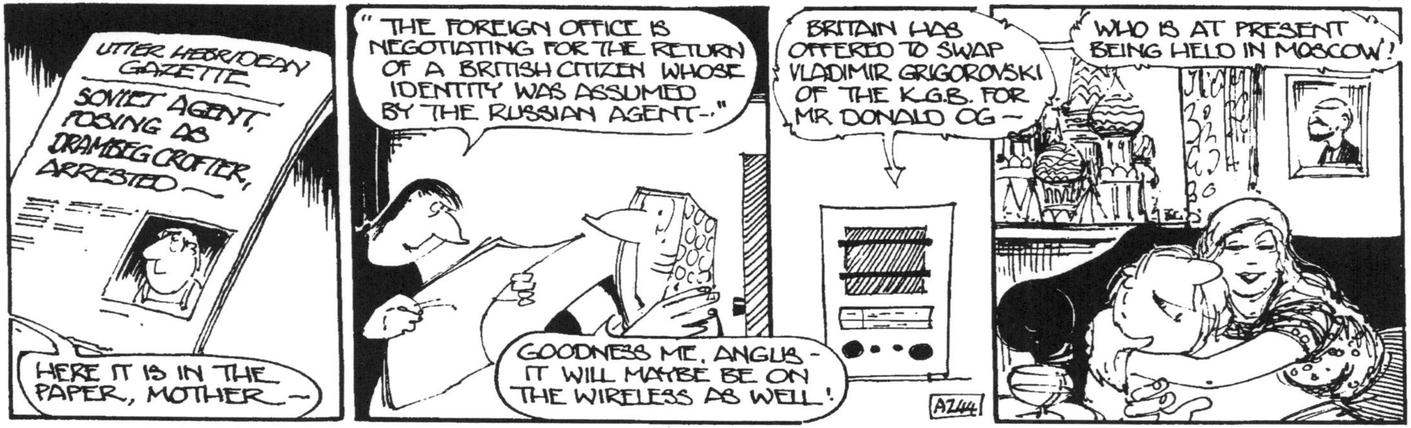
UTTER HEBRIDEAN GAZETTE
SOVIET AGENT, POSING AS DRAMBEG CROFTER, ARRESTED—
HERE IT IS IN THE PAPER, MOTHER—
"THE FOREIGN OFFICE IS NEGOTIATING FOR THE RETURN OF A BRITISH CITIZEN WHOSE IDENTITY WAS ASSUMED BY THE RUSSIAN AGENT—."
GOODNESS ME, ANGUS - IT WILL MAYBE BE ON THE WIRELESS AS WELL!
BRITAIN HAS OFFERED TO SWAP VLADIMIR GRIGOROVSKI OF THE K.G.B. FOR MR DONALD OG—
A244
WHO IS AT PRESENT BEING HELD IN MOSCOW!

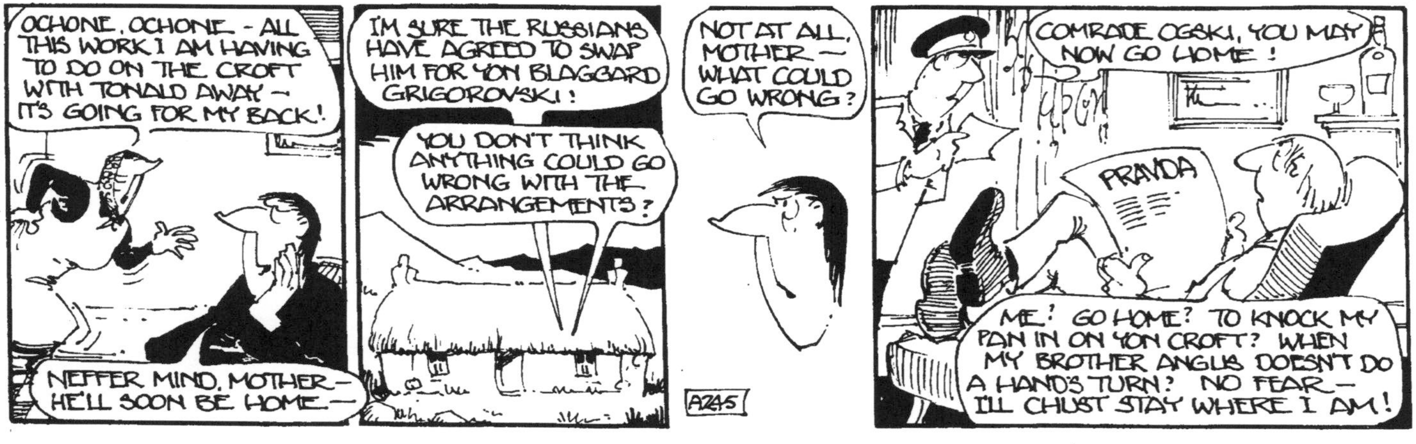
OCHONE, OCHONE - ALL THIS WORK I AM HAVING TO DO ON THE CROFT WITH TONALD AWAY - IT'S GOING FOR MY BACK!
NEFFER MIND, MOTHER - HE'LL SOON BE HOME—
I'M SURE THE RUSSIANS HAVE AGREED TO SWAP HIM FOR YON BLAGGARD GRIGOROVSKI!
YOU DON'T THINK ANYTHING COULD GO WRONG WITH THE ARRANGEMENTS?
NOT AT ALL, MOTHER - WHAT COULD GO WRONG?
A245
COMRADE OGSKI, YOU MAY NOW GO HOME!
PRAVDA
ME? GO HOME? TO KNOCK MY PAN IN ON YON CROFT? WHEN MY BROTHER ANGUS DOESN'T DO A HAND'S TURN? NO FEAR - I'LL CHUST STAY WHERE I AM!

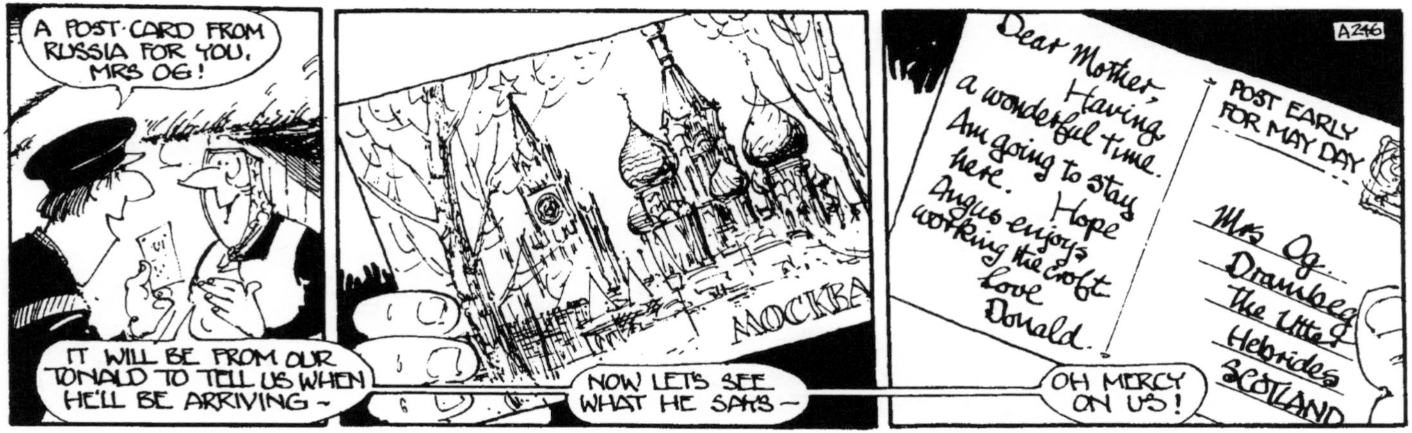
A POST-CARD FROM RUSSIA FOR YOU, MRS OG!
IT WILL BE FROM OUR TONALD TO TELL US WHEN HE'LL BE ARRIVING -
NOW LET'S SEE WHAT HE SAYS -
MOCKBA
A246
Dear Mother, Having a wonderful time. Am going to stay here. Hope Angus enjoys working the croft. Love Donald.
POST EARLY FOR MAY DAY
Mrs Og. Drambeg The Utter Hebrides SCOTLAND
OH MERCY ON US!

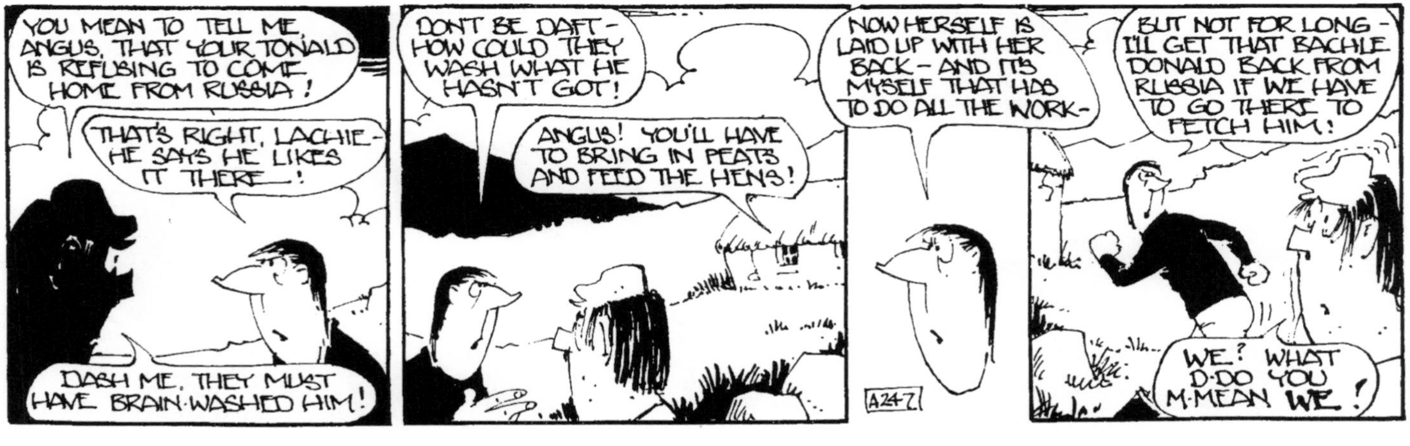
YOU MEAN TO TELL ME, ANGUS, THAT YOUR TONALD IS REFUSING TO COME HOME FROM RUSSIA!
THAT'S RIGHT, LACHIE - HE SAYS HE LIKES IT THERE - !
DASH ME, THEY MUST HAVE BRAIN-WASHED HIM!
DON'T BE DAFT - HOW COULD THEY WASH WHAT HE HASN'T GOT!
ANGUS! YOU'LL HAVE TO BRING IN PEATS AND FEED THE HENS!
A247
NOW HERSELF IS LAID UP WITH HER BACK - AND IT'S MYSELF THAT HAS TO DO ALL THE WORK -
BUT NOT FOR LONG - I'LL GET THAT BACHLE DONALD BACK FROM RUSSIA IF WE HAVE TO GO THERE TO FETCH HIM!
WE? WHAT D-DO YOU M-MEAN WE!

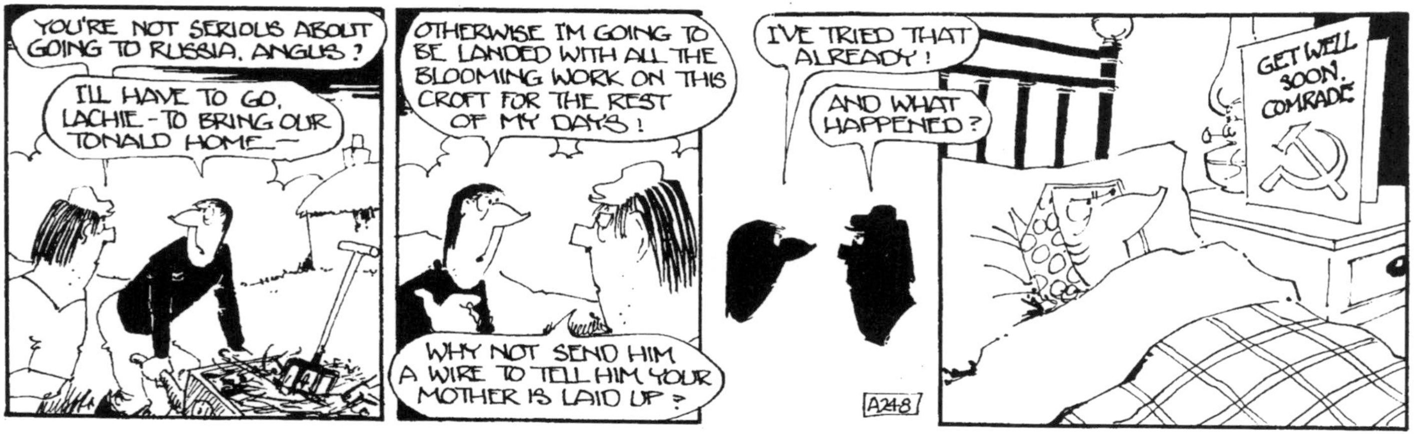
YOU'RE NOT SERIOUS ABOUT GOING TO RUSSIA, ANGUS?
I'LL HAVE TO GO, LACHIE - TO BRING OUR TONALD HOME —
OTHERWISE I'M GOING TO BE LANDED WITH ALL THE BLOOMING WORK ON THIS CROFT FOR THE REST OF MY DAYS!
WHY NOT SEND HIM A WIRE TO TELL HIM YOUR MOTHER IS LAID UP?
I'VE TRIED THAT ALREADY!
AND WHAT HAPPENED?
A248
GET WELL SOON, COMRADE

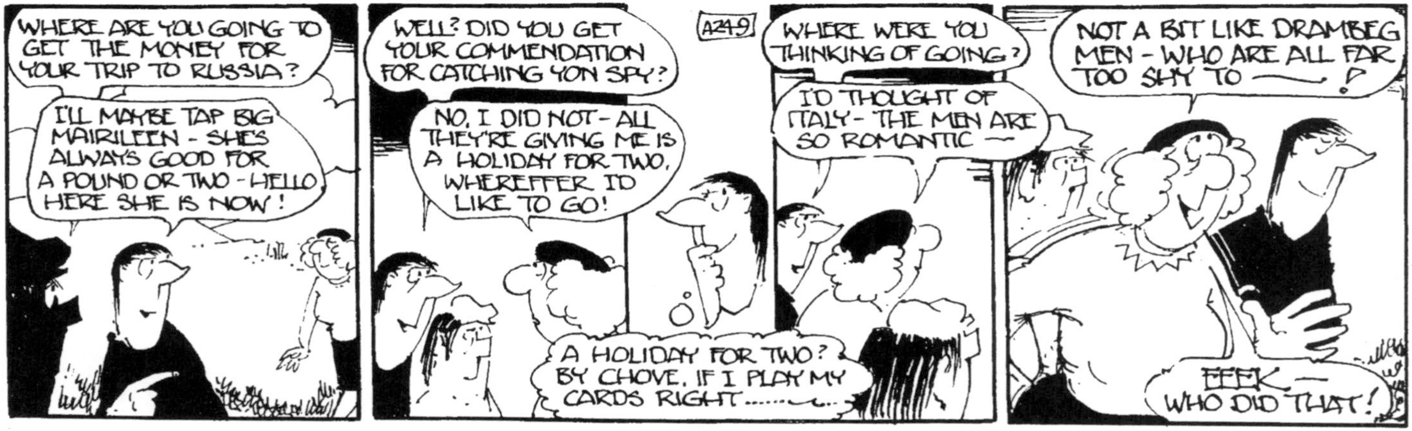
WHERE ARE YOU GOING TO GET THE MONEY FOR YOUR TRIP TO RUSSIA?
I'LL MAYBE TAP BIG MAIRILEEN - SHE'S ALWAYS GOOD FOR A POUND OR TWO - HELLO HERE SHE IS NOW!
WELL? DID YOU GET YOUR COMMENDATION FOR CATCHING YON SPY?
NO, I DID NOT - ALL THEY'RE GIVING ME IS A HOLIDAY FOR TWO, WHEREFFER I'D LIKE TO GO!
A HOLIDAY FOR TWO? BY CHOVE, IF I PLAY MY CARDS RIGHT ......
A249
WHERE WERE YOU THINKING OF GOING?
I'D THOUGHT OF ITALY - THE MEN ARE SO ROMANTIC —
NOT A BIT LIKE DRAMBEG MEN - WHO ARE ALL FAR TOO SHY TO — !
EEEK — WHO DID THAT!

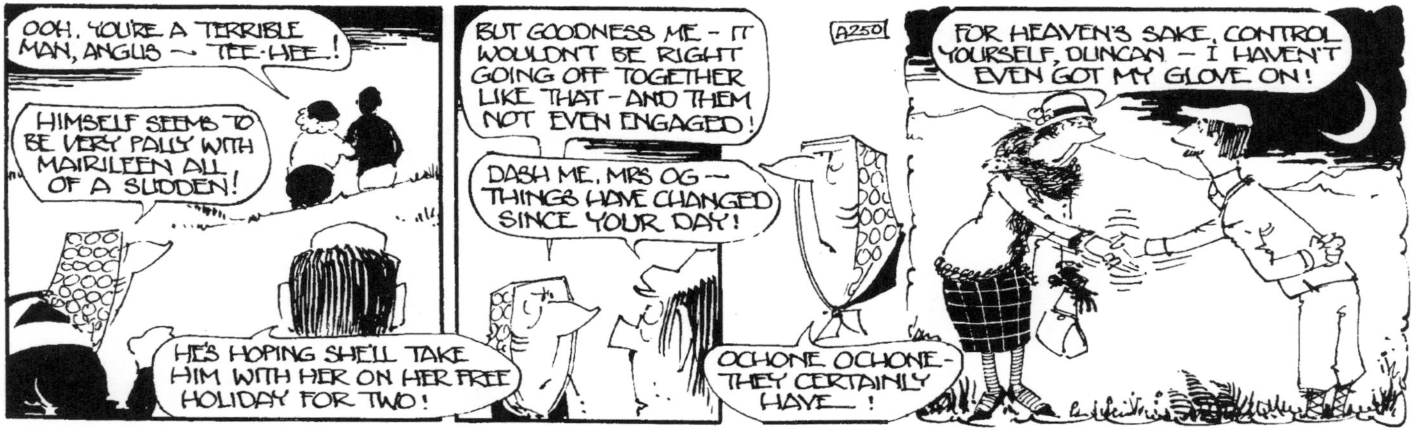
OOH. YOU'RE A TERRIBLE MAN, ANGUS — TEE-HEE!
HIMSELF SEEMS TO BE VERY PALLY WITH MAIRILEEN ALL OF A SUDDEN!
HE'S HOPING SHE'LL TAKE HIM WITH HER ON HER FREE HOLIDAY FOR TWO!
BUT GOODNESS ME — IT WOULDN'T BE RIGHT GOING OFF TOGETHER LIKE THAT — AND THEM NOT EVEN ENGAGED!
DASH ME, MRS OG — THINGS HAVE CHANGED SINCE YOUR DAY!
OCHONE OCHONE — THEY CERTAINLY HAVE!
A250
FOR HEAVEN'S SAKE, CONTROL YOURSELF, DUNCAN — I HAVEN'T EVEN GOT MY GLOVE ON!

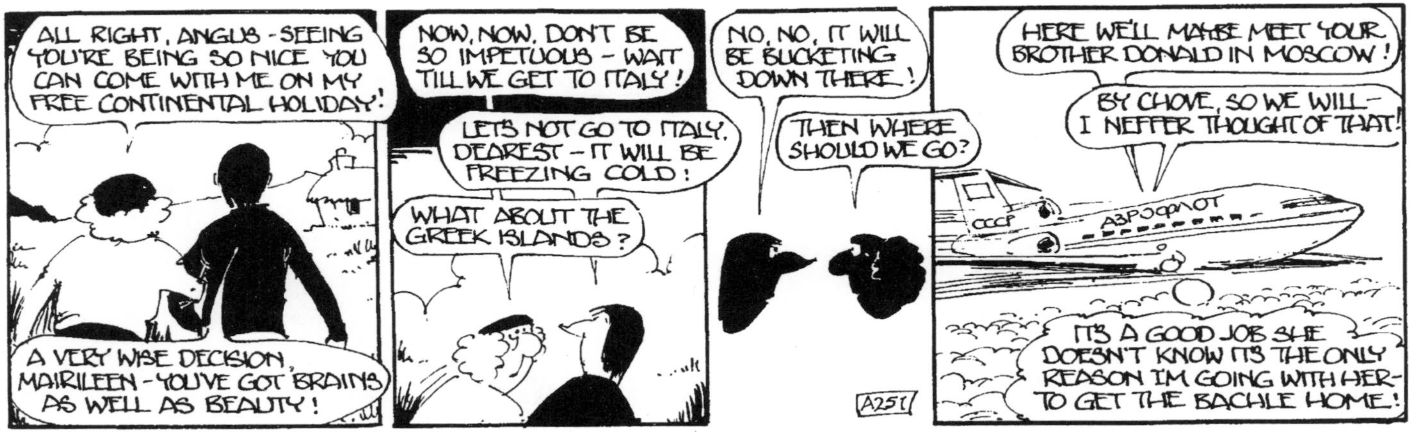
ALL RIGHT, ANGUS — SEEING YOU'RE BEING SO NICE YOU CAN COME WITH ME ON MY FREE CONTINENTAL HOLIDAY!
A VERY WISE DECISION, MAIRILEEN — YOU'VE GOT BRAINS AS WELL AS BEAUTY!
NOW, NOW, DON'T BE SO IMPETUOUS — WAIT TILL WE GET TO ITALY!
LET'S NOT GO TO ITALY, DEAREST — IT WILL BE FREEZING COLD!
WHAT ABOUT THE GREEK ISLANDS?
NO, NO, IT WILL BE BUCKETING DOWN THERE!
THEN WHERE SHOULD WE GO?
A251
HERE WE'LL MAYBE MEET YOUR BROTHER DONALD IN MOSCOW!
BY CHOVE, SO WE WILL — I NEFFER THOUGHT OF THAT!
CCCP
IT'S A GOOD JOB SHE DOESN'T KNOW IT'S THE ONLY REASON I'M GOING WITH HER — TO GET THE BACHLE HOME!

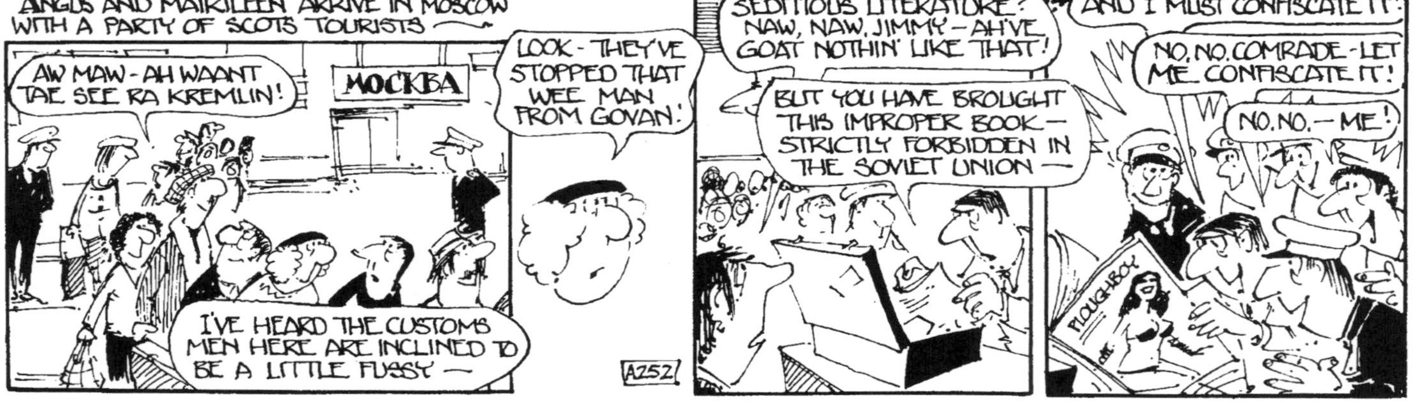
ANGUS AND MAIRILEEN ARRIVE IN MOSCOW WITH A PARTY OF SCOTS TOURISTS —
AW MAW - AH WAANT TAE SEE RA KREMLIN!
MOCKBA
I'VE HEARD THE CUSTOMS MEN HERE ARE INCLINED TO BE A LITTLE FUSSY —
LOOK - THEY'VE STOPPED THAT WEE MAN FROM GOVAN!
A252
SEDITIOUS LITERATURE? NAW, NAW, JIMMY — AH'VE GOAT NOTHIN' LIKE THAT!
BUT YOU HAVE BROUGHT THIS IMPROPER BOOK — STRICTLY FORBIDDEN IN THE SOVIET UNION —
AND I MUST CONFISCATE IT!
NO, NO, COMRADE - LET ME CONFISCATE IT!
NO, NO, — ME!
PLOUGHBOY

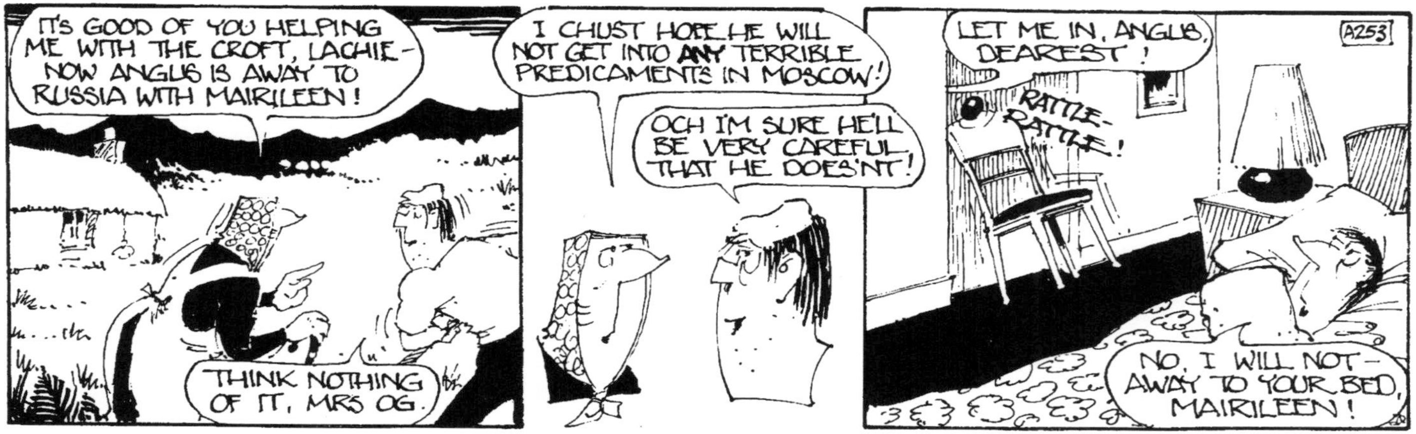
IT'S GOOD OF YOU HELPING ME WITH THE CROFT, LACHIE - NOW ANGUS IS AWAY TO RUSSIA WITH MAIRILEEN!
THINK NOTHING OF IT, MRS OG.
I CHUST HOPE HE WILL NOT GET INTO ANY TERRIBLE PREDICAMENTS IN MOSCOW!
OCH I'M SURE HE'LL BE VERY CAREFUL THAT HE DOES'NT!
A253
LET ME IN, ANGUS, DEAREST!
RATTLE-RATTLE!
NO, I WILL NOT - AWAY TO YOUR BED, MAIRILEEN!

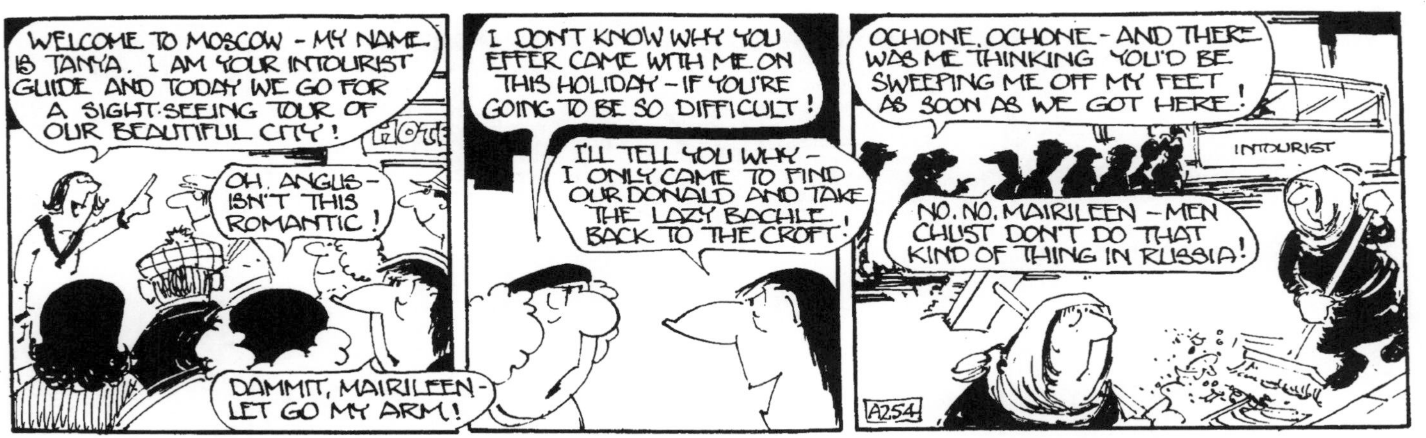

WELCOME TO MOSCOW - MY NAME IS TANYA. I AM YOUR INTOURIST GUIDE AND TODAY WE GO FOR A SIGHT-SEEING TOUR OF OUR BEAUTIFUL CITY!
OH, ANGUS - ISN'T THIS ROMANTIC!
DAMMIT, MAIRILEEN - LET GO MY ARM!
I DON'T KNOW WHY YOU EFFER CAME WITH ME ON THIS HOLIDAY - IF YOU'RE GOING TO BE SO DIFFICULT!
I'LL TELL YOU WHY - I ONLY CAME TO FIND OUR DONALD AND TAKE THE LAZY BACHLE BACK TO THE CROFT!
OCHONE, OCHONE - AND THERE WAS ME THINKING YOU'D BE SWEEPING ME OFF MY FEET AS SOON AS WE GOT HERE!
INTOURIST
NO, NO, MAIRILEEN - MEN CHUST DON'T DO THAT KIND OF THING IN RUSSIA!
A254

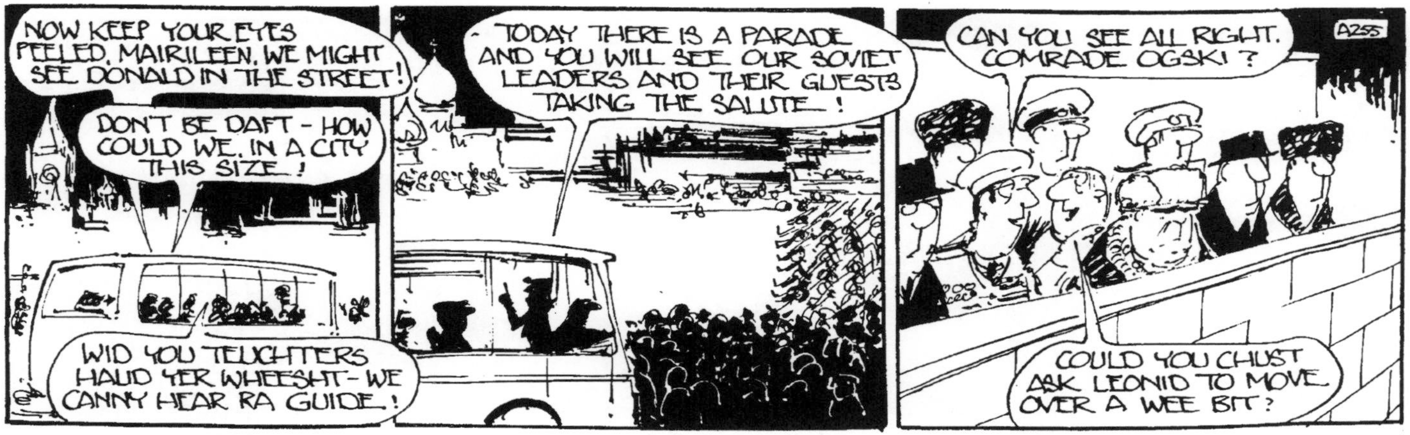

NOW KEEP YOUR EYES PEELED, MAIRILEEN, WE MIGHT SEE DONALD IN THE STREET!
DON'T BE DAFT - HOW COULD WE, IN A CITY THIS SIZE!
WID YOU TEUCHTERS HAUD YER WHEESHT - WE CANNY HEAR RA GUIDE!
TODAY THERE IS A PARADE AND YOU WILL SEE OUR SOVIET LEADERS AND THEIR GUESTS TAKING THE SALUTE!
CAN YOU SEE ALL RIGHT, COMRADE OGSKI?
A255
COULD YOU CHUST ASK LEONID TO MOVE OVER A WEE BIT?

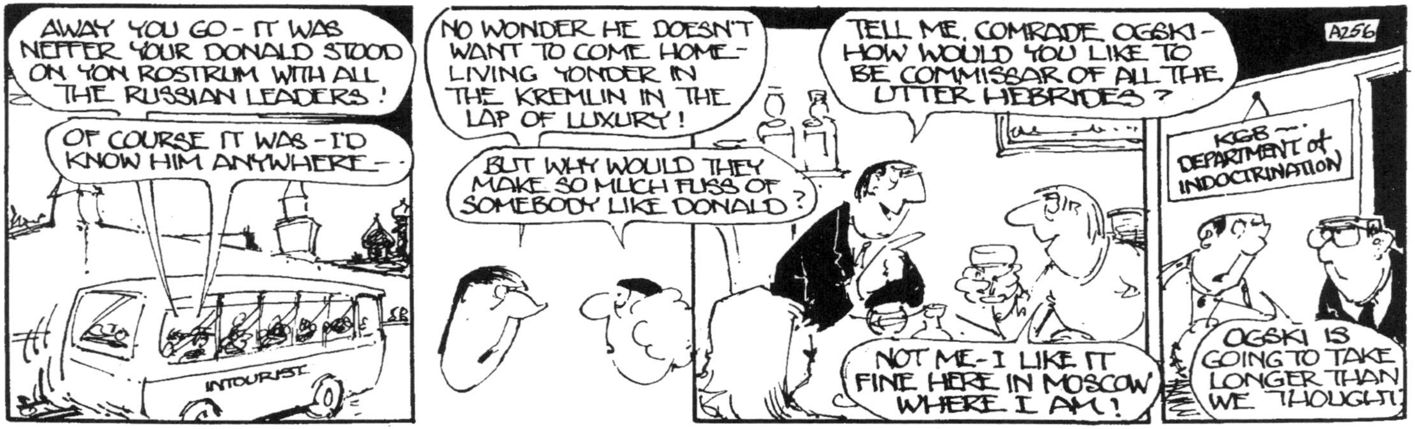
AWAY YOU GO - IT WAS NEFFER YOUR DONALD STOOD ON YON ROSTRUM WITH ALL THE RUSSIAN LEADERS!
OF COURSE IT WAS - I'D KNOW HIM ANYWHERE—
INTOURIST
NO WONDER HE DOESN'T WANT TO COME HOME— LIVING YONDER IN THE KREMLIN IN THE LAP OF LUXURY!
BUT WHY WOULD THEY MAKE SO MUCH FUSS OF SOMEBODY LIKE DONALD?
A256
TELL ME, COMRADE OGSKI - HOW WOULD YOU LIKE TO BE COMMISSAR OF ALL THE UTTER HEBRIDES?
NOT ME - I LIKE IT FINE HERE IN MOSCOW WHERE I AM!
KGB — DEPARTMENT of INDOCTRINATION
OGSKI IS GOING TO TAKE LONGER THAN WE THOUGHT!

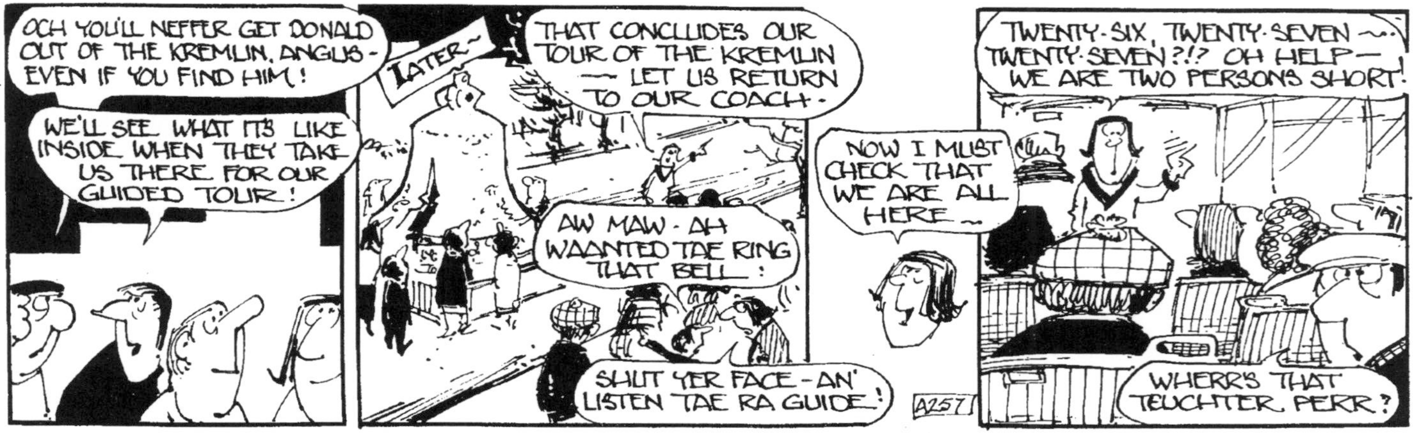
OCH YOU'LL NEFFER GET DONALD OUT OF THE KREMLIN, ANGUS - EVEN IF YOU FIND HIM!
WE'LL SEE WHAT IT'S LIKE INSIDE WHEN THEY TAKE US THERE FOR OUR GUIDED TOUR!
LATER—
THAT CONCLUDES OUR TOUR OF THE KREMLIN — LET US RETURN TO OUR COACH -
AW MAW - AH WAANTED TAE RING THAT BELL!
SHUT YER FACE - AN' LISTEN TAE RA GUIDE!
A257
NOW I MUST CHECK THAT WE ARE ALL HERE—
TWENTY-SIX, TWENTY-SEVEN — TWENTY-SEVEN?!? OH HELP— WE ARE TWO PERSONS SHORT!
WHERR'S THAT TEUCHTER, PERR?

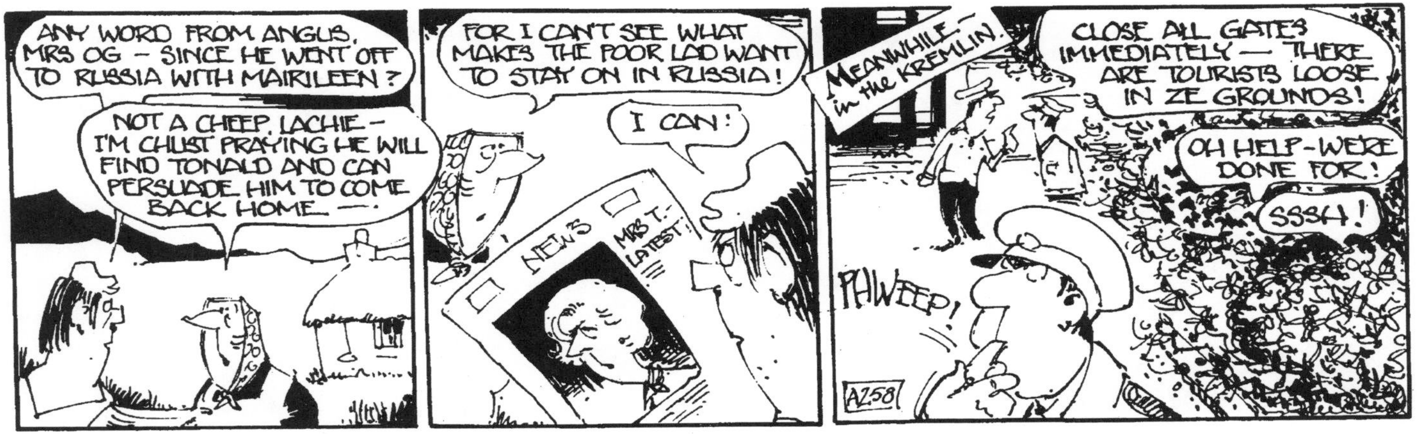
ANY WORD FROM ANGUS, MRS OG — SINCE HE WENT OFF TO RUSSIA WITH MAIRILEEN?
NOT A CHEEP, LACHIE — I'M CHUST PRAYING HE WILL FIND TONALD AND CAN PERSUADE HIM TO COME BACK HOME —
FOR I CAN'T SEE WHAT MAKES THE POOR LAD WANT TO STAY ON IN RUSSIA!
I CAN!
NEWS
MRS T. LATEST
MEANWHILE— in the KREMLIN.
CLOSE ALL GATES IMMEDIATELY — THERE ARE TOURISTS LOOSE IN ZE GROUNDS!
OH HELP—WE'RE DONE FOR!
SSSH!
PHWEEP!
A258

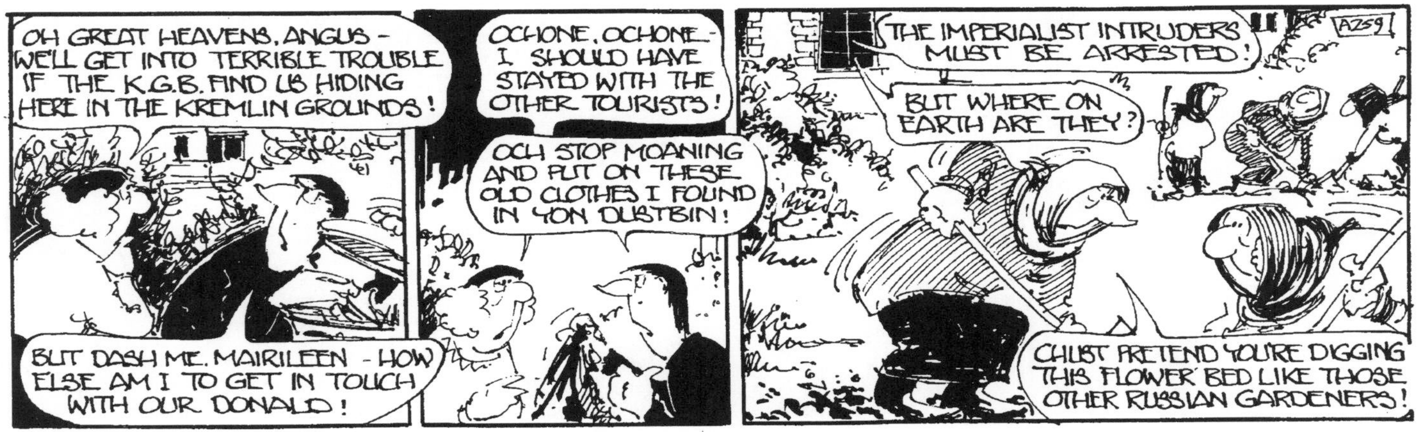
OH GREAT HEAVENS, ANGUS — WE'LL GET INTO TERRIBLE TROUBLE IF THE K.G.B. FIND US HIDING HERE IN THE KREMLIN GROUNDS!
BUT DASH ME, MAIRILEEN — HOW ELSE AM I TO GET IN TOUCH WITH OUR DONALD!
OCHONE, OCHONE — I SHOULD HAVE STAYED WITH THE OTHER TOURISTS!
OCH STOP MOANING AND PUT ON THESE OLD CLOTHES I FOUND IN YON DUSTBIN!
A259
THE IMPERIALIST INTRUDERS MUST BE ARRESTED!
BUT WHERE ON EARTH ARE THEY?
CHUST PRETEND YOU'RE DIGGING THIS FLOWER BED LIKE THOSE OTHER RUSSIAN GARDENERS!

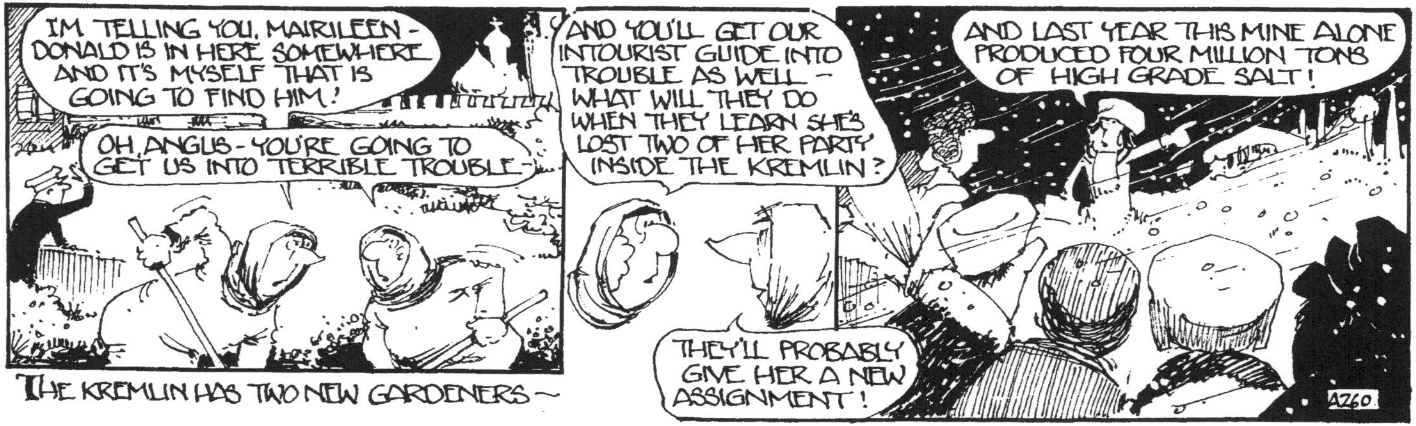
I'M TELLING YOU, MAIRILEEN - DONALD IS IN HERE SOMEWHERE AND IT'S MYSELF THAT IS GOING TO FIND HIM!
OH, ANGUS - YOU'RE GOING TO GET US INTO TERRIBLE TROUBLE -
THE KREMLIN HAS TWO NEW GARDENERS ~
AND YOU'LL GET OUR INTOURIST GUIDE INTO TROUBLE AS WELL - WHAT WILL THEY DO WHEN THEY LEARN SHE'S LOST TWO OF HER PARTY INSIDE THE KREMLIN?
THEY'LL PROBABLY GIVE HER A NEW ASSIGNMENT!
AND LAST YEAR THIS MINE ALONE PRODUCED FOUR MILLION TONS OF HIGH GRADE SALT!
A260

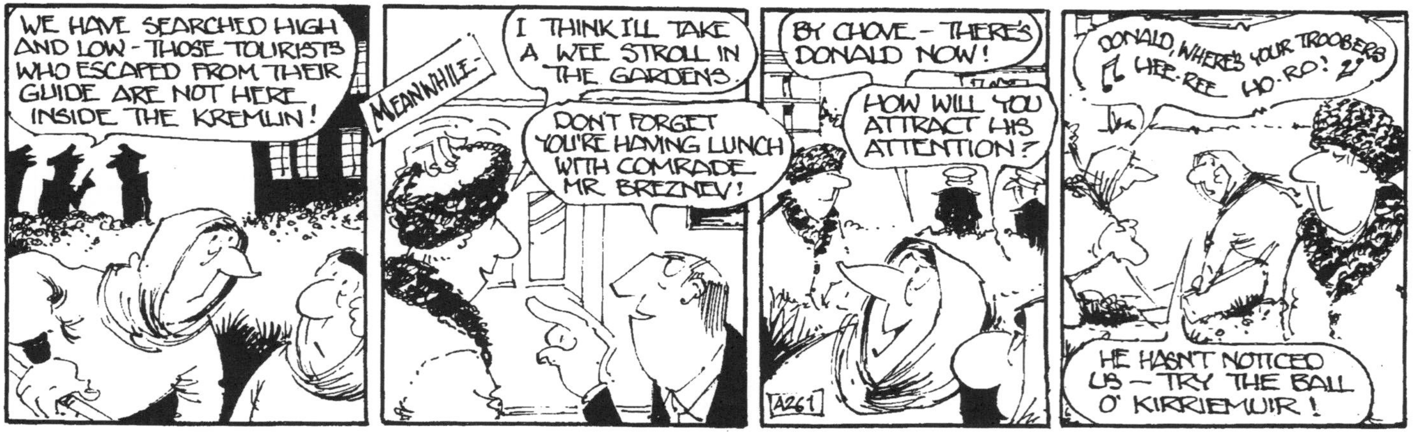
WE HAVE SEARCHED HIGH AND LOW - THOSE TOURISTS WHO ESCAPED FROM THEIR GUIDE ARE NOT HERE INSIDE THE KREMLIN!
MEANWHILE -
I THINK I'LL TAKE A WEE STROLL IN THE GARDENS.
DON'T FORGET YOU'RE HAVING LUNCH WITH COMRADE MR BREZNEV!
BY CHOVE - THERE'S DONALD NOW!
HOW WILL YOU ATTRACT HIS ATTENTION?
A261
DONALD, WHERE'S YOUR TROOBERS HEE-REE HO-RO!
HE HASN'T NOTICED US - TRY THE BALL O' KIRRIEMUIR!

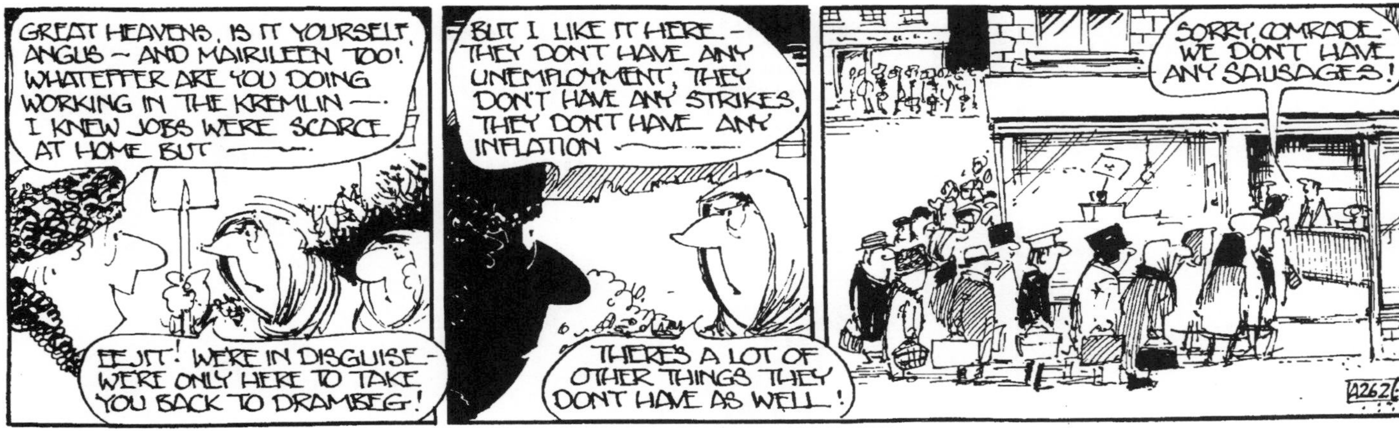
GREAT HEAVENS, IS IT YOURSELF ANGUS – AND MAIRILEEN TOO! WHATEFFER ARE YOU DOING WORKING IN THE KREMLIN – I KNEW JOBS WERE SCARCE AT HOME BUT –
EEJIT! WE'RE IN DISGUISE – WE'RE ONLY HERE TO TAKE YOU BACK TO DRAMBEG!
BUT I LIKE IT HERE – THEY DON'T HAVE ANY UNEMPLOYMENT, THEY DON'T HAVE ANY STRIKES, THEY DON'T HAVE ANY INFLATION –
THERE'S A LOT OF OTHER THINGS THEY DON'T HAVE AS WELL!
SORRY, COMRADE – WE DON'T HAVE ANY SAUSAGES!
A262

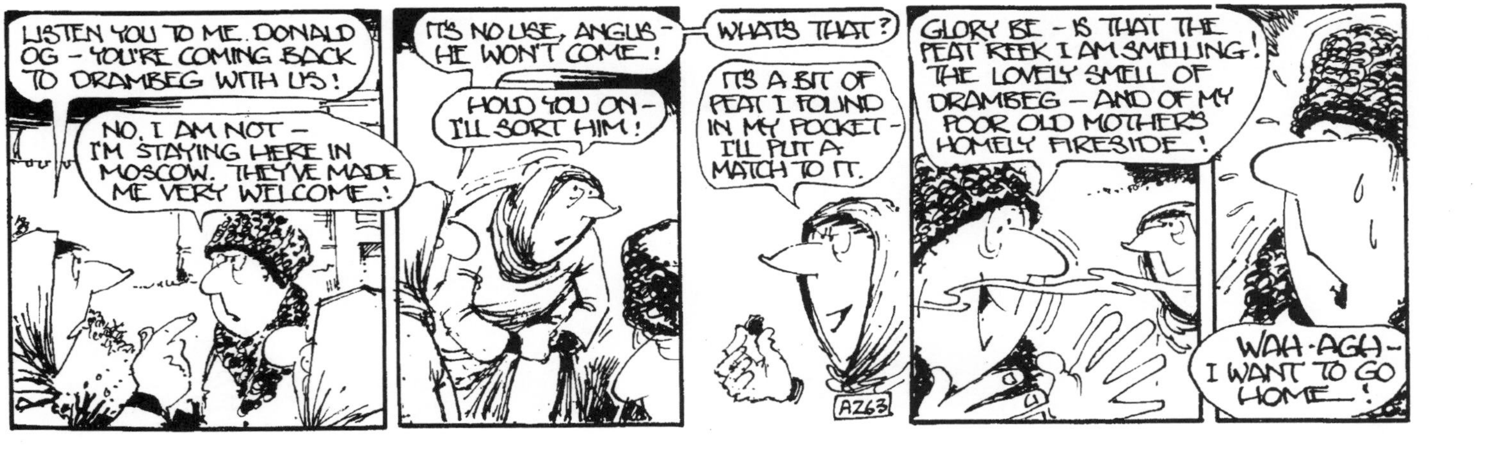
LISTEN YOU TO ME, DONALD OG – YOU'RE COMING BACK TO DRAMBEG WITH US!
NO, I AM NOT – I'M STAYING HERE IN MOSCOW. THEY'VE MADE ME VERY WELCOME!
IT'S NO USE, ANGUS – HE WON'T COME!
HOLD YOU ON – I'LL SORT HIM!
WHAT'S THAT?
IT'S A BIT OF PEAT I FOUND IN MY POCKET – I'LL PUT A MATCH TO IT.
A263
GLORY BE – IS THAT THE PEAT REEK I AM SMELLING! THE LOVELY SMELL OF DRAMBEG – AND OF MY POOR OLD MOTHER'S HOMELY FIRESIDE!
WAH-AGH – I WANT TO GO HOME!

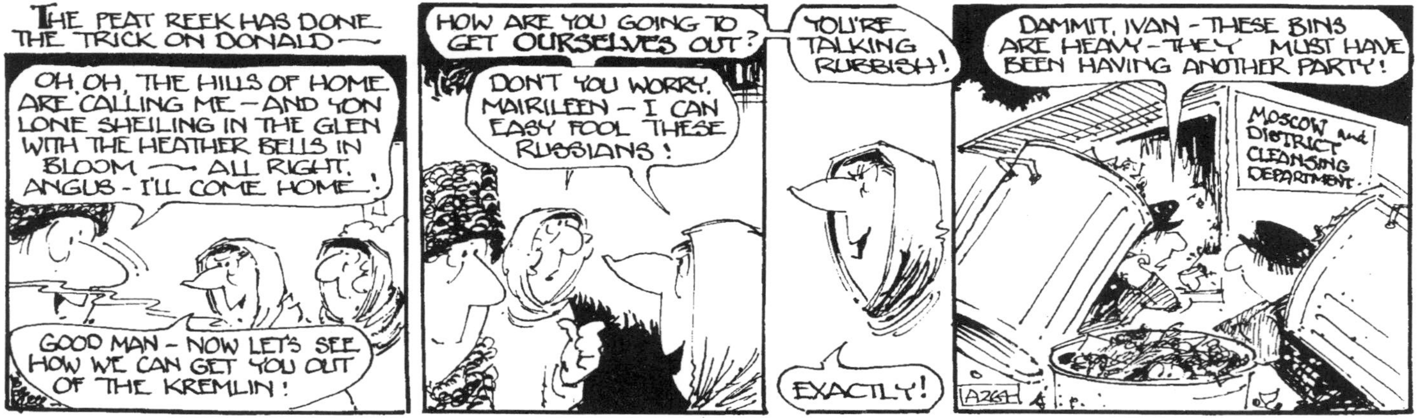
THE PEAT REEK HAS DONE THE TRICK ON DONALD—
OH, OH, THE HILLS OF HOME ARE CALLING ME — AND YON LONE SHEILING IN THE GLEN WITH THE HEATHER BELLS IN BLOOM — ALL RIGHT, ANGUS - I'LL COME HOME!
GOOD MAN — NOW LET'S SEE HOW WE CAN GET YOU OUT OF THE KREMLIN!
HOW ARE YOU GOING TO GET OURSELVES OUT?
DON'T YOU WORRY, MAIRILEEN — I CAN EASY FOOL THESE RUSSIANS!
YOU'RE TALKING RUBBISH!
EXACTLY!
DAMMIT, IVAN — THESE BINS ARE HEAVY — THEY MUST HAVE BEEN HAVING ANOTHER PARTY!
MOSCOW and DISTRICT CLEANSING DEPARTMENT
A264

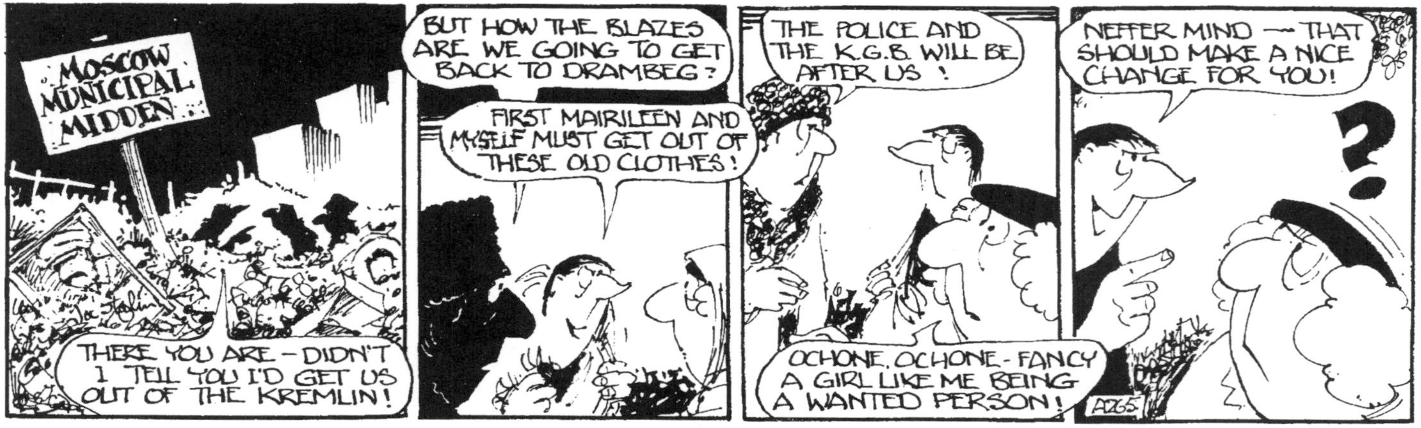
MOSCOW MUNICIPAL MIDDEN
THERE YOU ARE — DIDN'T I TELL YOU I'D GET US OUT OF THE KREMLIN!
BUT HOW THE BLAZES ARE WE GOING TO GET BACK TO DRAMBEG?
FIRST MAIRILEEN AND MYSELF MUST GET OUT OF THESE OLD CLOTHES!
THE POLICE AND THE K.G.B. WILL BE AFTER US!
OCHONE, OCHONE — FANCY A GIRL LIKE ME BEING A WANTED PERSON!
NEFFER MIND — THAT SHOULD MAKE A NICE CHANGE FOR YOU!
?
A265

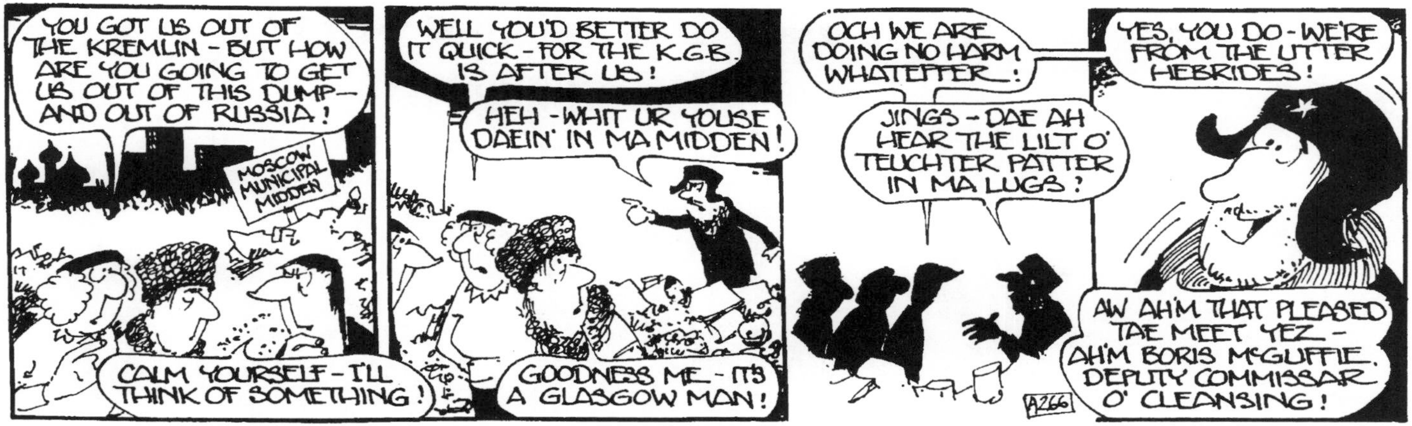
YOU GOT US OUT OF THE KREMLIN – BUT HOW ARE YOU GOING TO GET US OUT OF THIS DUMP– AND OUT OF RUSSIA!
MOSCOW MUNICIPAL MIDDEN
CALM YOURSELF – I'LL THINK OF SOMETHING!
WELL YOU'D BETTER DO IT QUICK – FOR THE K.G.B. IS AFTER US!
HEH – WHIT UR YOUSE DAEIN' IN MA MIDDEN!
GOODNESS ME – IT'S A GLASGOW MAN!
OCH WE ARE DOING NO HARM WHATEFFER!
JINGS – DAE AH HEAR THE LILT O' TEUCHTER PATTER IN MA LUGS?
A266
YES, YOU DO – WE'RE FROM THE UTTER HEBRIDES!
AW AH'M THAT PLEASED TAE MEET YEZ – AH'M BORIS McGUFFIE, DEPUTY COMMISSAR O' CLEANSING!

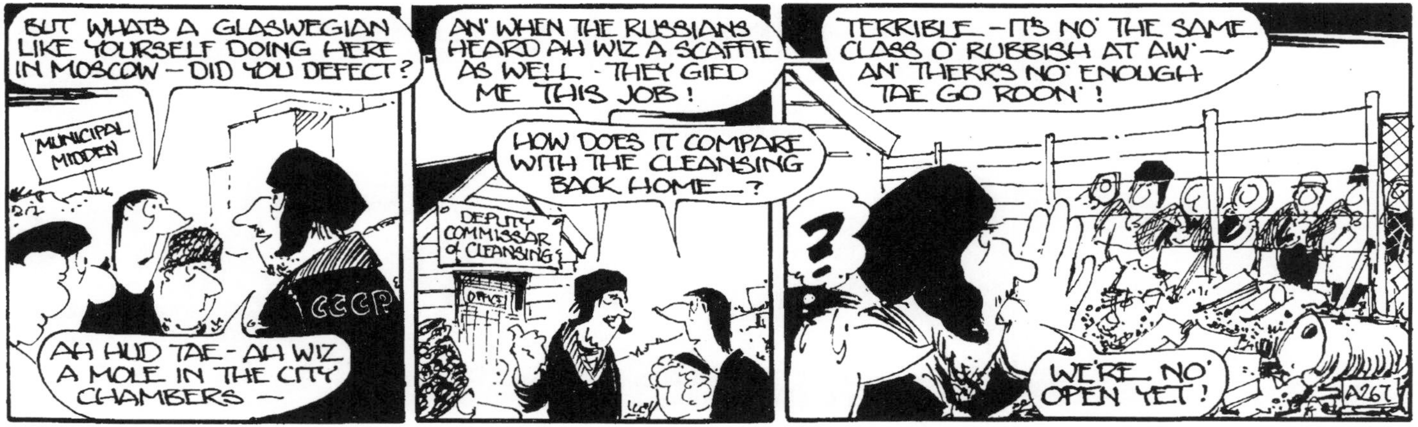
BUT WHATS A GLASWEGIAN LIKE YOURSELF DOING HERE IN MOSCOW – DID YOU DEFECT?
MUNICIPAL MIDDEN
AH HUD TAE – AH WIZ A MOLE IN THE CITY CHAMBERS –
AN' WHEN THE RUSSIANS HEARD AH WIZ A SCAFFIE AS WELL – THEY GIED ME THIS JOB!
HOW DOES IT COMPARE WITH THE CLEANSING BACK HOME?
DEPUTY COMMISSAR of CLEANSING
TERRIBLE – IT'S NO' THE SAME CLASS O' RUBBISH AT AW' – AN' THERR'S NO' ENOUGH TAE GO ROON'!
WE'RE NO' OPEN YET!
A267

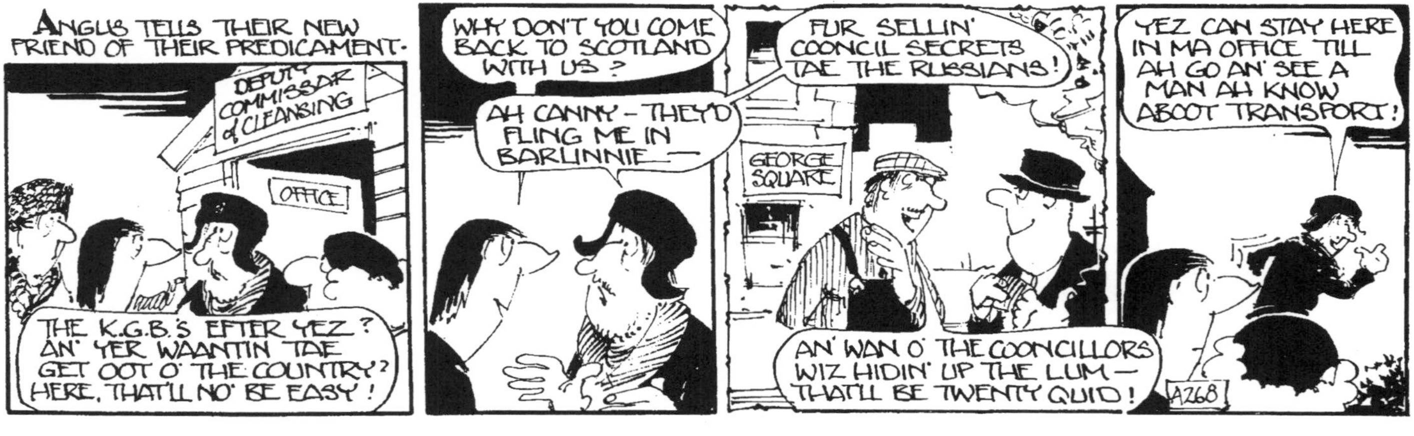
ANGUS TELLS THEIR NEW FRIEND OF THEIR PREDICAMENT.
DEPUTY COMMISSAR of CLEANSING
OFFICE
THE K.G.B.'S EFTER YEZ? AN' YER WAANTIN TAE GET OOT O' THE COUNTRY? HERE, THAT'LL NO' BE EASY!
WHY DON'T YOU COME BACK TO SCOTLAND WITH US?
AH CANNY – THEY'D FLING ME IN BARLINNIE —
FUR SELLIN' COONCIL SECRETS TAE THE RUSSIANS!
GEORGE SQUARE
AN' WAN O' THE COONCILLORS WIZ HIDIN' UP THE LUM – THAT'LL BE TWENTY QUID!
YEZ CAN STAY HERE IN MA OFFICE TILL AH GO AN' SEE A MAN AH KNOW ABOOT TRANSPORT!
A268

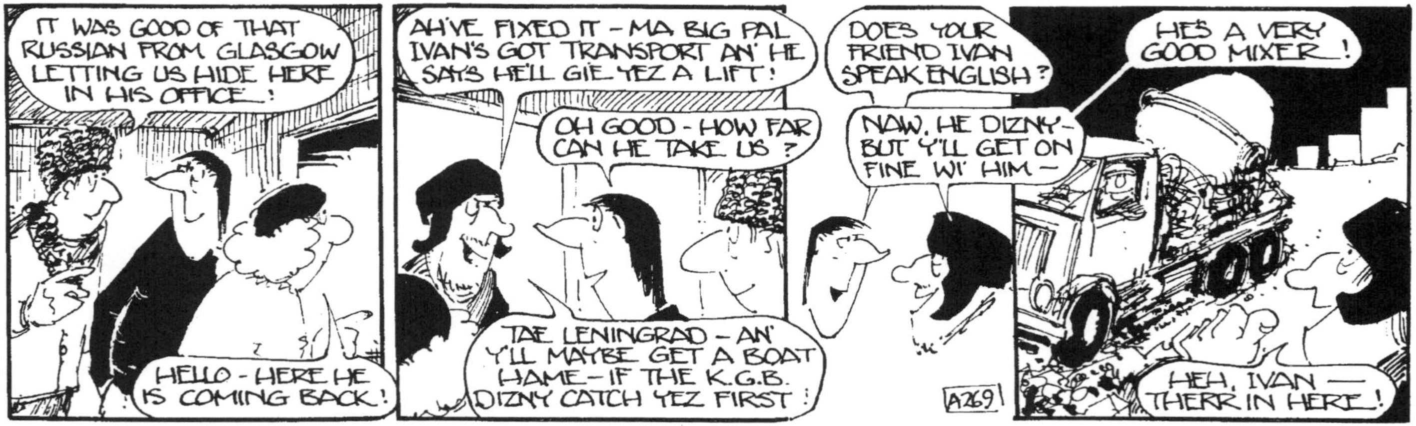
IT WAS GOOD OF THAT RUSSIAN FROM GLASGOW LETTING US HIDE HERE IN HIS OFFICE!
HELLO – HERE HE IS COMING BACK!
AH'VE FIXED IT – MA BIG PAL IVAN'S GOT TRANSPORT AN' HE SAYS HE'LL GIE YEZ A LIFT!
OH GOOD – HOW FAR CAN HE TAKE US?
TAE LENINGRAD – AN' Y'LL MAYBE GET A BOAT HAME – IF THE K.G.B. DIZNY CATCH YEZ FIRST!
DOES YOUR FRIEND IVAN SPEAK ENGLISH?
NAW, HE DIZNY – BUT Y'LL GET ON FINE WI' HIM –
A269
HE'S A VERY GOOD MIXER!
HEH, IVAN — THERR IN HERE!

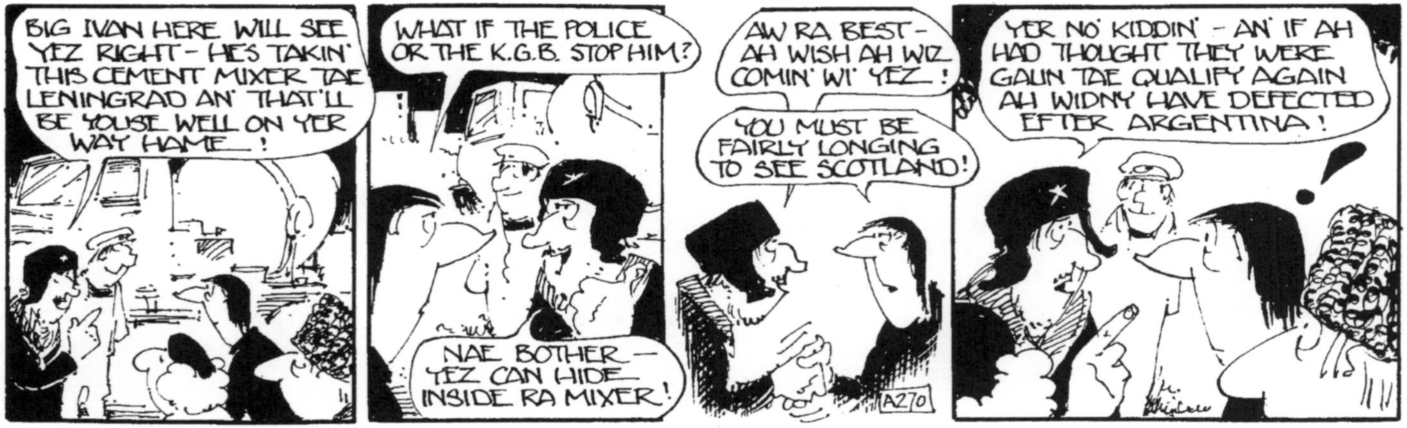
BIG IVAN HERE WILL SEE YEZ RIGHT - HE'S TAKIN' THIS CEMENT MIXER TAE LENINGRAD AN' THAT'LL BE YOUSE WELL ON YER WAY HAME — !
WHAT IF THE POLICE OR THE K.G.B. STOP HIM?
NAE BOTHER — YEZ CAN HIDE INSIDE RA MIXER!
AW RA BEST - AH WISH AH WIZ COMIN' WI' YEZ !
YOU MUST BE FAIRLY LONGING TO SEE SCOTLAND!
A270
YER NO' KIDDIN' - AN' IF AH HAD THOUGHT THEY WERE GAUN TAE QUALIFY AGAIN AH WIDNY HAVE DEFECTED EFTER ARGENTINA !
!

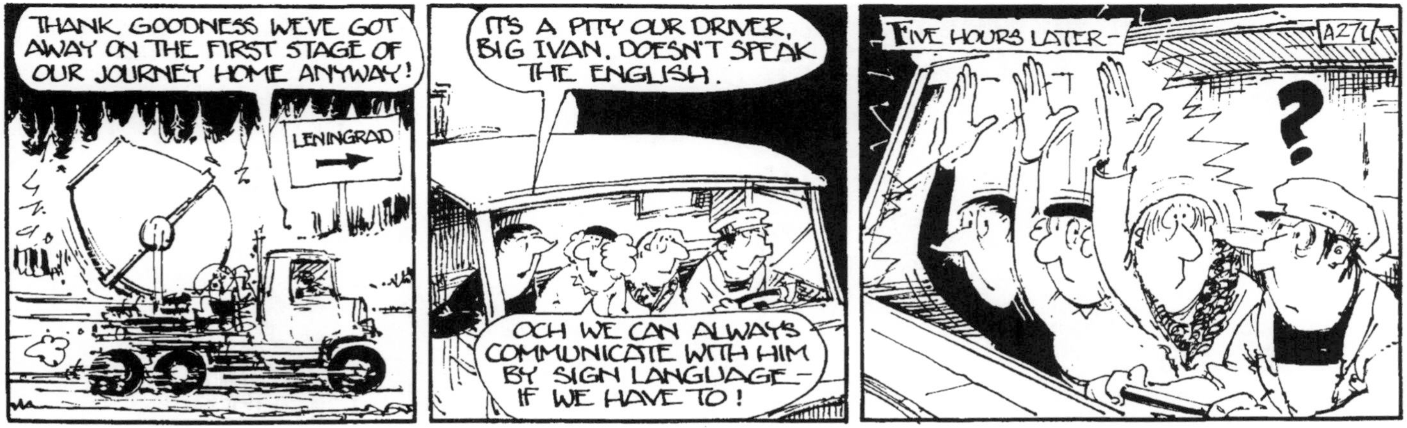
THANK GOODNESS WE'VE GOT AWAY ON THE FIRST STAGE OF OUR JOURNEY HOME ANYWAY!
LENINGRAD
IT'S A PITY OUR DRIVER, BIG IVAN, DOESN'T SPEAK THE ENGLISH.
OCH WE CAN ALWAYS COMMUNICATE WITH HIM BY SIGN LANGUAGE - IF WE HAVE TO !
FIVE HOURS LATER -
A271
?

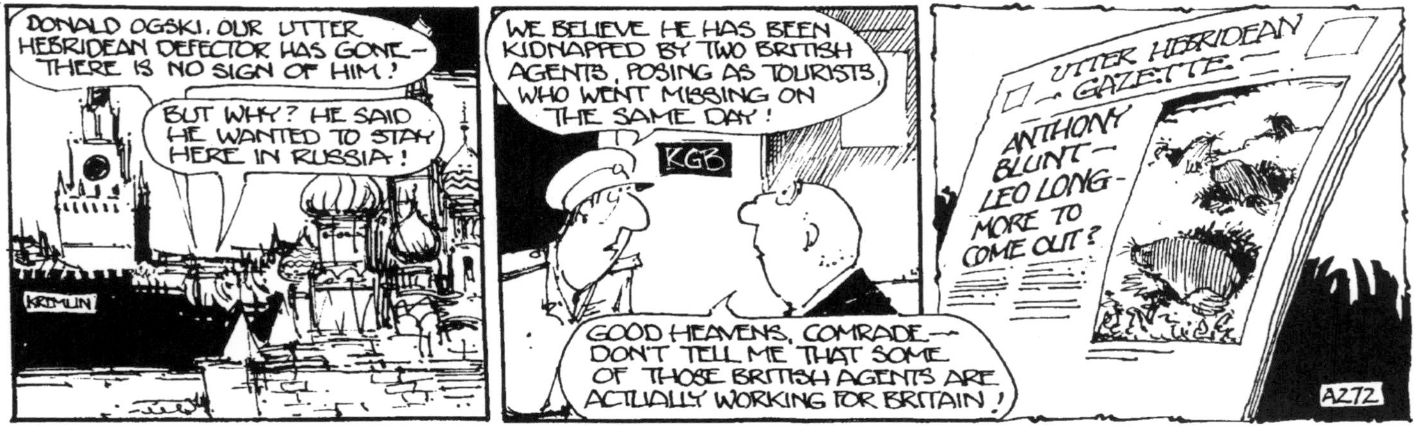
DONALD OGSKI, OUR UTTER HEBRIDEAN DEFECTOR HAS GONE — THERE IS NO SIGN OF HIM!
BUT WHY? HE SAID HE WANTED TO STAY HERE IN RUSSIA!
KREMLIN
WE BELIEVE HE HAS BEEN KIDNAPPED BY TWO BRITISH AGENTS, POSING AS TOURISTS, WHO WENT MISSING ON THE SAME DAY!
KGB
GOOD HEAVENS, COMRADE — DON'T TELL ME THAT SOME OF THOSE BRITISH AGENTS ARE ACTUALLY WORKING FOR BRITAIN!
UTTER HEBRIDEAN GAZETTE
ANTHONY BLUNT — LEO LONG — MORE TO COME OUT?
A272

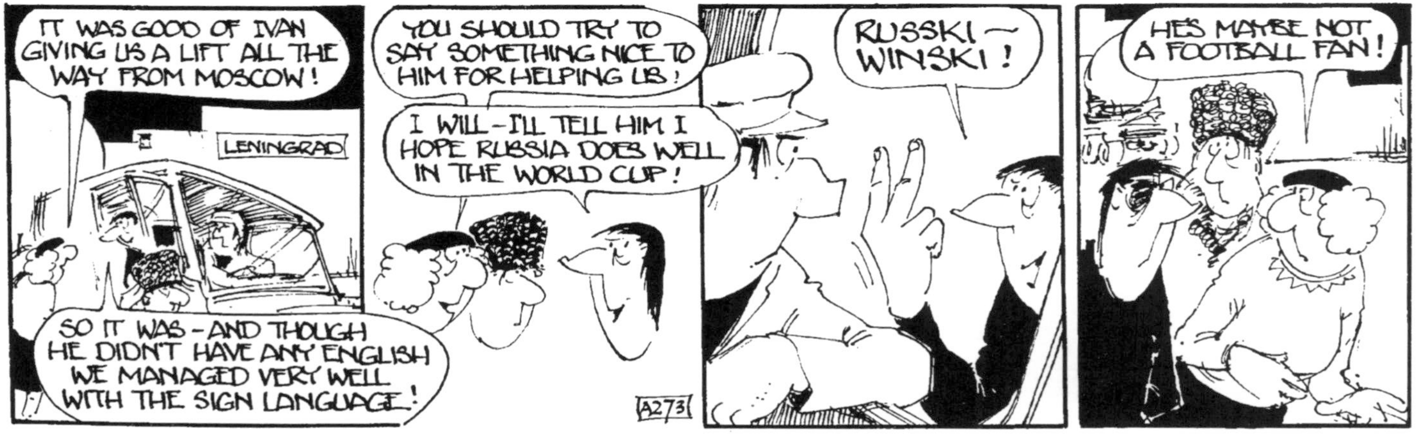
IT WAS GOOD OF IVAN GIVING US A LIFT ALL THE WAY FROM MOSCOW!
LENINGRAD
SO IT WAS — AND THOUGH HE DIDN'T HAVE ANY ENGLISH WE MANAGED VERY WELL WITH THE SIGN LANGUAGE!
YOU SHOULD TRY TO SAY SOMETHING NICE TO HIM FOR HELPING US!
I WILL — I'LL TELL HIM I HOPE RUSSIA DOES WELL IN THE WORLD CUP!
A273
RUSSKI — WINSKI!
HE'S MAYBE NOT A FOOTBALL FAN!

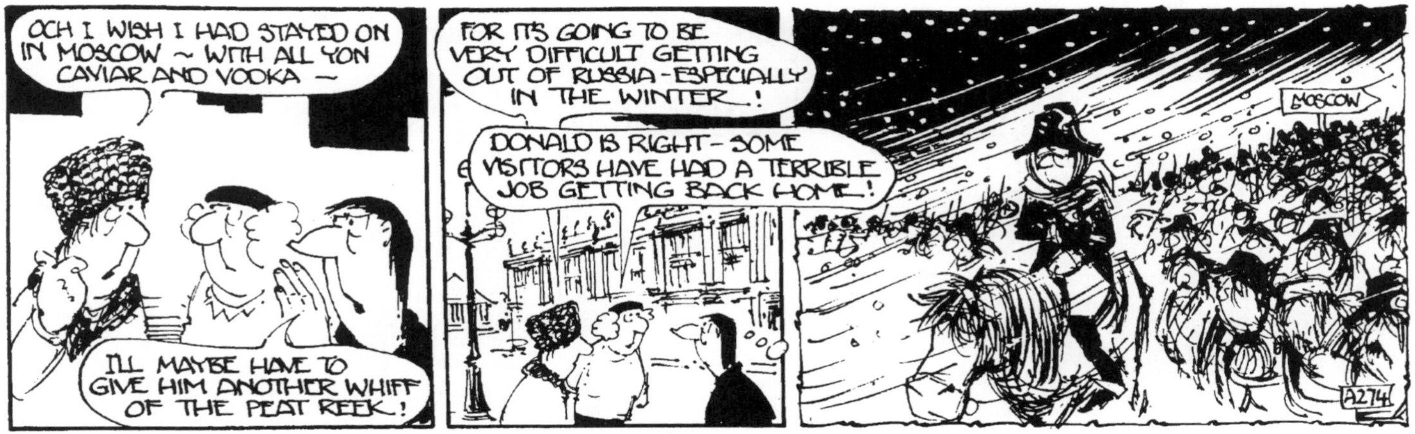
OCH I WISH I HAD STAYED ON IN MOSCOW ~ WITH ALL YON CAVIAR AND VODKA ~
I'LL MAYBE HAVE TO GIVE HIM ANOTHER WHIFF OF THE PEAT REEK!
FOR IT'S GOING TO BE VERY DIFFICULT GETTING OUT OF RUSSIA - ESPECIALLY IN THE WINTER...!
DONALD IS RIGHT - SOME VISITORS HAVE HAD A TERRIBLE JOB GETTING BACK HOME!
MOSCOW
A274

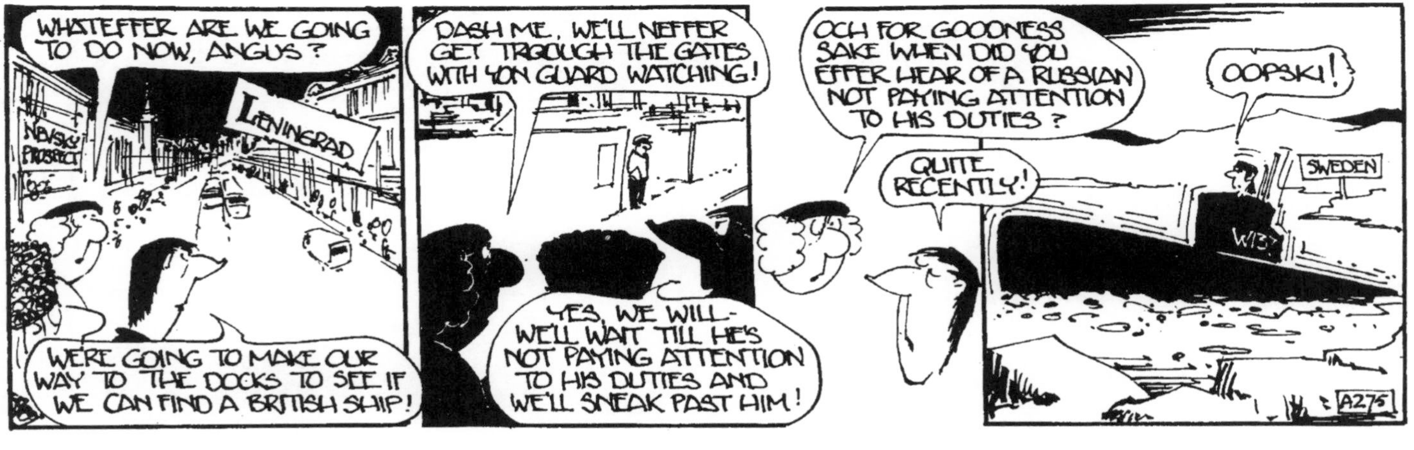
WHATEFFER ARE WE GOING TO DO NOW, ANGUS?
NEVSKY PROSPECT
LENINGRAD
WE'RE GOING TO MAKE OUR WAY TO THE DOCKS TO SEE IF WE CAN FIND A BRITISH SHIP!
DASH ME, WE'LL NEFFER GET TROUGH THE GATES WITH YON GUARD WATCHING!
YES, WE WILL - WE'LL WAIT TILL HE'S NOT PAYING ATTENTION TO HIS DUTIES AND WE'LL SNEAK PAST HIM!
OCH FOR GOOODNESS SAKE WHEN DID YOU EFFER HEAR OF A RUSSIAN NOT PAYING ATTENTION TO HIS DUTIES?
QUITE RECENTLY!
OOPSKI!
SWEDEN
A275

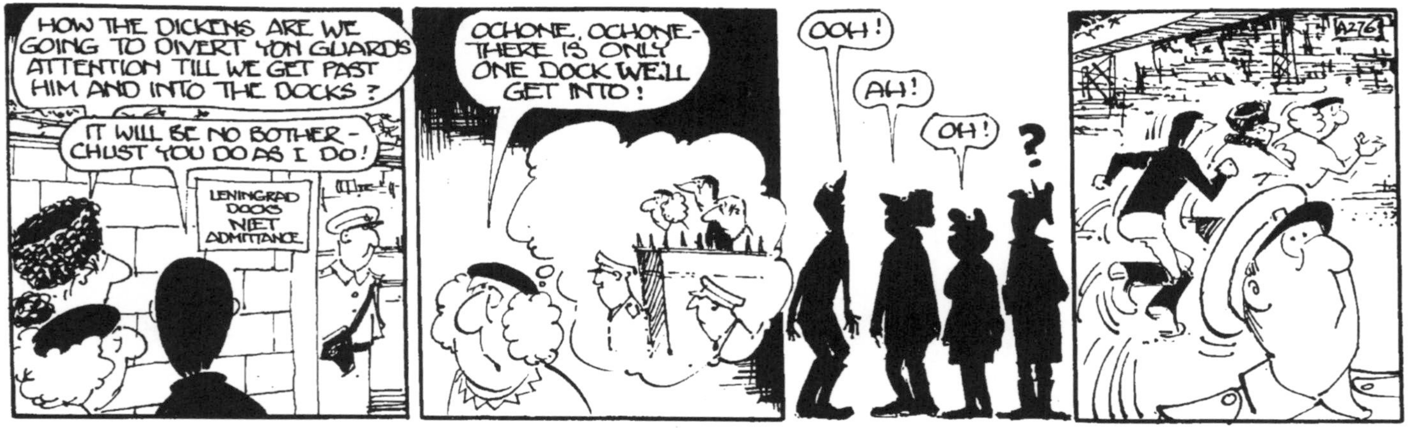
HOW THE DICKENS ARE WE GOING TO DIVERT YON GUARD'S ATTENTION TILL WE GET PAST HIM AND INTO THE DOCKS ?
IT WILL BE NO BOTHER - CHUST YOU DO AS I DO !
LENINGRAD DOCKS NIET ADMITTANCE
OCHONE, OCHONE - THERE IS ONLY ONE DOCK WE'LL GET INTO !
OOH !
AH !
OH !
?
A276

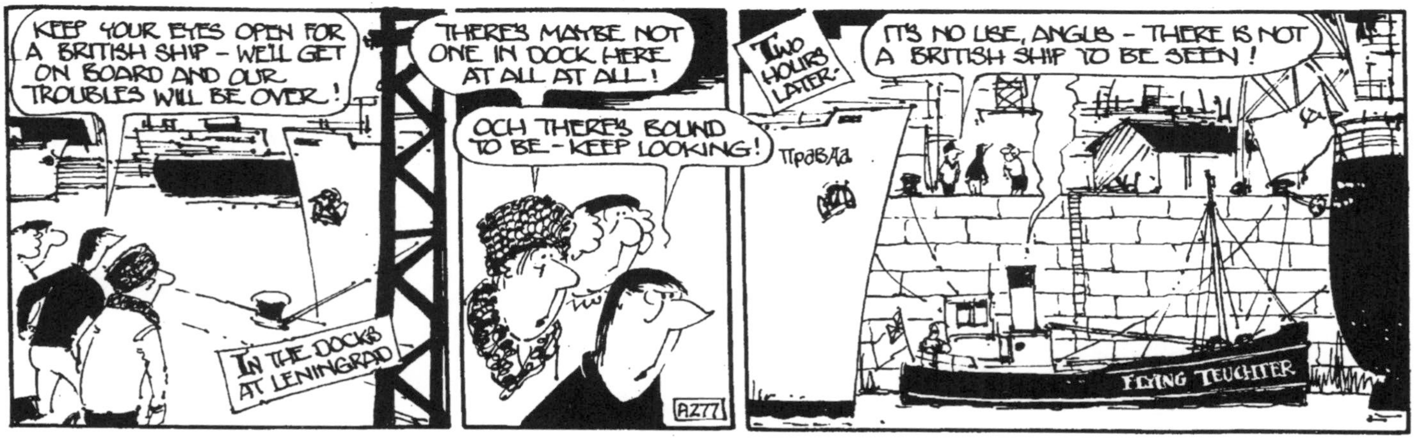
KEEP YOUR EYES OPEN FOR A BRITISH SHIP - WE'LL GET ON BOARD AND OUR TROUBLES WILL BE OVER !
IN THE DOCKS AT LENINGRAD
THERE'S MAYBE NOT ONE IN DOCK HERE AT ALL AT ALL !
OCH THERE'S BOUND TO BE - KEEP LOOKING !
A277
TWO HOURS LATER-
IT'S NO USE, ANGUS - THERE IS NOT A BRITISH SHIP TO BE SEEN !
Правда
FLYING TEUCHTER

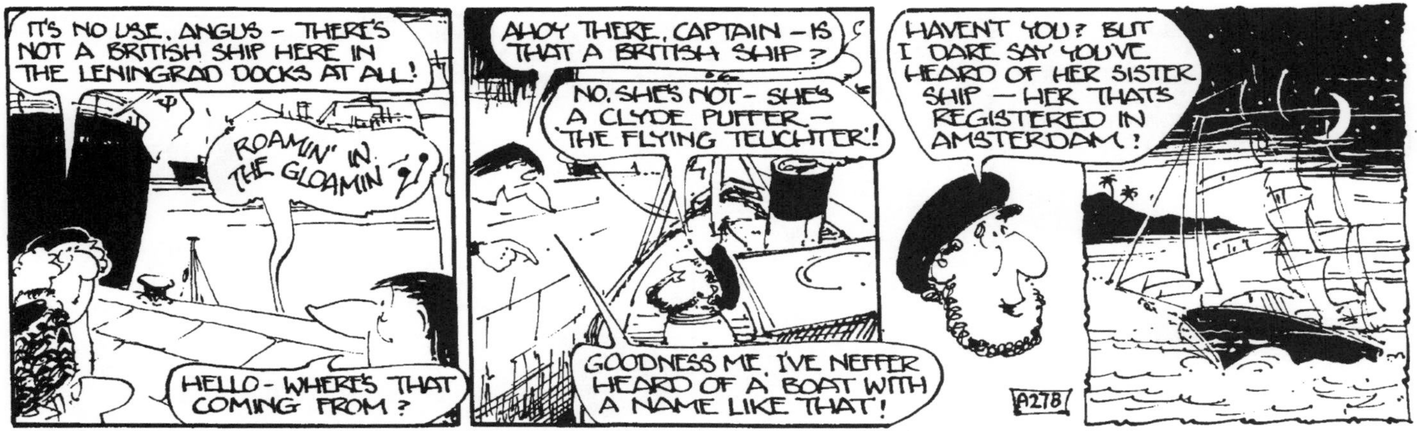
IT'S NO USE, ANGUS - THERE'S NOT A BRITISH SHIP HERE IN THE LENINGRAD DOCKS AT ALL!
ROAMIN' IN THE GLOAMIN
HELLO - WHERE'S THAT COMING FROM?
AHOY THERE, CAPTAIN - IS THAT A BRITISH SHIP?
NO, SHE'S NOT - SHE'S A CLYDE PUFFER - THE FLYING TEUCHTER!
GOODNESS ME, I'VE NEFFER HEARD OF A BOAT WITH A NAME LIKE THAT!
HAVEN'T YOU? BUT I DARE SAY YOU'VE HEARD OF HER SISTER SHIP - HER THAT'S REGISTERED IN AMSTERDAM!
A278

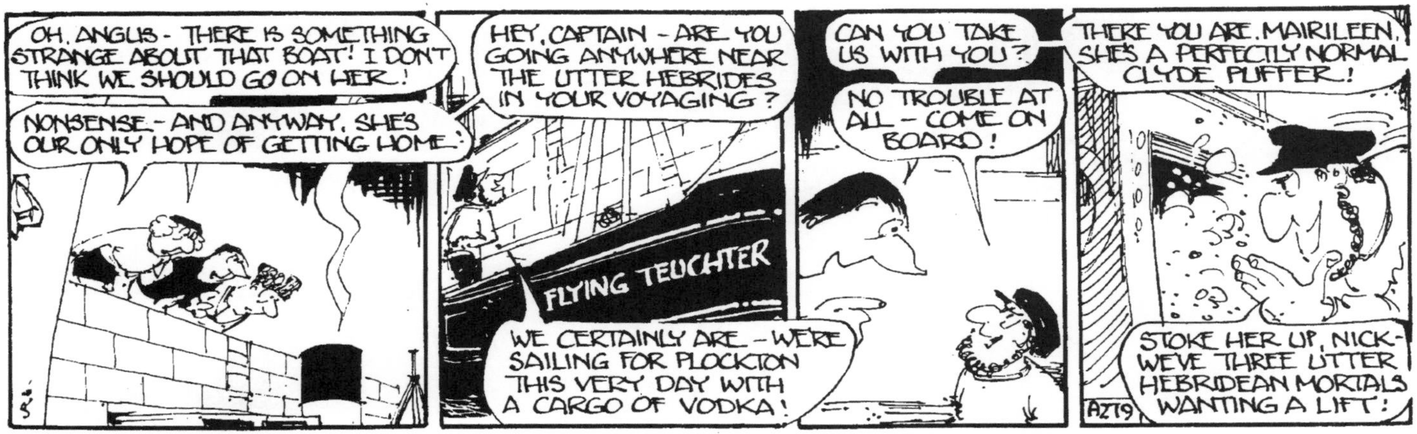
OH, ANGUS - THERE IS SOMETHING STRANGE ABOUT THAT BOAT! I DON'T THINK WE SHOULD GO ON HER!
NONSENSE - AND ANYWAY, SHE'S OUR ONLY HOPE OF GETTING HOME.
HEY, CAPTAIN - ARE YOU GOING ANYWHERE NEAR THE UTTER HEBRIDES IN YOUR VOYAGING?
FLYING TEUCHTER
WE CERTAINLY ARE - WE'RE SAILING FOR PLOCKTON THIS VERY DAY WITH A CARGO OF VODKA!
CAN YOU TAKE US WITH YOU?
NO TROUBLE AT ALL - COME ON BOARD!
THERE YOU ARE, MAIRILEEN, SHE'S A PERFECTLY NORMAL CLYDE PUFFER!
STOKE HER UP, NICK - WE'VE THREE UTTER HEBRIDEAN MORTALS WANTING A LIFT!
A279

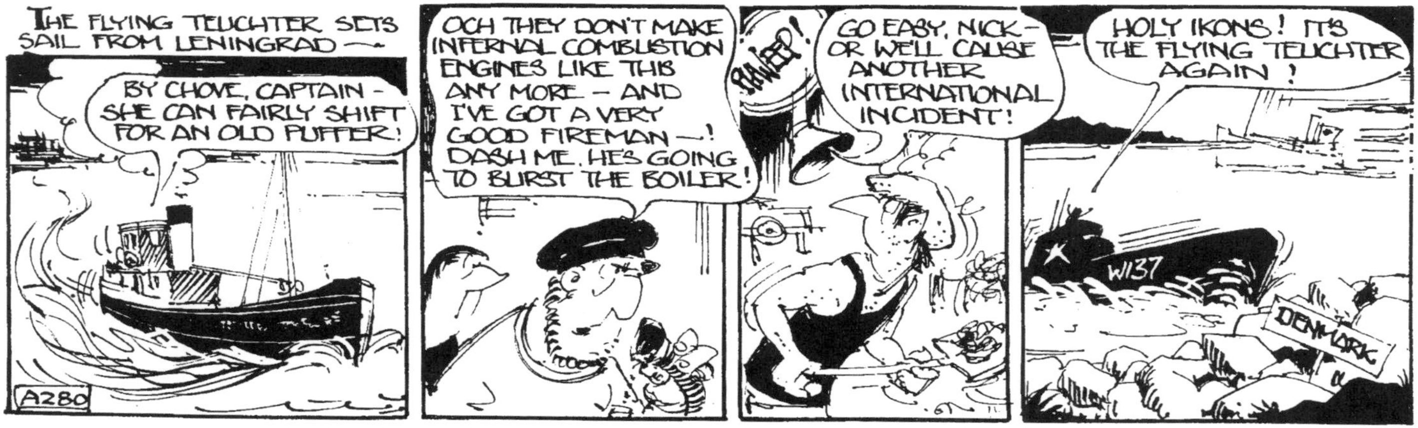
THE FLYING TEUCHTER SETS SAIL FROM LENINGRAD —
BY CHOVE, CAPTAIN - SHE CAN FAIRLY SHIFT FOR AN OLD PUFFER!
A280
OCH THEY DON'T MAKE INFERNAL COMBUSTION ENGINES LIKE THIS ANY MORE — AND I'VE GOT A VERY GOOD FIREMAN —! DASH ME. HE'S GOING TO BURST THE BOILER!
GO EASY, NICK — OR WE'LL CAUSE ANOTHER INTERNATIONAL INCIDENT!
HOLY IKONS! IT'S THE FLYING TEUCHTER AGAIN!
W137
DENMARK

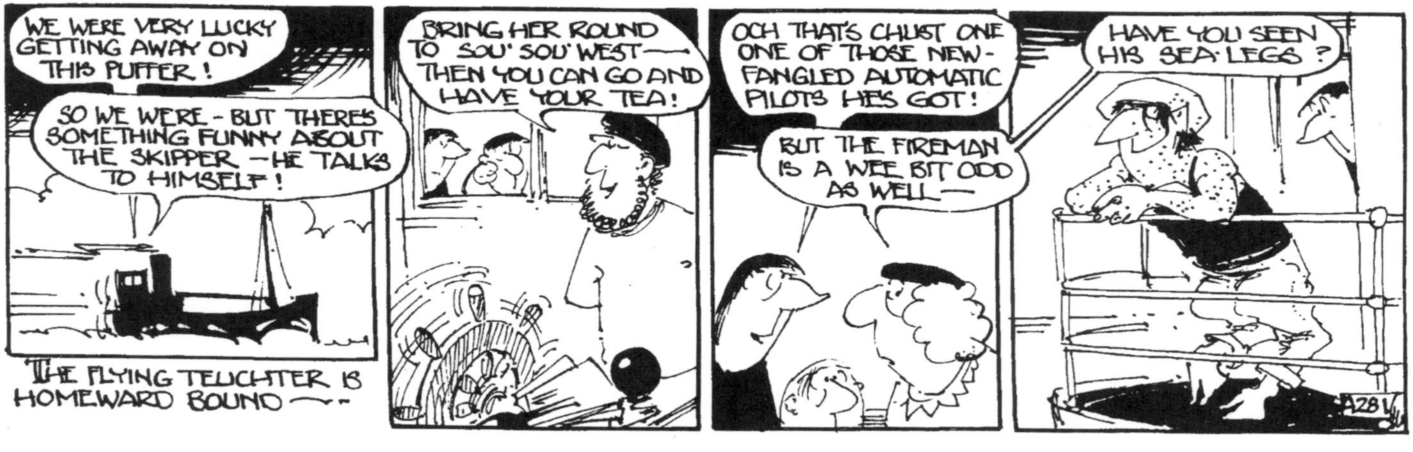
WE WERE VERY LUCKY GETTING AWAY ON THIS PUFFER!
SO WE WERE - BUT THERE'S SOMETHING FUNNY ABOUT THE SKIPPER — HE TALKS TO HIMSELF!
THE FLYING TEUCHTER IS HOMEWARD BOUND —
BRING HER ROUND TO SOU' SOU' WEST — THEN YOU CAN GO AND HAVE YOUR TEA!
OCH THAT'S CHUST ONE ONE OF THOSE NEW-FANGLED AUTOMATIC PILOTS HE'S GOT!
BUT THE FIREMAN IS A WEE BIT ODD AS WELL —
HAVE YOU SEEN HIS SEA-LEGS?
A281

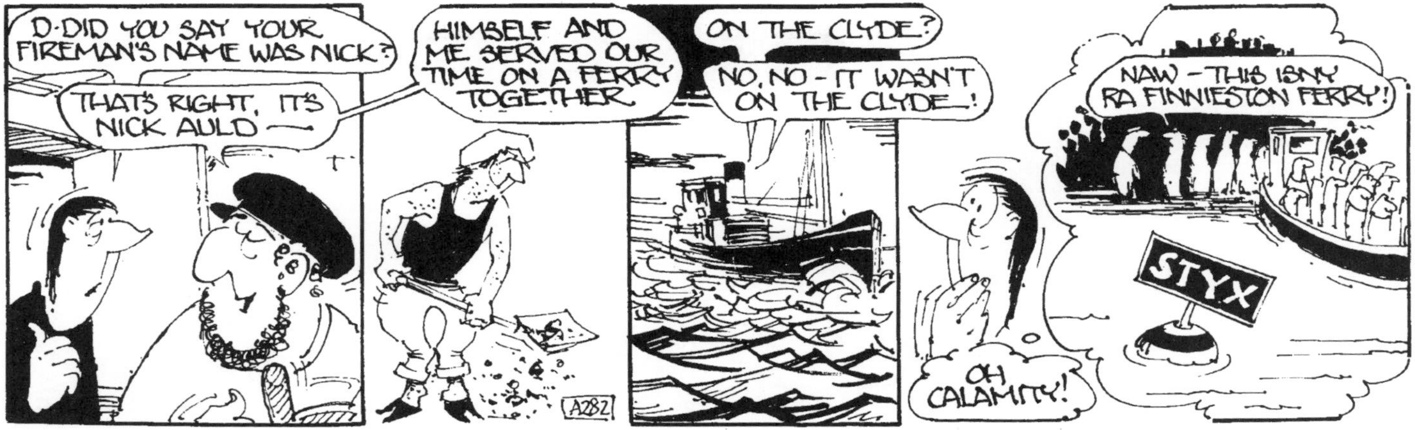
D-DID YOU SAY YOUR FIREMAN'S NAME WAS NICK?
THAT'S RIGHT, IT'S NICK AULD —
HIMSELF AND ME SERVED OUR TIME ON A FERRY TOGETHER.
A282
ON THE CLYDE?
NO, NO - IT WASN'T ON THE CLYDE...!
OH CALAMITY!
NAW - THIS ISNY RA FINNIESTON FERRY!
STYX

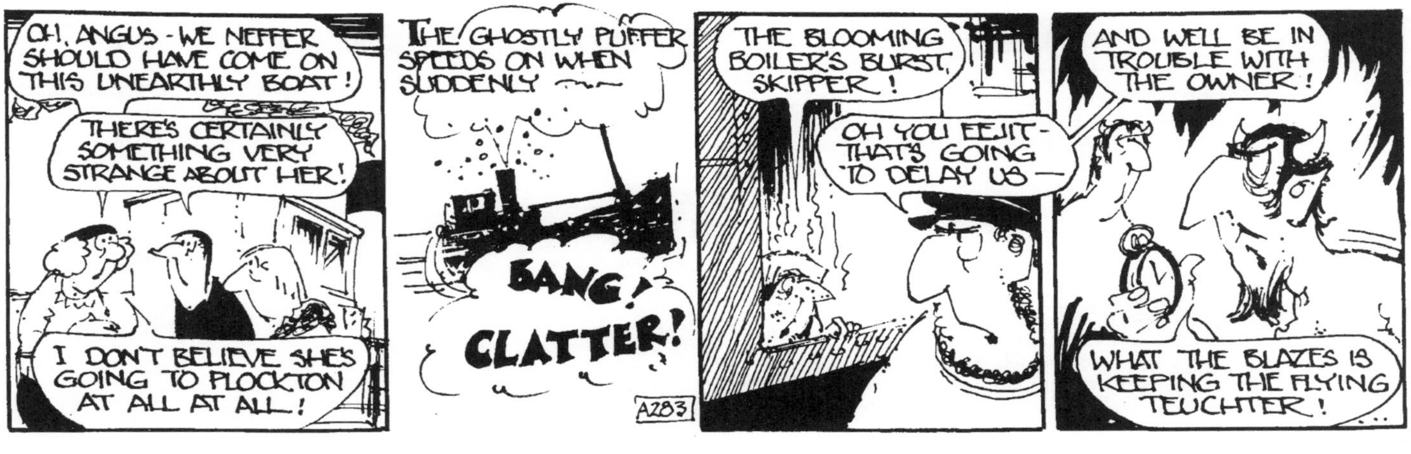
OH, ANGUS - WE NEFFER SHOULD HAVE COME ON THIS UNEARTHLY BOAT!
THERE'S CERTAINLY SOMETHING VERY STRANGE ABOUT HER!
I DON'T BELIEVE SHE'S GOING TO PLOCKTON AT ALL AT ALL!
THE GHOSTLY PUFFER SPEEDS ON WHEN SUDDENLY —
BANG!
CLATTER!
A283
THE BLOOMING BOILER'S BURST, SKIPPER!
OH YOU EEJIT - THAT'S GOING TO DELAY US —
AND WE'LL BE IN TROUBLE WITH THE OWNER!
WHAT THE BLAZES IS KEEPING THE FLYING TEUCHTER!

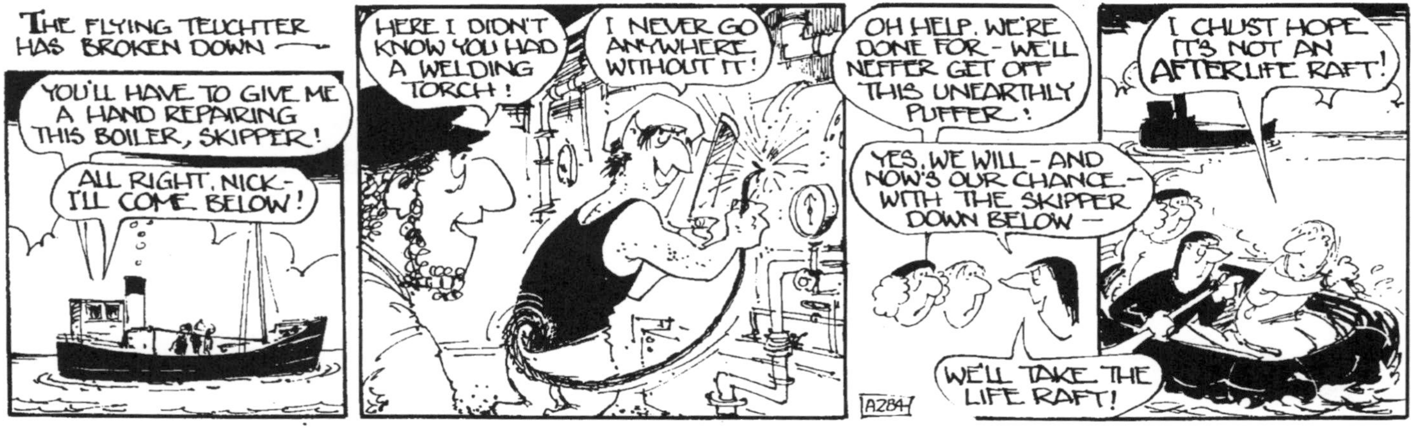
THE FLYING TEUCHTER HAS BROKEN DOWN —
YOU'LL HAVE TO GIVE ME A HAND REPAIRING THIS BOILER, SKIPPER!
ALL RIGHT, NICK — I'LL COME BELOW!
HERE I DIDN'T KNOW YOU HAD A WELDING TORCH!
I NEVER GO ANYWHERE WITHOUT IT!
OH HELP. WE'RE DONE FOR — WE'LL NEFFER GET OFF THIS UNEARTHLY PUFFER!
YES, WE WILL — AND NOW'S OUR CHANCE — WITH THE SKIPPER DOWN BELOW —
WE'LL TAKE THE LIFE RAFT!
A284
I CHUST HOPE IT'S NOT AN AFTERLIFE RAFT!

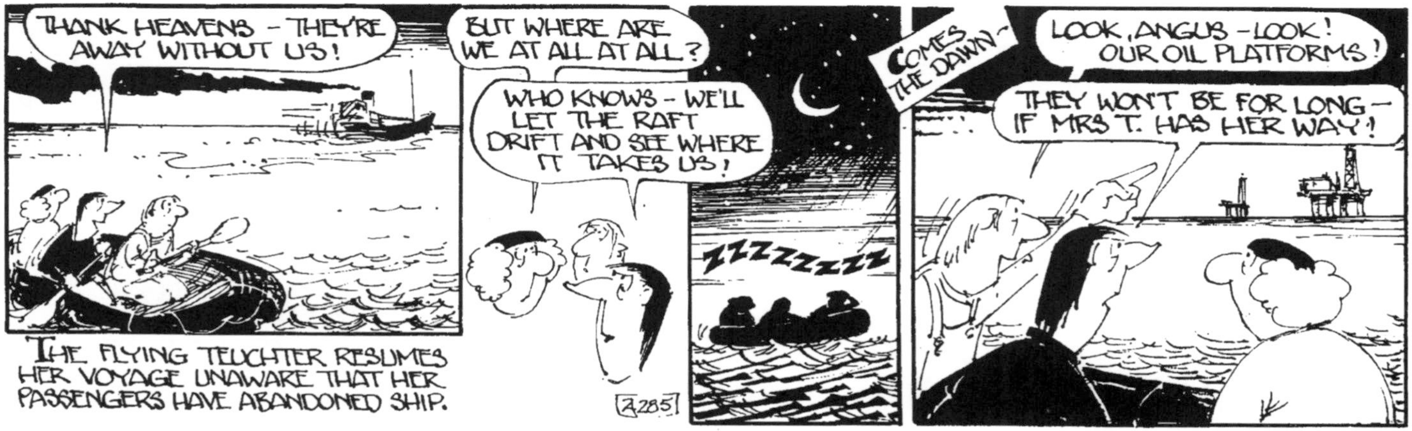
THANK HEAVENS — THEY'RE AWAY WITHOUT US!
THE FLYING TEUCHTER RESUMES HER VOYAGE UNAWARE THAT HER PASSENGERS HAVE ABANDONED SHIP.
BUT WHERE ARE WE AT ALL AT ALL?
WHO KNOWS — WE'LL LET THE RAFT DRIFT AND SEE WHERE IT TAKES US!
A285
ZZZZZZZZZ
COMES THE DAWN —
LOOK, ANGUS — LOOK! OUR OIL PLATFORMS!
THEY WON'T BE FOR LONG — IF MRS T. HAS HER WAY!

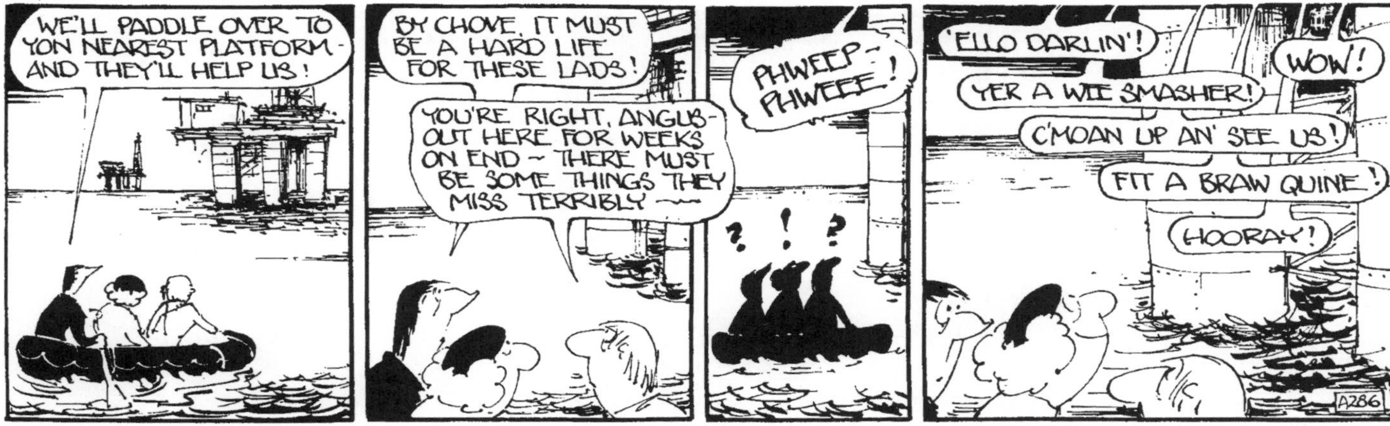
WE'LL PADDLE OVER TO YON NEAREST PLATFORM - AND THEY'LL HELP US!
BY CHOVE, IT MUST BE A HARD LIFE FOR THESE LADS!
YOU'RE RIGHT, ANGUS - OUT HERE FOR WEEKS ON END ~ THERE MUST BE SOME THINGS THEY MISS TERRIBLY ~~
PHWEEP - PHWEEE!
? ! ?
'ELLO DARLIN'!
WOW!
YER A WEE SMASHER!
C'MOAN UP AN' SEE US!
FIT A BRAW QUINE!
HOORAY!
A286

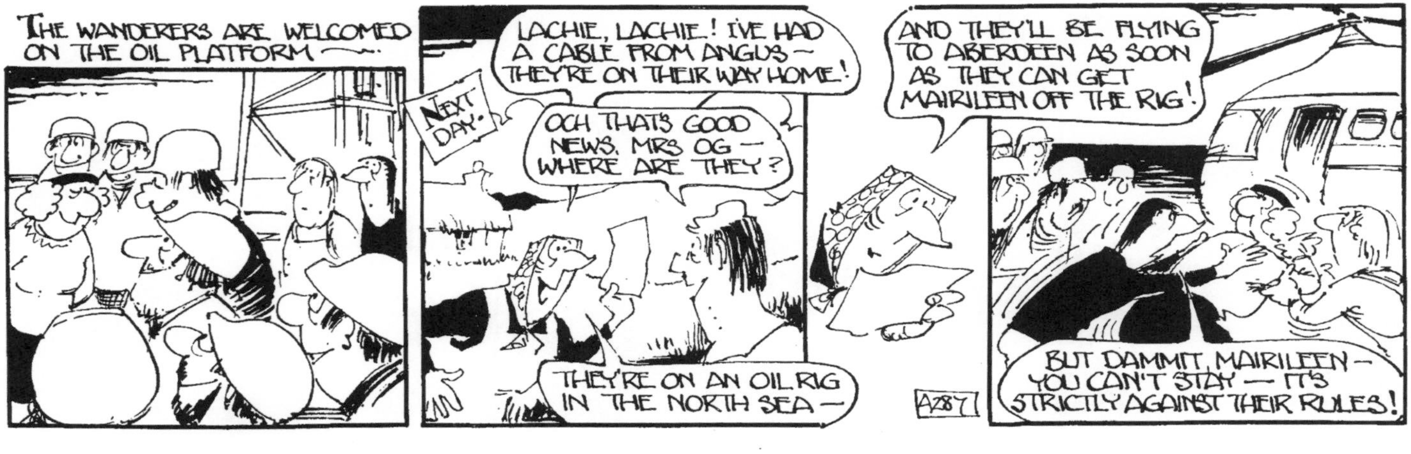
THE WANDERERS ARE WELCOMED ON THE OIL PLATFORM ~
NEXT DAY.
LACHIE, LACHIE! I'VE HAD A CABLE FROM ANGUS - THEY'RE ON THEIR WAY HOME!
OCH THAT'S GOOD NEWS, MRS OG - WHERE ARE THEY?
THEY'RE ON AN OIL RIG IN THE NORTH SEA -
AND THEY'LL BE FLYING TO ABERDEEN AS SOON AS THEY CAN GET MAIRILEEN OFF THE RIG!
BUT DAMMIT, MAIRILEEN - YOU CAN'T STAY — IT'S STRICTLY AGAINST THEIR RULES!
A287

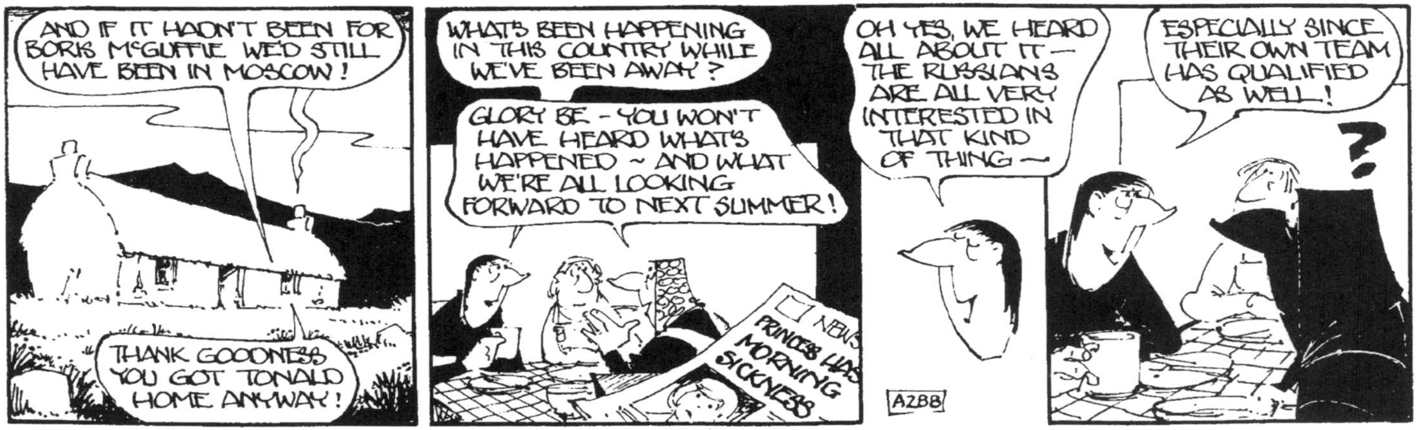
AND IF IT HADN'T BEEN FOR BORIS McGUFFIE WE'D STILL HAVE BEEN IN MOSCOW!
THANK GOOODNESS YOU GOT TONALD HOME ANYWAY!
WHAT'S BEEN HAPPENING IN THIS COUNTRY WHILE WE'VE BEEN AWAY?
GLORY BE - YOU WON'T HAVE HEARD WHAT'S HAPPENED ~ AND WHAT WE'RE ALL LOOKING FORWARD TO NEXT SUMMER!
NEWS
PRINCESS HAS MORNING SICKNESS
OH YES, WE HEARD ALL ABOUT IT - THE RUSSIANS ARE ALL VERY INTERESTED IN THAT KIND OF THING ~
A288
ESPECIALLY SINCE THEIR OWN TEAM HAS QUALIFIED AS WELL!
?

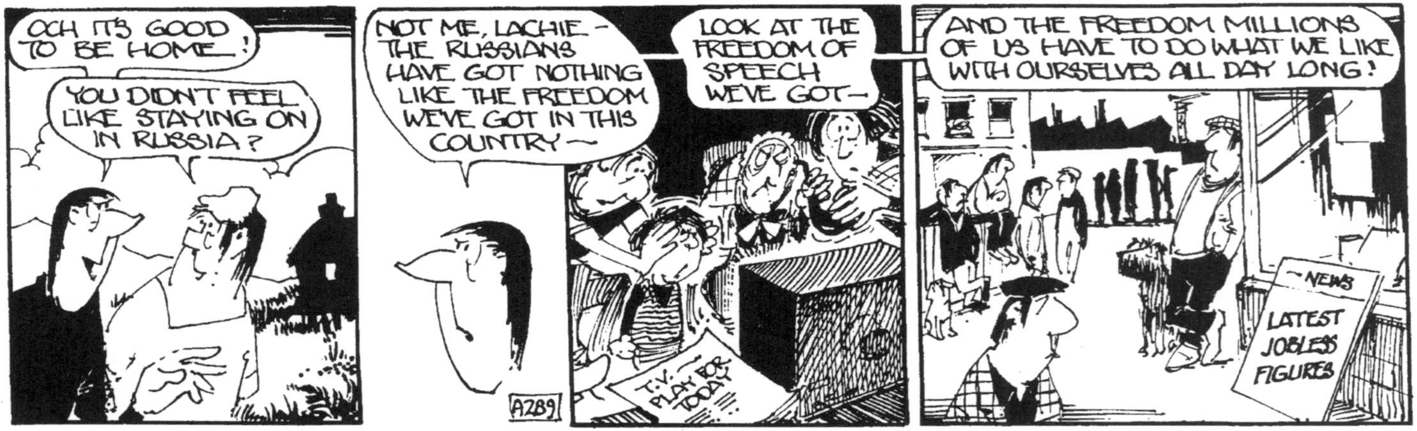
OCH IT'S GOOD TO BE HOME!
YOU DIDN'T FEEL LIKE STAYING ON IN RUSSIA?
NOT ME, LACHIE - THE RUSSIANS HAVE GOT NOTHING LIKE THE FREEDOM WE'VE GOT IN THIS COUNTRY ~
A289
LOOK AT THE FREEDOM OF SPEECH WE'VE GOT ~
T.V. - PLAY FOR TODAY
AND THE FREEDOM MILLIONS OF US HAVE TO DO WHAT WE LIKE WITH OURSELVES ALL DAY LONG!
~ NEWS
LATEST JOBLESS FIGURES

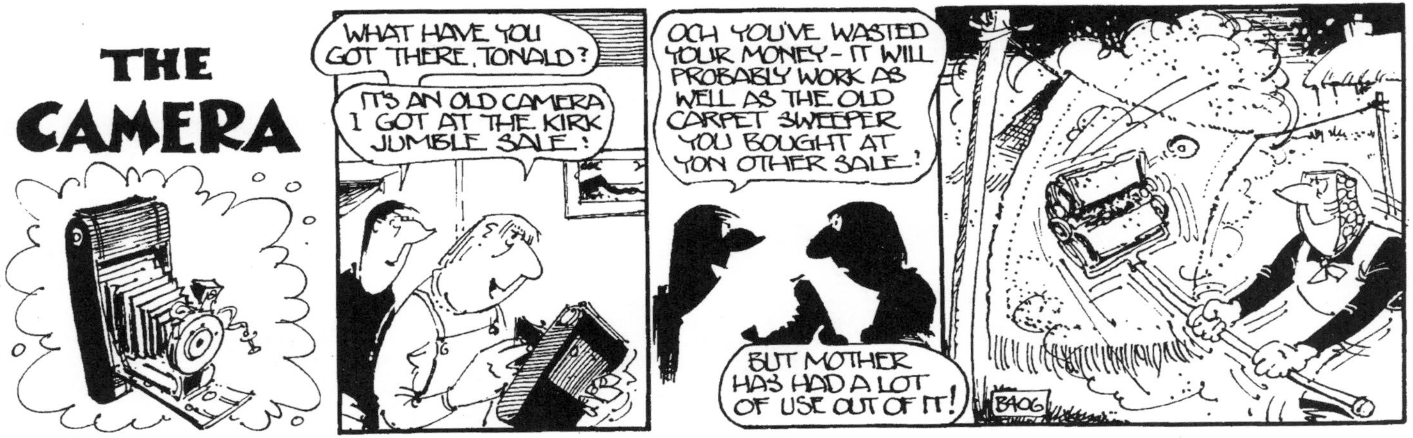
THE CAMERA
WHAT HAVE YOU GOT THERE, TONALD?
IT'S AN OLD CAMERA I GOT AT THE KIRK JUMBLE SALE!
OCH YOU'VE WASTED YOUR MONEY - IT WILL PROBABLY WORK AS WELL AS THE OLD CARPET SWEEPER YOU BOUGHT AT YON OTHER SALE!
BUT MOTHER HAS HAD A LOT OF USE OUT OF IT!

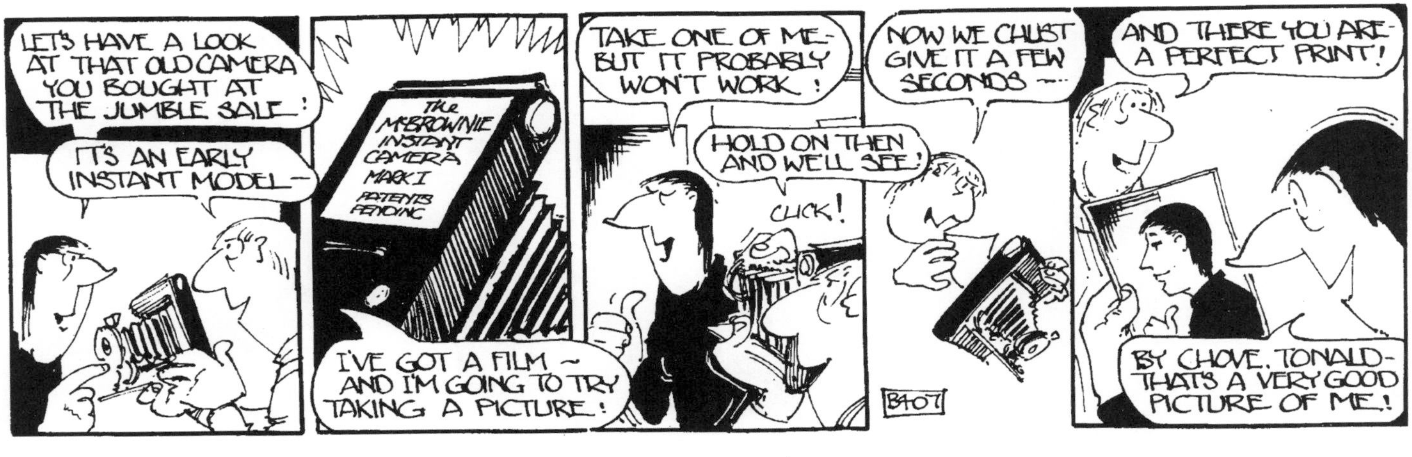
LET'S HAVE A LOOK AT THAT OLD CAMERA YOU BOUGHT AT THE JUMBLE SALE!
IT'S AN EARLY INSTANT MODEL—
The McBROWNIE INSTANT CAMERA MARK I PATENTS PENDING
I'VE GOT A FILM — AND I'M GOING TO TRY TAKING A PICTURE!
TAKE ONE OF ME- BUT IT PROBABLY WON'T WORK!
HOLD ON THEN AND WE'LL SEE!
CLICK!
NOW WE CHUST GIVE IT A FEW SECONDS —
AND THERE YOU ARE- A PERFECT PRINT!
BY CHOVE, TONALD- THAT'S A VERY GOOD PICTURE OF ME!

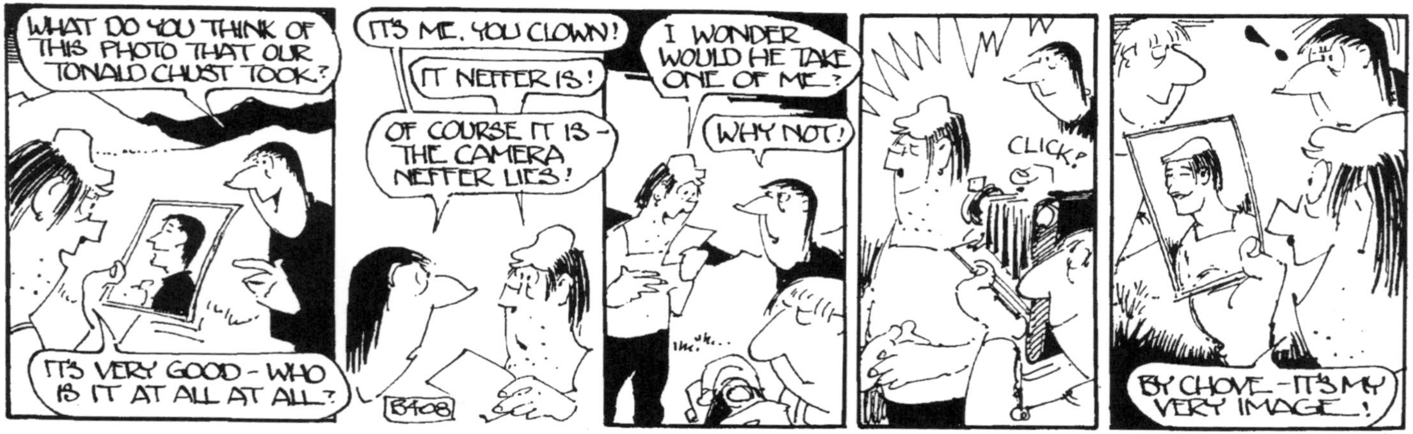
WHAT DO YOU THINK OF THIS PHOTO THAT OUR TONALD CHUST TOOK?
IT'S VERY GOOD - WHO IS IT AT ALL AT ALL?
IT'S ME, YOU CLOWN!
IT NEFFER IS!
OF COURSE IT IS - THE CAMERA NEFFER LIES!
B408
I WONDER WOULD HE TAKE ONE OF ME?
WHY NOT!
CLICK!
!
BY CHOVE - IT'S MY VERY IMAGE!

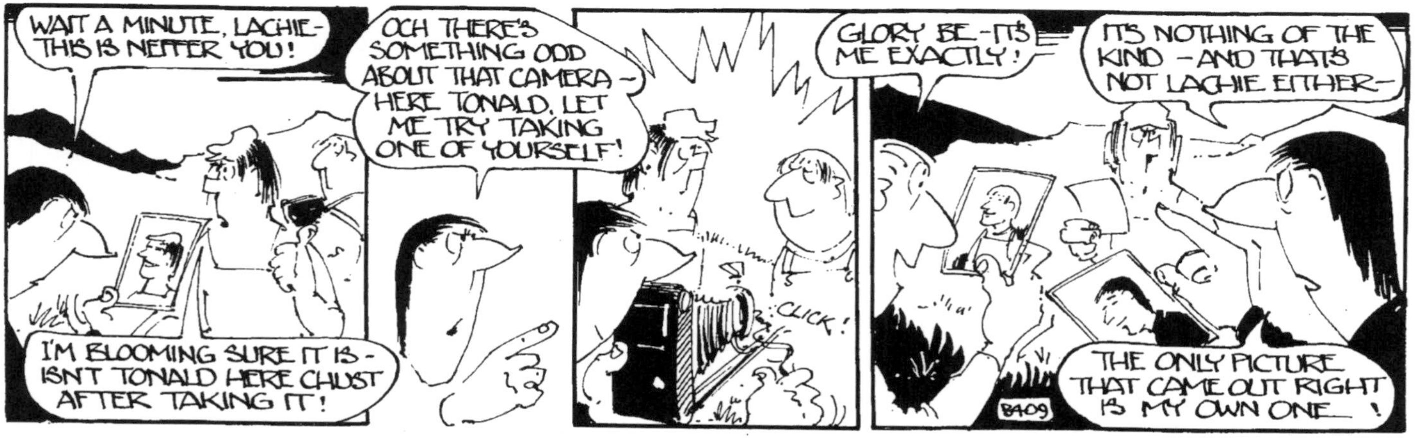
WAIT A MINUTE, LACHIE - THIS IS NEFFER YOU!
I'M BLOOMING SURE IT IS - ISN'T TONALD HERE CHUST AFTER TAKING IT!
OCH THERE'S SOMETHING ODD ABOUT THAT CAMERA - HERE TONALD, LET ME TRY TAKING ONE OF YOURSELF!
CLICK!
GLORY BE - IT'S ME EXACTLY!
IT'S NOTHING OF THE KIND - AND THAT'S NOT LACHIE EITHER -
THE ONLY PICTURE THAT CAME OUT RIGHT IS MY OWN ONE!
B409

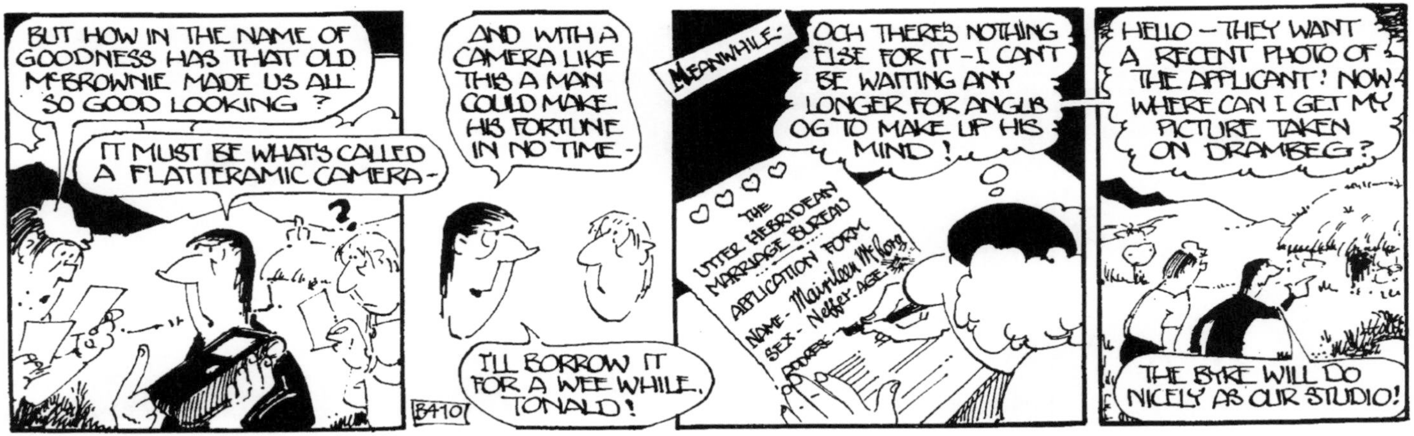
BUT HOW IN THE NAME OF GOODNESS HAS THAT OLD McBROWNIE MADE US ALL SO GOOD LOOKING ?
IT MUST BE WHAT'S CALLED A FLATTERAMIC CAMERA -
AND WITH A CAMERA LIKE THIS A MAN COULD MAKE HIS FORTUNE IN NO TIME -
I'LL BORROW IT FOR A WEE WHILE, TONALD !
B410
MEANWHILE:
OCH THERE'S NOTHING ELSE FOR IT - I CAN'T BE WAITING ANY LONGER FOR ANGUS OG TO MAKE UP HIS MIND !
THE
UTTER HEBRIDEAN
MARRIAGE BUREAU
APPLICATION FORM
NAME - Mairileen McRong
SEX - Neffer. AGE
HELLO - THEY WANT A RECENT PHOTO OF THE APPLICANT ! NOW WHERE CAN I GET MY PICTURE TAKEN ON DRAMBEG ?
THE BYRE WILL DO NICELY AS OUR STUDIO !

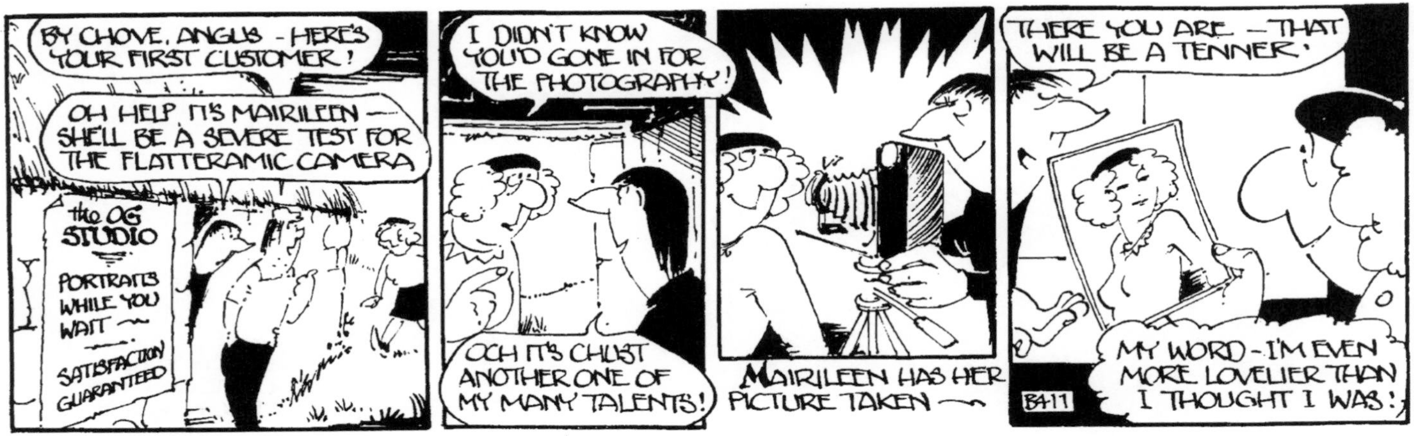
BY CHOVE, ANGUS - HERE'S YOUR FIRST CUSTOMER !
OH HELP IT'S MAIRILEEN - SHE'LL BE A SEVERE TEST FOR THE FLATTERAMIC CAMERA
the OG STUDIO
PORTRAITS WHILE YOU WAIT
SATISFACTION GUARANTEED
I DIDN'T KNOW YOU'D GONE IN FOR THE PHOTOGRAPHY !
OCH IT'S CHUST ANOTHER ONE OF MY MANY TALENTS !
MAIRILEEN HAS HER PICTURE TAKEN
THERE YOU ARE - THAT WILL BE A TENNER !
MY WORD - I'M EVEN MORE LOVELIER THAN I THOUGHT I WAS !
B411

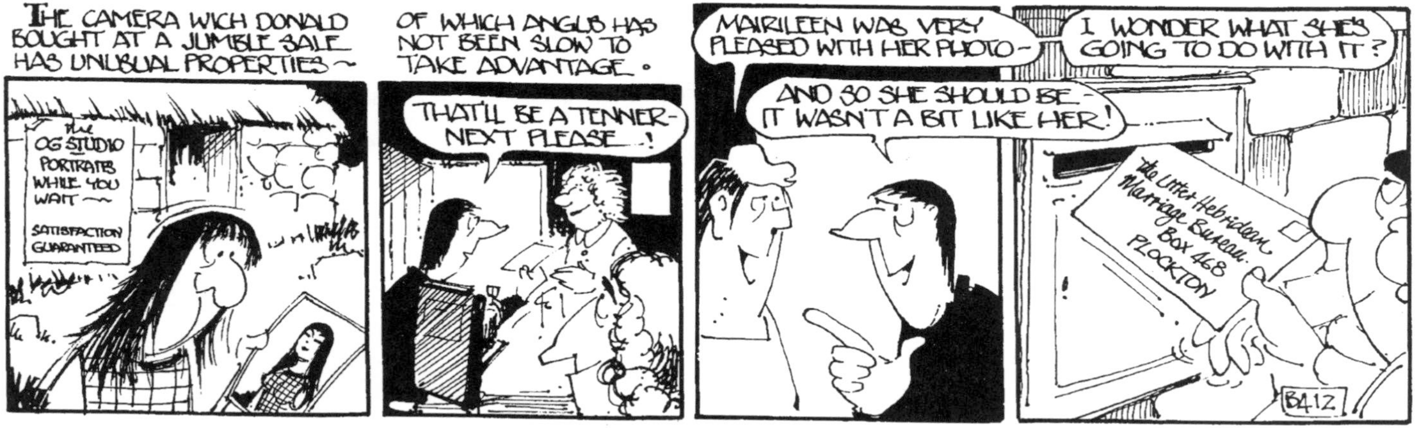
THE CAMERA WICH DONALD BOUGHT AT A JUMBLE SALE HAS UNUSUAL PROPERTIES ~
the OG STUDIO PORTRAITS WHILE YOU WAIT ~~ SATISFACTION GUARANTEED
OF WHICH ANGUS HAS NOT BEEN SLOW TO TAKE ADVANTAGE.
THAT'LL BE A TENNER- NEXT PLEASE ...!
MAIRILEEN WAS VERY PLEASED WITH HER PHOTO-
AND SO SHE SHOULD BE- IT WASN'T A BIT LIKE HER!
I WONDER WHAT SHE'S GOING TO DO WITH IT?
The Utter Hebridean Marriage Bureau. Box 468 PLOCKTON
B412

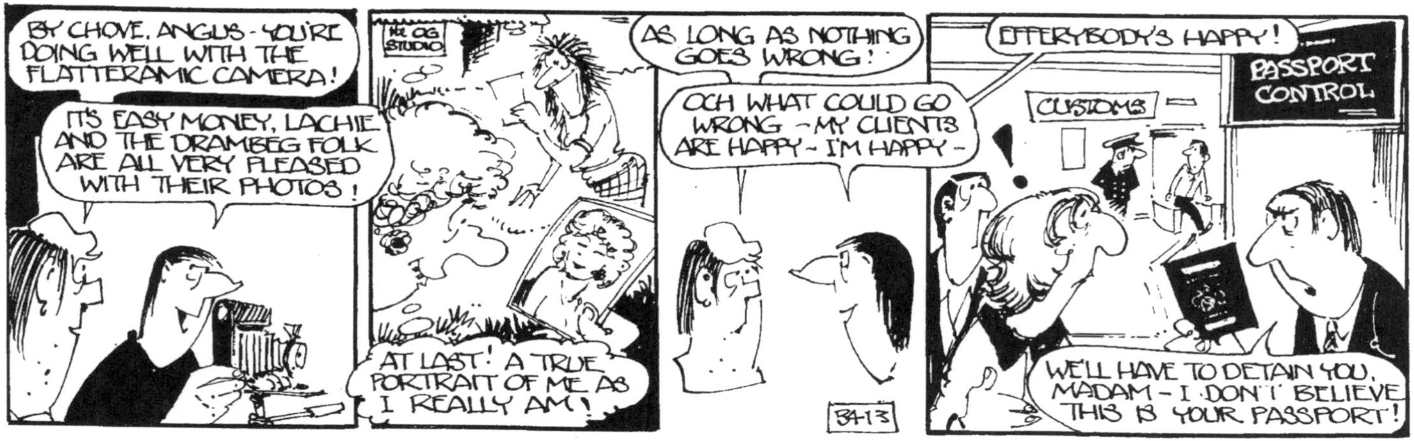
BY CHOVE, ANGUS - YOU'RE DOING WELL WITH THE FLATTERAMIC CAMERA!
IT'S EASY MONEY, LACHIE AND THE DRAMBEG FOLK ARE ALL VERY PLEASED WITH THEIR PHOTOS!
THE OG STUDIO
AT LAST! A TRUE PORTRAIT OF ME AS I REALLY AM!
AS LONG AS NOTHING GOES WRONG!
OCH WHAT COULD GO WRONG - MY CLIENTS ARE HAPPY - I'M HAPPY -
B413
EFFERYBODY'S HAPPY!
PASSPORT CONTROL
CUSTOMS
WE'LL HAVE TO DETAIN YOU, MADAM - I DON'T BELIEVE THIS IS YOUR PASSPORT!

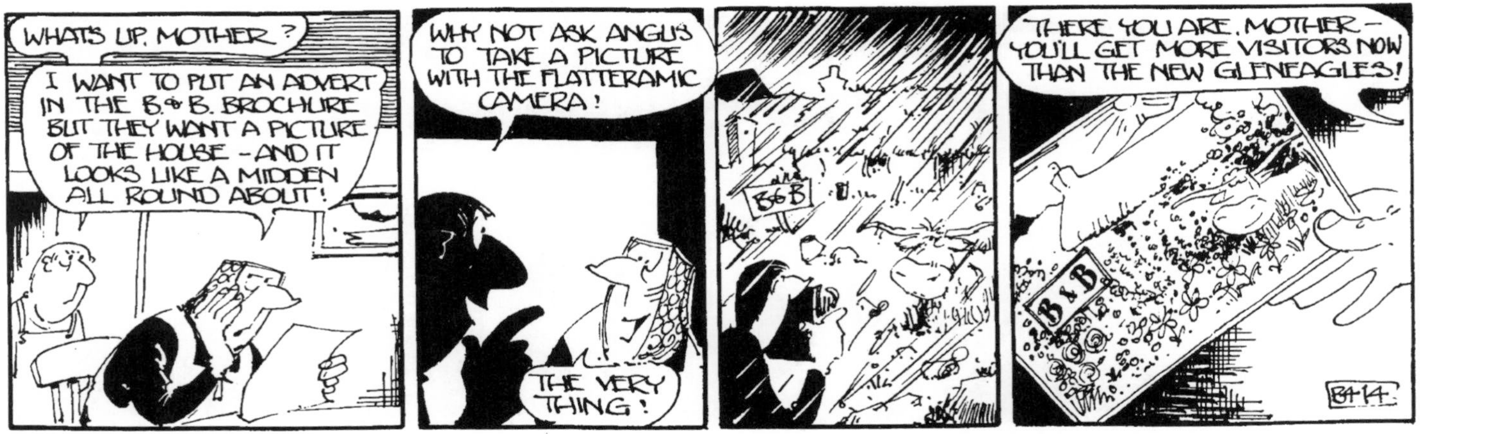
WHAT'S UP, MOTHER?
I WANT TO PUT AN ADVERT IN THE B.& B. BROCHURE BUT THEY WANT A PICTURE OF THE HOUSE - AND IT LOOKS LIKE A MIDDEN ALL ROUND ABOUT!
WHY NOT ASK ANGUS TO TAKE A PICTURE WITH THE FLATTERAMIC CAMERA!
THE VERY THING!
B&B
THERE YOU ARE, MOTHER - YOU'LL GET MORE VISITORS NOW THAN THE NEW GLENEAGLES!
B&B
B4-14

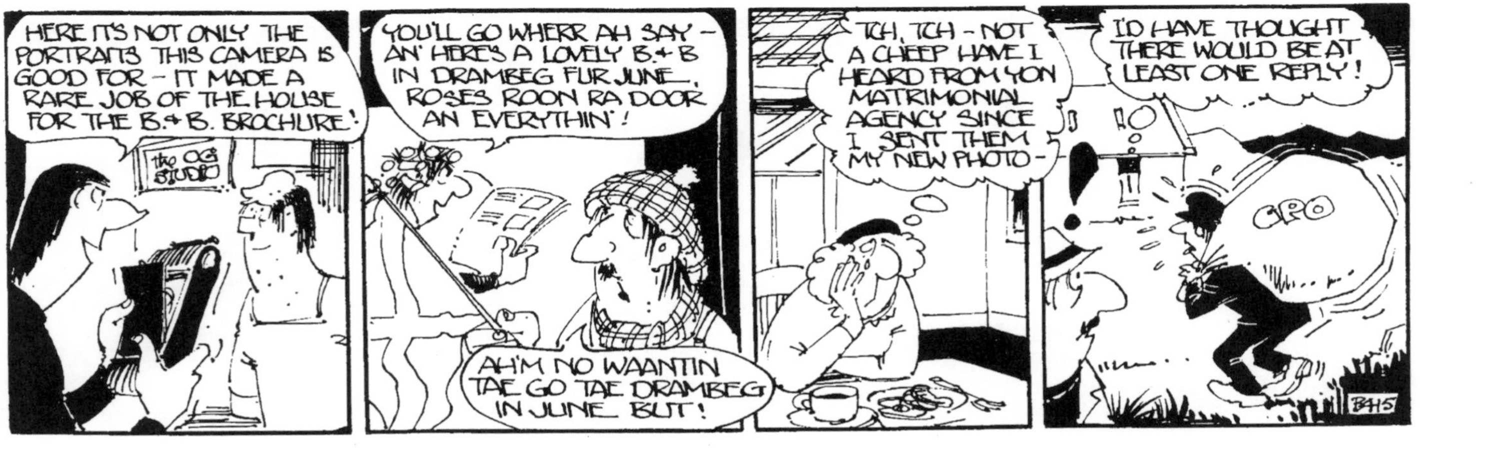
HERE IT'S NOT ONLY THE PORTRAITS THIS CAMERA IS GOOD FOR - IT MADE A RARE JOB OF THE HOUSE FOR THE B.& B. BROCHURE!
the OG STUDIO
YOU'LL GO WHERR AH SAY - AN' HERE'S A LOVELY B.& B IN DRAMBEG FUR JUNE, ROSES ROON RA DOOR AN EVERYTHIN'!
AH'M NO WAANTIN TAE GO TAE DRAMBEG IN JUNE BUT!
TCH, TCH - NOT A CHEEP HAVE I HEARD FROM YON MATRIMONIAL AGENCY SINCE I SENT THEM MY NEW PHOTO -
I'D HAVE THOUGHT THERE WOULD BE AT LEAST ONE REPLY!
GPO
B4-15

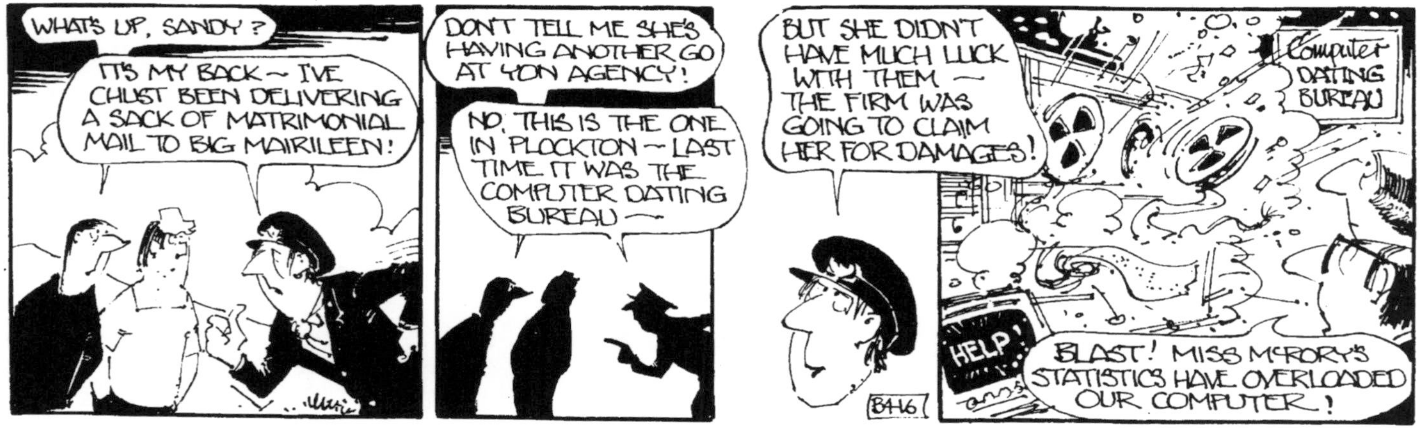
WHAT'S UP, SANDY ?
IT'S MY BACK ~ I'VE CHUST BEEN DELIVERING A SACK OF MATRIMONIAL MAIL TO BIG MAIRILEEN !
DON'T TELL ME SHE'S HAVING ANOTHER GO AT YON AGENCY !
NO, THIS IS THE ONE IN PLOCKTON ~ LAST TIME IT WAS THE COMPUTER DATING BUREAU ~
BUT SHE DIDN'T HAVE MUCH LUCK WITH THEM ~ THE FIRM WAS GOING TO CLAIM HER FOR DAMAGES !
B416
Computer DATING BUREAU
HELP
BLAST ! MISS McRORY'S STATISTICS HAVE OVERLOADED OUR COMPUTER !

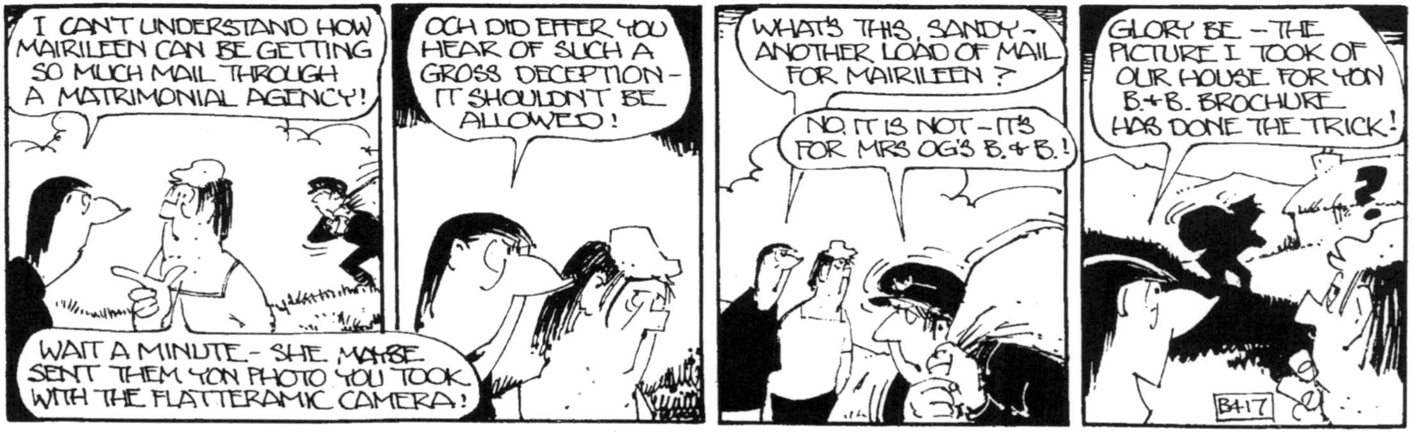
I CAN'T UNDERSTAND HOW MAIRILEEN CAN BE GETTING SO MUCH MAIL THROUGH A MATRIMONIAL AGENCY !
WAIT A MINUTE - SHE MAYBE SENT THEM YON PHOTO YOU TOOK WITH THE FLATTERAMIC CAMERA !
OCH DID EFFER YOU HEAR OF SUCH A GROSS DECEPTION - IT SHOULDN'T BE ALLOWED !
WHAT'S THIS, SANDY - ANOTHER LOAD OF MAIL FOR MAIRILEEN ?
NO, IT IS NOT - IT'S FOR MRS OG'S B. & B. !
GLORY BE - THE PICTURE I TOOK OF OUR HOUSE FOR YON B. & B. BROCHURE HAS DONE THE TRICK !
B417

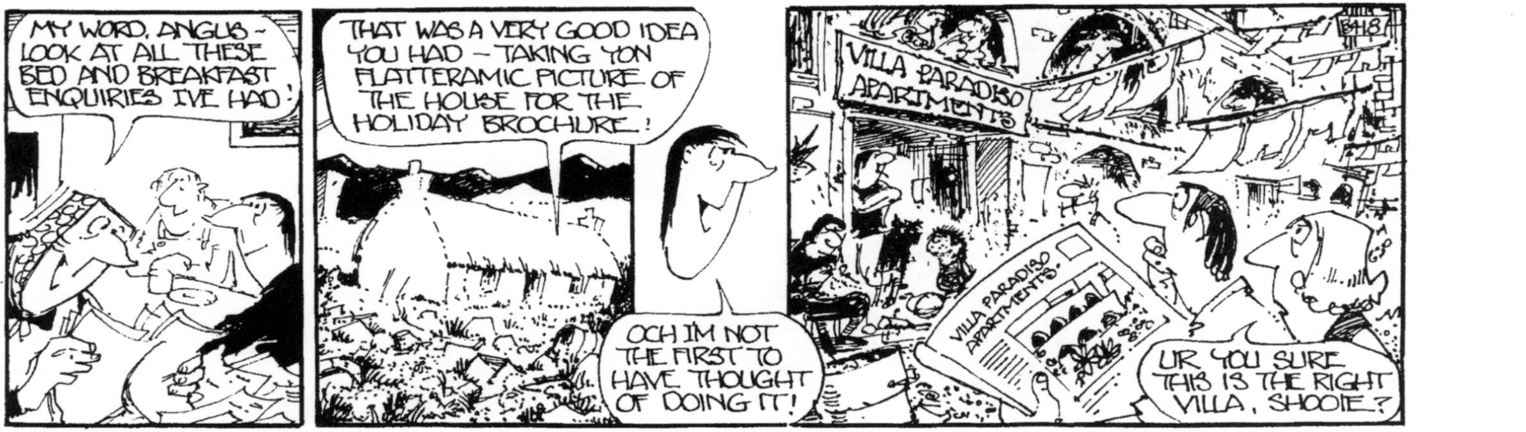
MY WORD, ANGUS – LOOK AT ALL THESE BED AND BREAKFAST ENQUIRIES I'VE HAD!
THAT WAS A VERY GOOD IDEA YOU HAD – TAKING YON FLATTERAMIC PICTURE OF THE HOUSE FOR THE HOLIDAY BROCHURE!
OCH I'M NOT THE FIRST TO HAVE THOUGHT OF DOING IT!
B418
VILLA PARADISO APARTMENTS
VILLA PARADISO APARTMENTS
UR YOU SURE THIS IS THE RIGHT VILLA, SHOOIE?

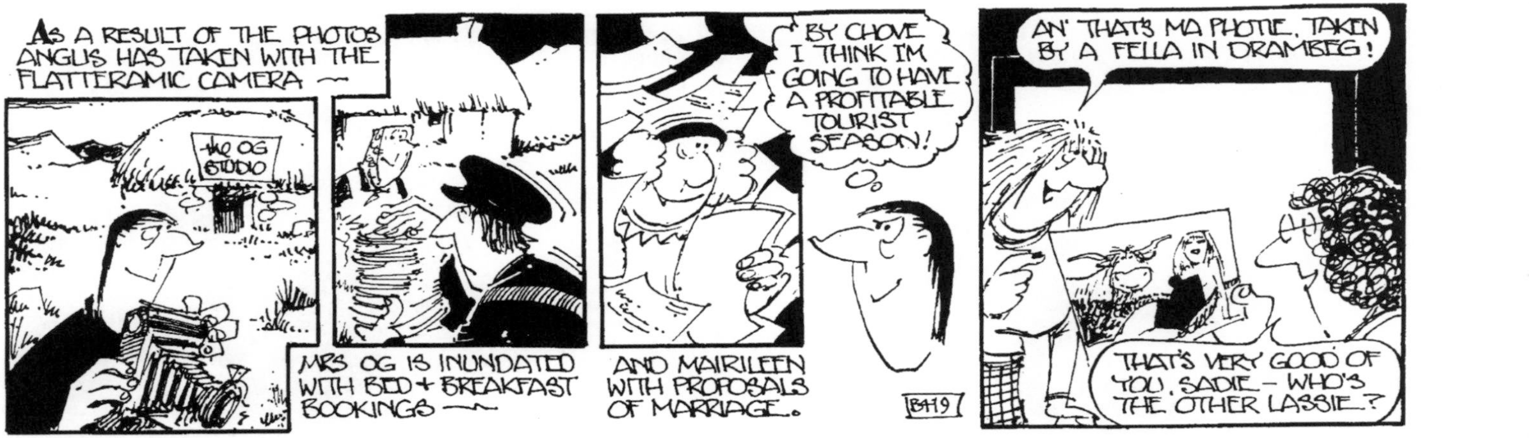
AS A RESULT OF THE PHOTOS ANGUS HAS TAKEN WITH THE FLATTERAMIC CAMERA ~
THE OG STUDIO
MRS OG IS INUNDATED WITH BED + BREAKFAST BOOKINGS ~
AND MAIRILEEN WITH PROPOSALS OF MARRIAGE.
BY CHOVE I THINK I'M GOING TO HAVE A PROFITABLE TOURIST SEASON!
B419
AN' THAT'S MA PHOTIE, TAKEN BY A FELLA IN DRAMBEG!
THAT'S VERY GOOD OF YOU, SADIE – WHO'S THE OTHER LASSIE?

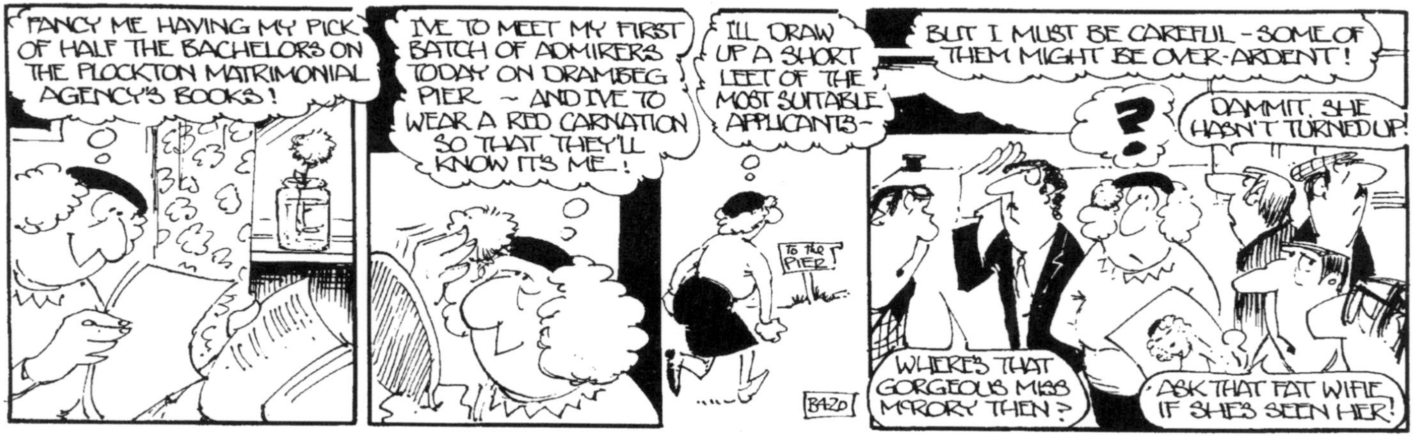
FANCY ME HAVING MY PICK OF HALF THE BACHELORS ON THE PLOCKTON MATRIMONIAL AGENCY'S BOOKS!
I'VE TO MEET MY FIRST BATCH OF ADMIRERS TODAY ON DRAMBEG PIER ~ AND I'VE TO WEAR A RED CARNATION SO THAT THEY'LL KNOW IT'S ME!
I'LL DRAW UP A SHORT LEET OF THE MOST SUITABLE APPLICANTS~
To the PIER!
B4-20
BUT I MUST BE CAREFUL - SOME OF THEM MIGHT BE OVER-ARDENT!
?
DAMMIT, SHE HASN'T TURNED UP!
WHERE'S THAT GORGEOUS MISS McRORY THEN?
ASK THAT FAT WIFIE IF SHE'S SEEN HER!

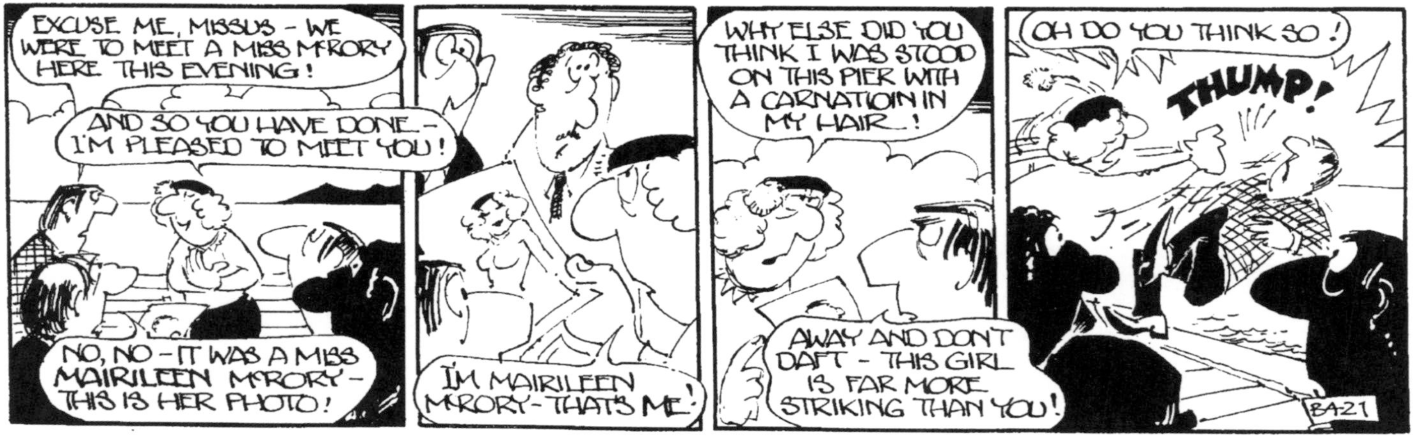
EXCUSE ME, MISSUS - WE WERE TO MEET A MISS McRORY HERE THIS EVENING!
AND SO YOU HAVE DONE - I'M PLEASED TO MEET YOU!
NO, NO - IT WAS A MISS MAIRILEEN McRORY - THIS IS HER PHOTO!
I'M MAIRILEEN McRORY - THAT'S ME!
WHY ELSE DID YOU THINK I WAS STOOD ON THIS PIER WITH A CARNATIOIN IN MY HAIR...!
AWAY AND DON'T DAFT - THIS GIRL IS FAR MORE STRIKING THAN YOU!
OH DO YOU THINK SO!
THUMP!
B4-21

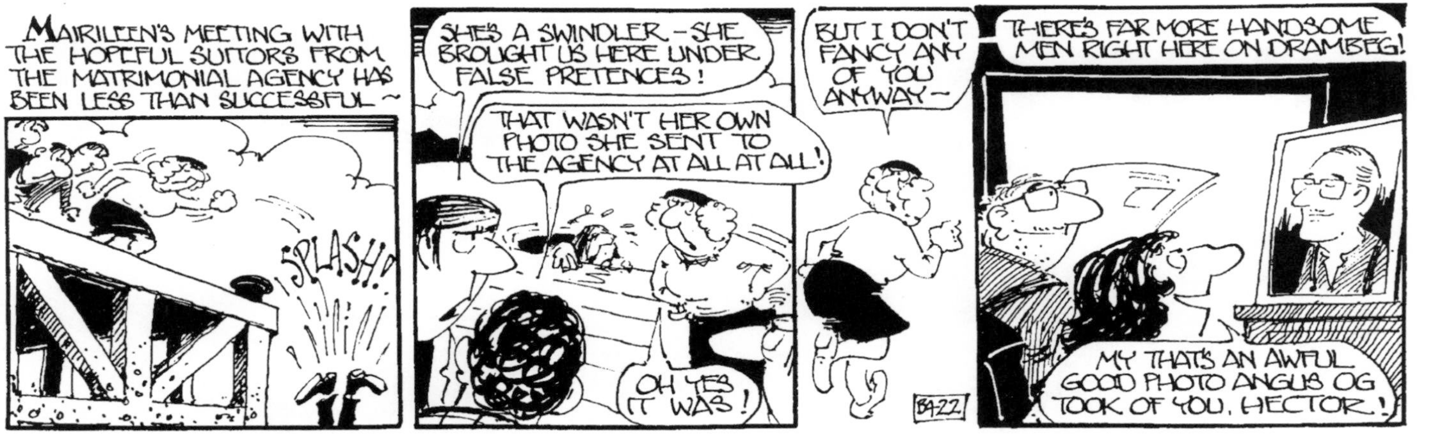
MAIRILEEN'S MEETING WITH THE HOPEFUL SUITORS FROM THE MATRIMONIAL AGENCY HAS BEEN LESS THAN SUCCESSFUL ~
SPLASH!
SHE'S A SWINDLER – SHE BROUGHT US HERE UNDER FALSE PRETENCES!
THAT WASN'T HER OWN PHOTO SHE SENT TO THE AGENCY AT ALL AT ALL!
OH YES IT WAS!
BUT I DON'T FANCY ANY OF YOU ANYWAY –
THERE'S FAR MORE HANDSOME MEN RIGHT HERE ON DRAMBEG!
B4-22
MY THAT'S AN AWFUL GOOD PHOTO ANGUS OG TOOK OF YOU, HECTOR!

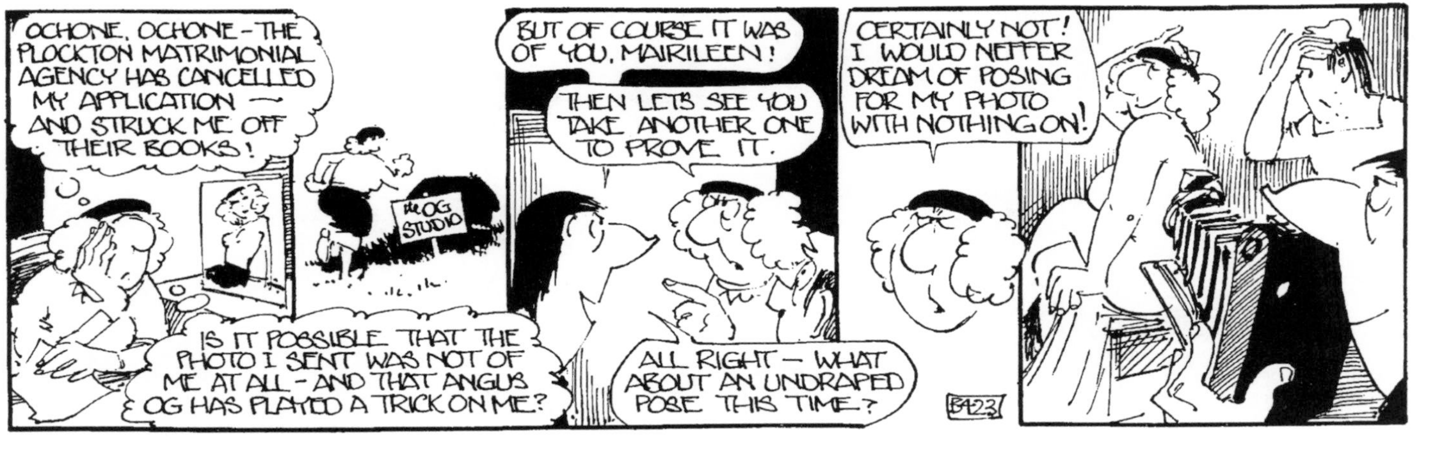
OCHONE, OCHONE – THE PLOCKTON MATRIMONIAL AGENCY HAS CANCELLED MY APPLICATION — AND STRUCK ME OFF THEIR BOOKS!
IS IT POSSIBLE THAT THE PHOTO I SENT WAS NOT OF ME AT ALL – AND THAT ANGUS OG HAS PLAYED A TRICK ON ME?
the OG STUDIO
BUT OF COURSE IT WAS OF YOU, MAIRILEEN!
THEN LETS SEE YOU TAKE ANOTHER ONE TO PROVE IT.
ALL RIGHT – WHAT ABOUT AN UNDRAPED POSE THIS TIME?
B4-23
CERTAINLY NOT! I WOULD NEFFER DREAM OF POSING FOR MY PHOTO WITH NOTHING ON!

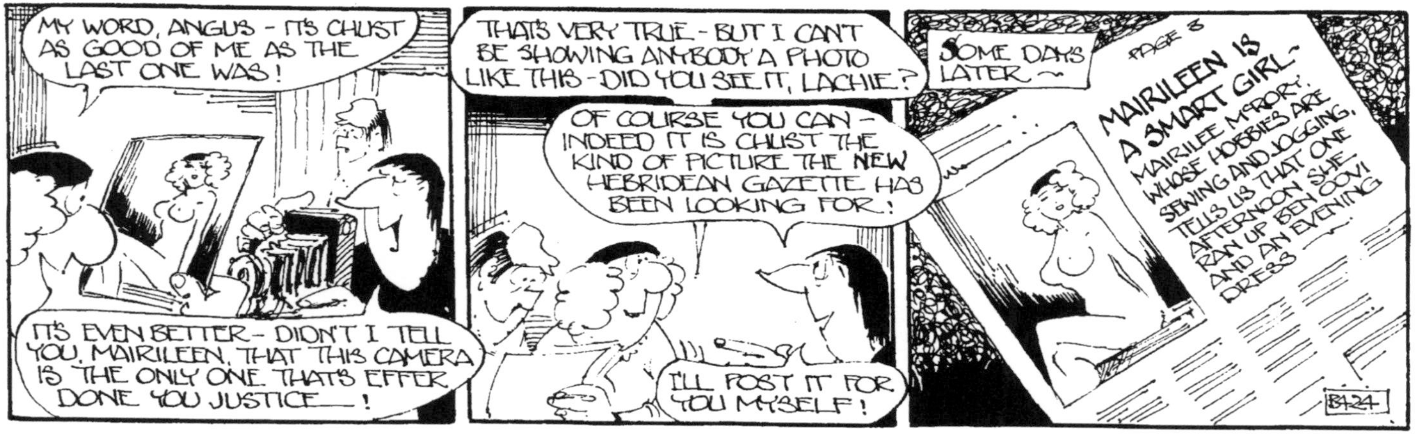
MY WORD, ANGUS - IT'S CHUST AS GOOD OF ME AS THE LAST ONE WAS!
IT'S EVEN BETTER - DIDN'T I TELL YOU, MAIRILEEN, THAT THIS CAMERA IS THE ONLY ONE THAT'S EFFER DONE YOU JUSTICE—!
THAT'S VERY TRUE - BUT I CAN'T BE SHOWING ANYBODY A PHOTO LIKE THIS - DID YOU SEE IT, LACHIE?
OF COURSE YOU CAN - INDEED IT IS CHUST THE KIND OF PICTURE THE NEW HEBRIDEAN GAZETTE HAS BEEN LOOKING FOR!
I'LL POST IT FOR YOU MYSELF!
SOME DAYS LATER ~
PAGE 8
MAIRILEEN IS A SMART GIRL ~
MAIRILEE McRORY WHOSE HOBBIES ARE SEWING AND JOGGING, TELLS US THAT ONE AFTERNOON SHE RAN UP BEN OOVI AND AN EVENING DRESS
8424

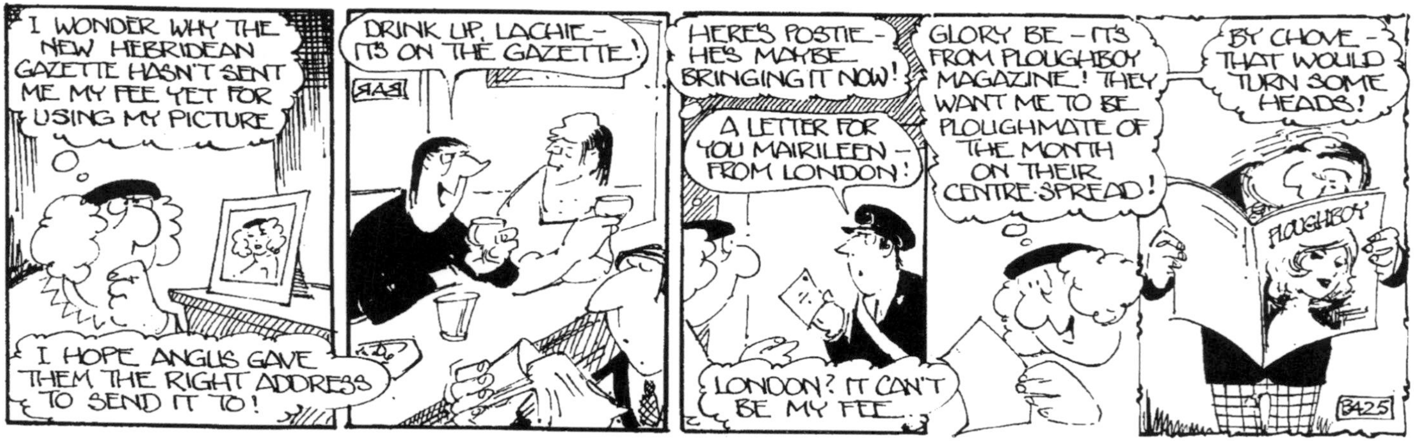
I WONDER WHY THE NEW HEBRIDEAN GAZETTE HASN'T SENT ME MY FEE YET FOR USING MY PICTURE
I HOPE ANGUS GAVE THEM THE RIGHT ADDRESS TO SEND IT TO!
DRINK UP, LACHIE - IT'S ON THE GAZETTE!
HERE'S POSTIE - HE'S MAYBE BRINGING IT NOW!
A LETTER FOR YOU MAIRILEEN - FROM LONDON!
LONDON? IT CAN'T BE MY FEE.
GLORY BE - IT'S FROM PLOUGHBOY MAGAZINE! THEY WANT ME TO BE PLOUGHMATE OF THE MONTH ON THEIR CENTRE-SPREAD!
BY CHOVE - THAT WOULD TURN SOME HEADS!
PLOUGHBOY
8425

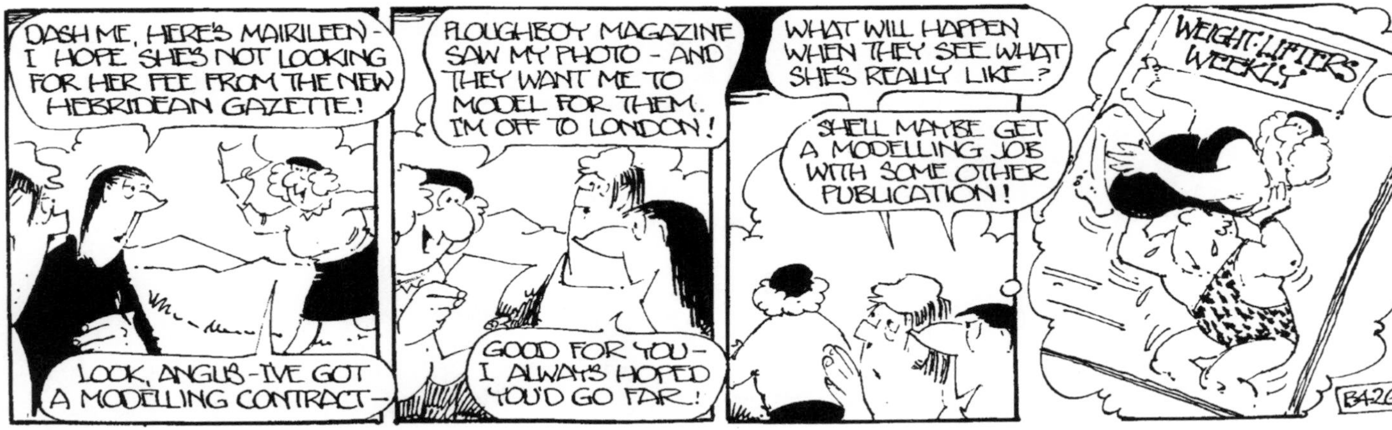
DASH ME, HERE'S MAIRILEEN - I HOPE SHE'S NOT LOOKING FOR HER FEE FROM THE NEW HEBRIDEAN GAZETTE!
LOOK, ANGUS - I'VE GOT A MODELLING CONTRACT -
PLOUGHBOY MAGAZINE SAW MY PHOTO - AND THEY WANT ME TO MODEL FOR THEM. I'M OFF TO LONDON!
GOOD FOR YOU - I ALWAYS HOPED YOU'D GO FAR!
WHAT WILL HAPPEN WHEN THEY SEE WHAT SHE'S REALLY LIKE?
SHE'LL MAYBE GET A MODELLING JOB WITH SOME OTHER PUBLICATION!
WEIGHT-LIFTERS WEEKLY
B426

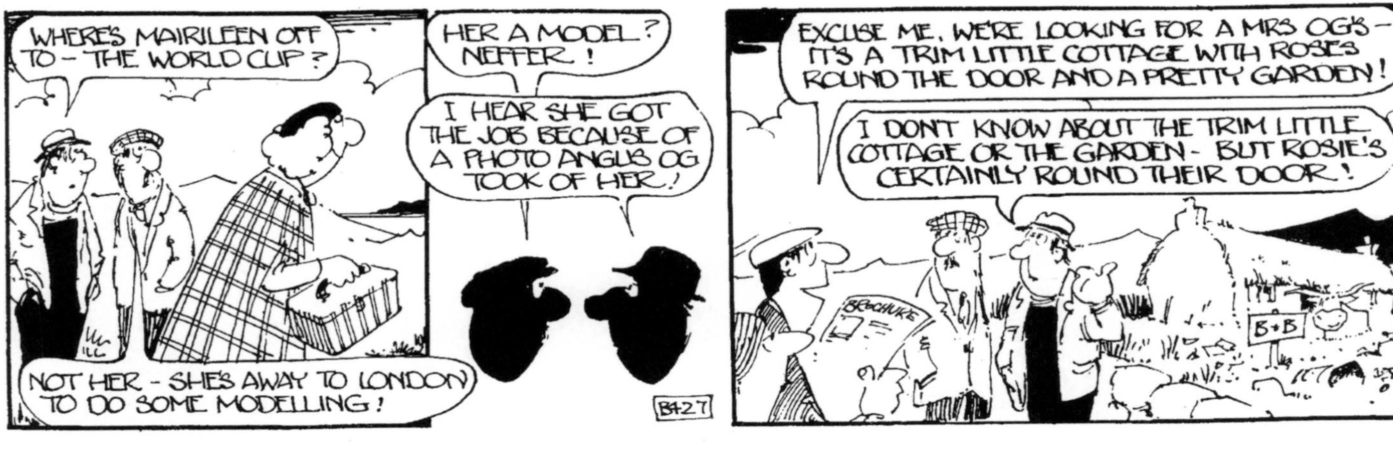
WHERE'S MAIRILEEN OFF TO - THE WORLD CUP?
NOT HER - SHE'S AWAY TO LONDON TO DO SOME MODELLING!
HER A MODEL? NEFFER!
I HEAR SHE GOT THE JOB BECAUSE OF A PHOTO ANGUS OG TOOK OF HER!
B427
EXCUSE ME, WE'RE LOOKING FOR A MRS OG'S - IT'S A TRIM LITTLE COTTAGE WITH ROSES ROUND THE DOOR AND A PRETTY GARDEN!
I DON'T KNOW ABOUT THE TRIM LITTLE COTTAGE OR THE GARDEN - BUT ROSIE'S CERTAINLY ROUND THEIR DOOR!
BROCHURE
B+B

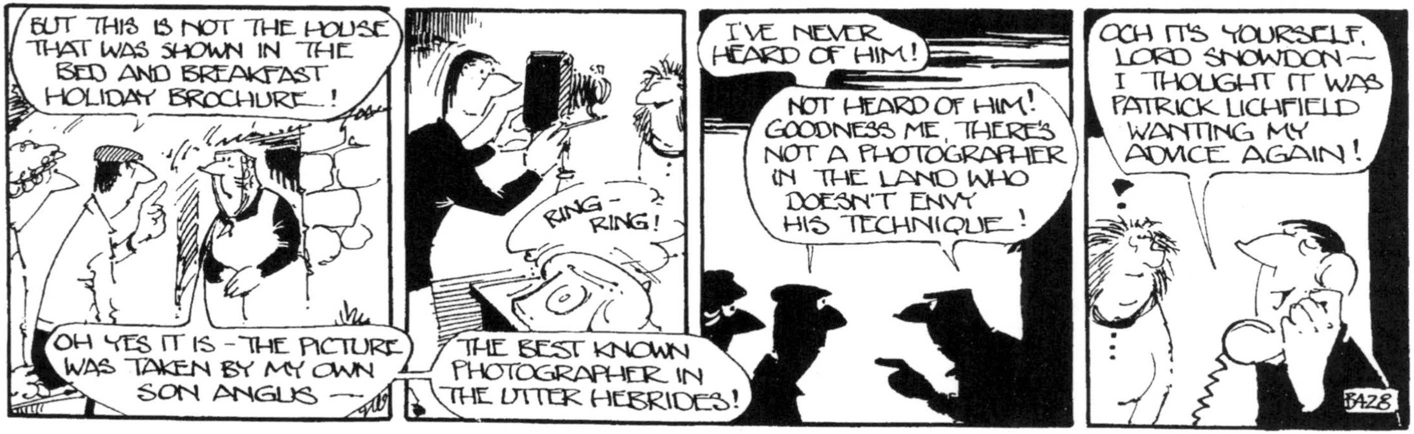
BUT THIS IS NOT THE HOUSE THAT WAS SHOWN IN THE BED AND BREAKFAST HOLIDAY BROCHURE!
OH YES IT IS – THE PICTURE WAS TAKEN BY MY OWN SON ANGUS –
THE BEST KNOWN PHOTOGRAPHER IN THE UTTER HEBRIDES!
RING – RING!
I'VE NEVER HEARD OF HIM!
NOT HEARD OF HIM! GOODNESS ME, THERE'S NOT A PHOTOGRAPHER IN THE LAND WHO DOESN'T ENVY HIS TECHNIQUE!
OCH IT'S YOURSELF, LORD SNOWDON – I THOUGHT IT WAS PATRICK LICHFIELD WANTING MY ADVICE AGAIN!
8428

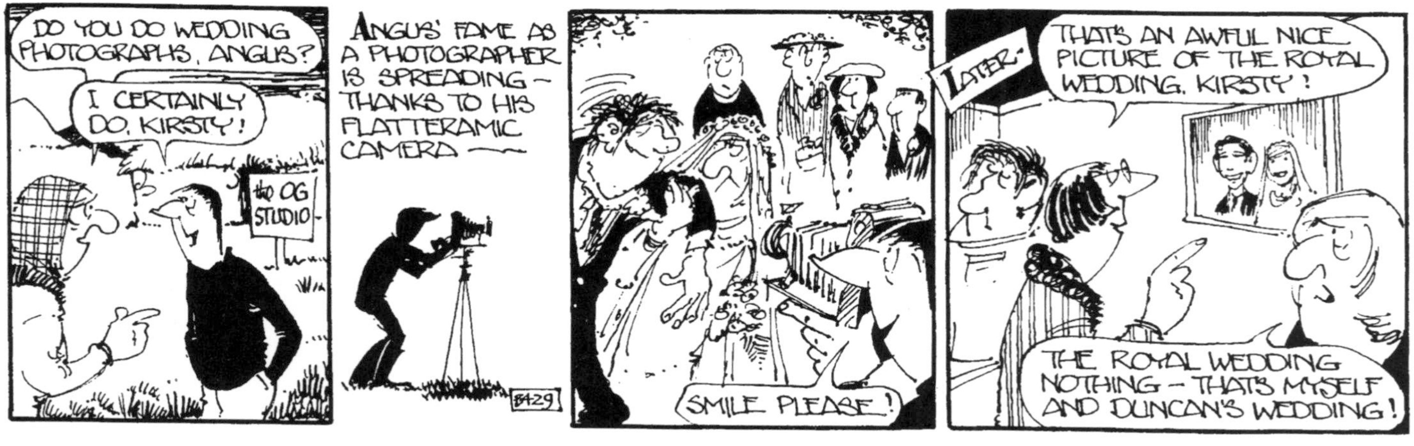
DO YOU DO WEDDING PHOTOGRAPHS, ANGUS?
I CERTAINLY DO, KIRSTY!
the OG STUDIO
ANGUS' FAME AS A PHOTOGRAPHER IS SPREADING – THANKS TO HIS FLATTERAMIC CAMERA —
8429
SMILE PLEASE!
LATER-
THAT'S AN AWFUL NICE PICTURE OF THE ROYAL WEDDING, KIRSTY!
THE ROYAL WEDDING NOTHING – THAT'S MYSELF AND DUNCAN'S WEDDING!

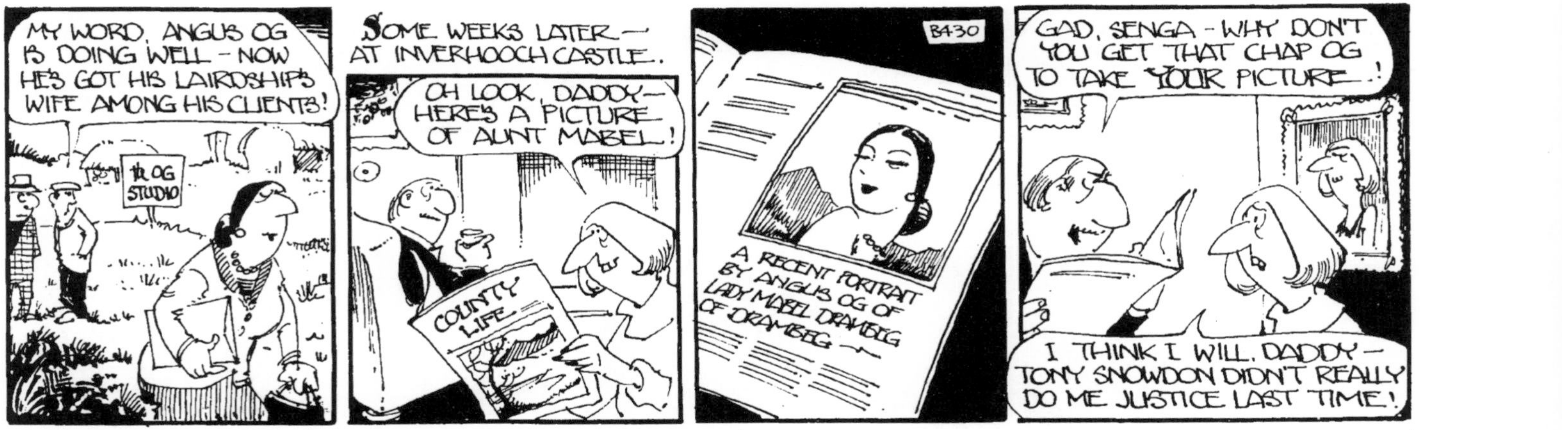
MY WORD, ANGUS OG IS DOING WELL - NOW HE'S GOT HIS LAIRDSHIP'S WIFE AMONG HIS CLIENTS!
OG
STUDIO
SOME WEEKS LATER — AT INVERHOOCH CASTLE.
OH LOOK, DADDY— HERE'S A PICTURE OF AUNT MABEL!
COUNTY LIFE
B430
A RECENT PORTRAIT BY ANGUS OG OF LADY MABEL DRAMBEG OF DRAMBEG
GAD, SENGA - WHY DON'T YOU GET THAT CHAP OG TO TAKE YOUR PICTURE!
I THINK I WILL, DADDY— TONY SNOWDON DIDN'T REALLY DO ME JUSTICE LAST TIME!

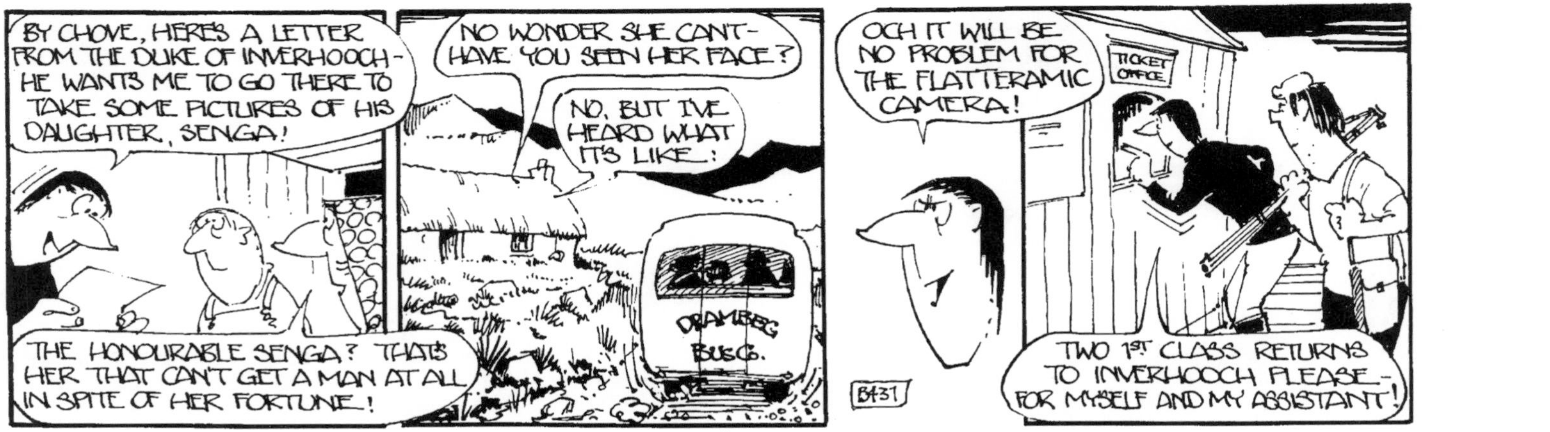
BY CHOVE, HERE'S A LETTER FROM THE DUKE OF INVERHOOCH - HE WANTS ME TO GO THERE TO TAKE SOME PICTURES OF HIS DAUGHTER, SENGA!
THE HONOURABLE SENGA? THAT'S HER THAT CAN'T GET A MAN AT ALL IN SPITE OF HER FORTUNE!
NO WONDER SHE CAN'T - HAVE YOU SEEN HER FACE?
NO, BUT I'VE HEARD WHAT IT'S LIKE!
DRAMBEG BUS Co.
B437
OCH IT WILL BE NO PROBLEM FOR THE FLATTERAMIC CAMERA!
TICKET OFFICE
TWO 1ST CLASS RETURNS TO INVERHOOCH PLEASE - FOR MYSELF AND MY ASSISTANT!

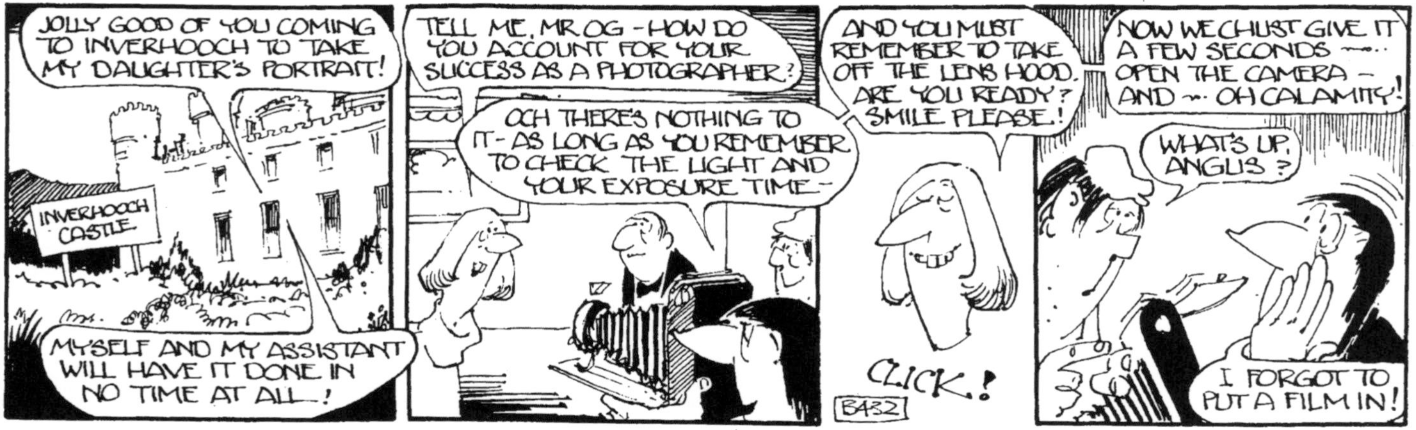
JOLLY GOOD OF YOU COMING TO INVERHOOCH TO TAKE MY DAUGHTER'S PORTRAIT!
INVERHOOCH CASTLE
MYSELF AND MY ASSISTANT WILL HAVE IT DONE IN NO TIME AT ALL!
TELL ME, MR OG – HOW DO YOU ACCOUNT FOR YOUR SUCCESS AS A PHOTOGRAPHER?
OCH THERE'S NOTHING TO IT – AS LONG AS YOU REMEMBER TO CHECK THE LIGHT AND YOUR EXPOSURE TIME –
AND YOU MUST REMEMBER TO TAKE OFF THE LENS HOOD. ARE YOU READY? SMILE PLEASE!
CLICK!
B432
NOW WE CHUST GIVE IT A FEW SECONDS ... OPEN THE CAMERA – AND ... OH CALAMITY!
WHAT'S UP, ANGUS?
I FORGOT TO PUT A FILM IN!

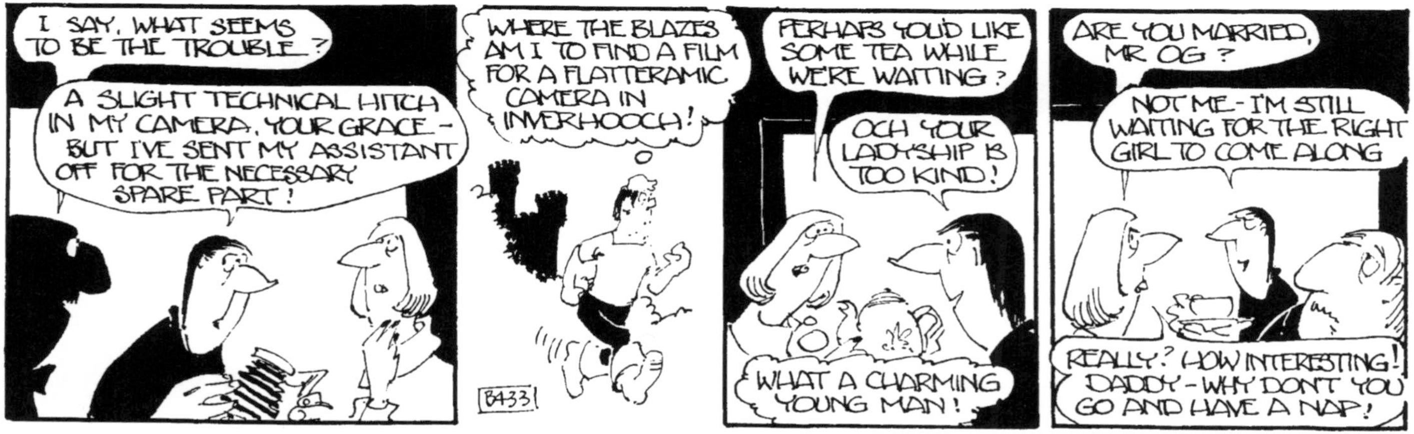
I SAY, WHAT SEEMS TO BE THE TROUBLE?
A SLIGHT TECHNICAL HITCH IN MY CAMERA, YOUR GRACE – BUT I'VE SENT MY ASSISTANT OFF FOR THE NECESSARY SPARE PART!
WHERE THE BLAZES AM I TO FIND A FILM FOR A FLATTERAMIC CAMERA IN INVERHOOCH!
B433
PERHAPS YOU'D LIKE SOME TEA WHILE WE'RE WAITING?
OCH YOUR LADYSHIP IS TOO KIND!
WHAT A CHARMING YOUNG MAN!
ARE YOU MARRIED, MR OG?
NOT ME – I'M STILL WAITING FOR THE RIGHT GIRL TO COME ALONG
REALLY? HOW INTERESTING! DADDY – WHY DON'T YOU GO AND HAVE A NAP!

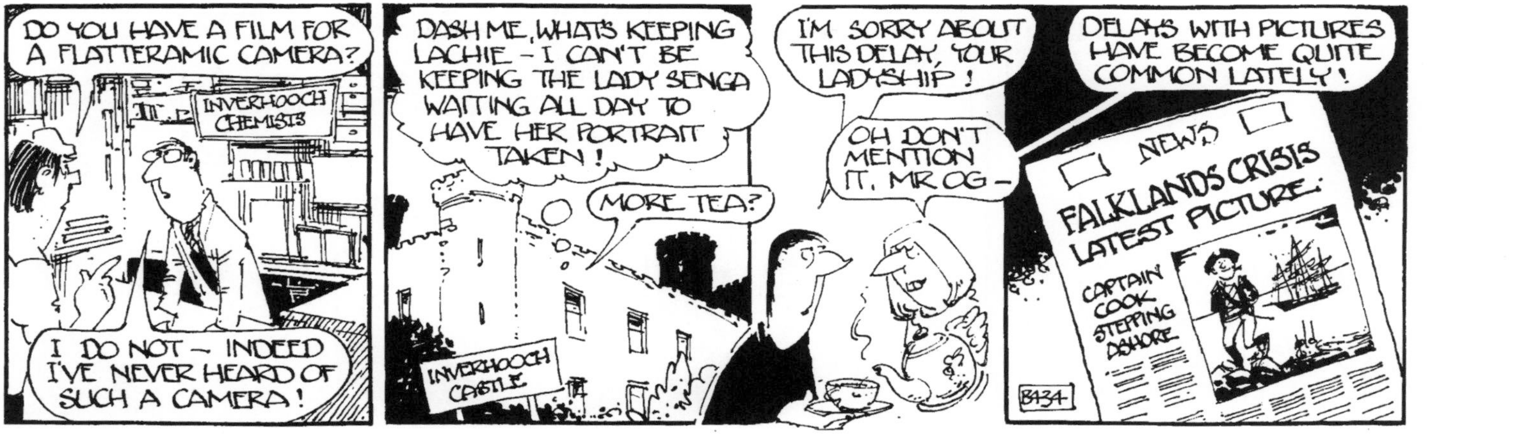
DO YOU HAVE A FILM FOR A FLATTERAMIC CAMERA?
INVERHOOCH CHEMISTS
I DO NOT – INDEED I'VE NEVER HEARD OF SUCH A CAMERA!
DASH ME, WHAT'S KEEPING LACHIE – I CAN'T BE KEEPING THE LADY SENGA WAITING ALL DAY TO HAVE HER PORTRAIT TAKEN!
MORE TEA?
INVERHOOCH CASTLE
I'M SORRY ABOUT THIS DELAY, YOUR LADYSHIP!
OH DON'T MENTION IT, MR OG –
DELAYS WITH PICTURES HAVE BECOME QUITE COMMON LATELY!
NEWS
FALKLANDS CRISIS
LATEST PICTURE
CAPTAIN COOK STEPPING ASHORE
8434

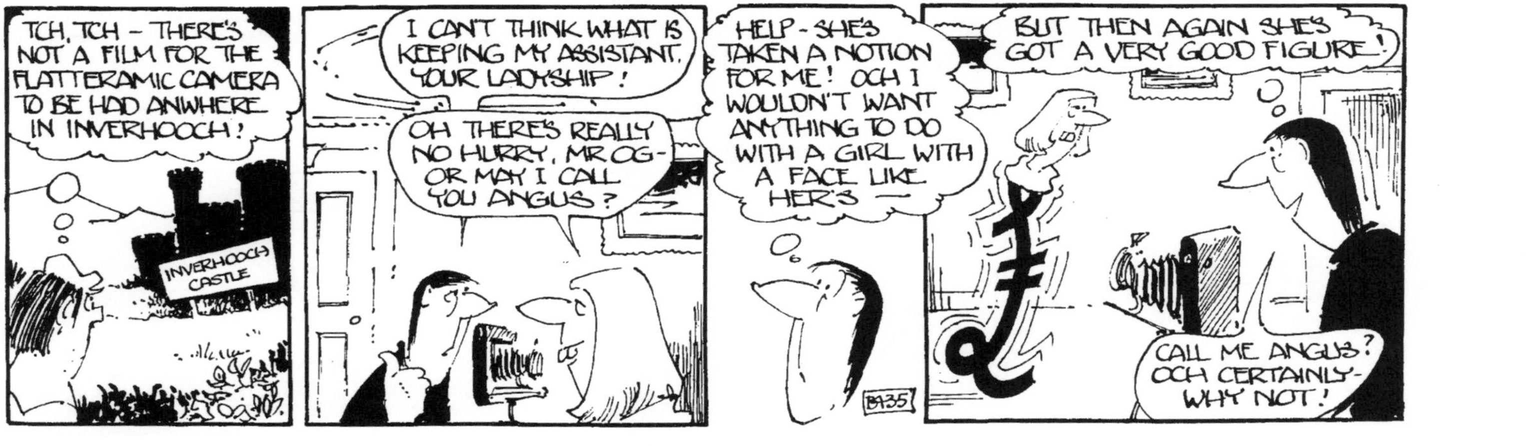
TCH, TCH – THERE'S NOT A FILM FOR THE FLATTERAMIC CAMERA TO BE HAD ANWHERE IN INVERHOOCH!
INVERHOOCH CASTLE
I CAN'T THINK WHAT IS KEEPING MY ASSISTANT, YOUR LADYSHIP!
OH THERE'S REALLY NO HURRY, MR OG – OR MAY I CALL YOU ANGUS?
HELP – SHE'S TAKEN A NOTION FOR ME! OCH I WOULDN'T WANT ANYTHING TO DO WITH A GIRL WITH A FACE LIKE HER'S –
8435
BUT THEN AGAIN SHE'S GOT A VERY GOOD FIGURE!
CALL ME ANGUS? OCH CERTAINLY – WHY NOT!

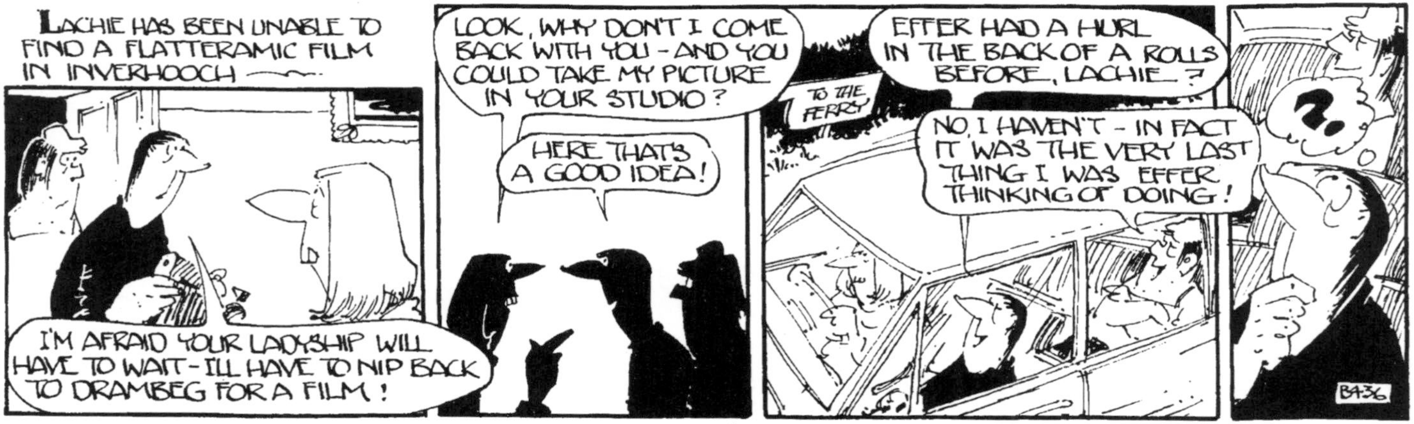
LACHIE HAS BEEN UNABLE TO FIND A FLATTERAMIC FILM IN INVERHOOCH
I'M AFRAID YOUR LADYSHIP WILL HAVE TO WAIT - I'LL HAVE TO NIP BACK TO DRAMBEG FOR A FILM!
LOOK, WHY DON'T I COME BACK WITH YOU - AND YOU COULD TAKE MY PICTURE IN YOUR STUDIO?
HERE THAT'S A GOOD IDEA!
TO THE FERRY
EFFER HAD A HURL IN THE BACK OF A ROLLS BEFORE, LACHIE?
NO, I HAVEN'T - IN FACT IT WAS THE VERY LAST THING I WAS EFFER THINKING OF DOING!
?
B436

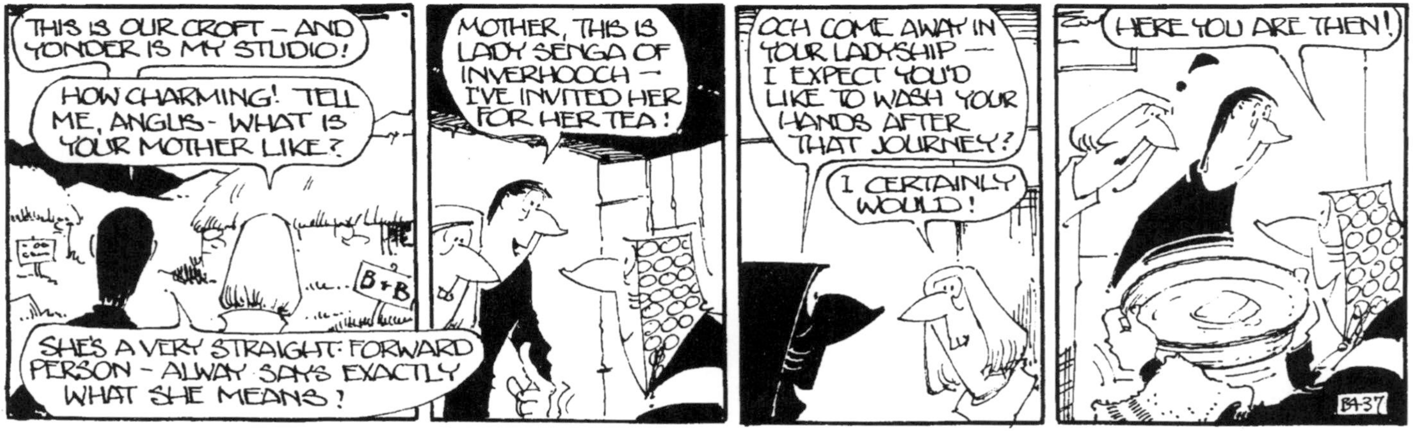
THIS IS OUR CROFT - AND YONDER IS MY STUDIO!
HOW CHARMING! TELL ME, ANGUS - WHAT IS YOUR MOTHER LIKE?
B+B
SHE'S A VERY STRAIGHT-FORWARD PERSON - ALWAY SAYS EXACTLY WHAT SHE MEANS!
MOTHER, THIS IS LADY SENGA OF INVERHOOCH - I'VE INVITED HER FOR HER TEA!
OCH COME AWAY IN YOUR LADYSHIP - I EXPECT YOU'D LIKE TO WASH YOUR HANDS AFTER THAT JOURNEY?
I CERTAINLY WOULD!
HERE YOU ARE THEN!
B437

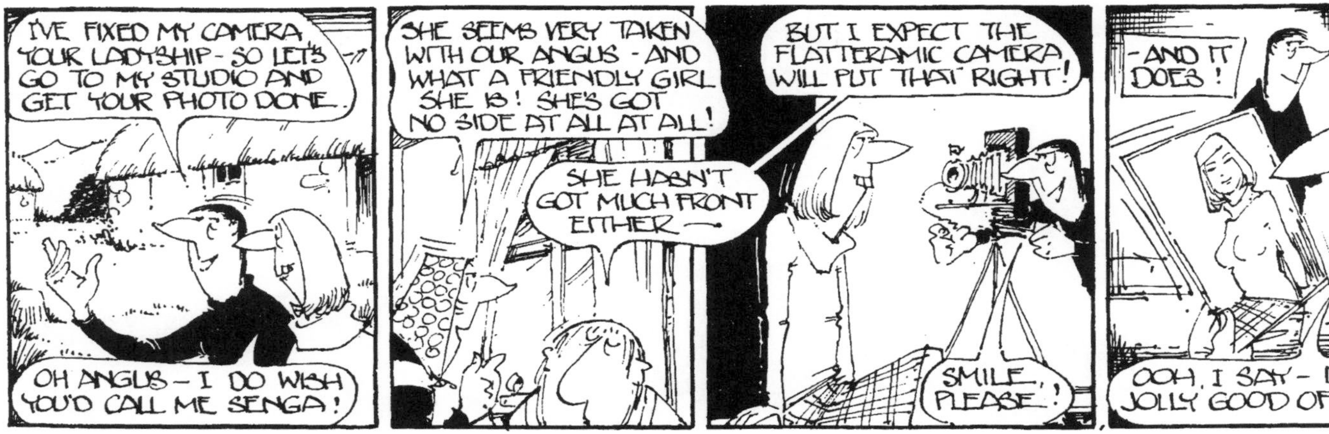
I'VE FIXED MY CAMERA YOUR LADYSHIP - SO LET'S GO TO MY STUDIO AND GET YOUR PHOTO DONE.
OH ANGUS - I DO WISH YOU'D CALL ME SENGA!
SHE SEEMS VERY TAKEN WITH OUR ANGUS - AND WHAT A FRIENDLY GIRL SHE IS! SHE'S GOT NO SIDE AT ALL AT ALL!
SHE HASN'T GOT MUCH FRONT EITHER -
BUT I EXPECT THE FLATTERAMIC CAMERA WILL PUT THAT RIGHT!
SMILE, PLEASE!
B438
- AND IT DOES!
OOH, I SAY - IT'S JOLLY GOOD OF ME

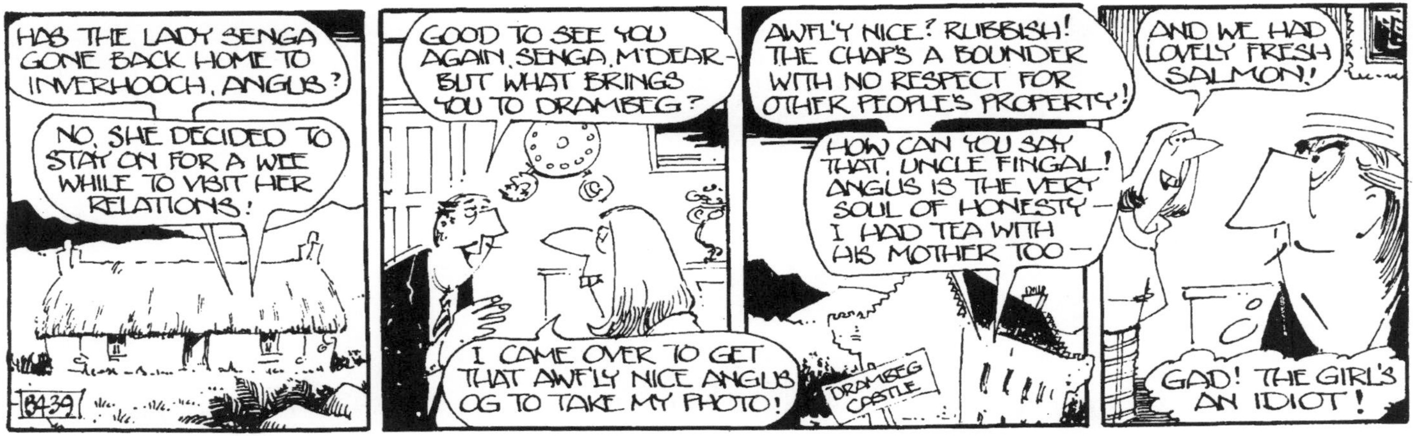
HAS THE LADY SENGA GONE BACK HOME TO INVERHOOCH, ANGUS?
NO, SHE DECIDED TO STAY ON FOR A WEE WHILE TO VISIT HER RELATIONS!
B439
GOOD TO SEE YOU AGAIN, SENGA, M'DEAR - BUT WHAT BRINGS YOU TO DRAMBEG?
I CAME OVER TO GET THAT AWF'LY NICE ANGUS OG TO TAKE MY PHOTO!
AWF'LY NICE? RUBBISH! THE CHAP'S A BOUNDER WITH NO RESPECT FOR OTHER PEOPLE'S PROPERTY!
HOW CAN YOU SAY THAT, UNCLE FINGAL! ANGUS IS THE VERY SOUL OF HONESTY - I HAD TEA WITH HIS MOTHER TOO -
DRAMBEG CASTLE
AND WE HAD LOVELY FRESH SALMON!
GAD! THE GIRL'S AN IDIOT!

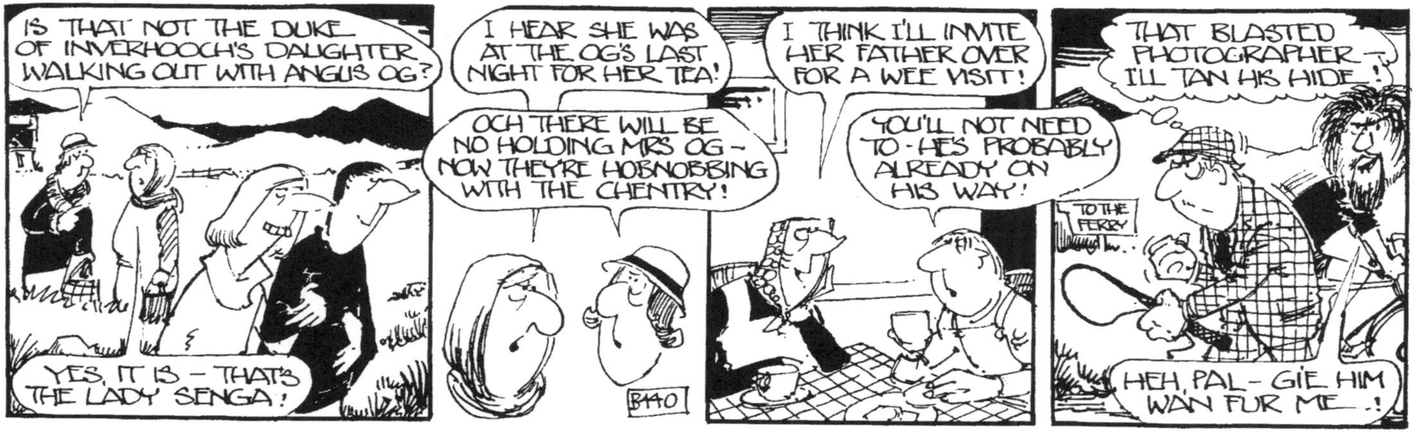
IS THAT NOT THE DUKE OF INVERHOOCH'S DAUGHTER WALKING OUT WITH ANGUS OG?
YES, IT IS – THAT'S THE LADY SENGA!
I HEAR SHE WAS AT THE OG'S LAST NIGHT FOR HER TEA!
OCH THERE WILL BE NO HOLDING MRS OG – NOW THEY'RE HOBNOBBING WITH THE CHENTRY!
B440
I THINK I'LL INVITE HER FATHER OVER FOR A WEE VISIT!
YOU'LL NOT NEED TO – HE'S PROBABLY ALREADY ON HIS WAY!
THAT BLASTED PHOTOGRAPHER – I'LL TAN HIS HIDE!
TO THE FERRY
HEH, PAL – GIE HIM WAN FUR ME!

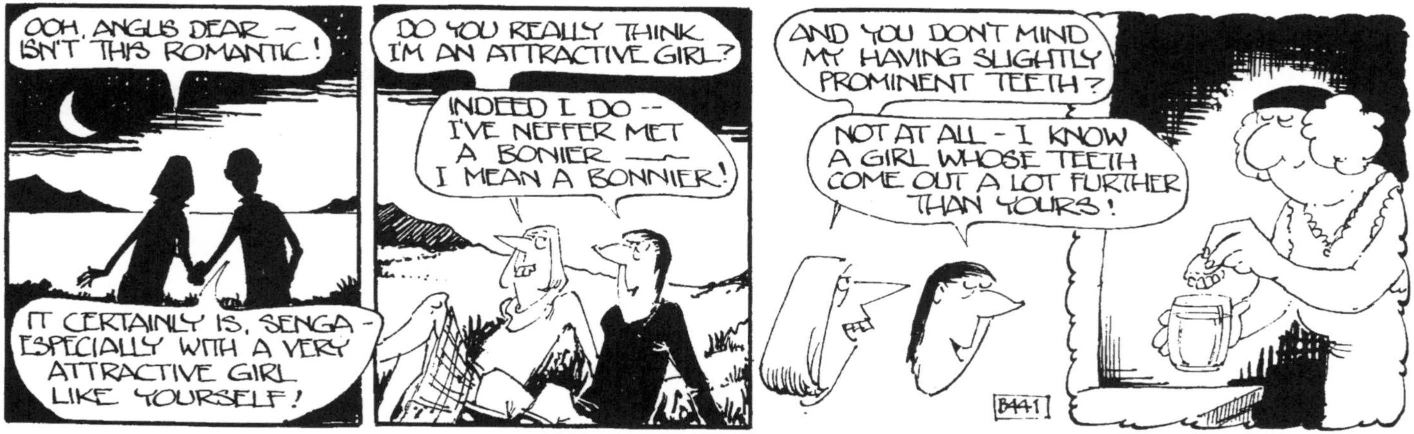
OOH, ANGUS DEAR – ISN'T THIS ROMANTIC!
IT CERTAINLY IS, SENGA – ESPECIALLY WITH A VERY ATTRACTIVE GIRL LIKE YOURSELF!
DO YOU REALLY THINK I'M AN ATTRACTIVE GIRL?
INDEED I DO – I'VE NEFFER MET A BONIER — I MEAN A BONNIER!
AND YOU DON'T MIND MY HAVING SLIGHTLY PROMINENT TEETH?
NOT AT ALL – I KNOW A GIRL WHOSE TEETH COME OUT A LOT FURTHER THAN YOURS!
B441

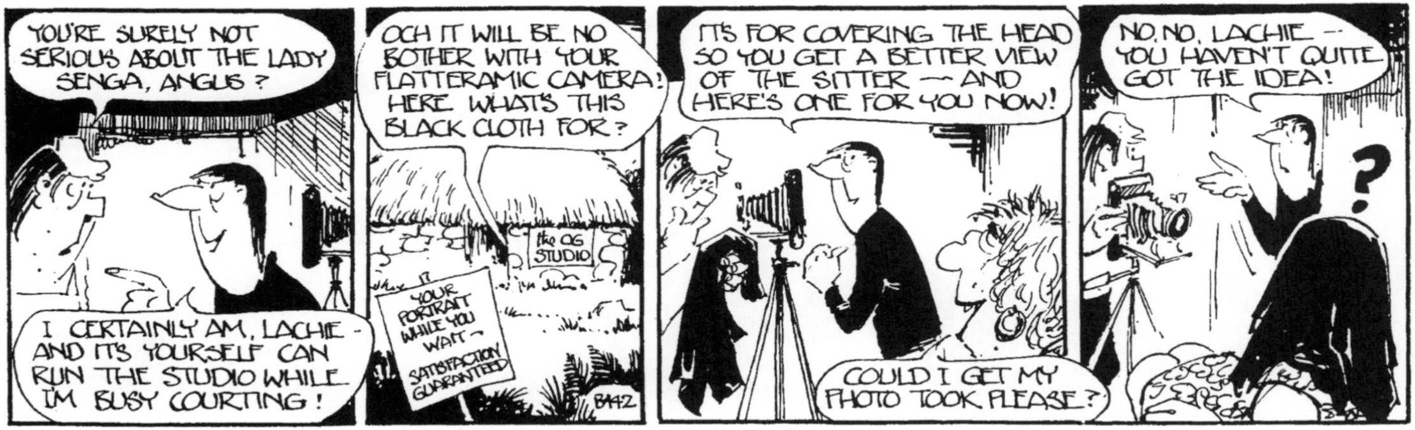
YOU'RE SURELY NOT SERIOUS ABOUT THE LADY SENGA, ANGUS?
I CERTAINLY AM, LACHIE - AND IT'S YOURSELF CAN RUN THE STUDIO WHILE I'M BUSY COURTING!
OCH IT WILL BE NO BOTHER WITH YOUR FLATTERAMIC CAMERA! HERE WHAT'S THIS BLACK CLOTH FOR?
the OG STUDIO
YOUR PORTRAIT WHILE YOU WAIT — SATISFACTION GUARANTEED
B442
IT'S FOR COVERING THE HEAD SO YOU GET A BETTER VIEW OF THE SITTER — AND HERE'S ONE FOR YOU NOW!
COULD I GET MY PHOTO TOOK PLEASE?
NO, NO, LACHIE — YOU HAVEN'T QUITE GOT THE IDEA!
?

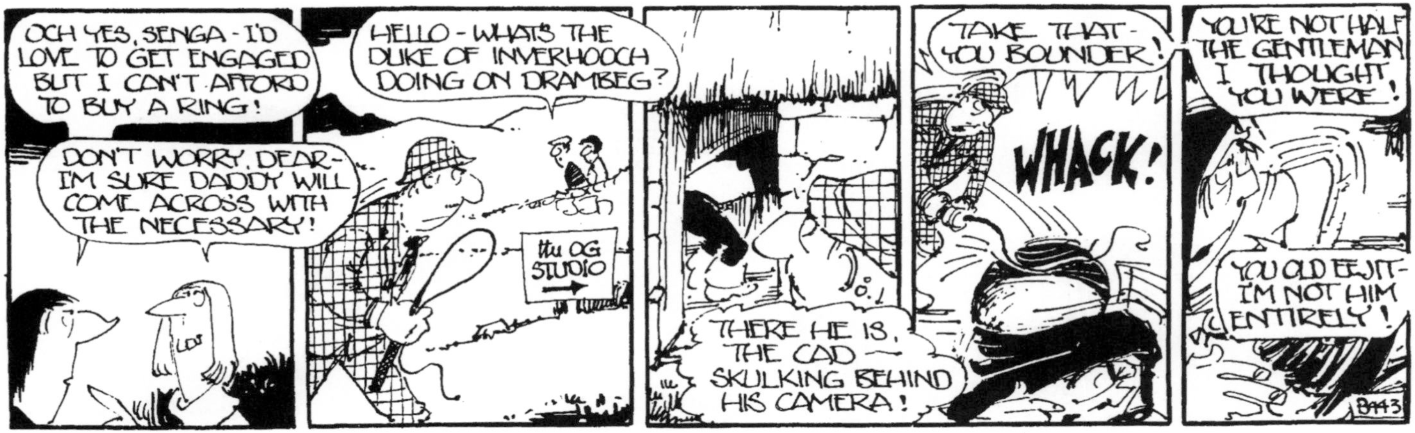
OCH YES, SENGA - I'D LOVE TO GET ENGAGED BUT I CAN'T AFFORD TO BUY A RING!
DON'T WORRY, DEAR - I'M SURE DADDY WILL COME ACROSS WITH THE NECESSARY!
HELLO - WHAT'S THE DUKE OF INVERHOOCH DOING ON DRAMBEG?
the OG STUDIO
THERE HE IS, THE CAD — SKULKING BEHIND HIS CAMERA!
TAKE THAT - YOU BOUNDER!
WHACK!
YOU'RE NOT HALF THE GENTLEMAN I THOUGHT YOU WERE!
YOU OLD EEJIT - I'M NOT HIM ENTIRELY!
B443

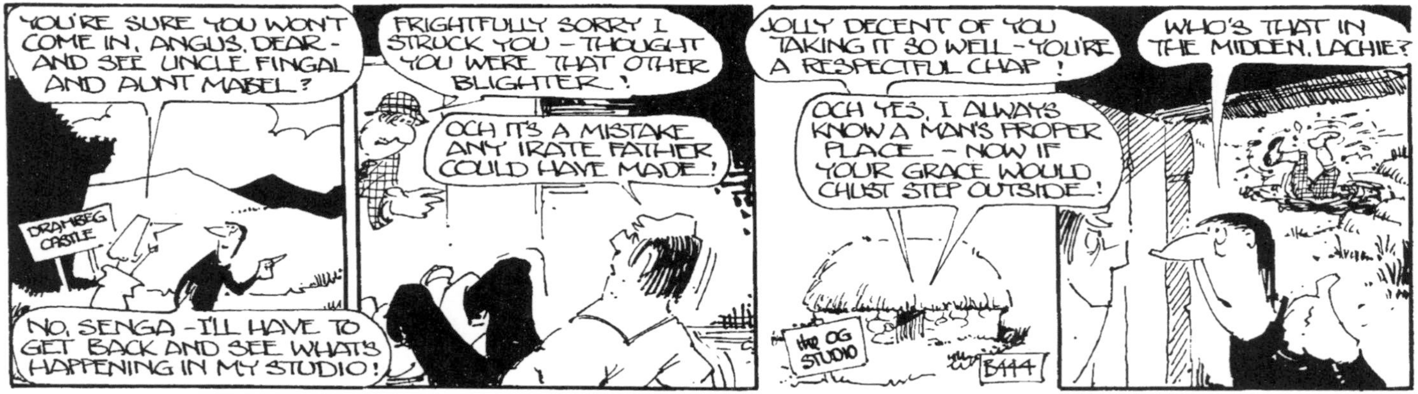
YOU'RE SURE YOU WON'T COME IN, ANGUS, DEAR - AND SEE UNCLE FINGAL AND AUNT MABEL?
DRAMBEG CASTLE
NO, SENGA - I'LL HAVE TO GET BACK AND SEE WHAT'S HAPPENING IN MY STUDIO!
FRIGHTFULLY SORRY I STRUCK YOU - THOUGHT YOU WERE THAT OTHER BLIGHTER!
OCH IT'S A MISTAKE ANY IRATE FATHER COULD HAVE MADE!
JOLLY DECENT OF YOU TAKING IT SO WELL - YOU'RE A RESPECTFUL CHAP!
OCH YES, I ALWAYS KNOW A MAN'S PROPER PLACE - NOW IF YOUR GRACE WOULD CHUST STEP OUTSIDE!
THE OG STUDIO
B444
WHO'S THAT IN THE MIDDEN, LACHIE?

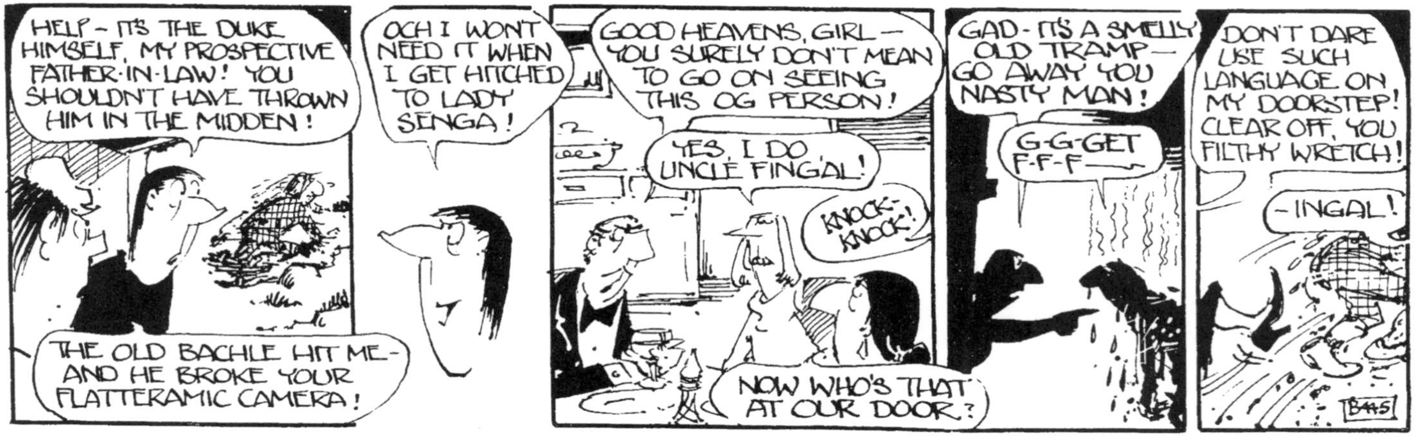
HELP - IT'S THE DUKE HIMSELF, MY PROSPECTIVE FATHER-IN-LAW! YOU SHOULDN'T HAVE THROWN HIM IN THE MIDDEN!
THE OLD BACHLE HIT ME - AND HE BROKE YOUR FLATTERAMIC CAMERA!
OCH I WON'T NEED IT WHEN I GET HITCHED TO LADY SENGA!
GOOD HEAVENS, GIRL - YOU SURELY DON'T MEAN TO GO ON SEEING THIS OG PERSON!
YES, I DO UNCLE FINGAL!
KNOCK-KNOCK!
NOW WHO'S THAT AT OUR DOOR?
GAD - IT'S A SMELLY OLD TRAMP - GO AWAY YOU NASTY MAN!
G-G-GET F-F-F
DON'T DARE USE SUCH LANGUAGE ON MY DOORSTEP! CLEAR OFF, YOU FILTHY WRETCH!
-INGAL!
B445

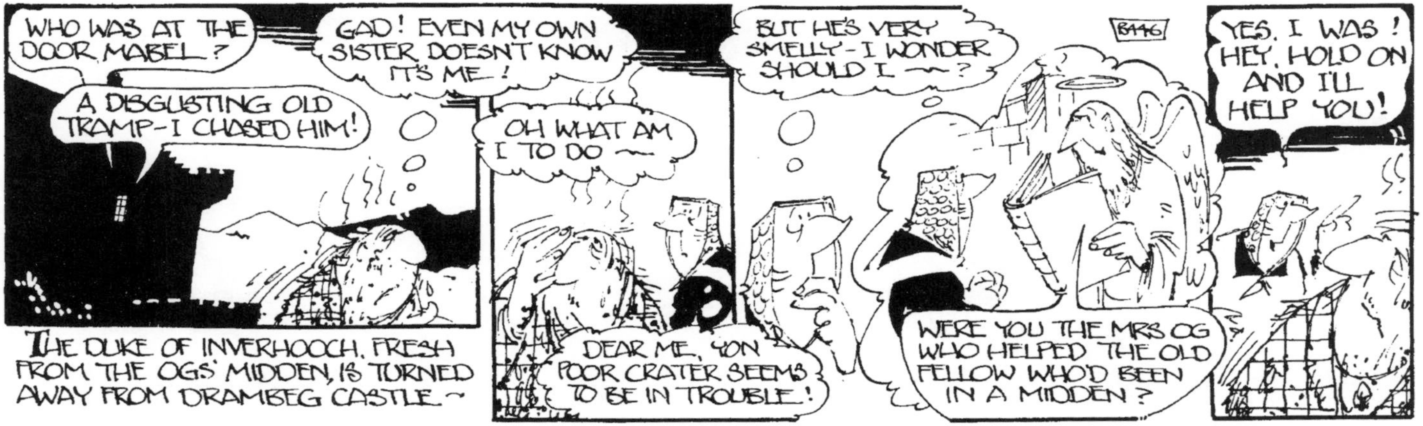
WHO WAS AT THE DOOR, MABEL?
A DISGUSTING OLD TRAMP—I CHASED HIM!
GAD! EVEN MY OWN SISTER DOESN'T KNOW IT'S ME!
THE DUKE OF INVERHOOCH, FRESH FROM THE OGS' MIDDEN, IS TURNED AWAY FROM DRAMBEG CASTLE ~
OH WHAT AM I TO DO ~
DEAR ME, YON POOR CRATER SEEMS TO BE IN TROUBLE!
BUT HE'S VERY SMELLY—I WONDER SHOULD I ~ ?
B446
WERE YOU THE MRS OG WHO HELPED THE OLD FELLOW WHO'D BEEN IN A MIDDEN?
YES, I WAS! HEY, HOLD ON AND I'LL HELP YOU!

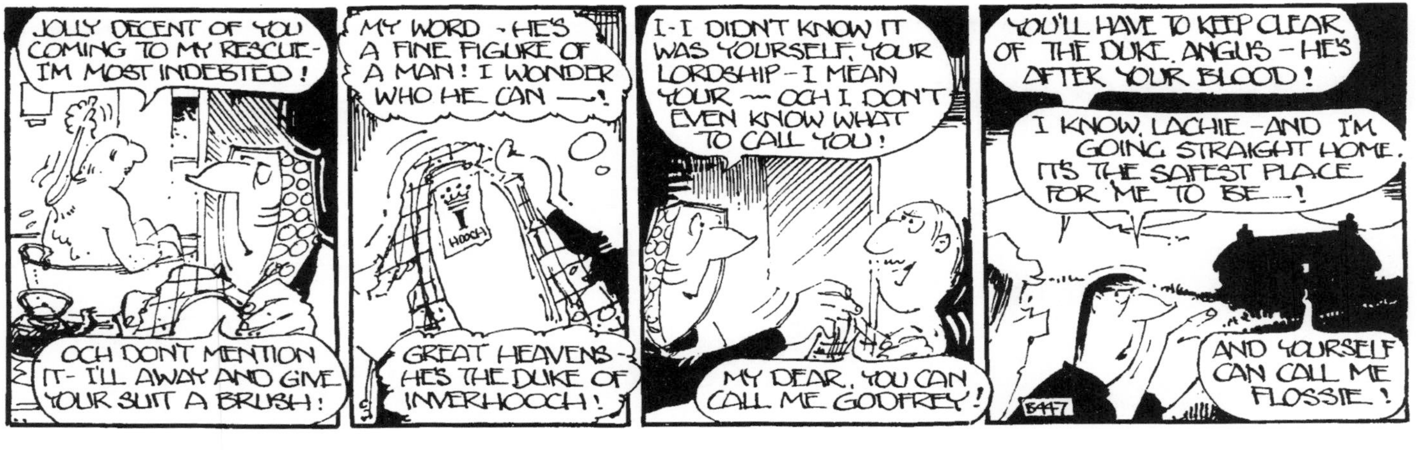
JOLLY DECENT OF YOU COMING TO MY RESCUE—I'M MOST INDEBTED!
OCH DON'T MENTION IT—I'LL AWAY AND GIVE YOUR SUIT A BRUSH!
MY WORD—HE'S A FINE FIGURE OF A MAN! I WONDER WHO HE CAN —!
HOOCH
GREAT HEAVENS—HE'S THE DUKE OF INVERHOOCH!
I-I DIDN'T KNOW IT WAS YOURSELF, YOUR LORDSHIP—I MEAN YOUR ~ OCH I DON'T EVEN KNOW WHAT TO CALL YOU!
MY DEAR, YOU CAN CALL ME GODFREY!
B447
YOU'LL HAVE TO KEEP CLEAR OF THE DUKE, ANGUS—HE'S AFTER YOUR BLOOD!
I KNOW, LACHIE—AND I'M GOING STRAIGHT HOME. IT'S THE SAFEST PLACE FOR ME TO BE—!
AND YOURSELF CAN CALL ME FLOSSIE!

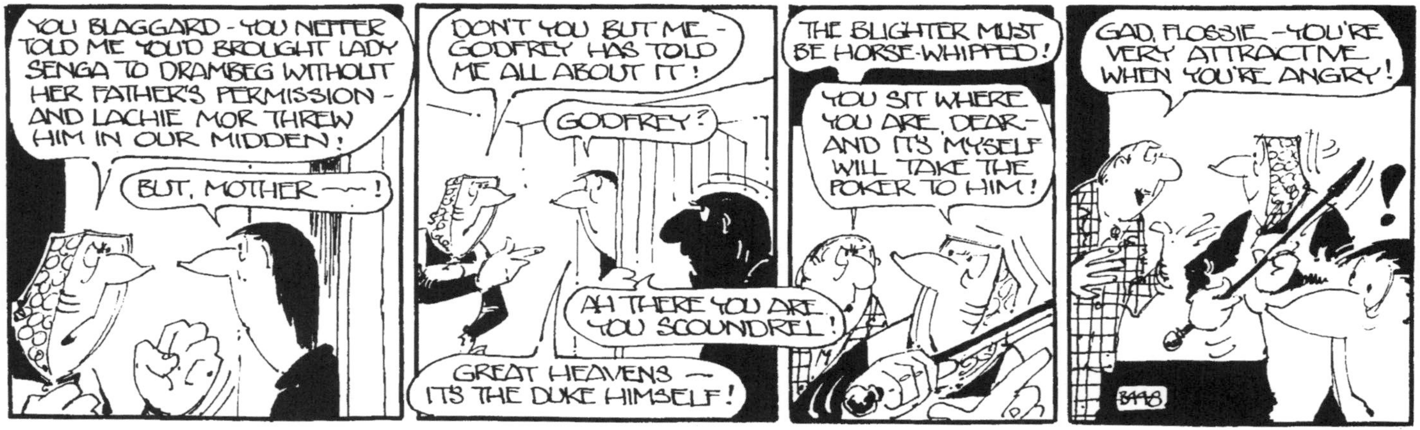
YOU BLAGGARD - YOU NEFFER TOLD ME YOU'D BROUGHT LADY SENGA TO DRAMBEG WITHOUT HER FATHER'S PERMISSION - AND LACHIE MOR THREW HIM IN OUR MIDDEN!
BUT, MOTHER ~~!
DON'T YOU BUT ME - GODFREY HAS TOLD ME ALL ABOUT IT!
GODFREY?
AH THERE YOU ARE YOU SCOUNDREL!
GREAT HEAVENS — IT'S THE DUKE HIMSELF!
THE BLIGHTER MUST BE HORSE-WHIPPED!
YOU SIT WHERE YOU ARE, DEAR - AND IT'S MYSELF WILL TAKE THE POKER TO HIM!
GAD, FLOSSIE - YOU'RE VERY ATTRACTIVE WHEN YOU'RE ANGRY!
!
B448

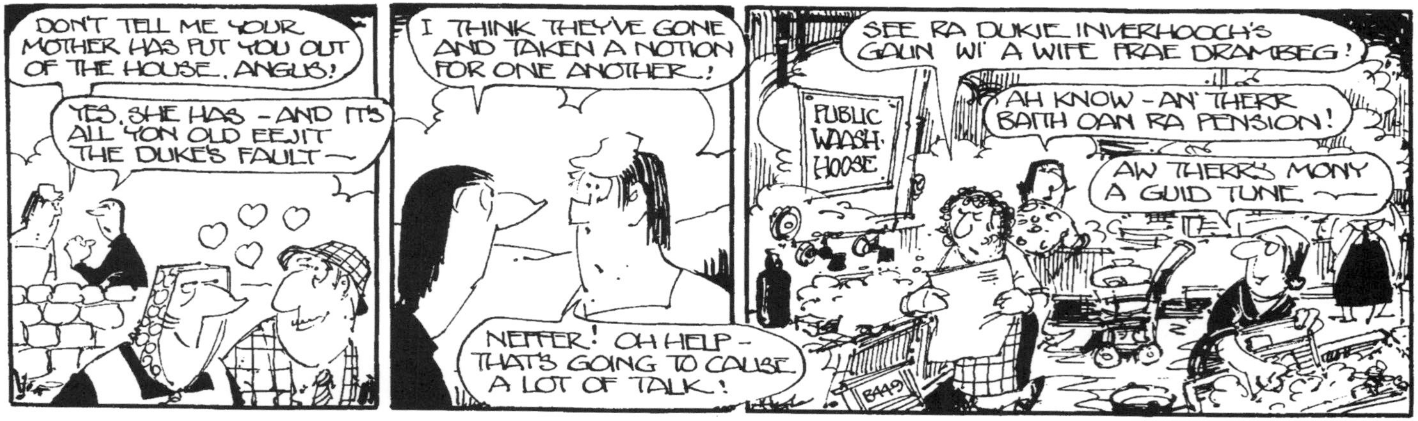
DON'T TELL ME YOUR MOTHER HAS PUT YOU OUT OF THE HOUSE, ANGUS!
YES, SHE HAS - AND IT'S ALL YON OLD EEJIT THE DUKE'S FAULT ~
I THINK THEY'VE GONE AND TAKEN A NOTION FOR ONE ANOTHER!
NEFFER! OH HELP - THAT'S GOING TO CAUSE A LOT OF TALK!
SEE RA DUKIE INVERHOOCH'S GAUN WI' A WIFE FRAE DRAMBEG!
AH KNOW - AN' THERR BAITH OAN RA PENSION!
AW THERR'S MONY A GUID TUNE ~
PUBLIC WAASH-HOOSE
B449

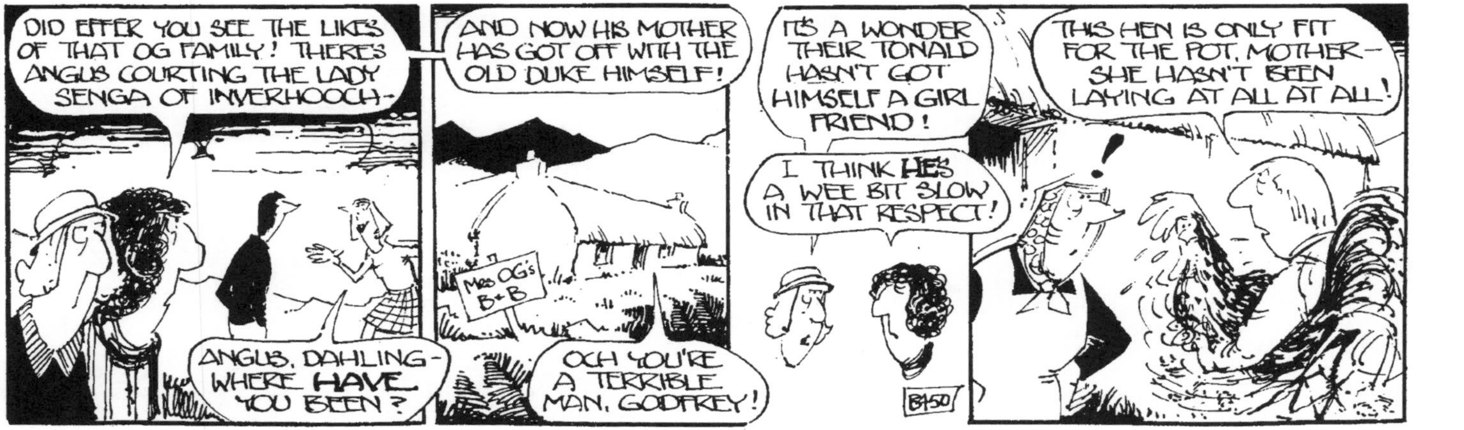
DID EFFER YOU SEE THE LIKES OF THAT OG FAMILY! THERE'S ANGUS COURTING THE LADY SENGA OF INVERHOOCH-
ANGUS, DAHLING- WHERE HAVE YOU BEEN?
AND NOW HIS MOTHER HAS GOT OFF WITH THE OLD DUKE HIMSELF!
MRS OG'S B&B
OCH YOU'RE A TERRIBLE MAN, GODFREY!
IT'S A WONDER THEIR TONALD HASN'T GOT HIMSELF A GIRL FRIEND!
I THINK HE'S A WEE BIT SLOW IN THAT RESPECT!
B450
THIS HEN IS ONLY FIT FOR THE POT, MOTHER- SHE HASN'T BEEN LAYING AT ALL AT ALL!
!

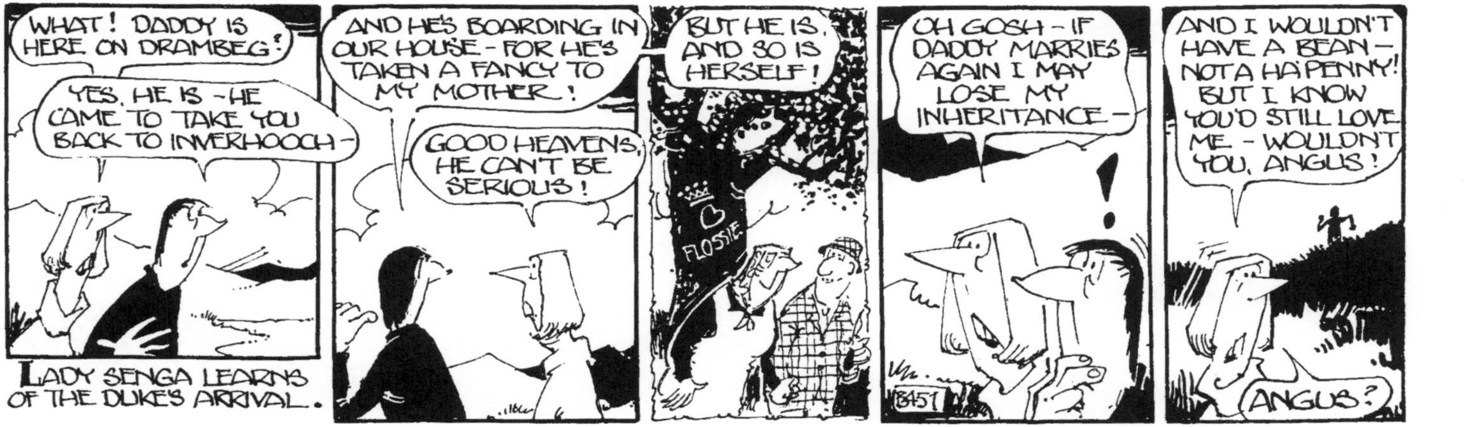
WHAT! DADDY IS HERE ON DRAMBEG?
YES, HE IS -HE CAME TO TAKE YOU BACK TO INVERHOOCH-
AND HE'S BOARDING IN OUR HOUSE - FOR HE'S TAKEN A FANCY TO MY MOTHER!
GOOD HEAVENS, HE CAN'T BE SERIOUS!
BUT HE IS, AND SO IS HERSELF!
FLOSSIE
OH GOSH - IF DADDY MARRIES AGAIN I MAY LOSE MY INHERITANCE-
!
B451
AND I WOULDN'T HAVE A BEAN- NOT A HA'PENNY! BUT I KNOW YOU'D STILL LOVE ME - WOULDN'T YOU, ANGUS!
ANGUS?

LADY SENGA LEARNS OF THE DUKE'S ARRIVAL.

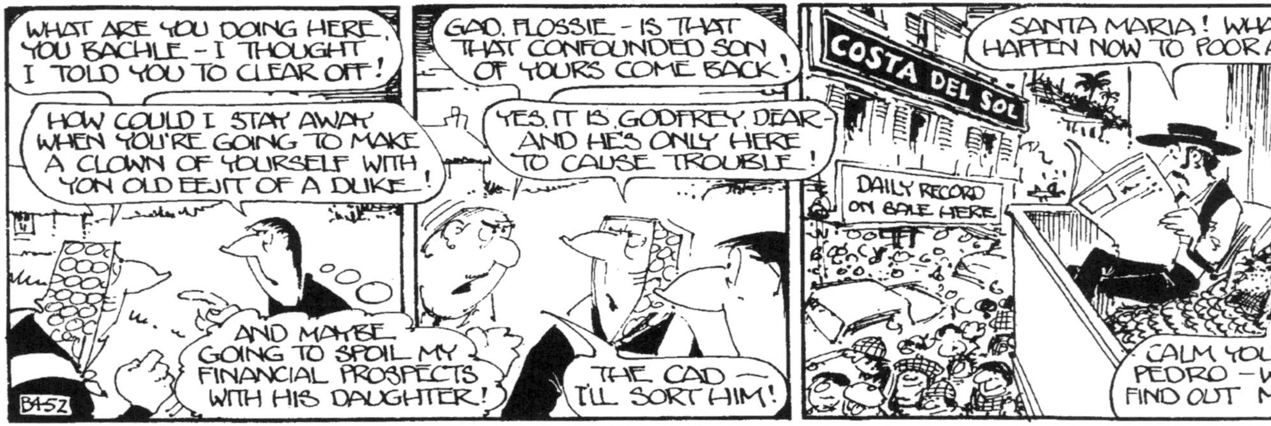
WHAT ARE YOU DOING HERE, YOU BACHLE - I THOUGHT I TOLD YOU TO CLEAR OFF!
HOW COULD I STAY AWAY WHEN YOU'RE GOING TO MAKE A CLOWN OF YOURSELF WITH YON OLD EEJIT OF A DUKE!
AND MAYBE GOING TO SPOIL MY FINANCIAL PROSPECTS WITH HIS DAUGHTER!
B452
GAD, FLOSSIE - IS THAT THAT CONFOUNDED SON OF YOURS COME BACK!
YES, IT IS, GODFREY, DEAR - AND HE'S ONLY HERE TO CAUSE TROUBLE!
THE CAD - I'LL SORT HIM!
COSTA DEL SOL
DAILY RECORD ON SALE HERE
SANTA MARIA! WHAT WILL HAPPEN NOW TO POOR ANGUS?
CALM YOURSELF, PEDRO - WE WILL FIND OUT MAÑANA!

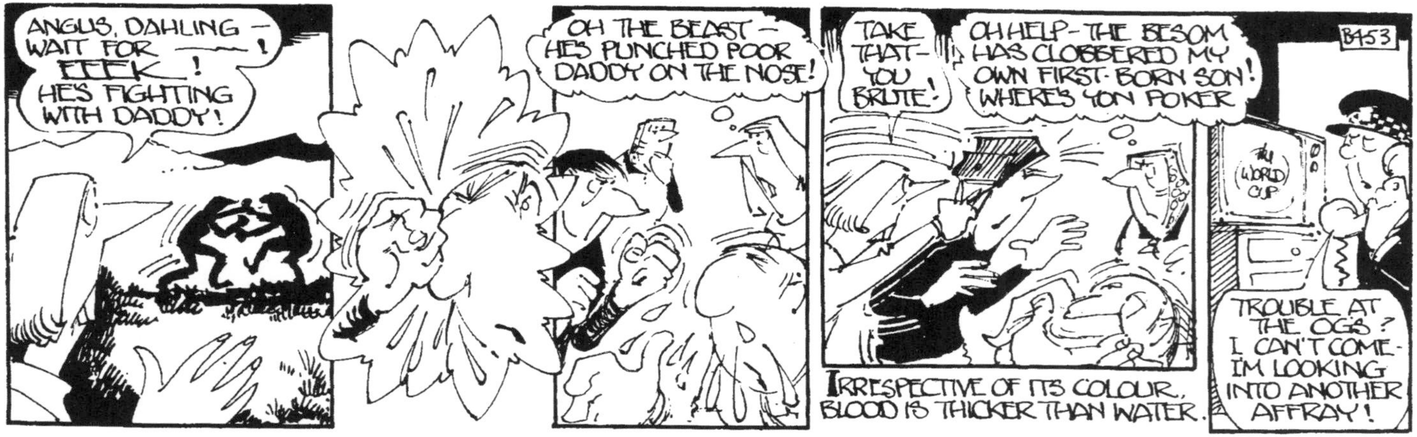
ANGUS, DAHLING - WAIT FOR ——!
EEEK!
HE'S FIGHTING WITH DADDY!
OH THE BEAST - HE'S PUNCHED POOR DADDY ON THE NOSE!
TAKE THAT - YOU BRUTE!
OH HELP - THE BESOM HAS CLOBBERED MY OWN FIRST-BORN SON! WHERE'S YON POKER
IRRESPECTIVE OF ITS COLOUR, BLOOD IS THICKER THAN WATER.
B453
THE WORLD CUP
TROUBLE AT THE OGS? I CAN'T COME - I'M LOOKING INTO ANOTHER AFFRAY!

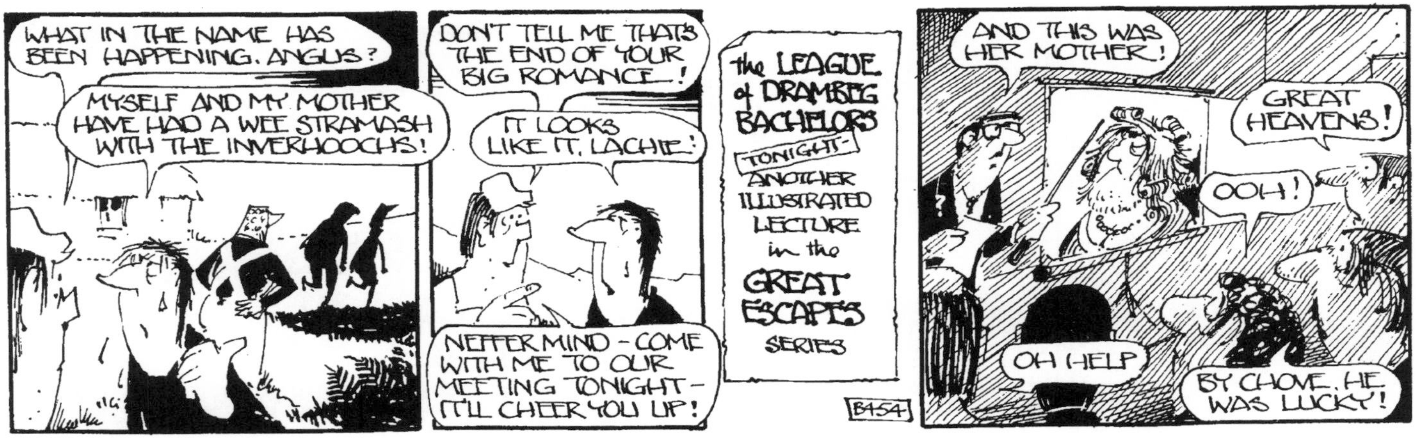
WHAT IN THE NAME HAS BEEN HAPPENING, ANGUS?
MYSELF AND MY MOTHER HAVE HAD A WEE STRAMASH WITH THE INVERHOOCHS!
DON'T TELL ME THAT'S THE END OF YOUR BIG ROMANCE!
IT LOOKS LIKE IT, LACHIE!
NEFFER MIND – COME WITH ME TO OUR MEETING TONIGHT – IT'LL CHEER YOU UP!
the LEAGUE of DRAMBEG BACHELORS
TONIGHT –
ANOTHER ILLUSTRATED LECTURE in the GREAT ESCAPES SERIES
B454
AND THIS WAS HER MOTHER!
GREAT HEAVENS!
OOH!
OH HELP
BY CHOVE, HE WAS LUCKY!

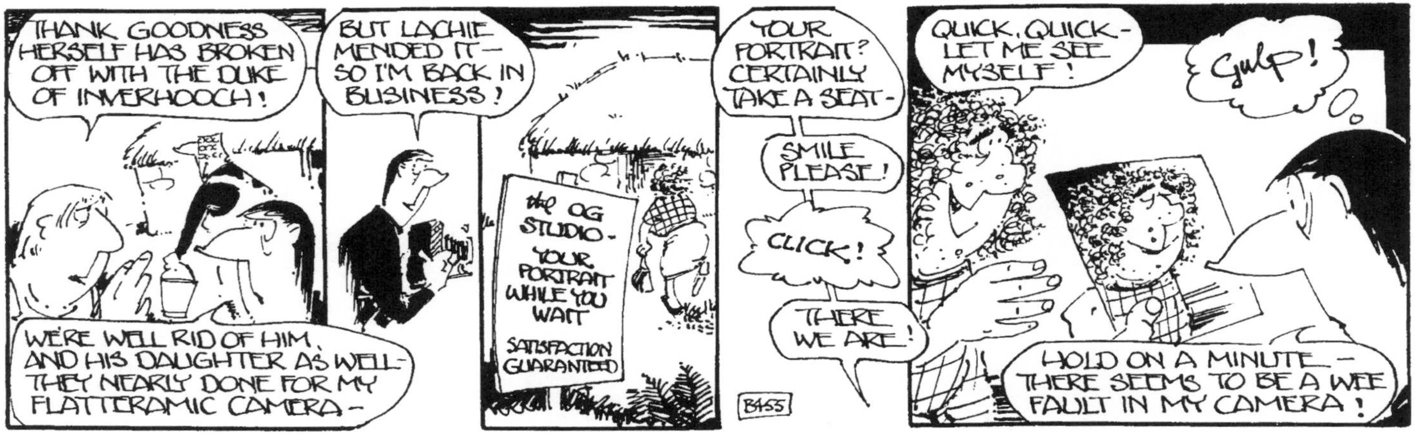
THANK GOODNESS HERSELF HAS BROKEN OFF WITH THE DUKE OF INVERHOOCH!
WE'RE WELL RID OF HIM, AND HIS DAUGHTER AS WELL – THEY NEARLY DONE FOR MY FLATTERAMIC CAMERA –
BUT LACHIE MENDED IT – SO I'M BACK IN BUSINESS!
the OG STUDIO – YOUR PORTRAIT WHILE YOU WAIT
SATISFACTION GUARANTEED
YOUR PORTRAIT? CERTAINLY TAKE A SEAT –
SMILE PLEASE!
CLICK!
THERE WE ARE!
B455
QUICK, QUICK – LET ME SEE MYSELF!
Gulp!
HOLD ON A MINUTE – THERE SEEMS TO BE A WEE FAULT IN MY CAMERA!

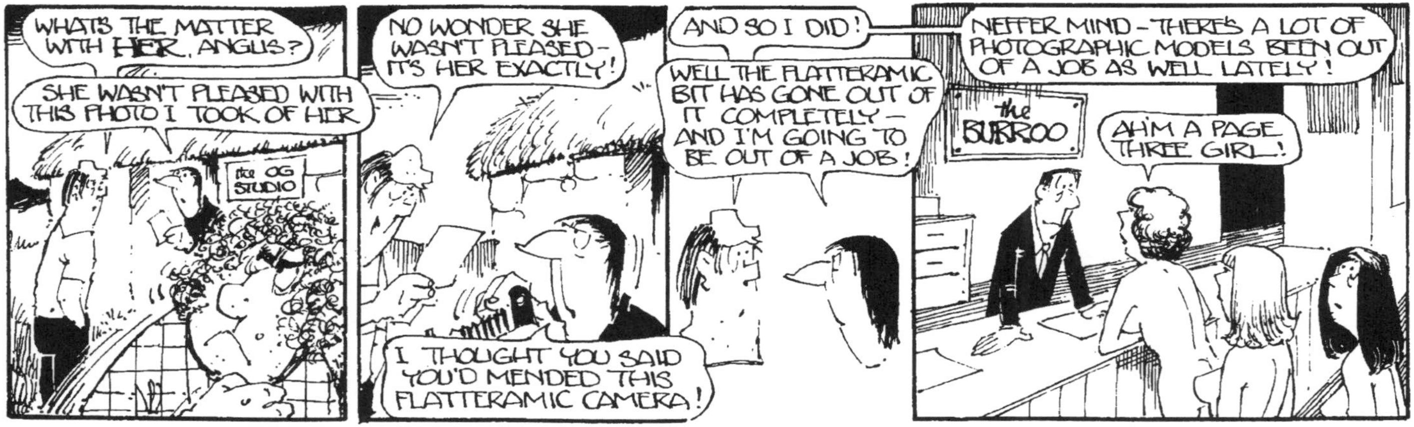
WHAT'S THE MATTER WITH HER, ANGUS?
SHE WASN'T PLEASED WITH THIS PHOTO I TOOK OF HER
the OG STUDIO
NO WONDER SHE WASN'T PLEASED — IT'S HER EXACTLY!
I THOUGHT YOU SAID YOU'D MENDED THIS FLATTERAMIC CAMERA!
AND SO I DID!
WELL THE FLATTERAMIC BIT HAS GONE OUT OF IT COMPLETELY — AND I'M GOING TO BE OUT OF A JOB!
NEFFER MIND — THERE'S A LOT OF PHOTOGRAPHIC MODELS BEEN OUT OF A JOB AS WELL LATELY!
the BURROO
AH'M A PAGE THREE GIRL!

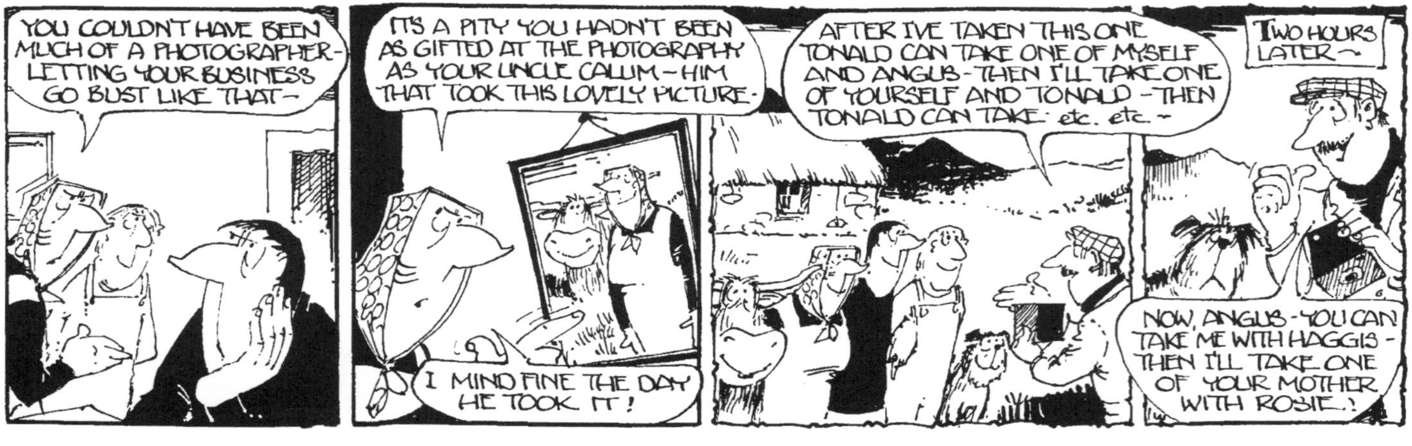
YOU COULDN'T HAVE BEEN MUCH OF A PHOTOGRAPHER — LETTING YOUR BUSINESS GO BUST LIKE THAT —
IT'S A PITY YOU HADN'T BEEN AS GIFTED AT THE PHOTOGRAPHY AS YOUR UNCLE CALUM — HIM THAT TOOK THIS LOVELY PICTURE —
I MIND FINE THE DAY HE TOOK IT!
AFTER I'VE TAKEN THIS ONE TONALD CAN TAKE ONE OF MYSELF AND ANGUS — THEN I'LL TAKE ONE OF YOURSELF AND TONALD — THEN TONALD CAN TAKE etc. etc. ~
TWO HOURS LATER ~
NOW, ANGUS — YOU CAN TAKE ME WITH HAGGIS — THEN I'LL TAKE ONE OF YOUR MOTHER WITH ROSIE!

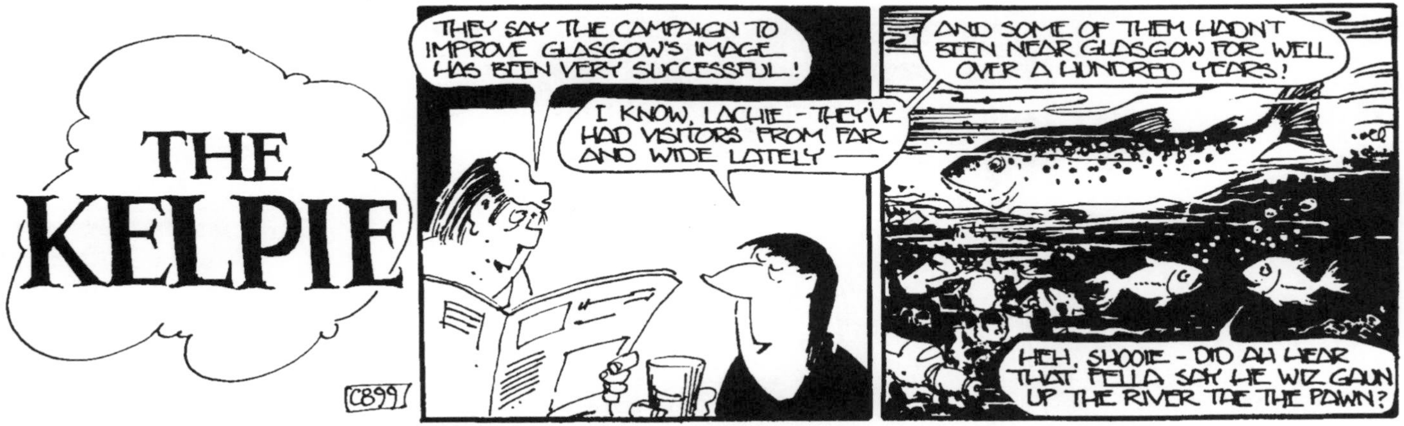
THE KELPIE
C899
THEY SAY THE CAMPAIGN TO IMPROVE GLASGOW'S IMAGE HAS BEEN VERY SUCCESSFUL!
I KNOW, LACHIE - THEY'VE HAD VISITORS FROM FAR AND WIDE LATELY —
AND SOME OF THEM HADN'T BEEN NEAR GLASGOW FOR WELL OVER A HUNDRED YEARS!
HEH, SHOOIE - DID AH HEAR THAT FELLA SAY HE WIZ GAUN UP THE RIVER TAE THE PAWN?

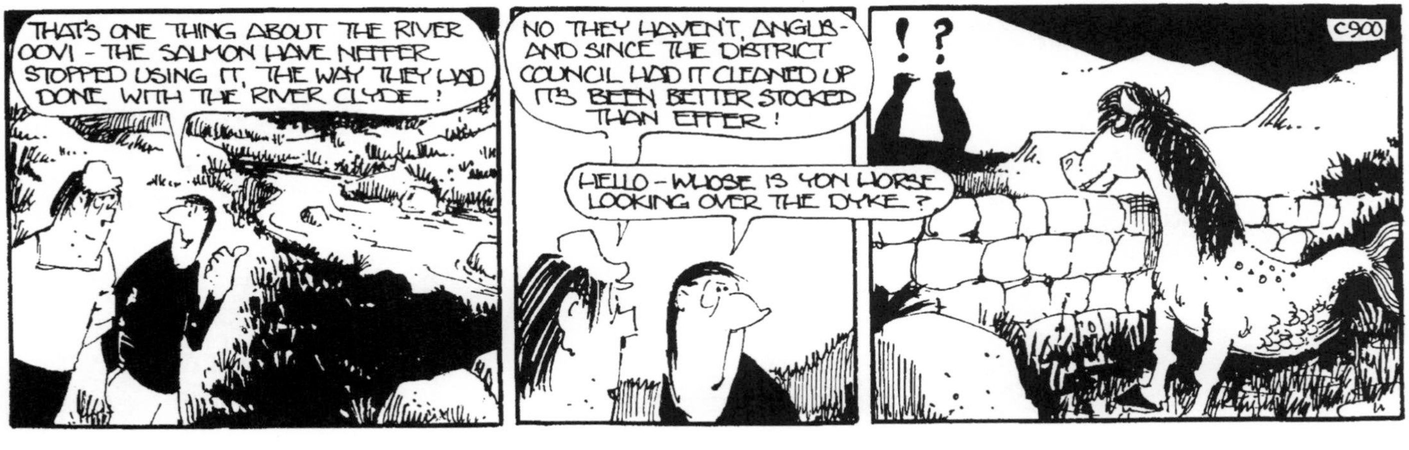
THAT'S ONE THING ABOUT THE RIVER OOVI - THE SALMON HAVE NEFFER STOPPED USING IT, THE WAY THEY HAD DONE WITH THE RIVER CLYDE!
NO THEY HAVEN'T, ANGUS - AND SINCE THE DISTRICT COUNCIL HAD IT CLEANED UP IT'S BEEN BETTER STOCKED THAN EFFER!
HELLO - WHOSE IS YON HORSE LOOKING OVER THE DYKE?
C900
! ?

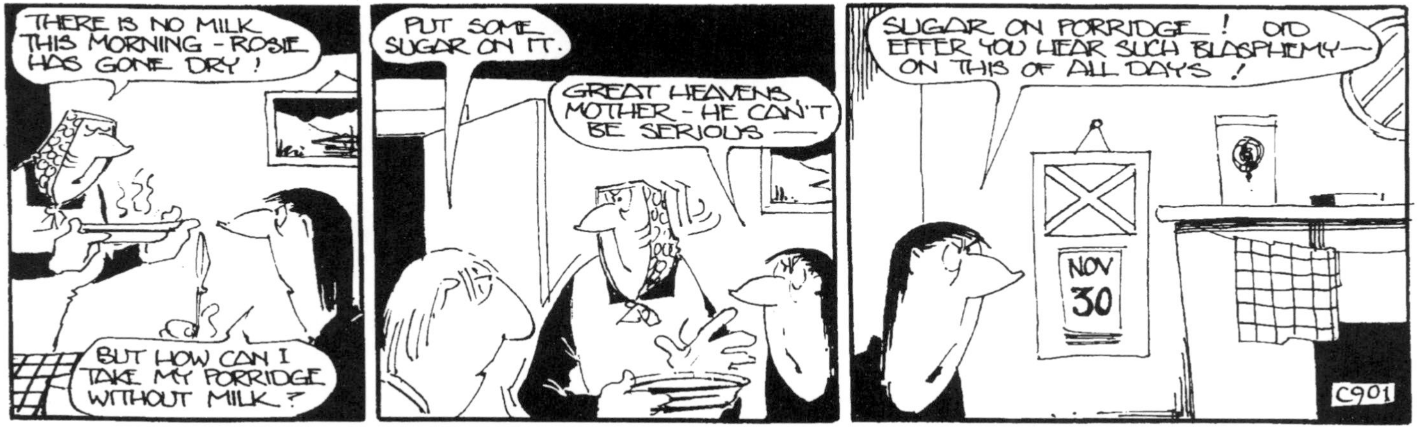
THERE IS NO MILK THIS MORNING - ROSIE HAS GONE DRY !
BUT HOW CAN I TAKE MY PORRIDGE WITHOUT MILK ?
PUT SOME SUGAR ON IT.
GREAT HEAVENS, MOTHER - HE CAN'T BE SERIOUS —
SUGAR ON PORRIDGE ! DID EFFER YOU HEAR SUCH BLASPHEMY — ON THIS OF ALL DAYS !
NOV 30
C901

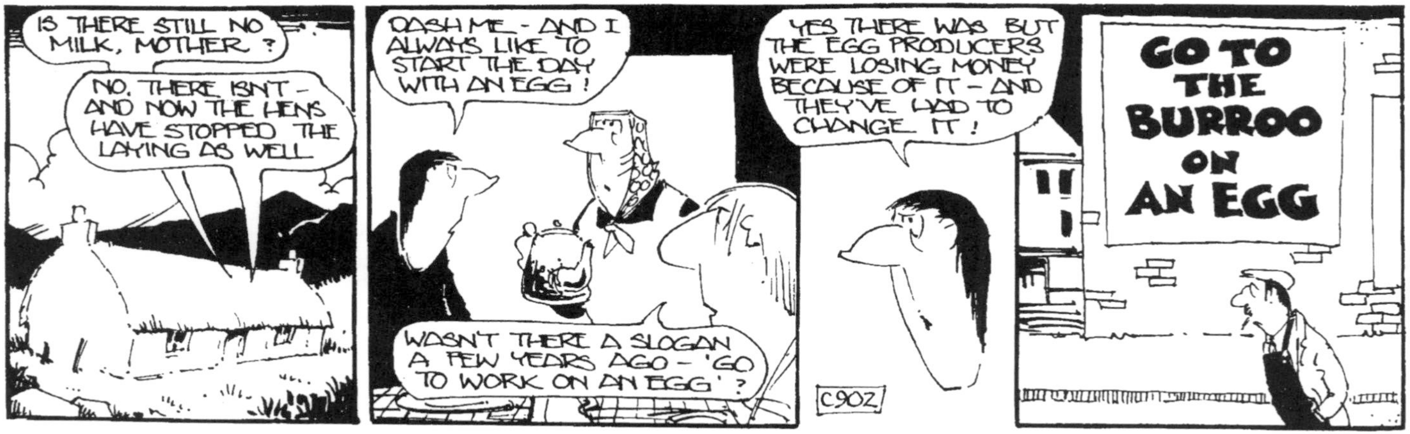
IS THERE STILL NO MILK, MOTHER ?
NO, THERE ISN'T - AND NOW THE HENS HAVE STOPPED THE LAYING AS WELL
DASH ME - AND I ALWAYS LIKE TO START THE DAY WITH AN EGG !
WASN'T THERE A SLOGAN A FEW YEARS AGO - 'GO TO WORK ON AN EGG' ?
YES THERE WAS BUT THE EGG PRODUCERS WERE LOSING MONEY BECAUSE OF IT - AND THEY'VE HAD TO CHANGE IT !
GO TO THE BURROO ON AN EGG
C902

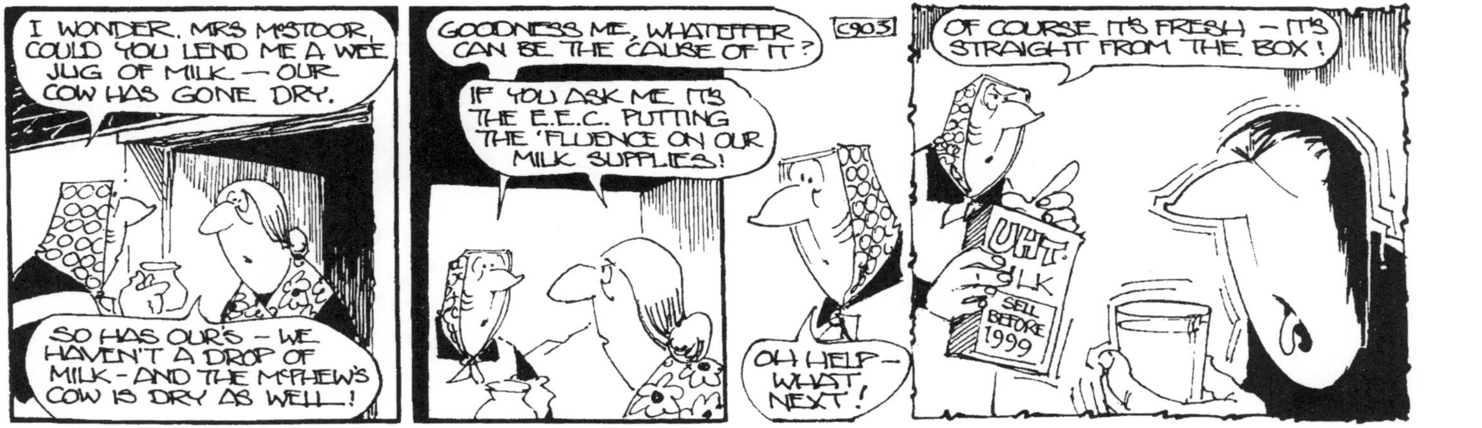
I WONDER, MRS McSTOOR, COULD YOU LEND ME A WEE JUG OF MILK — OUR COW HAS GONE DRY.
SO HAS OUR'S — WE HAVEN'T A DROP OF MILK - AND THE McPHEW'S COW IS DRY AS WELL!
GOODNESS ME, WHATEFFER CAN BE THE CAUSE OF IT?
C903
IF YOU ASK ME IT'S THE E.E.C. PUTTING THE 'FLUENCE ON OUR MILK SUPPLIES!
OH HELP— WHAT NEXT!
OF COURSE IT'S FRESH — IT'S STRAIGHT FROM THE BOX!
UHT
SELL BEFORE 1999

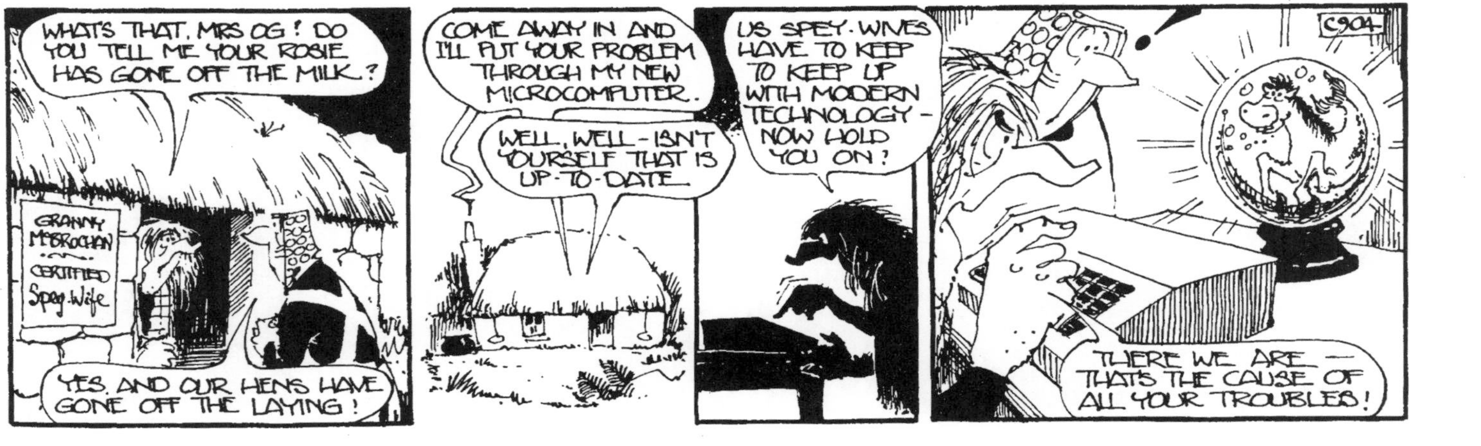
WHAT'S THAT, MRS OG! DO YOU TELL ME YOUR ROSIE HAS GONE OFF THE MILK?
GRANNY McBROCHAN CERTIFIED Spey-Wife
YES, AND OUR HENS HAVE GONE OFF THE LAYING!
COME AWAY IN AND I'LL PUT YOUR PROBLEM THROUGH MY NEW MICROCOMPUTER.
WELL, WELL - ISN'T YOURSELF THAT IS UP-TO-DATE.
US SPEY-WIVES HAVE TO KEEP TO KEEP UP WITH MODERN TECHNOLOGY - NOW HOLD YOU ON!
C904
THERE WE ARE — THAT'S THE CAUSE OF ALL YOUR TROUBLES!

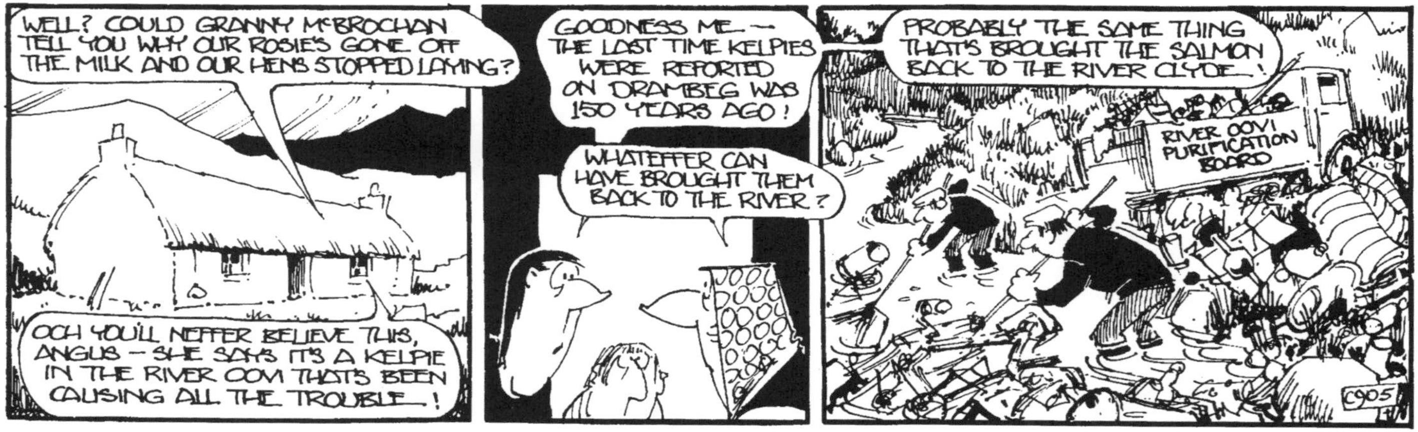

WELL? COULD GRANNY McBROCHAN TELL YOU WHY OUR ROSIE'S GONE OFF THE MILK AND OUR HENS STOPPED LAYING?
OCH YOU'LL NEFFER BELIEVE THIS, ANGUS – SHE SAYS IT'S A KELPIE IN THE RIVER OOVI THAT'S BEEN CAUSING ALL THE TROUBLE!
GOODNESS ME – THE LAST TIME KELPIES WERE REPORTED ON DRAMBEG WAS 150 YEARS AGO!
WHATEFFER CAN HAVE BROUGHT THEM BACK TO THE RIVER?
PROBABLY THE SAME THING THAT'S BROUGHT THE SALMON BACK TO THE RIVER CLYDE!
RIVER OOVI PURIFICATION BOARD
C905

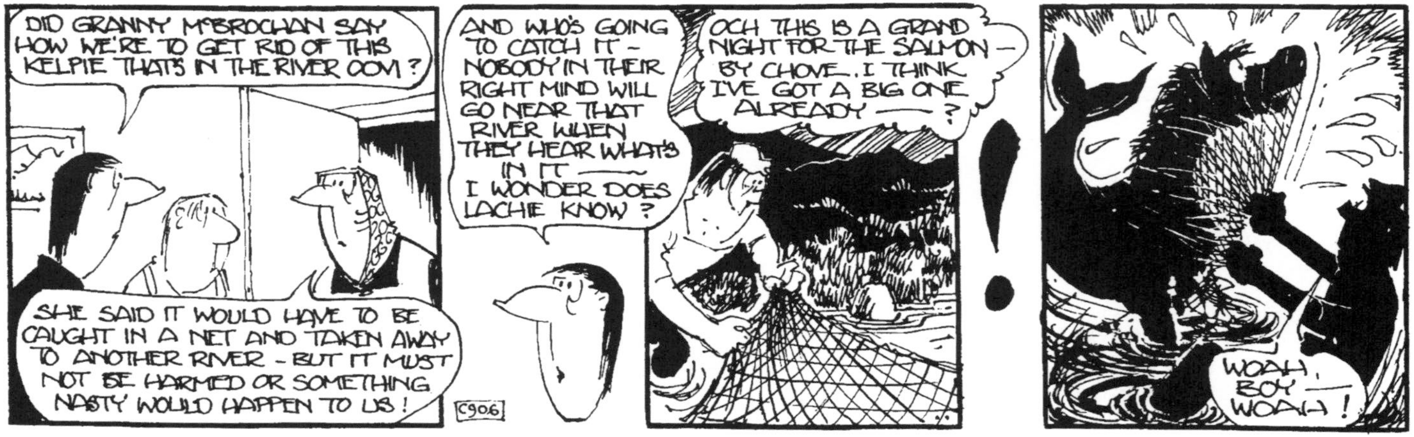

DID GRANNY McBROCHAN SAY HOW WE'RE TO GET RID OF THIS KELPIE THAT'S IN THE RIVER OOVI?
SHE SAID IT WOULD HAVE TO BE CAUGHT IN A NET AND TAKEN AWAY TO ANOTHER RIVER – BUT IT MUST NOT BE HARMED OR SOMETHING NASTY WOULD HAPPEN TO US!
AND WHO'S GOING TO CATCH IT – NOBODY IN THEIR RIGHT MIND WILL GO NEAR THAT RIVER WHEN THEY HEAR WHAT'S IN IT — I WONDER DOES LACHIE KNOW?
C906
OCH THIS IS A GRAND NIGHT FOR THE SALMON – BY CHOVE. I THINK I'VE GOT A BIG ONE ALREADY —?
!
WOAH, BOY — WOAH!

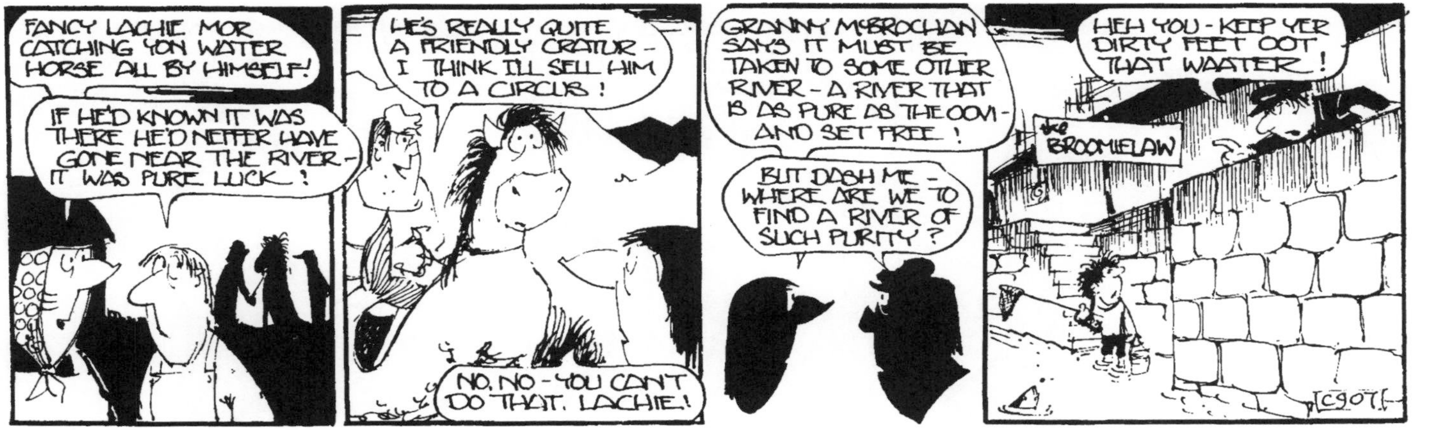
FANCY LACHIE MOR CATCHING YON WATER HORSE ALL BY HIMSELF!
IF HE'D KNOWN IT WAS THERE HE'D NEFFER HAVE GONE NEAR THE RIVER - IT WAS PURE LUCK!
HE'S REALLY QUITE A FRIENDLY CRATUR - I THINK I'LL SELL HIM TO A CIRCUS!
NO, NO - YOU CAN'T DO THAT, LACHIE!
GRANNY McBROCHAN SAYS IT MUST BE TAKEN TO SOME OTHER RIVER - A RIVER THAT IS AS PURE AS THE OOVI AND SET FREE!
BUT DASH ME - WHERE ARE WE TO FIND A RIVER OF SUCH PURITY?
HEH YOU - KEEP YER DIRTY FEET OOT THAT WAATER!
the BROOMIELAW
C907

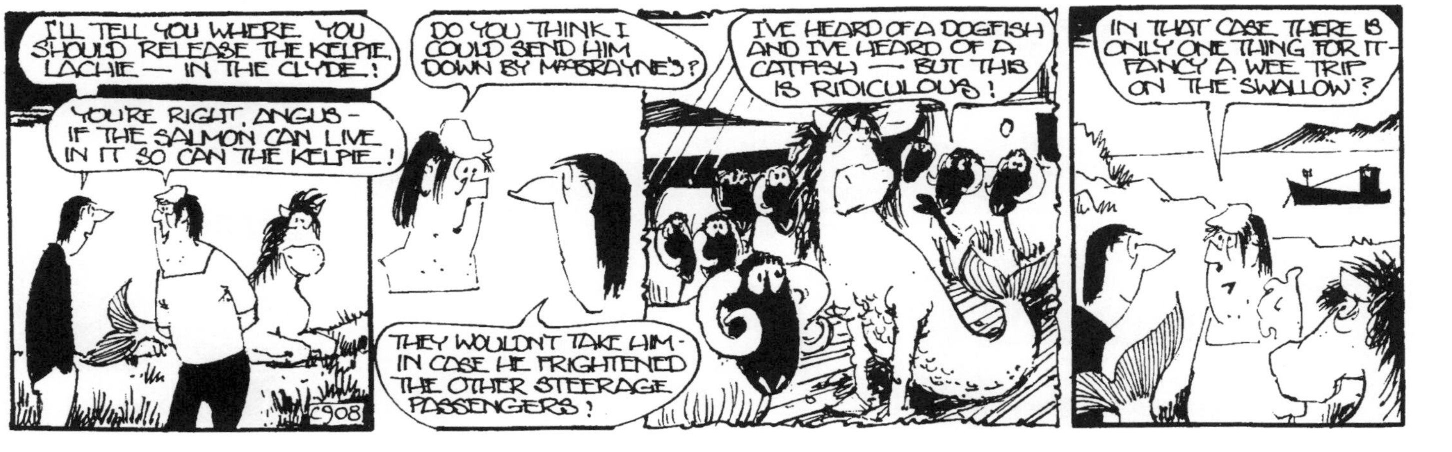
I'LL TELL YOU WHERE YOU SHOULD RELEASE THE KELPIE, LACHIE — IN THE CLYDE!
YOU'RE RIGHT, ANGUS - IF THE SALMON CAN LIVE IN IT SO CAN THE KELPIE!
C908
DO YOU THINK I COULD SEND HIM DOWN BY MacBRAYNE'S?
THEY WOULDN'T TAKE HIM - IN CASE HE FRIGHTENED THE OTHER STEERAGE PASSENGERS!
I'VE HEARD OF A DOGFISH AND I'VE HEARD OF A CATFISH — BUT THIS IS RIDICULOUS!
IN THAT CASE THERE IS ONLY ONE THING FOR IT - FANCY A WEE TRIP ON THE 'SWALLOW'?

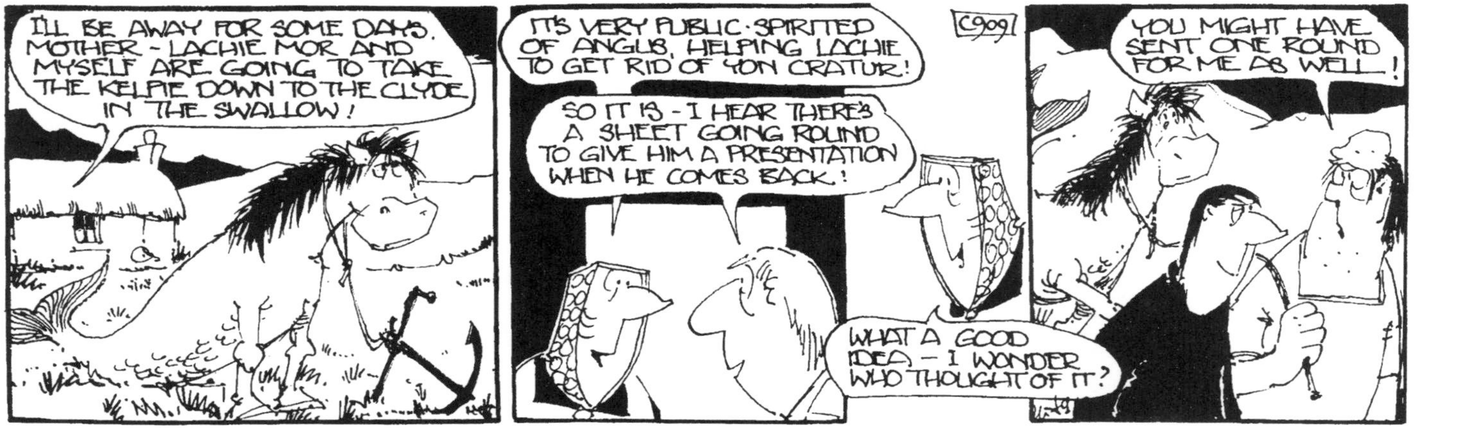
I'LL BE AWAY FOR SOME DAYS, MOTHER - LACHIE MOR AND MYSELF ARE GOING TO TAKE THE KELPIE DOWN TO THE CLYDE IN THE SWALLOW!
IT'S VERY PUBLIC-SPIRITED OF ANGUS, HELPING LACHIE TO GET RID OF YON CRATUR!
SO IT IS - I HEAR THERE'S A SHEET GOING ROUND TO GIVE HIM A PRESENTATION WHEN HE COMES BACK!
WHAT A GOOD IDEA - I WONDER WHO THOUGHT OF IT?
C909
YOU MIGHT HAVE SENT ONE ROUND FOR ME AS WELL!

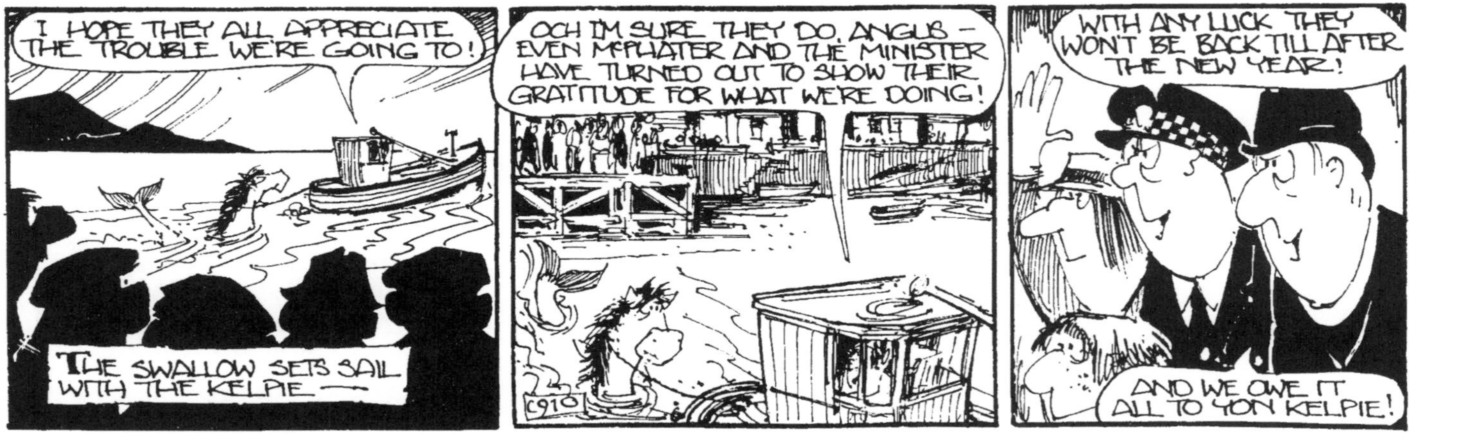
THE SWALLOW SETS SAIL WITH THE KELPIE —
I HOPE THEY ALL APPRECIATE THE TROUBLE WE'RE GOING TO!
OCH I'M SURE THEY DO, ANGUS - EVEN McPHATER AND THE MINISTER HAVE TURNED OUT TO SHOW THEIR GRATITUDE FOR WHAT WE'RE DOING!
C910
WITH ANY LUCK THEY WON'T BE BACK TILL AFTER THE NEW YEAR!
AND WE OWE IT ALL TO YON KELPIE!

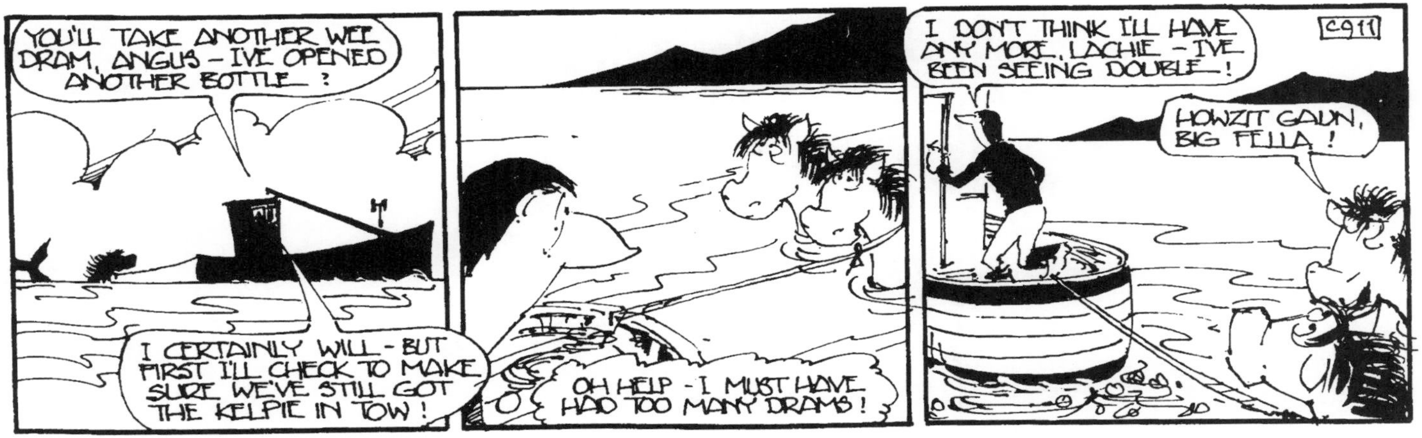
YOU'LL TAKE ANOTHER WEE DRAM, ANGUS – I'VE OPENED ANOTHER BOTTLE ?
I CERTAINLY WILL – BUT FIRST I'LL CHECK TO MAKE SURE WE'VE STILL GOT THE KELPIE IN TOW !
OH HELP – I MUST HAVE HAD TOO MANY DRAMS !
I DON'T THINK I'LL HAVE ANY MORE, LACHIE – I'VE BEEN SEEING DOUBLE !
C911
HOWZIT GAUN, BIG FELLA !

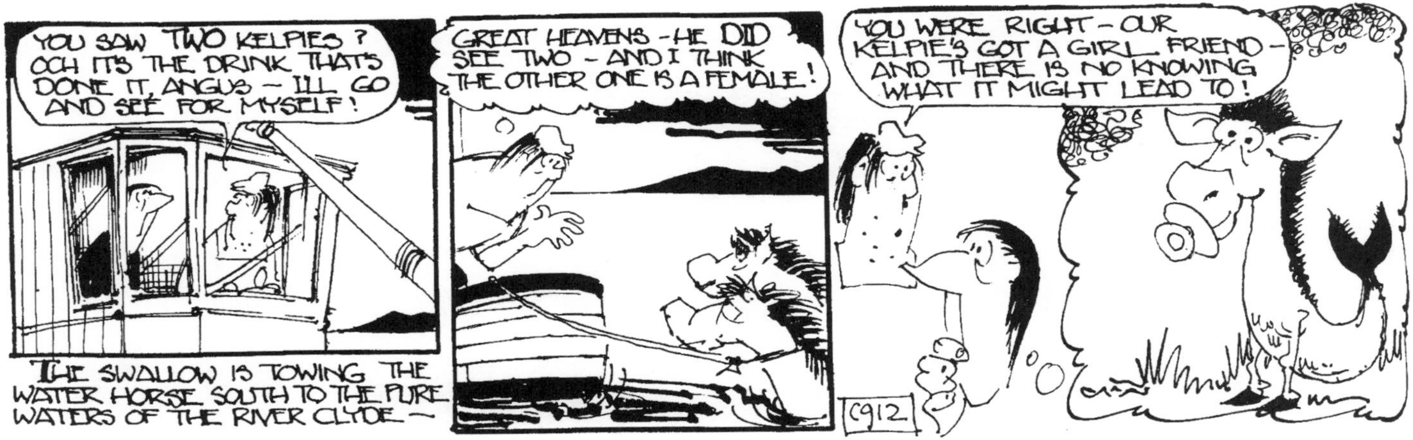
YOU SAW TWO KELPIES ? OCH IT'S THE DRINK THAT'S DONE IT, ANGUS – I'LL GO AND SEE FOR MYSELF !
THE SWALLOW IS TOWING THE WATER HORSE SOUTH TO THE PURE WATERS OF THE RIVER CLYDE –
GREAT HEAVENS – HE DID SEE TWO – AND I THINK THE OTHER ONE IS A FEMALE !
YOU WERE RIGHT – OUR KELPIE'S GOT A GIRL FRIEND – AND THERE IS NO KNOWING WHAT IT MIGHT LEAD TO !
C912

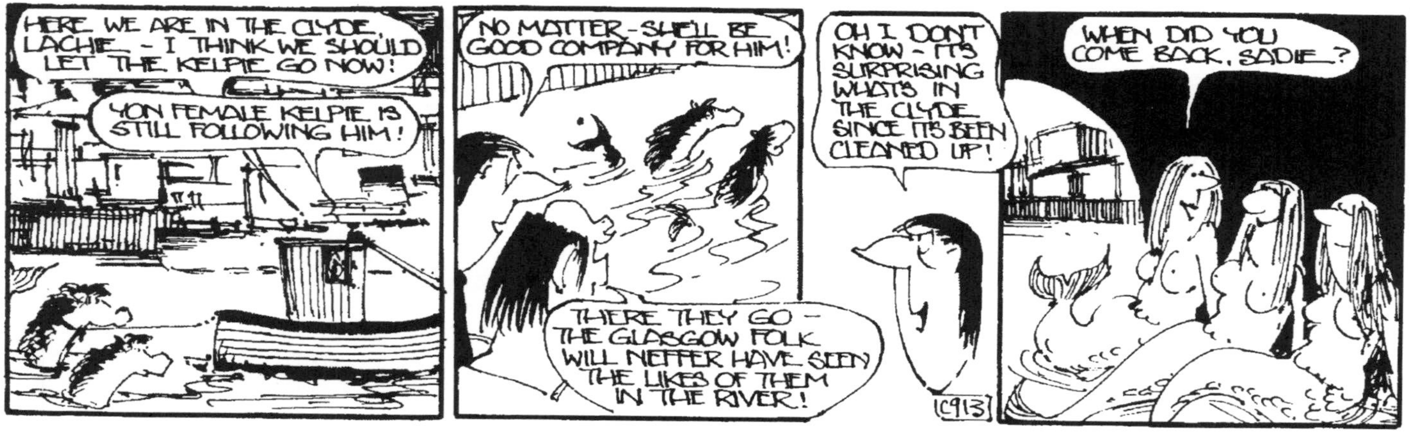
HERE WE ARE IN THE CLYDE, LACHIE - I THINK WE SHOULD LET THE KELPIE GO NOW!
YON FEMALE KELPIE IS STILL FOLLOWING HIM!
NO MATTER - SHE'LL BE GOOD COMPANY FOR HIM!
THERE THEY GO - THE GLASGOW FOLK WILL NEFFER HAVE SEEN THE LIKES OF THEM IN THE RIVER!
OH I DON'T KNOW - IT'S SURPRISING WHAT'S IN THE CLYDE SINCE IT'S BEEN CLEANED UP!
C913
WHEN DID YOU COME BACK, SADIE?

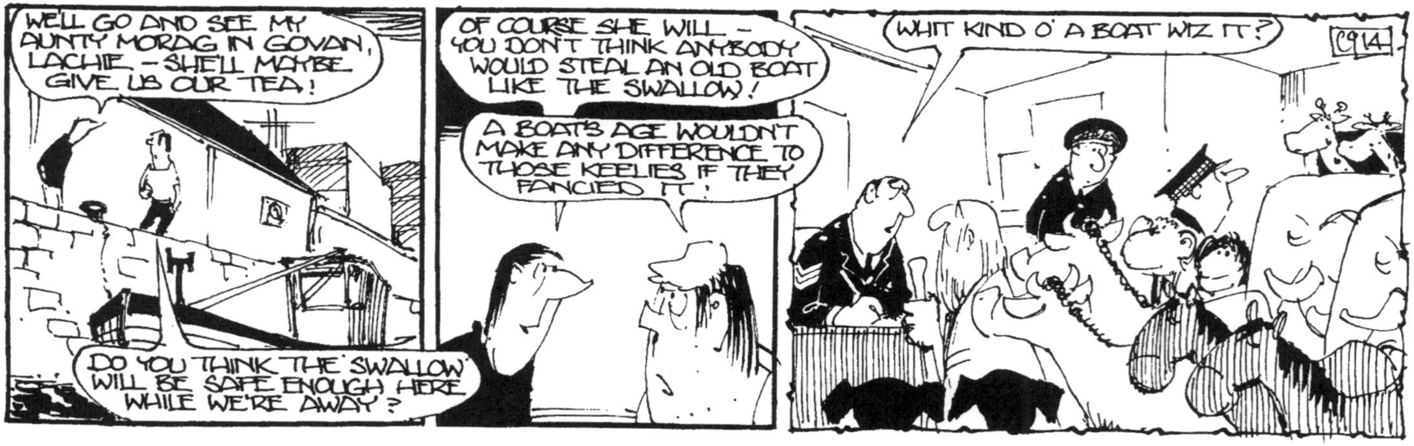
WE'LL GO AND SEE MY AUNTY MORAG IN GOVAN, LACHIE - SHE'LL MAYBE GIVE US OUR TEA!
DO YOU THINK THE SWALLOW WILL BE SAFE ENOUGH HERE WHILE WE'RE AWAY?
OF COURSE SHE WILL - YOU DON'T THINK ANYBODY WOULD STEAL AN OLD BOAT LIKE THE SWALLOW!
A BOAT'S AGE WOULDN'T MAKE ANY DIFFERENCE TO THOSE KEELIES IF THEY FANCIED IT!
WHIT KIND O' A BOAT WIZ IT?
C914

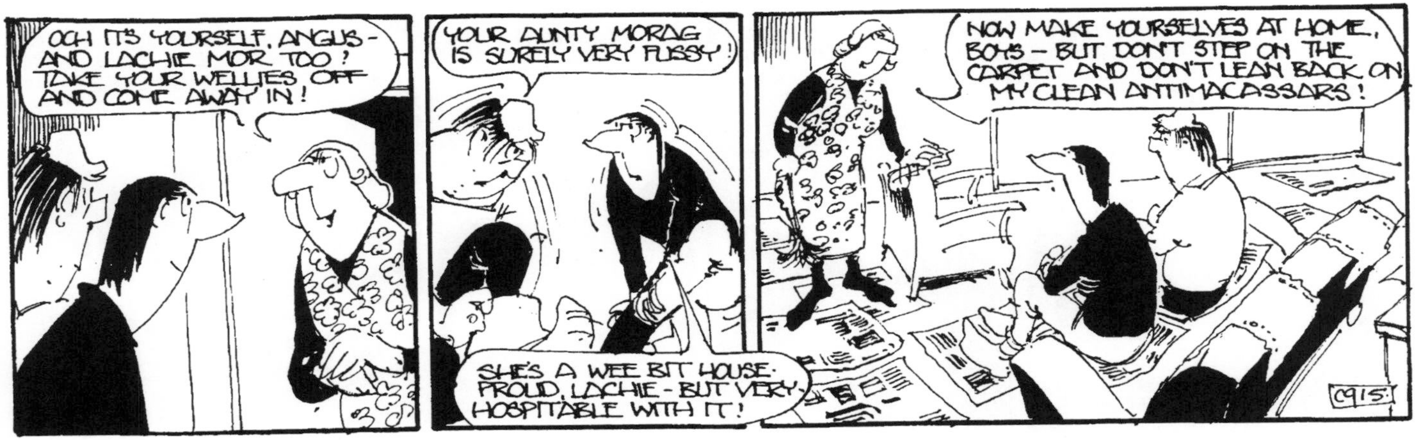
OCH IT'S YOURSELF, ANGUS - AND LACHIE MOR TOO? TAKE YOUR WELLIES OFF AND COME AWAY IN!
YOUR AUNTY MORAG IS SURELY VERY FUSSY!
SHE'S A WEE BIT HOUSE-PROUD, LACHIE - BUT VERY HOSPITABLE WITH IT!
NOW MAKE YOURSELVES AT HOME, BOYS - BUT DON'T STEP ON THE CARPET AND DON'T LEAN BACK ON MY CLEAN ANTIMACASSARS!
C915

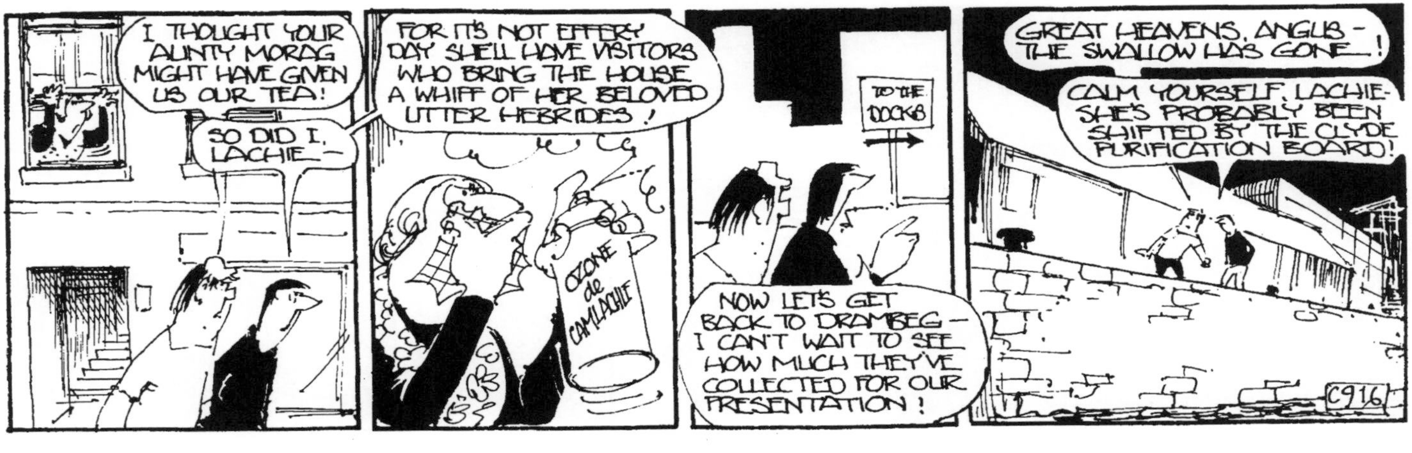
I THOUGHT YOUR AUNTY MORAG MIGHT HAVE GIVEN US OUR TEA!
SO DID I, LACHIE -
FOR IT'S NOT EFFERY DAY SHE'LL HAVE VISITORS WHO BRING THE HOUSE A WHIFF OF HER BELOVED UTTER HEBRIDES!
OZONE de CAMLACHIE
TO THE DOCKS
NOW LET'S GET BACK TO DRAMBEG - I CAN'T WAIT TO SEE HOW MUCH THEY'VE COLLECTED FOR OUR PRESENTATION!
GREAT HEAVENS, ANGUS - THE SWALLOW HAS GONE!
CALM YOURSELF, LACHIE - SHE'S PROBABLY BEEN SHIFTED BY THE CLYDE PURIFICATION BOARD!
C916

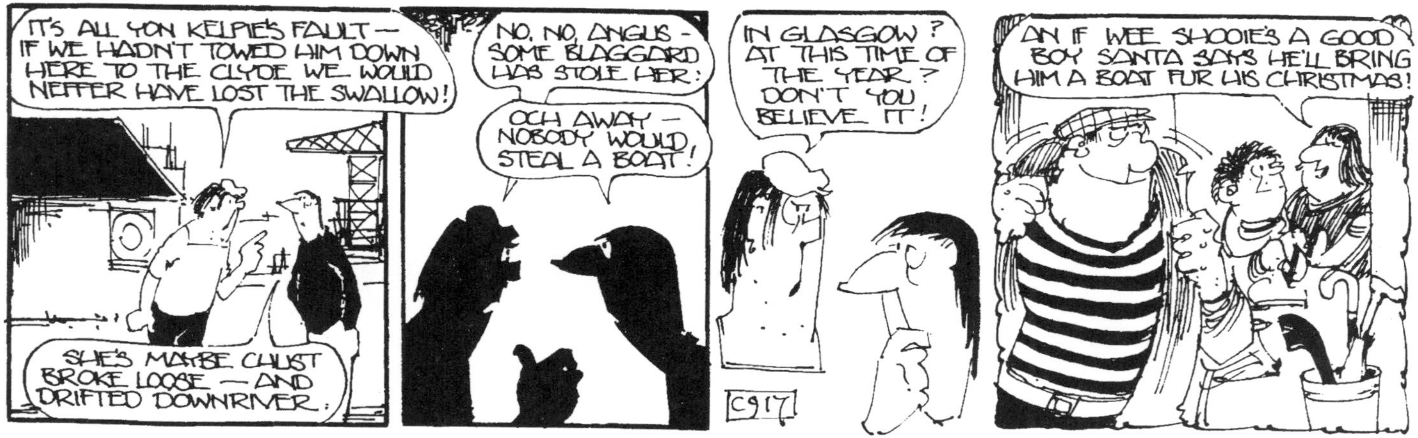
IT'S ALL YON KELPIE'S FAULT — IF WE HADN'T TOWED HIM DOWN HERE TO THE CLYDE WE WOULD NEFFER HAVE LOST THE SWALLOW!
SHE'S MAYBE CHUST BROKE LOOSE — AND DRIFTED DOWNRIVER.
NO, NO, ANGUS - SOME BLAGGARD HAS STOLE HER!
OCH AWAY — NOBODY WOULD STEAL A BOAT!
IN GLASGOW? AT THIS TIME OF THE YEAR? DON'T YOU BELIEVE IT!
C917
AN IF WEE SHOOIE'S A GOOD BOY SANTA SAYS HE'LL BRING HIM A BOAT FUR HIS CHRISTMAS!

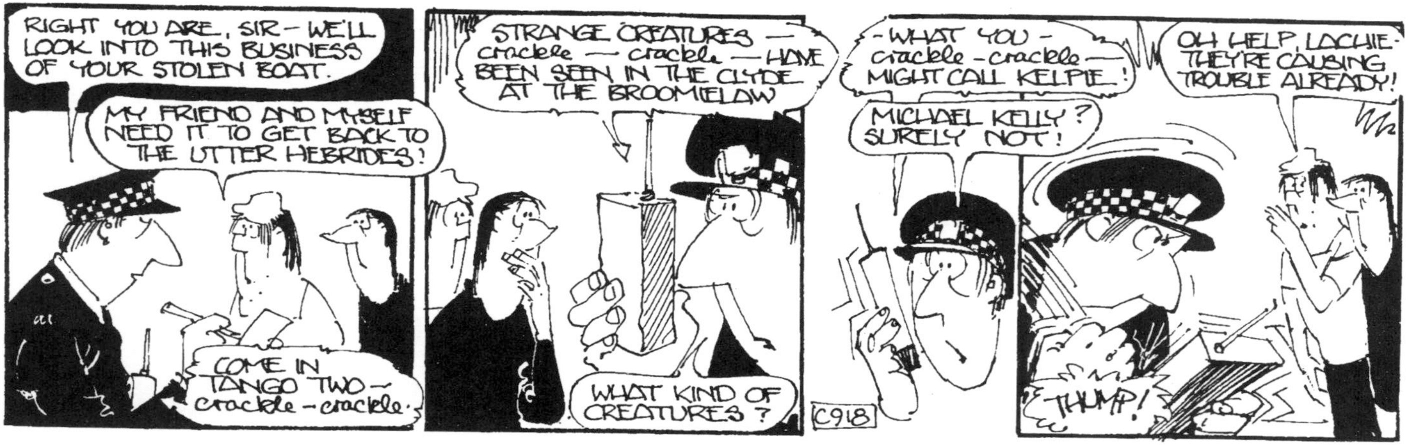
RIGHT YOU ARE, SIR — WE'LL LOOK INTO THIS BUSINESS OF YOUR STOLEN BOAT.
MY FRIEND AND MYSELF NEED IT TO GET BACK TO THE UTTER HEBRIDES!
COME IN TANGO TWO — crackle - crackle.
STRANGE CREATURES — crackle — crackle — HAVE BEEN SEEN IN THE CLYDE AT THE BROOMIELAW
WHAT KIND OF CREATURES?
C918
- WHAT YOU - crackle - crackle - MIGHT CALL KELPIE!
MICHAEL KELLY? SURELY NOT!
OH HELP, LACHIE - THEY'RE CAUSING TROUBLE ALREADY!
THUMP!

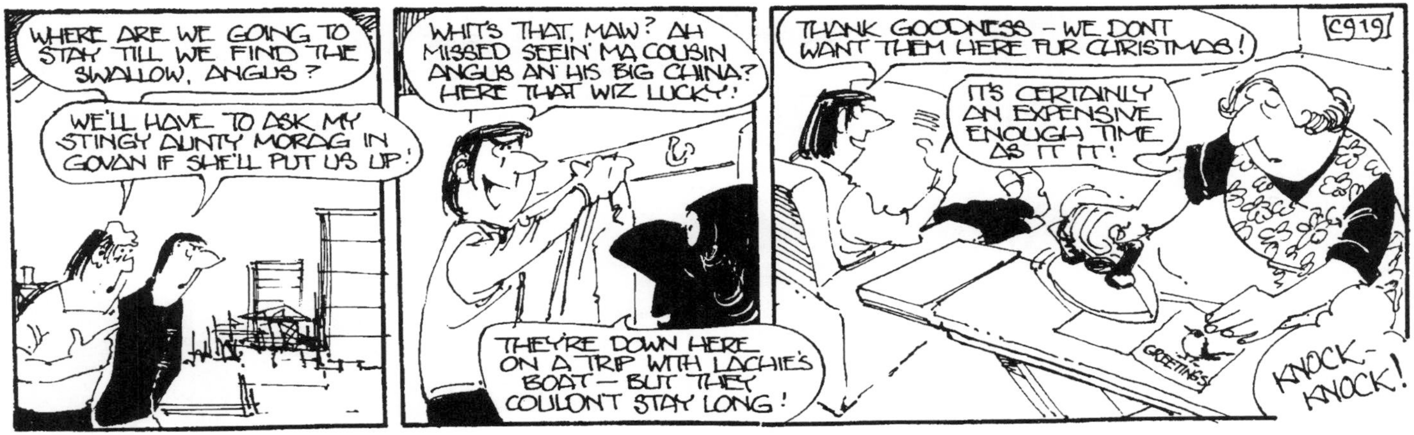
WHERE ARE WE GOING TO STAY TILL WE FIND THE SWALLOW, ANGUS?
WE'LL HAVE TO ASK MY STINGY AUNTY MORAG IN GOVAN IF SHE'LL PUT US UP!
WHIT'S THAT, MAW? AH MISSED SEEIN' MA COUSIN ANGUS AN' HIS BIG CHINA? HERE THAT WIZ LUCKY!
THEY'RE DOWN HERE ON A TRIP WITH LACHIE'S BOAT — BUT THEY COULDN'T STAY LONG!
C919
THANK GOODNESS — WE DONT WANT THEM HERE FUR CHRISTMAS!
IT'S CERTAINLY AN EXPENSIVE ENOUGH TIME AS IT IT!
GREETINGS
KNOCK-KNOCK!

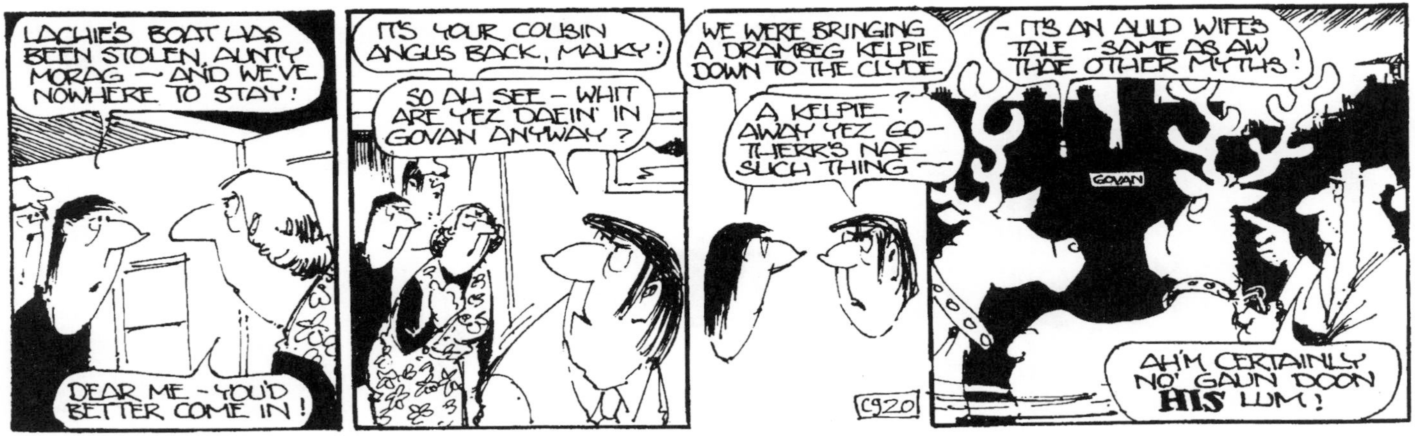
LACHIE'S BOAT HAS BEEN STOLEN, AUNTY MORAG — AND WE'VE NOWHERE TO STAY!
DEAR ME — YOU'D BETTER COME IN!
IT'S YOUR COUSIN ANGUS BACK, MALKY!
SO AH SEE — WHIT ARE YEZ DAEIN' IN GOVAN ANYWAY?
WE WERE BRINGING A DRAMBEG KELPIE DOWN TO THE CLYDE
A KELPIE? AWAY YEZ GO— THERR'S NAE SUCH THING—
C920
— IT'S AN AULD WIFE'S TALE — SAME AS AW THAE OTHER MYTHS!
GOVAN
AH'M CERTAINLY NO' GAUN DOON HIS LUM!

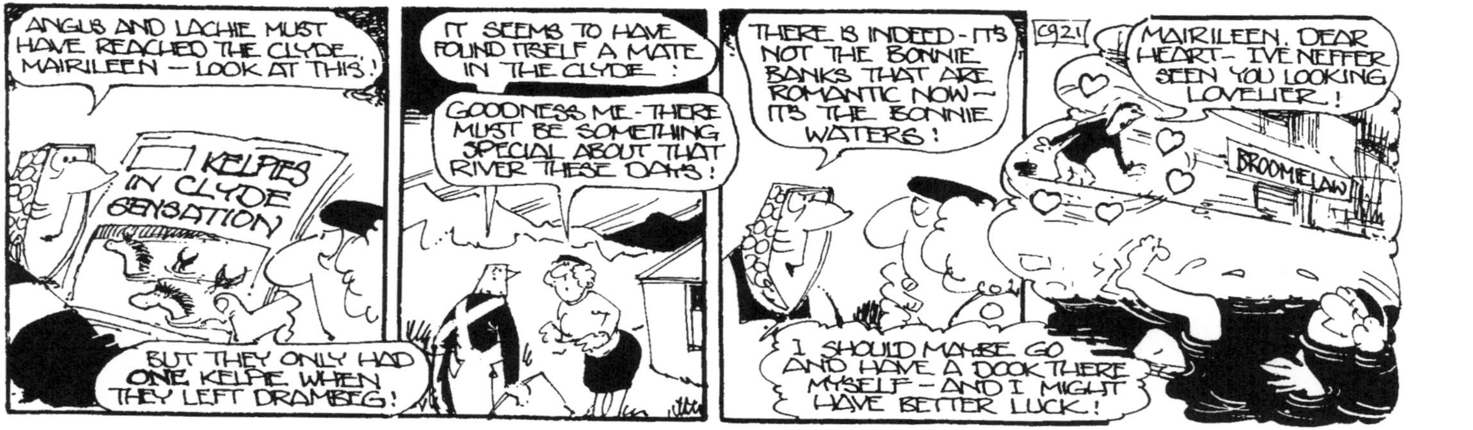
ANGUS AND LACHIE MUST HAVE REACHED THE CLYDE, MAIRILEEN — LOOK AT THIS!
KELPIES IN CLYDE SENSATION
BUT THEY ONLY HAD ONE KELPIE WHEN THEY LEFT DRAMBEG!
IT SEEMS TO HAVE FOUND ITSELF A MATE IN THE CLYDE!
GOODNESS ME - THERE MUST BE SOMETHING SPECIAL ABOUT THAT RIVER THESE DAYS!
THERE IS INDEED - IT'S NOT THE BONNIE BANKS THAT ARE ROMANTIC NOW - IT'S THE BONNIE WATERS!
I SHOULD MAYBE GO AND HAVE A DOOK THERE MYSELF - AND I MIGHT HAVE BETTER LUCK!
C921
MAIRILEEN, DEAR HEART - I'VE NEFFER SEEN YOU LOOKING LOVELIER!
BROOMIELAW

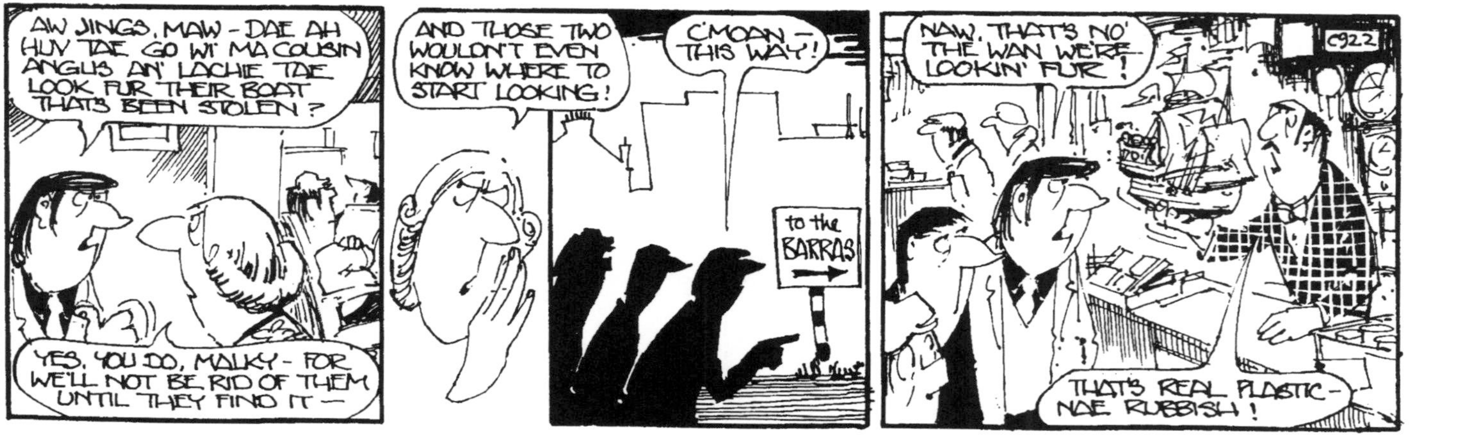
AW JINGS, MAW - DAE AH HUV TAE GO WI' MA COUSIN ANGUS AN' LACHIE TAE LOOK FUR THEIR BOAT THAT'S BEEN STOLEN?
YES, YOU DO, MALKY - FOR WE'LL NOT BE RID OF THEM UNTIL THEY FIND IT —
AND THOSE TWO WOULDN'T EVEN KNOW WHERE TO START LOOKING!
C'MOAN - THIS WAY!
to the BARRAS
C922
NAW, THAT'S NO' THE WAN WE'RE LOOKIN' FUR!
THAT'S REAL PLASTIC - NAE RUBBISH!

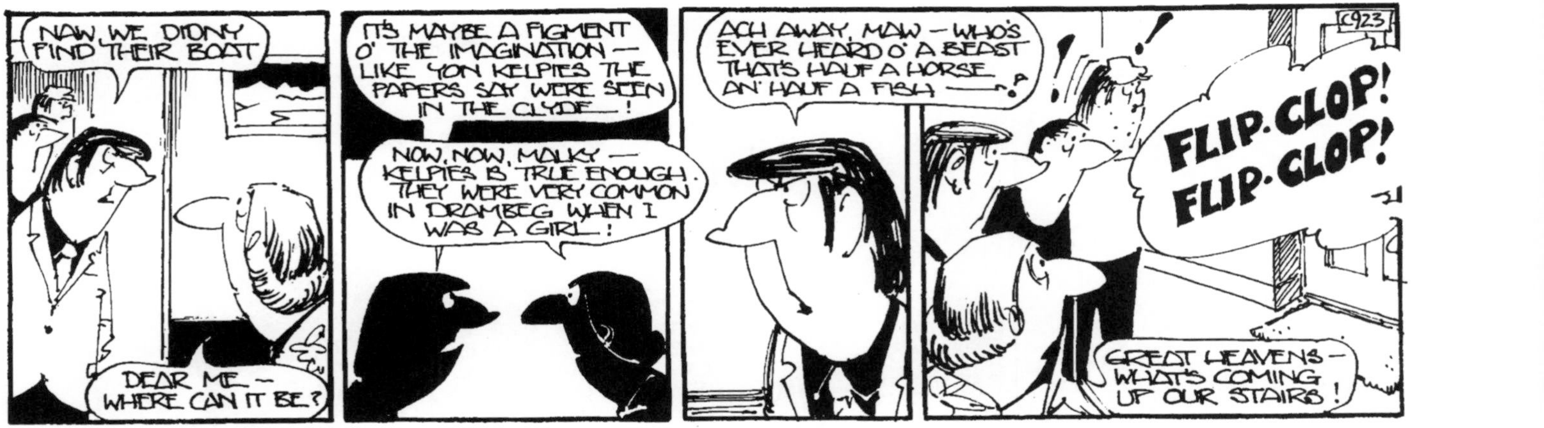
NAW, WE DIDNY FIND THEIR BOAT
DEAR ME — WHERE CAN IT BE?
IT'S MAYBE A FIGMENT O' THE IMAGINATION — LIKE YON KELPIES THE PAPERS SAY WERE SEEN IN THE CLYDE —!
NOW, NOW, MALKY — KELPIES IS TRUE ENOUGH. THEY WERE VERY COMMON IN DRAMBEG WHEN I WAS A GIRL!
ACH AWAY, MAW — WHO'S EVER HEARD O' A BEAST THAT'S HAUF A HORSE AN' HAUF A FISH —?
C923
FLIP-CLOP! FLIP-CLOP!
GREAT HEAVENS — WHAT'S COMING UP OUR STAIRS!

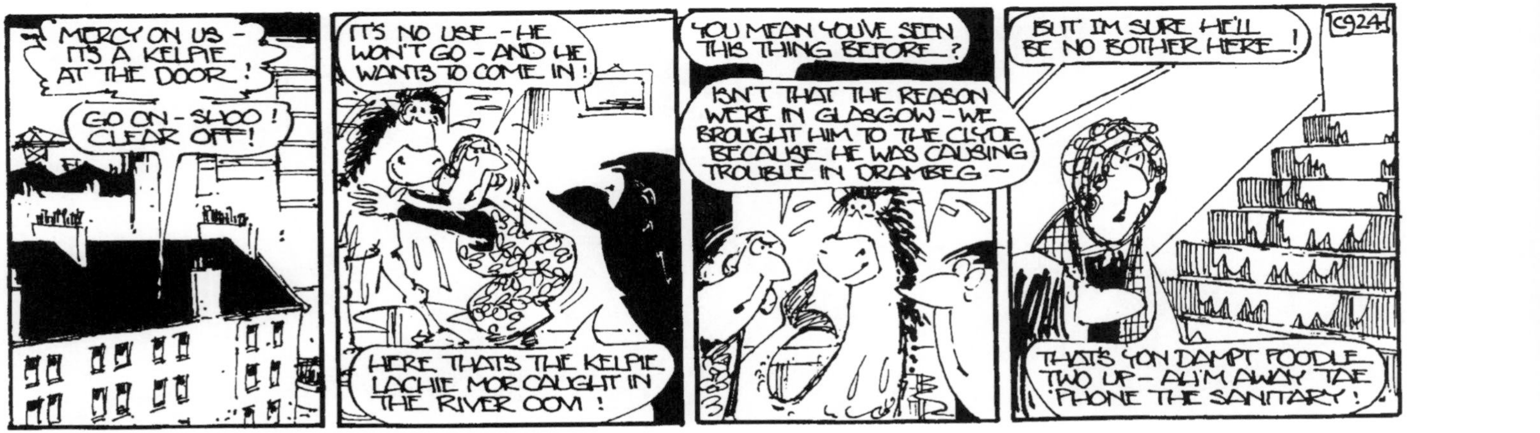
MERCY ON US — IT'S A KELPIE AT THE DOOR!
GO ON - SHOO! CLEAR OFF!
IT'S NO USE - HE WON'T GO - AND HE WANTS TO COME IN!
HERE THAT'S THE KELPIE LACHIE MOR CAUGHT IN THE RIVER OOM!
YOU MEAN YOU'VE SEEN THIS THING BEFORE?
ISN'T THAT THE REASON WE'RE IN GLASGOW - WE BROUGHT HIM TO THE CLYDE BECAUSE HE WAS CAUSING TROUBLE IN DRAMBEG —
C924
BUT I'M SURE HE'LL BE NO BOTHER HERE!
THAT'S YON DAMPT POODLE TWO UP - AH'M AWAY TAE 'PHONE THE SANITARY!

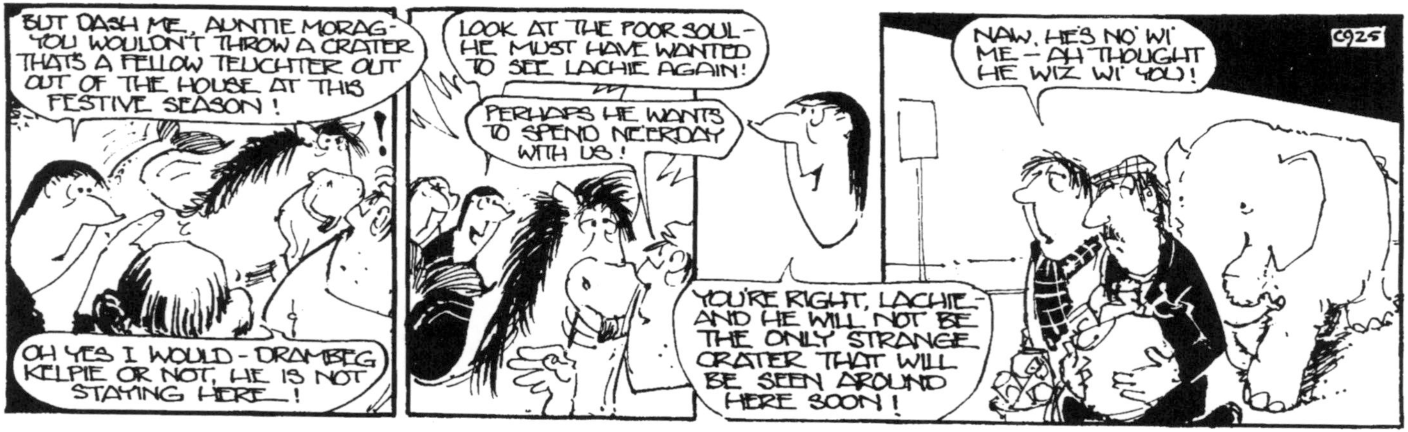
BUT DASH ME, AUNTIE MORAG- YOU WOULDN'T THROW A CRATER THAT'S A FELLOW TEUCHTER OUT OUT OF THE HOUSE AT THIS FESTIVE SEASON!
OH YES I WOULD - DRAMBEG KELPIE OR NOT, HE IS NOT STAYING HERE!
LOOK AT THE POOR SOUL- HE MUST HAVE WANTED TO SEE LACHIE AGAIN!
PERHAPS HE WANTS TO SPEND NEERDAY WITH US!
YOU'RE RIGHT, LACHIE- AND HE WILL NOT BE THE ONLY STRANGE CRATER THAT WILL BE SEEN AROUND HERE SOON!
C925
NAW, HE'S NO' WI' ME - AH THOUGHT HE WIZ WI' YOU!

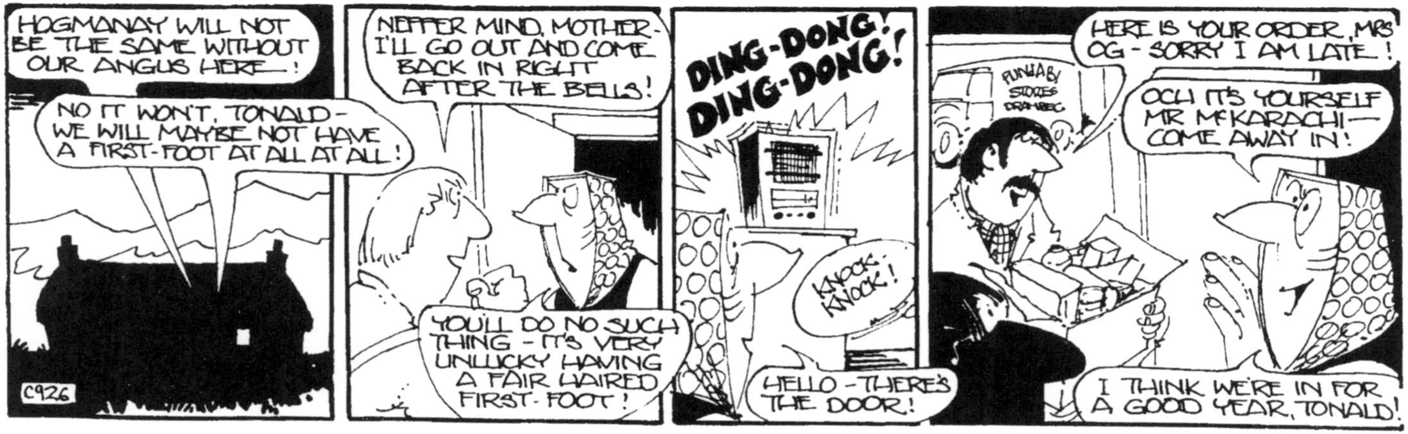
HOGMANAY WILL NOT BE THE SAME WITHOUT OUR ANGUS HERE!
NO IT WON'T, TONALD- WE WILL MAYBE NOT HAVE A FIRST-FOOT AT ALL AT ALL!
C926
NEFFER MIND, MOTHER- I'LL GO OUT AND COME BACK IN RIGHT AFTER THE BELLS!
YOU'LL DO NO SUCH THING - IT'S VERY UNLUCKY HAVING A FAIR HAIRED FIRST-FOOT!
DING-DONG! DING-DONG!
KNOCK KNOCK!
HELLO - THERE'S THE DOOR!
PUNJABI STORES DRAMBEG
HERE IS YOUR ORDER, MRS OG - SORRY I AM LATE!
OCH IT'S YOURSELF MR McKARACHI— COME AWAY IN!
I THINK WE'RE IN FOR A GOOD YEAR, TONALD!

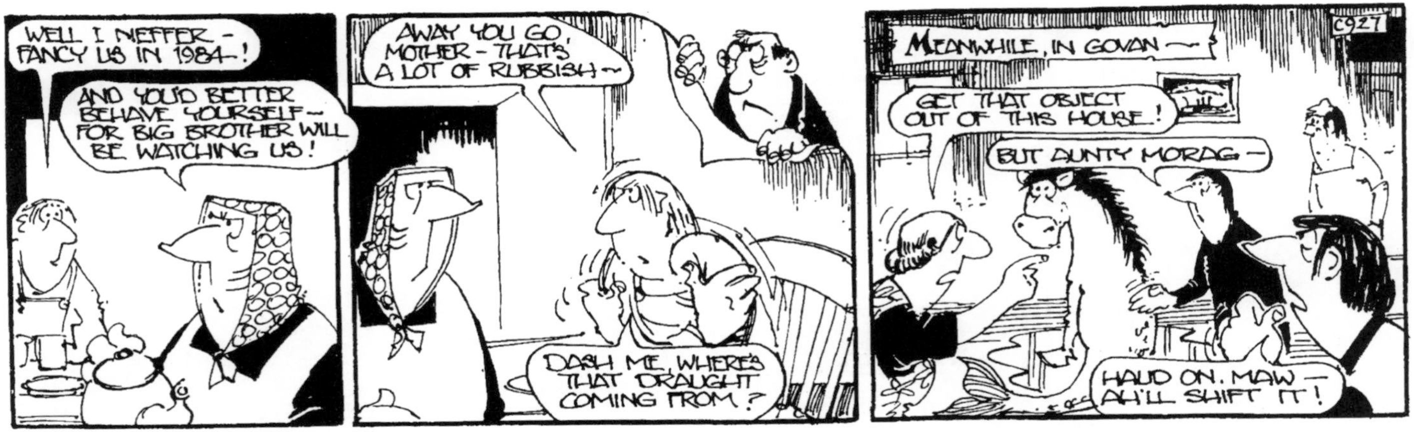
WELL I NEFFER - FANCY US IN 1984!
AND YOU'D BETTER BEHAVE YOURSELF - FOR BIG BROTHER WILL BE WATCHING US!
AWAY YOU GO, MOTHER - THAT'S A LOT OF RUBBISH ~
DASH ME, WHERE'S THAT DRAUGHT COMING FROM?
C927
MEANWHILE, IN GOVAN ~
GET THAT OBJECT OUT OF THIS HOUSE!
BUT AUNTY MORAG -
HAUD ON, MAW - AH'LL SHIFT IT!

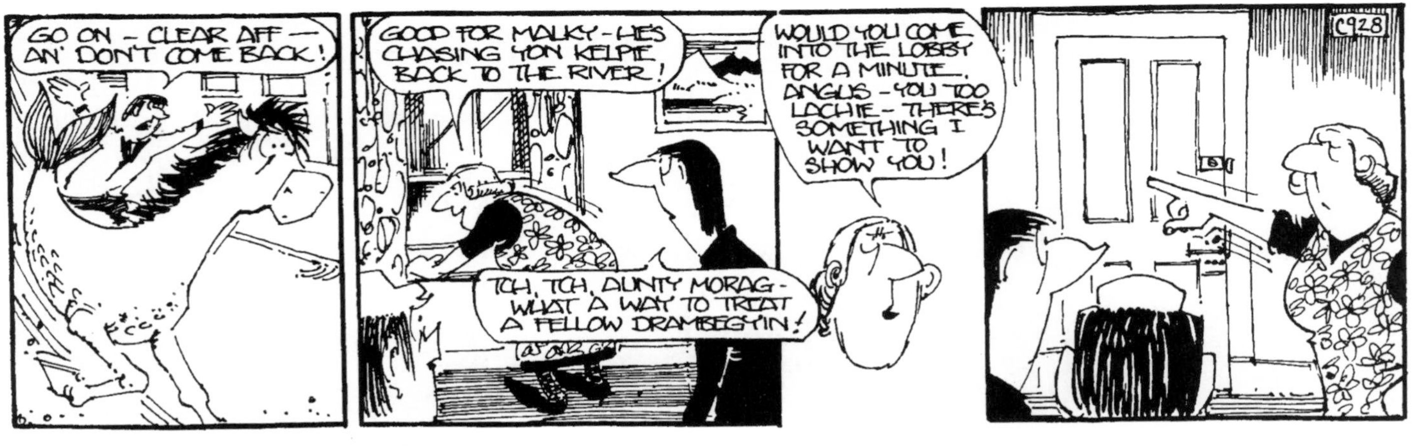
GO ON - CLEAR AFF - AN' DON'T COME BACK!
GOOD FOR MALKY - HE'S CHASING YON KELPIE BACK TO THE RIVER!
TCH, TCH, AUNTY MORAG - WHAT A WAY TO TREAT A FELLOW DRAMBEGYIN!
WOULD YOU COME INTO THE LOBBY FOR A MINUTE, ANGUS - YOU TOO LACHIE - THERE'S SOMETHING I WANT TO SHOW YOU!
C928

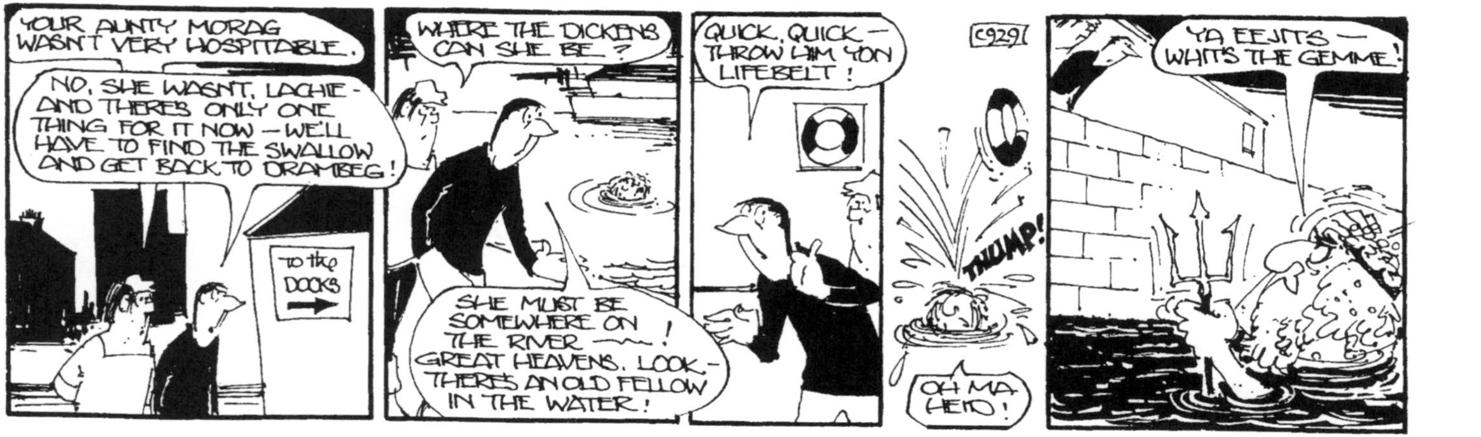
YOUR AUNTY MORAG WASN'T VERY HOSPITABLE.
NO, SHE WASN'T, LACHIE - AND THERE'S ONLY ONE THING FOR IT NOW - WE'LL HAVE TO FIND THE SWALLOW AND GET BACK TO DRAMBEG!
TO the DOCKS
WHERE THE DICKENS CAN SHE BE?
SHE MUST BE SOMEWHERE ON THE RIVER ~~! GREAT HEAVENS, LOOK - THERE'S AN OLD FELLOW IN THE WATER!
QUICK, QUICK - THROW HIM YON LIFEBELT!
c929
THUMP!
OH MA HEID!
YA EEJITS - WHIT'S THE GEMME!

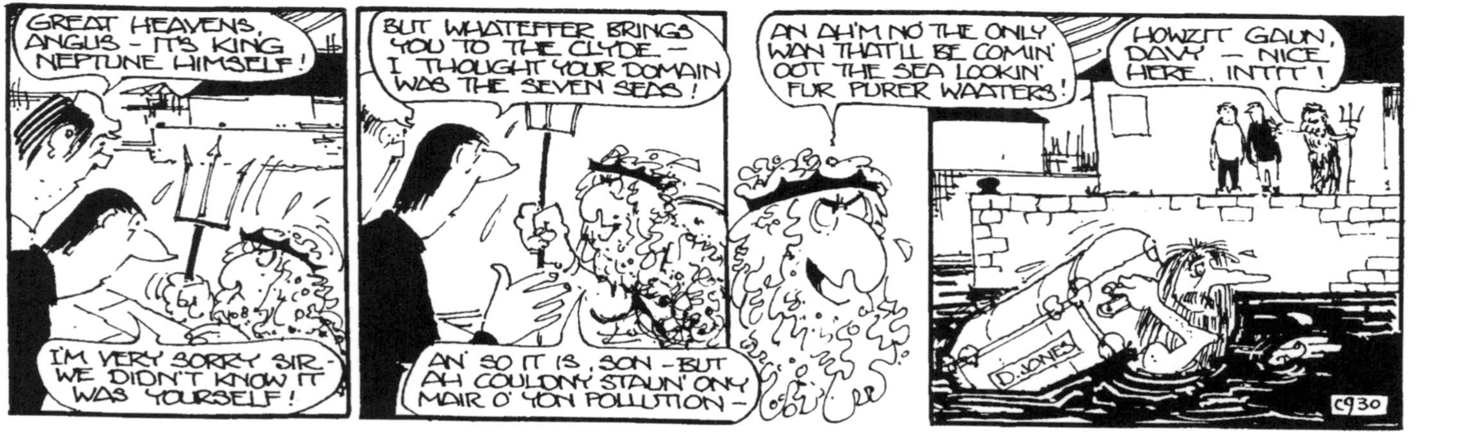
GREAT HEAVENS, ANGUS - IT'S KING NEPTUNE HIMSELF!
I'M VERY SORRY SIR - WE DIDN'T KNOW IT WAS YOURSELF!
BUT WHATEFFER BRINGS YOU TO THE CLYDE - I THOUGHT YOUR DOMAIN WAS THE SEVEN SEAS!
AN' SO IT IS, SON - BUT AH COULDNY STAUN' ONY MAIR O' YON POLLUTION -
AN AH'M NO THE ONLY WAN THAT'LL BE COMIN' OOT THE SEA LOOKIN' FUR PURER WAATERS!
HOWZIT GAUN, DAVY - NICE HERE, INTIT!
D. JONES
c930

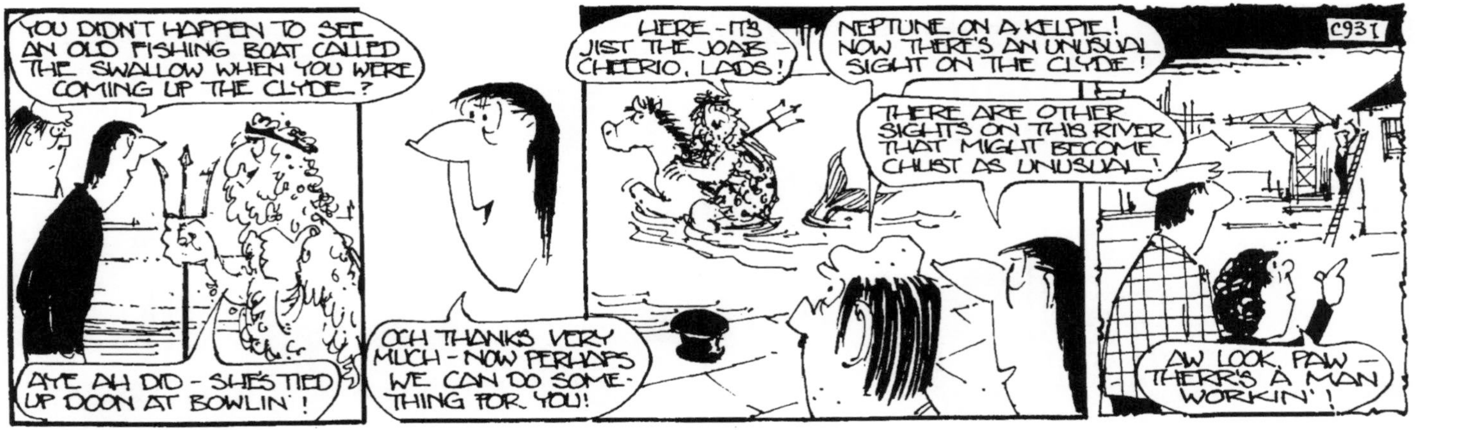
YOU DIDN'T HAPPEN TO SEE AN OLD FISHING BOAT CALLED THE SWALLOW WHEN YOU WERE COMING UP THE CLYDE?
AYE AH DID - SHE'S TIED UP DOON AT BOWLIN'!
OCH THANKS VERY MUCH - NOW PERHAPS WE CAN DO SOMETHING FOR YOU!
HERE - IT'S JIST THE JOAB - CHEERIO, LADS!
NEPTUNE ON A KELPIE! NOW THERE'S AN UNUSUAL SIGHT ON THE CLYDE!
THERE ARE OTHER SIGHTS ON THIS RIVER THAT MIGHT BECOME CHUST AS UNUSUAL!
C931
AW LOOK, PAW - THERR'S A MAN WORKIN'!

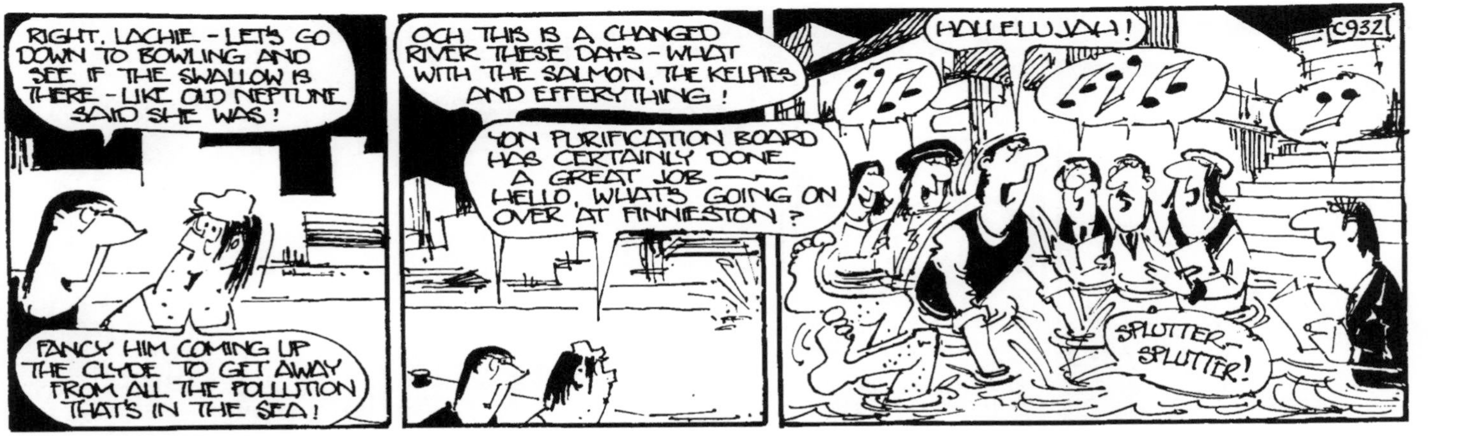
RIGHT, LACHIE - LET'S GO DOWN TO BOWLING AND SEE IF THE SWALLOW IS THERE - LIKE OLD NEPTUNE SAID SHE WAS!
FANCY HIM COMING UP THE CLYDE TO GET AWAY FROM ALL THE POLLUTION THAT'S IN THE SEA!
OCH THIS IS A CHANGED RIVER THESE DAYS - WHAT WITH THE SALMON, THE KELPIES AND EFFERYTHING!
YON PURIFICATION BOARD HAS CERTAINLY DONE A GREAT JOB — HELLO, WHAT'S GOING ON OVER AT FINNIESTON?
HALLELUJAH!
C932
SPLUTTER - SPLUTTER!

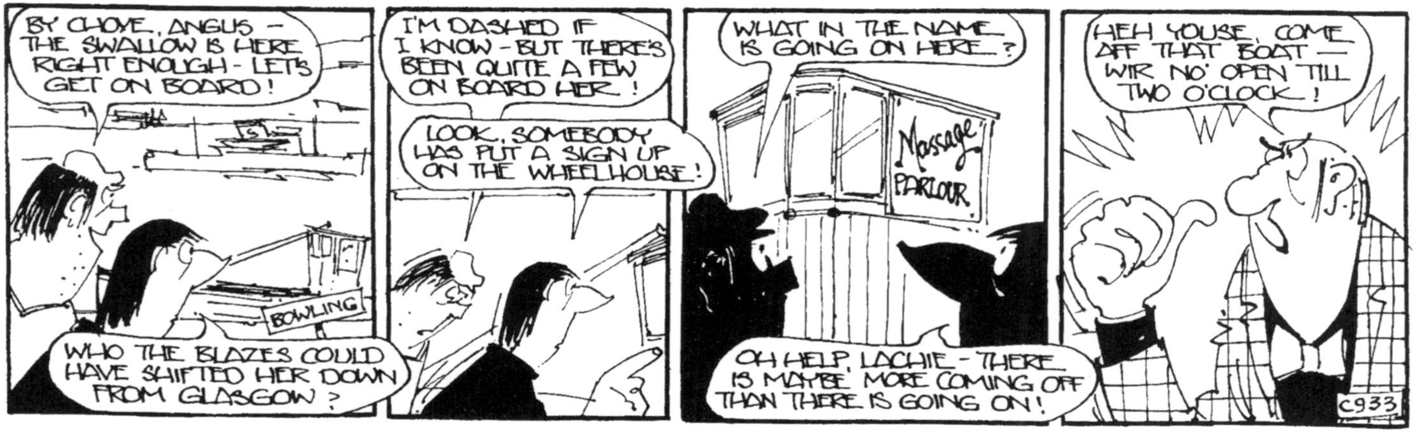
BY CHOYE, ANGUS — THE SWALLOW IS HERE RIGHT ENOUGH — LET'S GET ON BOARD!
BOWLING
WHO THE BLAZES COULD HAVE SHIFTED HER DOWN FROM GLASGOW?
I'M DASHED IF I KNOW — BUT THERE'S BEEN QUITE A FEW ON BOARD HER!
LOOK, SOMEBODY HAS PUT A SIGN UP ON THE WHEELHOUSE!
WHAT IN THE NAME IS GOING ON HERE?
Massage PARLOUR
OH HELP, LACHIE — THERE IS MAYBE MORE COMING OFF THAN THERE IS GOING ON!
HEH YOUSE, COME AFF THAT BOAT — WIR NO' OPEN TILL TWO O'CLOCK!
C933

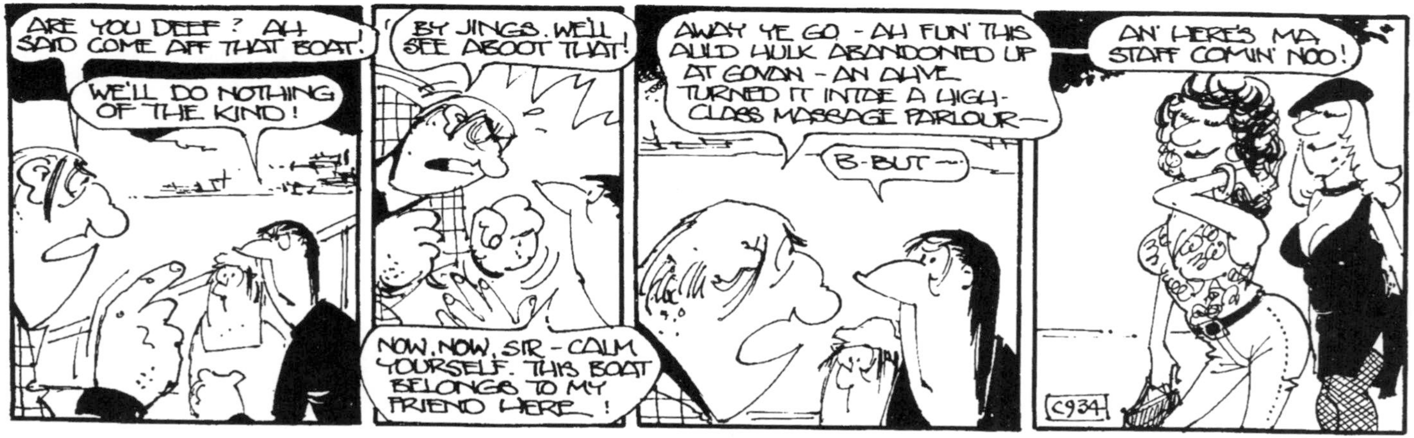
ARE YOU DEEF? AH SAID COME AFF THAT BOAT!
WE'LL DO NOTHING OF THE KIND!
BY JINGS, WE'LL SEE ABOOT THAT!
NOW, NOW, SIR — CALM YOURSELF. THIS BOAT BELONGS TO MY FRIEND HERE!
AWAY YE GO — AH FUN' THIS AULD HULK ABANDONED UP AT GOVAN — AN' AH'VE TURNED IT INTAE A HIGH-CLASS MASSAGE PARLOUR—
B-BUT—
AN' HERE'S MA STAFF COMIN' NOO!
C934

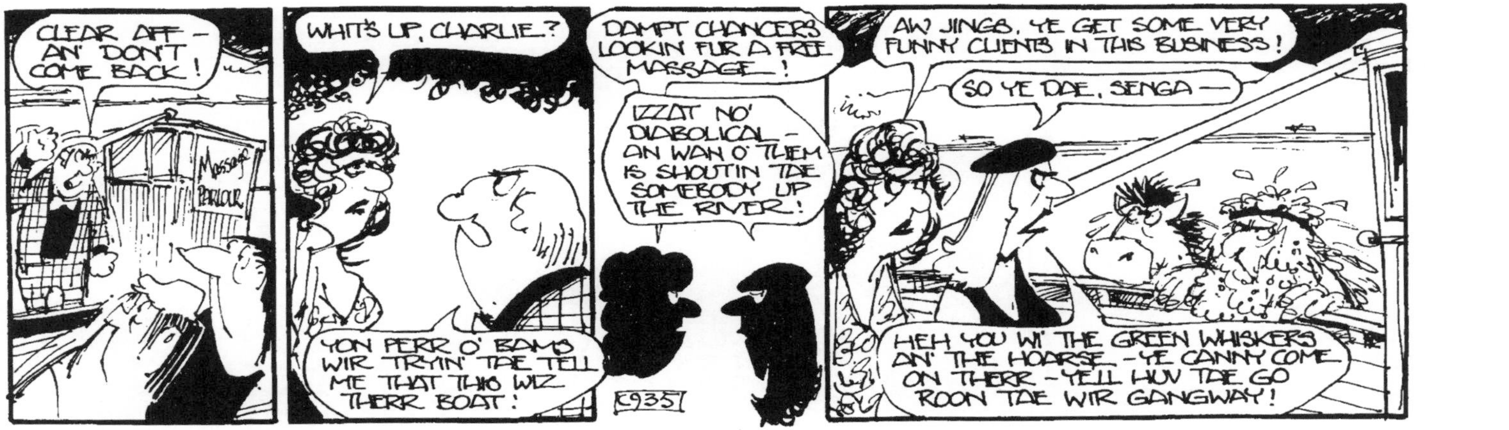
CLEAR AFF — AN' DON'T COME BACK!
Massage PARLOUR
WHIT'S UP, CHARLIE?
YON PERR O' BAMS WIR TRYIN' TAE TELL ME THAT THIS WIZ THERR BOAT!
DAMPT CHANCERS LOOKIN' FUR A FREE MASSAGE!
IZZAT NO' DIABOLICAL — AN WAN O' THEM IS SHOUTIN TAE SOMEBODY UP THE RIVER!
C935
AW JINGS, YE GET SOME VERY FUNNY CLIENTS IN THIS BUSINESS!
SO YE DAE, SENGA —
HEH YOU WI' THE GREEN WHISKERS AN' THE HOARSE — YE CANNY COME ON THERR — YE'LL HUV TAE GO ROON TAE WIR GANGWAY!

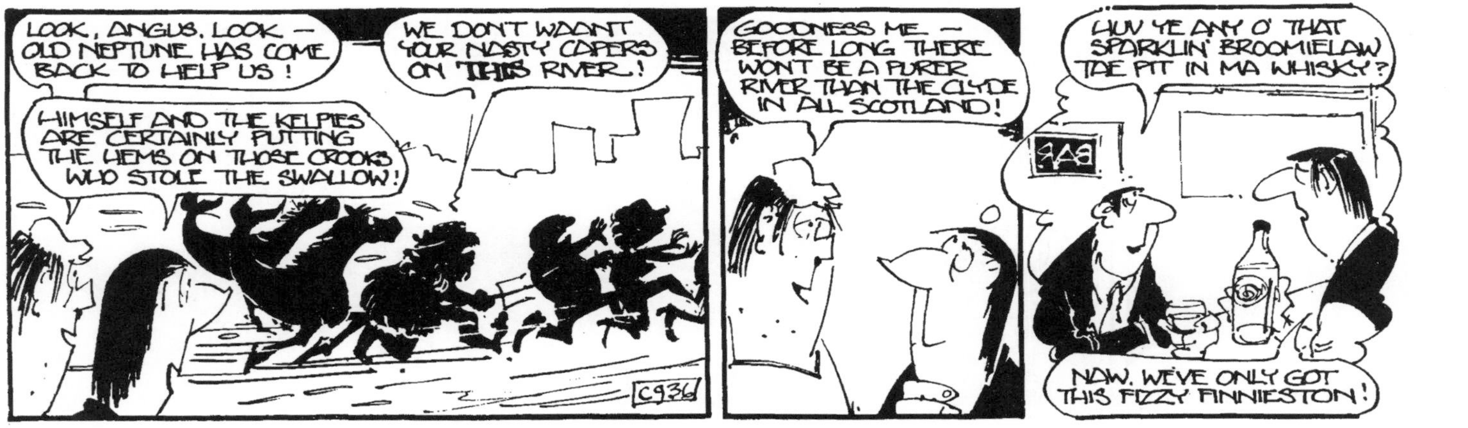
LOOK, ANGUS, LOOK — OLD NEPTUNE HAS COME BACK TO HELP US!
HIMSELF AND THE KELPIES ARE CERTAINLY PUTTING THE HEMS ON THOSE CROOKS WHO STOLE THE SWALLOW!
WE DON'T WAANT YOUR NASTY CAPERS ON THIS RIVER!
C936
GOODNESS ME — BEFORE LONG THERE WON'T BE A PURER RIVER THAN THE CLYDE IN ALL SCOTLAND!
HUV YE ANY O' THAT SPARKLIN' BROOMIELAW TAE PIT IN MA WHISKY?
NAW. WE'VE ONLY GOT THIS FIZZY FINNIESTON!

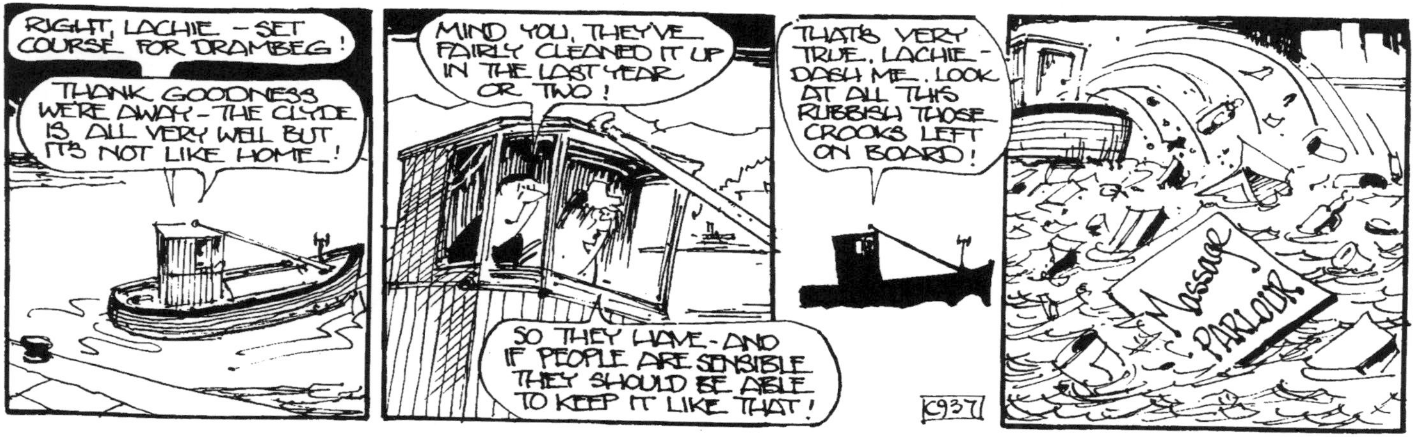
RIGHT, LACHIE - SET COURSE FOR DRAMBEG!
THANK GOODNESS WE'RE AWAY - THE CLYDE IS ALL VERY WELL BUT IT'S NOT LIKE HOME!
MIND YOU, THEY'VE FAIRLY CLEANED IT UP IN THE LAST YEAR OR TWO!
SO THEY HAVE - AND IF PEOPLE ARE SENSIBLE THEY SHOULD BE ABLE TO KEEP IT LIKE THAT!
THAT'S VERY TRUE, LACHIE - DASH ME, LOOK AT ALL THIS RUBBISH THOSE CROOKS LEFT ON BOARD!
K937
MASSAGE PARLOUR

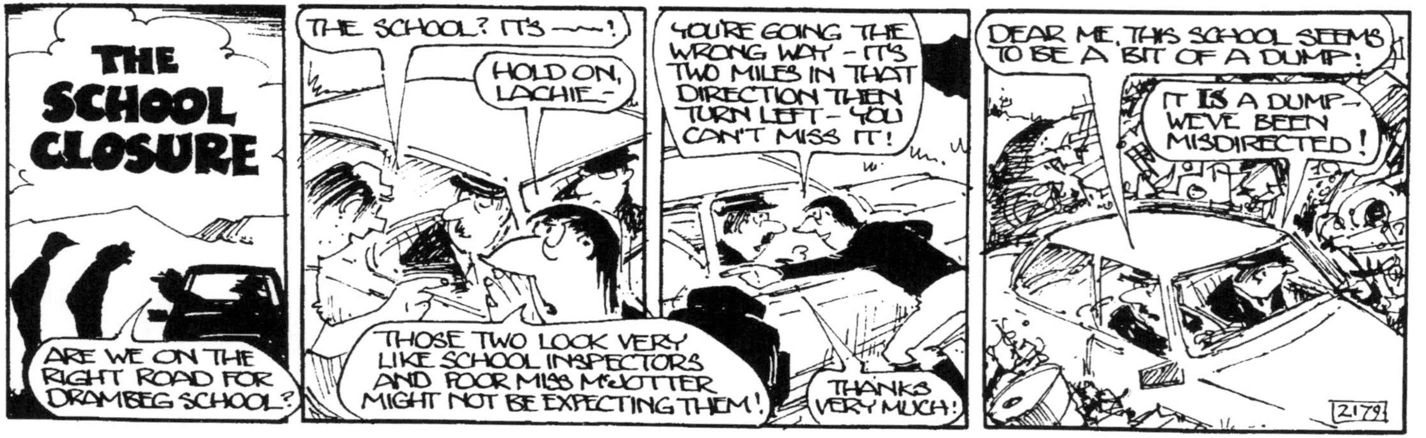
THE SCHOOL CLOSURE
ARE WE ON THE RIGHT ROAD FOR DRAMBEG SCHOOL?
THE SCHOOL? IT'S ---!
HOLD ON, LACHIE -
THOSE TWO LOOK VERY LIKE SCHOOL INSPECTORS AND POOR MISS McJOTTER MIGHT NOT BE EXPECTING THEM!
YOU'RE GOING THE WRONG WAY - IT'S TWO MILES IN THAT DIRECTION THEN TURN LEFT - YOU CAN'T MISS IT!
THANKS VERY MUCH!
DEAR ME, THIS SCHOOL SEEMS TO BE A BIT OF A DUMP!
IT IS A DUMP - WE'VE BEEN MISDIRECTED!
2179

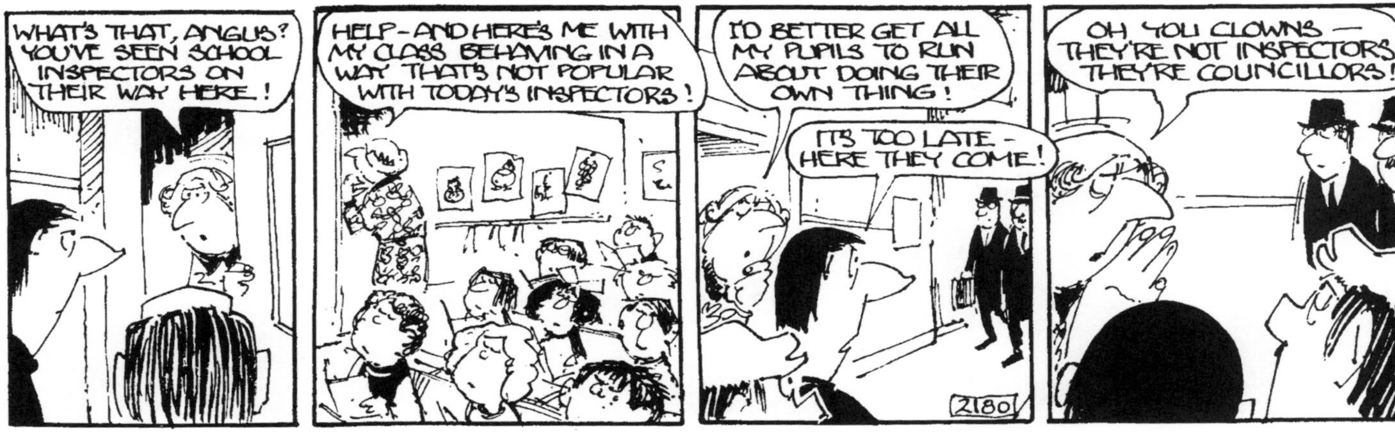
WHAT'S THAT, ANGUS? YOU'VE SEEN SCHOOL INSPECTORS ON THEIR WAY HERE!
HELP - AND HERE'S ME WITH MY CLASS BEHAVING IN A WAY THAT'S NOT POPULAR WITH TODAY'S INSPECTORS!
I'D BETTER GET ALL MY PUPILS TO RUN ABOUT DOING THEIR OWN THING!
IT'S TOO LATE - HERE THEY COME!
2180
OH YOU CLOWNS - THEY'RE NOT INSPECTORS - THEY'RE COUNCILLORS!

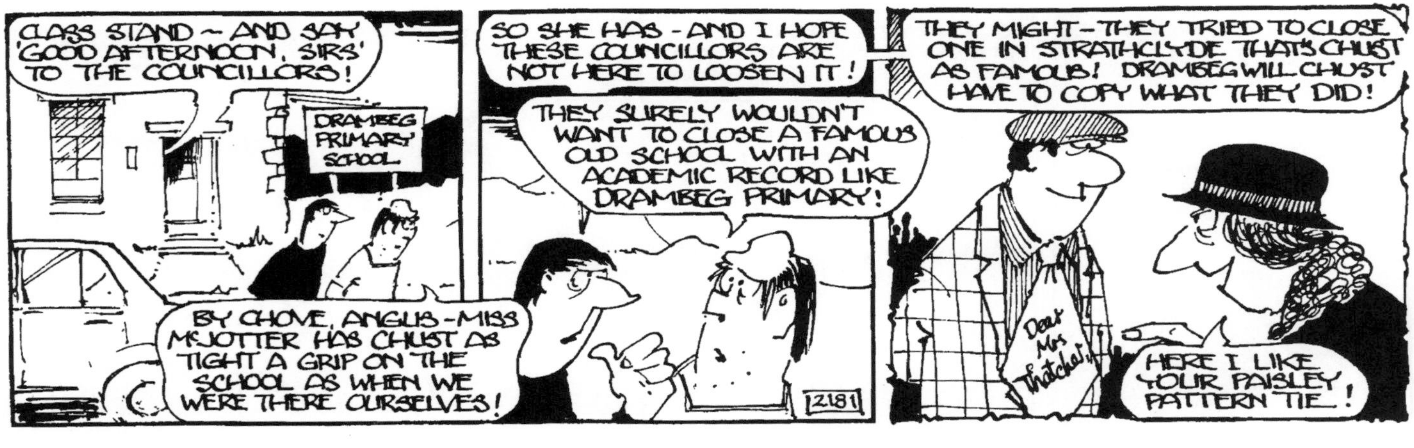
CLASS STAND - AND SAY 'GOOD AFTERNOON, SIRS' TO THE COUNCILLORS!
DRAMBEG PRIMARY SCHOOL
BY CHOVE, ANGUS - MISS McJOTTER HAS CHUST AS TIGHT A GRIP ON THE SCHOOL AS WHEN WE WERE THERE OURSELVES!
SO SHE HAS - AND I HOPE THESE COUNCILLORS ARE NOT HERE TO LOOSEN IT!
THEY SURELY WOULDN'T WANT TO CLOSE A FAMOUS OLD SCHOOL WITH AN ACADEMIC RECORD LIKE DRAMBEG PRIMARY!
2181
THEY MIGHT - THEY TRIED TO CLOSE ONE IN STRATHCLYDE THAT'S CHUST AS FAMOUS! DRAMBEG WILL CHUST HAVE TO COPY WHAT THEY DID!
Dear Mrs Thatcher
HERE I LIKE YOUR PAISLEY PATTERN TIE!

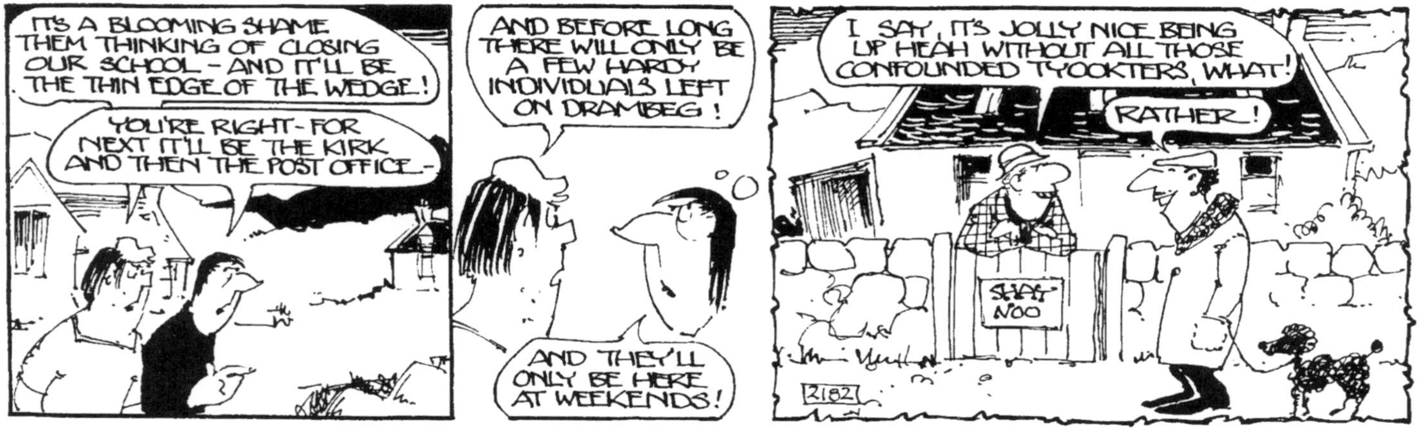
IT'S A BLOOMING SHAME THEM THINKING OF CLOSING OUR SCHOOL - AND IT'LL BE THE THIN EDGE OF THE WEDGE!
YOU'RE RIGHT - FOR NEXT IT'LL BE THE KIRK AND THEN THE POST OFFICE -
AND BEFORE LONG THERE WILL ONLY BE A FEW HARDY INDIVIDUALS LEFT ON DRAMBEG!
AND THEY'LL ONLY BE HERE AT WEEKENDS!
I SAY, IT'S JOLLY NICE BEING UP HEAH WITHOUT ALL THOSE CONFOUNDED TYOOKTERS, WHAT!
RATHER!
2182

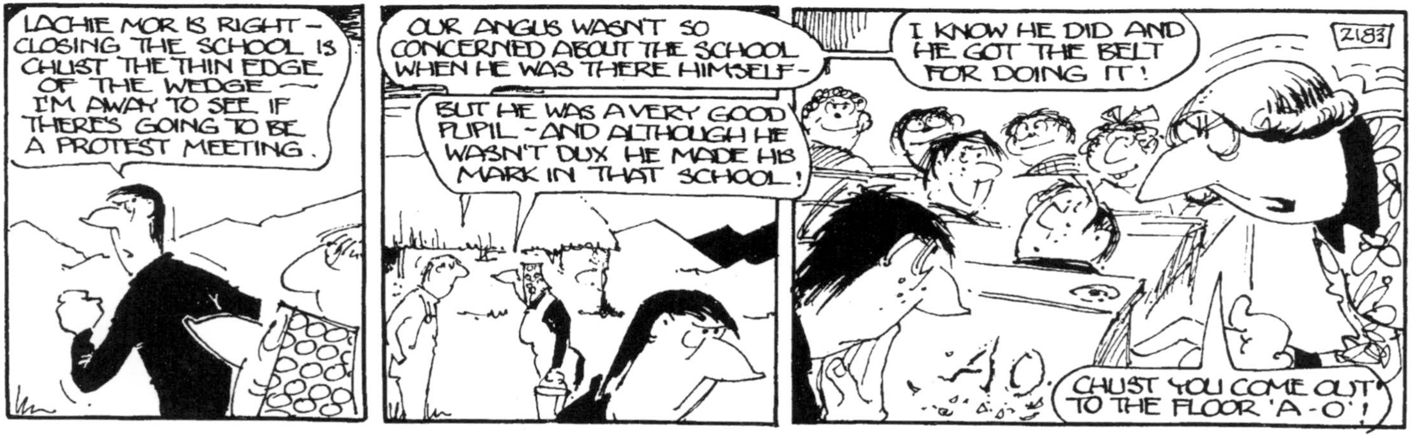
LACHIE MOR IS RIGHT - CLOSING THE SCHOOL IS CHUST THE THIN EDGE OF THE WEDGE - I'M AWAY TO SEE IF THERE'S GOING TO BE A PROTEST MEETING.
OUR ANGUS WASN'T SO CONCERNED ABOUT THE SCHOOL WHEN HE WAS THERE HIMSELF -
BUT HE WAS A VERY GOOD PUPIL - AND ALTHOUGH HE WASN'T DUX HE MADE HIS MARK IN THAT SCHOOL!
I KNOW HE DID AND HE GOT THE BELT FOR DOING IT!
2183
CHUST YOU COME OUT TO THE FLOOR 'A - O'!

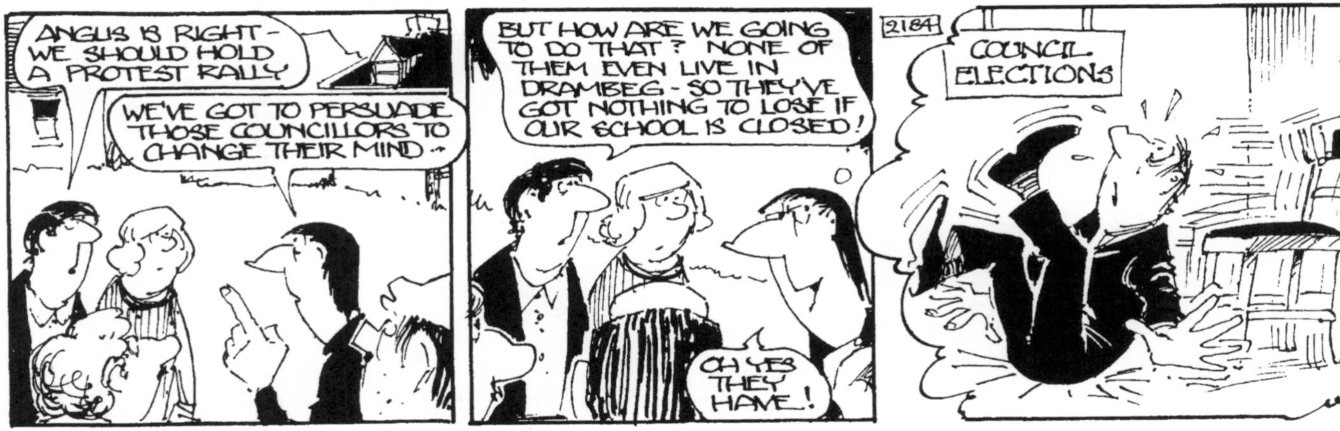
ANGUS IS RIGHT - WE SHOULD HOLD A PROTEST RALLY
WE'VE GOT TO PERSUADE THOSE COUNCILLORS TO CHANGE THEIR MIND -
BUT HOW ARE WE GOING TO DO THAT? NONE OF THEM EVEN LIVE IN DRAMBEG - SO THEY'VE GOT NOTHING TO LOSE IF OUR SCHOOL IS CLOSED!
OH YES THEY HAVE!
2184
COUNCIL ELECTIONS

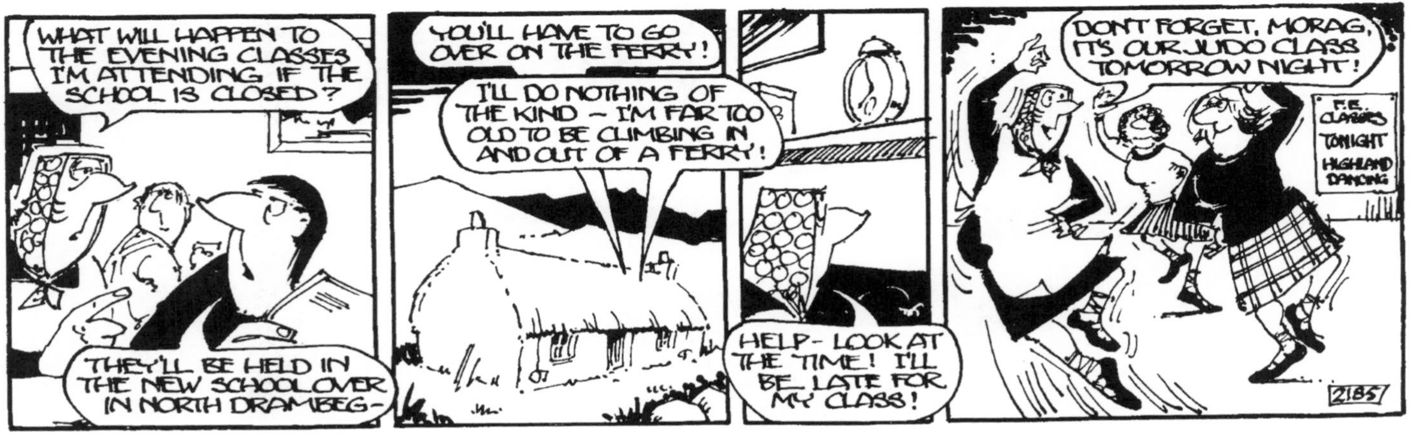
WHAT WILL HAPPEN TO THE EVENING CLASSES I'M ATTENDING IF THE SCHOOL IS CLOSED?
THEY'LL BE HELD IN THE NEW SCHOOL OVER IN NORTH DRAMBEG -
YOU'LL HAVE TO GO OVER ON THE FERRY!
I'LL DO NOTHING OF THE KIND - I'M FAIR TOO OLD TO BE CLIMBING IN AND OUT OF A FERRY!
HELP - LOOK AT THE TIME! I'LL BE LATE FOR MY CLASS!
DON'T FORGET, MORAG, IT'S OUR JUDO CLASS TOMORROW NIGHT!
F.E. CLASSES
TONIGHT
HIGHLAND DANCING
2185

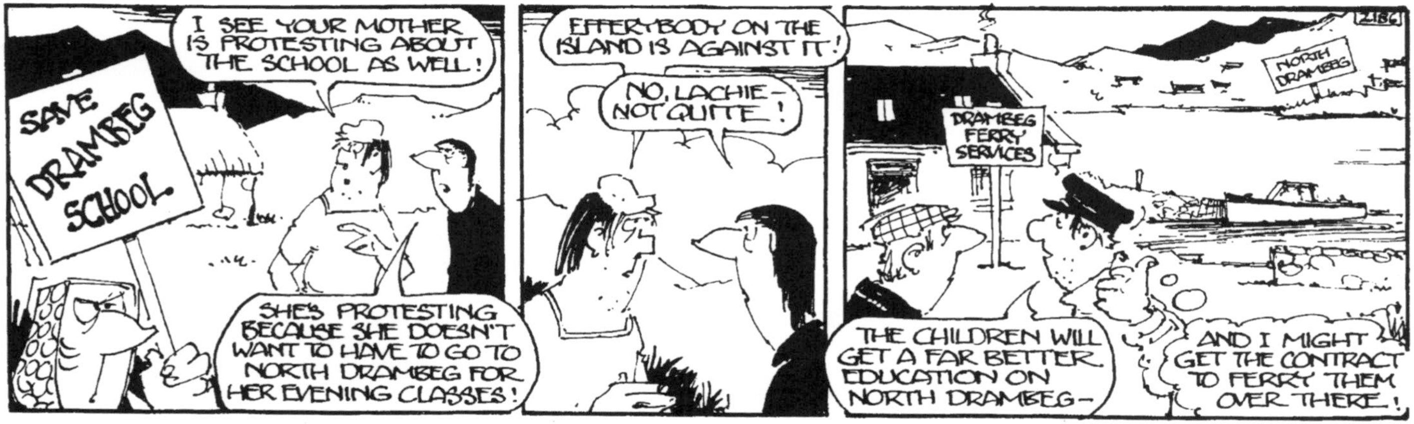
I SEE YOUR MOTHER IS PROTESTING ABOUT THE SCHOOL AS WELL!
SAVE DRAMBEG SCHOOL
SHE'S PROTESTING BECAUSE SHE DOESN'T WANT TO HAVE TO GO TO NORTH DRAMBEG FOR HER EVENING CLASSES!
EFFERYBODY ON THE ISLAND IS AGAINST IT!
NO, LACHIE - NOT QUITE!
2186
NORTH DRAMBEG
DRAMBEG FERRY SERVICES
THE CHILDREN WILL GET A FAR BETTER EDUCATION ON NORTH DRAMBEG -
AND I MIGHT GET THE CONTRACT TO FERRY THEM OVER THERE!

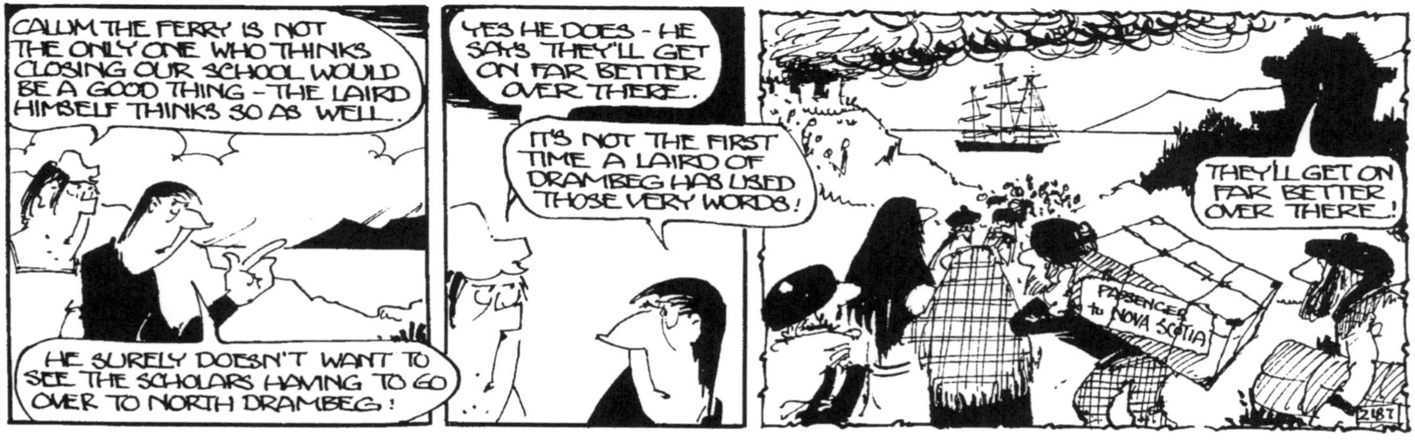
CALUM THE FERRY IS NOT THE ONLY ONE WHO THINKS CLOSING OUR SCHOOL WOULD BE A GOOD THING - THE LAIRD HIMSELF THINKS SO AS WELL.
HE SURELY DOESN'T WANT TO SEE THE SCHOLARS HAVING TO GO OVER TO NORTH DRAMBEG!
YES HE DOES - HE SAYS THEY'LL GET ON FAR BETTER OVER THERE.
IT'S NOT THE FIRST TIME A LAIRD OF DRAMBEG HAS USED THOSE VERY WORDS!
THEY'LL GET ON FAR BETTER OVER THERE!
PASSENGER to NOVA SCOTIA
2187

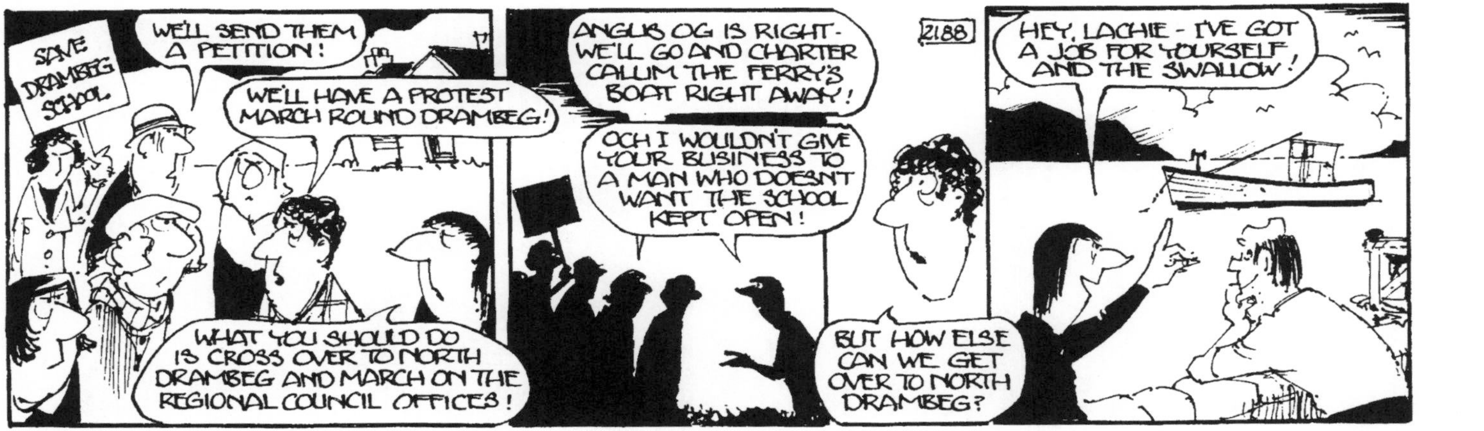
SAVE DRAMBEG SCHOOL
WE'LL SEND THEM A PETITION!
WE'LL HAVE A PROTEST MARCH ROUND DRAMBEG!
WHAT YOU SHOULD DO IS CROSS OVER TO NORTH DRAMBEG AND MARCH ON THE REGIONAL COUNCIL OFFICES!
ANGUS OG IS RIGHT - WE'LL GO AND CHARTER CALUM THE FERRY'S BOAT RIGHT AWAY!
OCH I WOULDN'T GIVE YOUR BUSINESS TO A MAN WHO DOESN'T WANT THE SCHOOL KEPT OPEN!
BUT HOW ELSE CAN WE GET OVER TO NORTH DRAMBEG?
2188
HEY, LACHIE - I'VE GOT A JOB FOR YOURSELF AND THE SWALLOW!

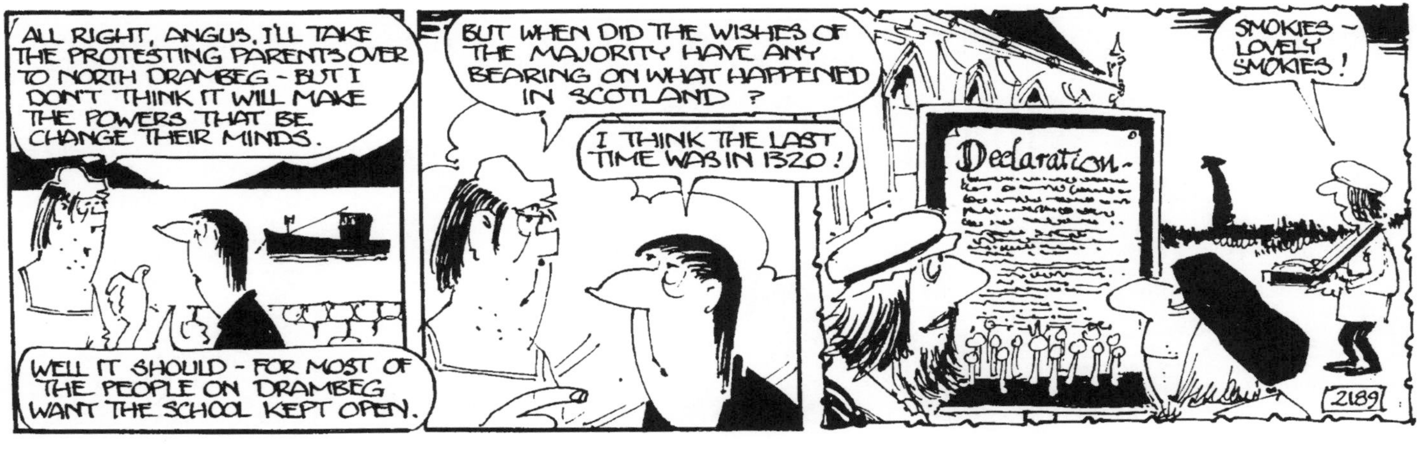
ALL RIGHT, ANGUS, I'LL TAKE THE PROTESTING PARENTS OVER TO NORTH DRAMBEG - BUT I DON'T THINK IT WILL MAKE THE POWERS THAT BE CHANGE THEIR MINDS.
WELL IT SHOULD - FOR MOST OF THE PEOPLE ON DRAMBEG WANT THE SCHOOL KEPT OPEN.
BUT WHEN DID THE WISHES OF THE MAJORITY HAVE ANY BEARING ON WHAT HAPPENED IN SCOTLAND?
I THINK THE LAST TIME WAS IN 1320!
Declaration
SMOKIES ~ LOVELY SMOKIES!
2189

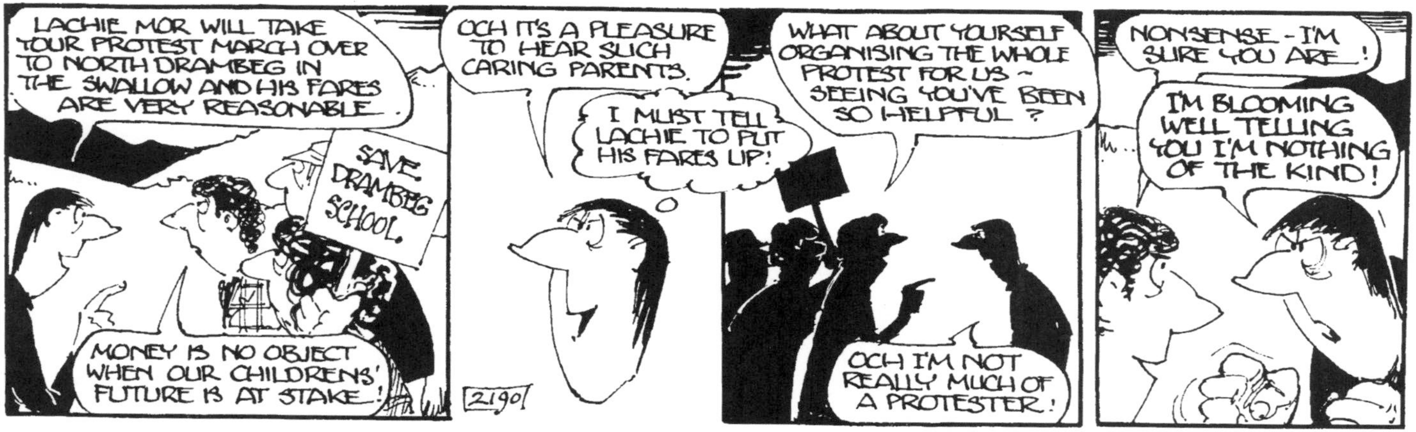
LACHIE MOR WILL TAKE YOUR PROTEST MARCH OVER TO NORTH DRAMBEG IN THE SWALLOW AND HIS FARES ARE VERY REASONABLE.
SAVE DRAMBEG SCHOOL.
MONEY IS NO OBJECT WHEN OUR CHILDRENS' FUTURE IS AT STAKE!
OCH IT'S A PLEASURE TO HEAR SUCH CARING PARENTS.
I MUST TELL LACHIE TO PUT HIS FARES UP!
2190
WHAT ABOUT YOURSELF ORGANISING THE WHOLE PROTEST FOR US ~ SEEING YOU'VE BEEN SO HELPFUL?
OCH I'M NOT REALLY MUCH OF A PROTESTER!
NONSENSE - I'M SURE YOU ARE!
I'M BLOOMING WELL TELLING YOU I'M NOTHING OF THE KIND!

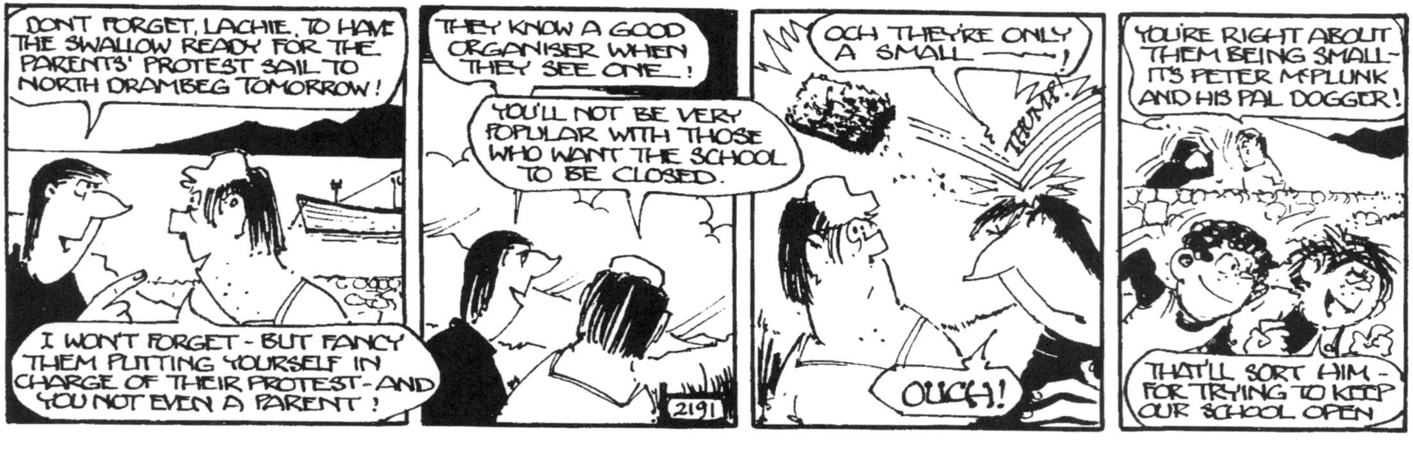
DON'T FORGET, LACHIE, TO HAVE THE SWALLOW READY FOR THE PARENTS' PROTEST SAIL TO NORTH DRAMBEG TOMORROW!
I WON'T FORGET - BUT FANCY THEM PUTTING YOURSELF IN CHARGE OF THEIR PROTEST - AND YOU NOT EVEN A PARENT!
THEY KNOW A GOOD ORGANISER WHEN THEY SEE ONE!
YOU'LL NOT BE VERY POPULAR WITH THOSE WHO WANT THE SCHOOL TO BE CLOSED.
2191
OCH THEY'RE ONLY A SMALL ——!
THUMP!
OUCH!
YOU'RE RIGHT ABOUT THEM BEING SMALL - IT'S PETER McPLUNK AND HIS PAL DOGGER!
THAT'LL SORT HIM - FOR TRYING TO KEEP OUR SCHOOL OPEN

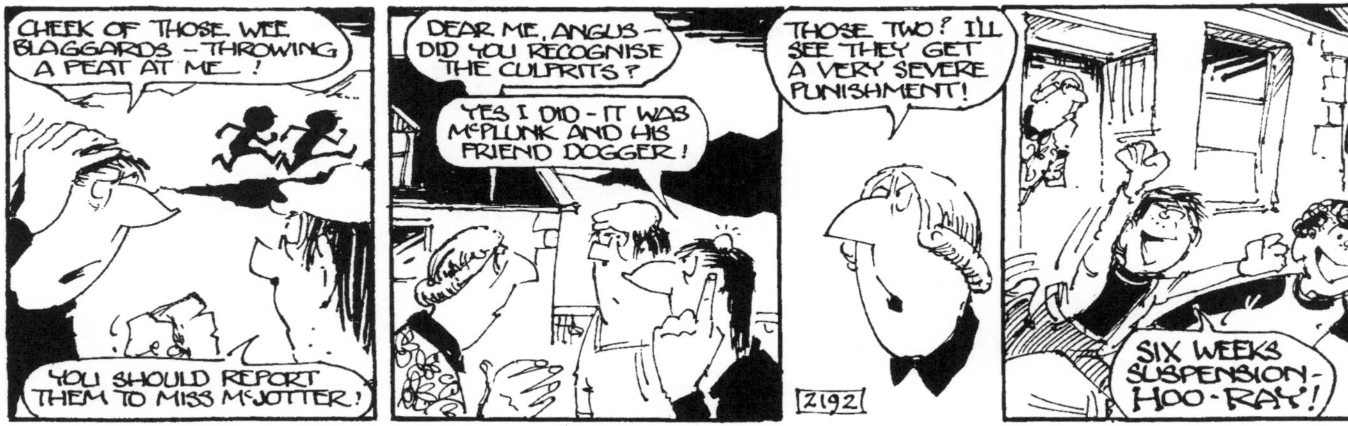
CHEEK OF THOSE WEE BLAGGARDS – THROWING A PEAT AT ME!
YOU SHOULD REPORT THEM TO MISS McJOTTER!
DEAR ME, ANGUS – DID YOU RECOGNISE THE CULPRITS?
YES I DID – IT WAS McPLUNK AND HIS FRIEND DOGGER!
THOSE TWO? I'LL SEE THEY GET A VERY SEVERE PUNISHMENT!
2192
SIX WEEKS SUSPENSION – HOO-RAY!

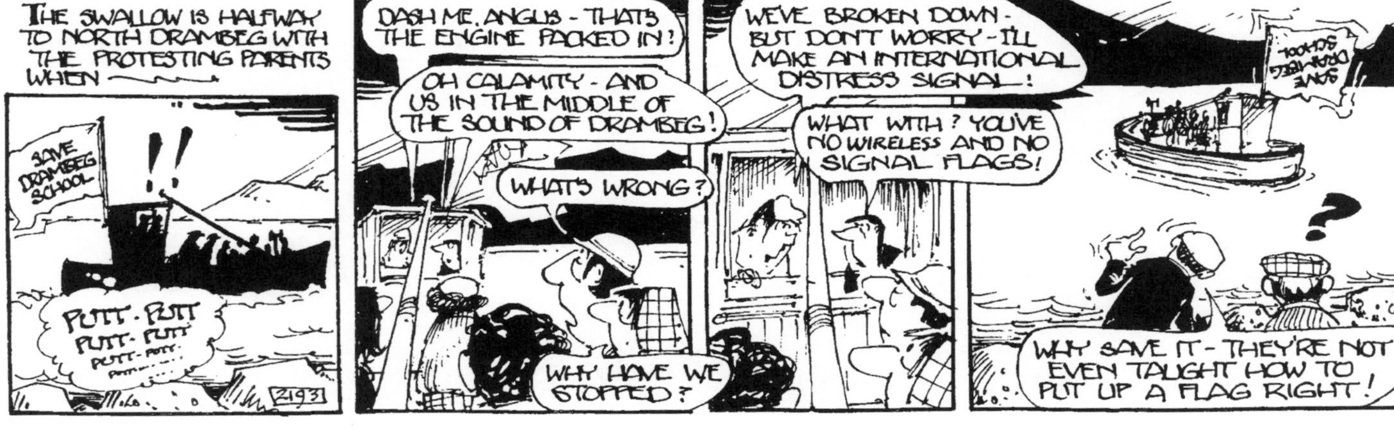
THE SWALLOW IS HALFWAY TO NORTH DRAMBEG WITH THE PROTESTING PARENTS WHEN —
SAVE DRAMBEG SCHOOL
!!
PUTT-PUTT
PUTT-PUTT
PUTT-PUTT...
2193
DASH ME, ANGUS – THAT'S THE ENGINE PACKED IN!
OH CALAMITY – AND US IN THE MIDDLE OF THE SOUND OF DRAMBEG!
WHAT'S WRONG?
WHY HAVE WE STOPPED?
WE'VE BROKEN DOWN – BUT DON'T WORRY – I'LL MAKE AN INTERNATIONAL DISTRESS SIGNAL!
WHAT WITH? YOU'VE NO WIRELESS AND NO SIGNAL FLAGS!
SAVE DRAMBEG SCHOOL
?
WHY SAVE IT – THEY'RE NOT EVEN TAUGHT HOW TO PUT UP A FLAG RIGHT!

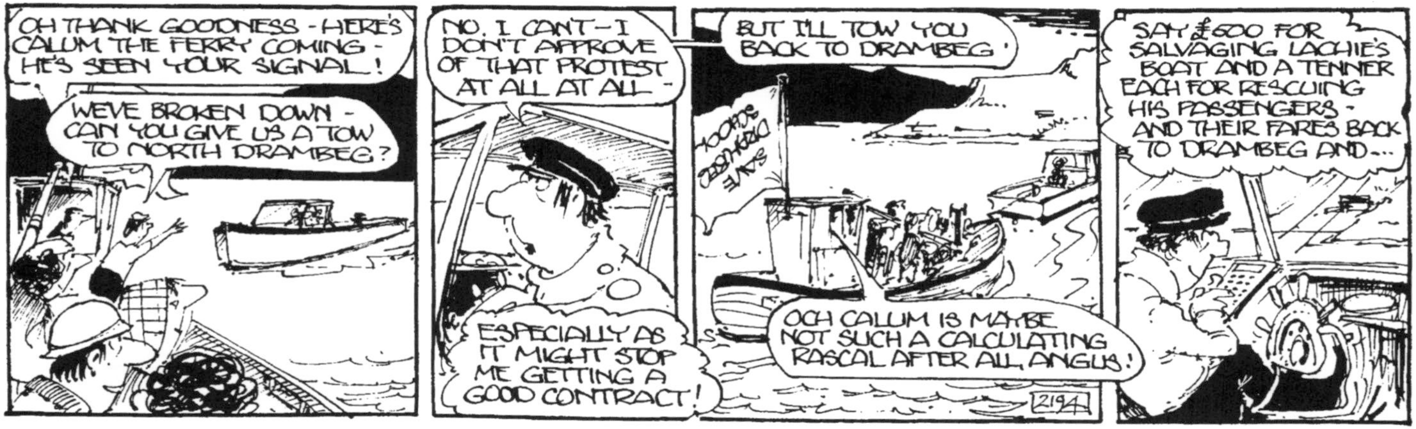
OH THANK GOODNESS - HERE'S CALUM THE FERRY COMING - HE'S SEEN YOUR SIGNAL!
WE'VE BROKEN DOWN - CAN YOU GIVE US A TOW TO NORTH DRAMBEG?
NO, I CAN'T - I DON'T APPROVE OF THAT PROTEST AT ALL AT ALL -
ESPECIALLY AS IT MIGHT STOP ME GETTING A GOOD CONTRACT!
BUT I'LL TOW YOU BACK TO DRAMBEG!
SAVE DRAMBEG SCHOOL
OCH CALUM IS MAYBE NOT SUCH A CALCULATING RASCAL AFTER ALL, ANGUS!
2194
SAY £600 FOR SALVAGING LACHIE'S BOAT AND A TENNER EACH FOR RESCUING HIS PASSENGERS - AND THEIR FARES BACK TO DRAMBEG AND...

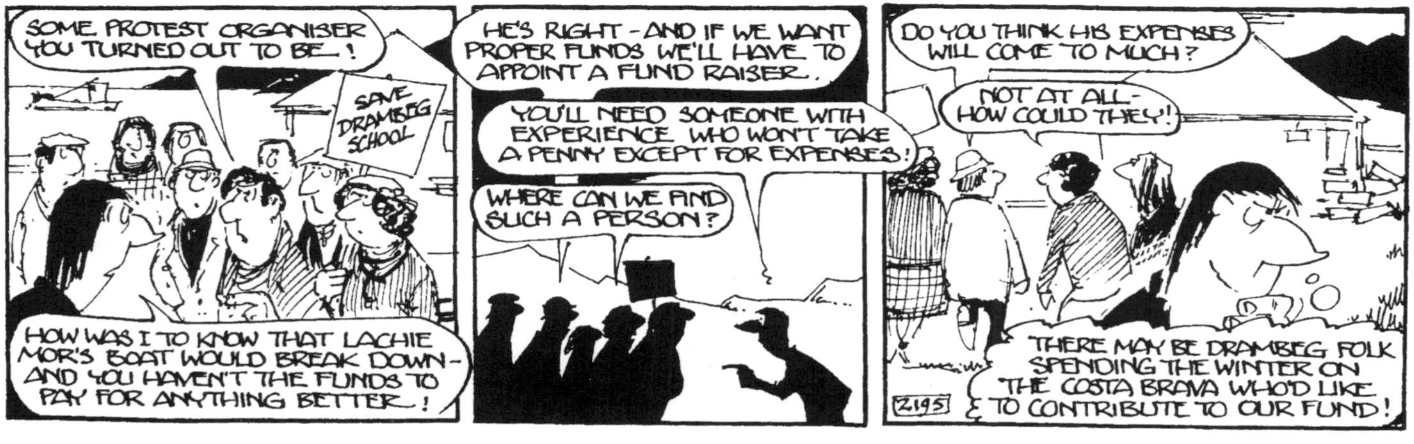
SOME PROTEST ORGANISER YOU TURNED OUT TO BE!
SAVE DRAMBEG SCHOOL
HOW WAS I TO KNOW THAT LACHIE MOR'S BOAT WOULD BREAK DOWN - AND YOU HAVEN'T THE FUNDS TO PAY FOR ANYTHING BETTER!
HE'S RIGHT - AND IF WE WANT PROPER FUNDS WE'LL HAVE TO APPOINT A FUND RAISER.
YOU'LL NEED SOMEONE WITH EXPERIENCE WHO WON'T TAKE A PENNY EXCEPT FOR EXPENSES!
WHERE CAN WE FIND SUCH A PERSON?
DO YOU THINK HIS EXPENSES WILL COME TO MUCH?
NOT AT ALL - HOW COULD THEY!
THERE MAY BE DRAMBEG FOLK SPENDING THE WINTER ON THE COSTA BRAVA WHO'D LIKE TO CONTRIBUTE TO OUR FUND!
2195

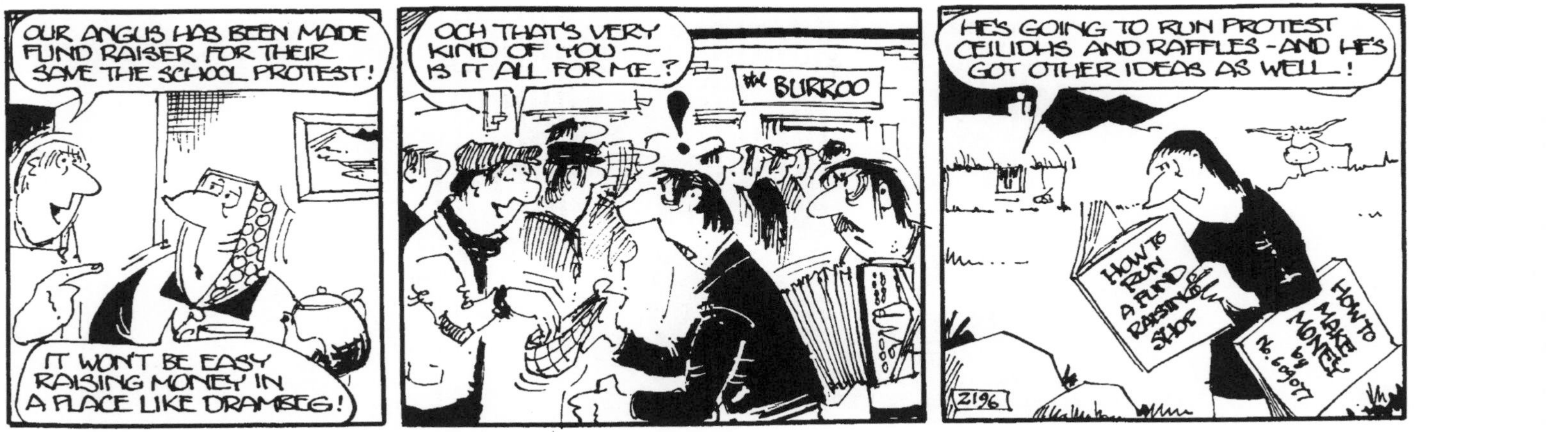
OUR ANGUS HAS BEEN MADE FUND RAISER FOR THEIR SAVE THE SCHOOL PROTEST!
IT WON'T BE EASY RAISING MONEY IN A PLACE LIKE DRAMBEG!
OCH THAT'S VERY KIND OF YOU — IS IT ALL FOR ME?
BURROO
!
HE'S GOING TO RUN PROTEST CEILIDHS AND RAFFLES - AND HE'S GOT OTHER IDEAS AS WELL!
HOW TO RUN A FUND RAISING SHOP
HOW TO MAKE MONEY
2196

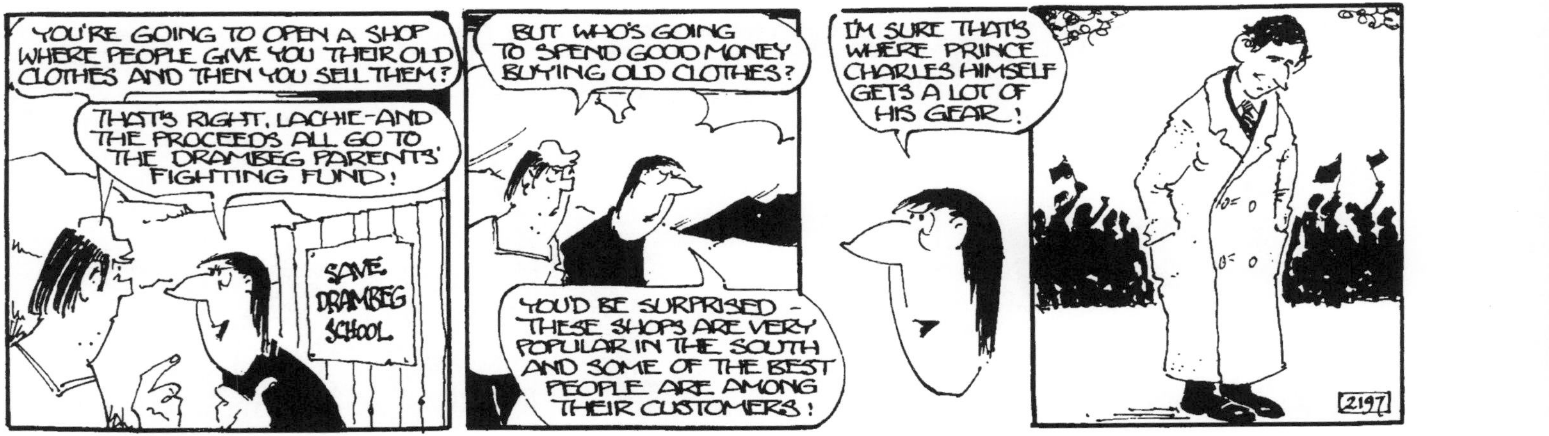
YOU'RE GOING TO OPEN A SHOP WHERE PEOPLE GIVE YOU THEIR OLD CLOTHES AND THEN YOU SELL THEM?
THAT'S RIGHT, LACHIE - AND THE PROCEEDS ALL GO TO THE DRAMBEG PARENTS' FIGHTING FUND!
SAVE DRAMBEG SCHOOL
BUT WHO'S GOING TO SPEND GOOD MONEY BUYING OLD CLOTHES?
YOU'D BE SURPRISED - THESE SHOPS ARE VERY POPULAR IN THE SOUTH AND SOME OF THE BEST PEOPLE ARE AMONG THEIR CUSTOMERS!
I'M SURE THAT'S WHERE PRINCE CHARLES HIMSELF GETS A LOT OF HIS GEAR!
2197

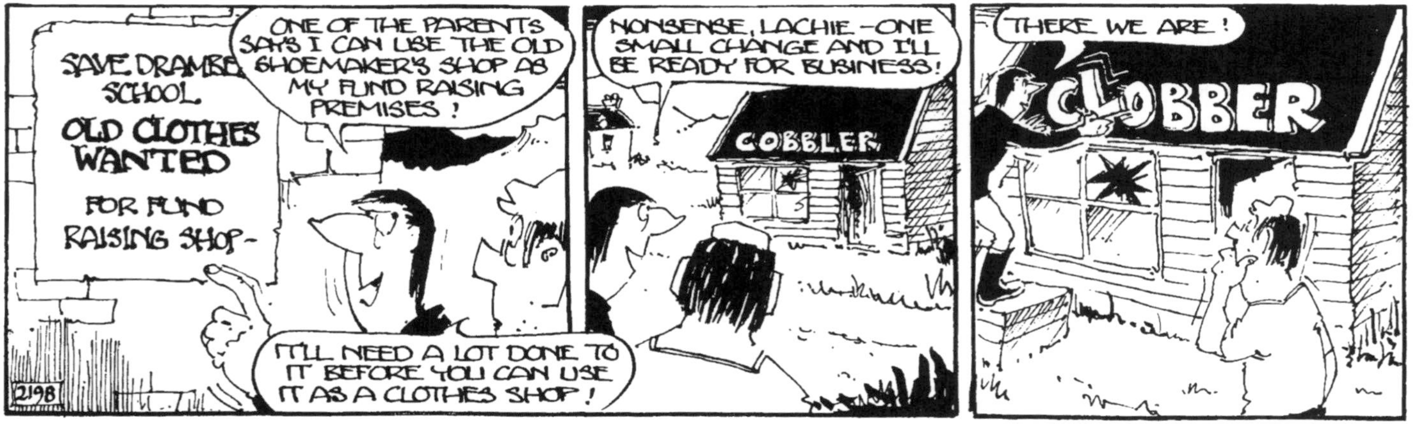
SAVE DRAMBE
SCHOOL
OLD CLOTHES WANTED
FOR FUND RAISING SHOP-
ONE OF THE PARENTS SAYS I CAN USE THE OLD SHOEMAKER'S SHOP AS MY FUND RAISING PREMISES!
I'LL NEED A LOT DONE TO IT BEFORE YOU CAN USE IT AS A CLOTHES SHOP!
2198
NONSENSE, LACHIE - ONE SMALL CHANGE AND I'LL BE READY FOR BUSINESS!
COBBLER
THERE WE ARE!
CLOBBER

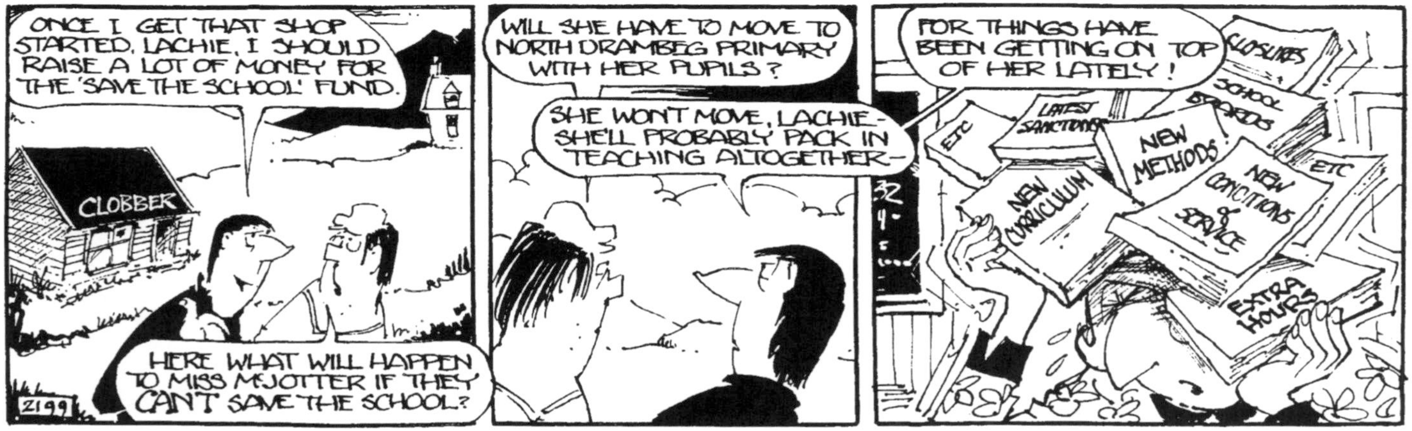
ONCE I GET THAT SHOP STARTED, LACHIE, I SHOULD RAISE A LOT OF MONEY FOR THE 'SAVE THE SCHOOL' FUND.
CLOBBER
HERE WHAT WILL HAPPEN TO MISS McJOTTER IF THEY CAN'T SAVE THE SCHOOL?
2199
WILL SHE HAVE TO MOVE TO NORTH DRAMBEG PRIMARY WITH HER PUPILS?
SHE WON'T MOVE, LACHIE - SHE'LL PROBABLY PACK IN TEACHING ALTOGETHER-
FOR THINGS HAVE BEEN GETTING ON TOP OF HER LATELY!
CLOSURES
SCHOOL BOARDS
LATEST SANCTIONS
ETC
NEW METHODS
ETC
NEW CURRICULUM
NEW CONDITIONS OF SERVICE
EXTRA HOURS

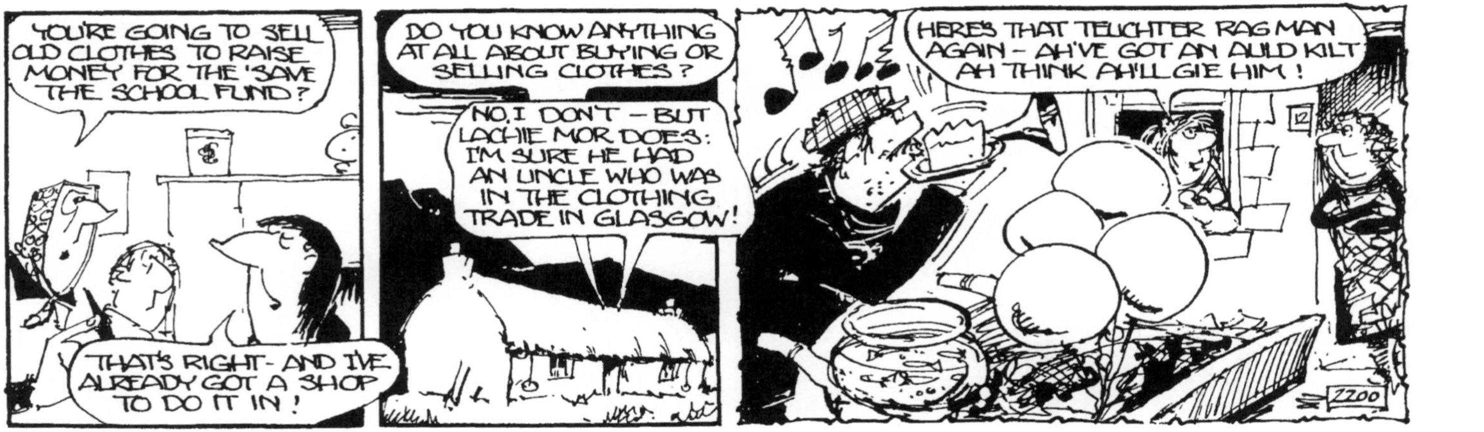
YOU'RE GOING TO SELL OLD CLOTHES TO RAISE MONEY FOR THE 'SAVE THE SCHOOL FUND?
THAT'S RIGHT - AND I'VE ALREADY GOT A SHOP TO DO IT IN!
DO YOU KNOW ANYTHING AT ALL ABOUT BUYING OR SELLING CLOTHES?
NO, I DON'T - BUT LACHIE MOR DOES: I'M SURE HE HAD AN UNCLE WHO WAS IN THE CLOTHING TRADE IN GLASGOW!
HERE'S THAT TEUCHTER RAG MAN AGAIN - AH'VE GOT AN AULD KILT AH THINK AH'LL GIE HIM!
2200

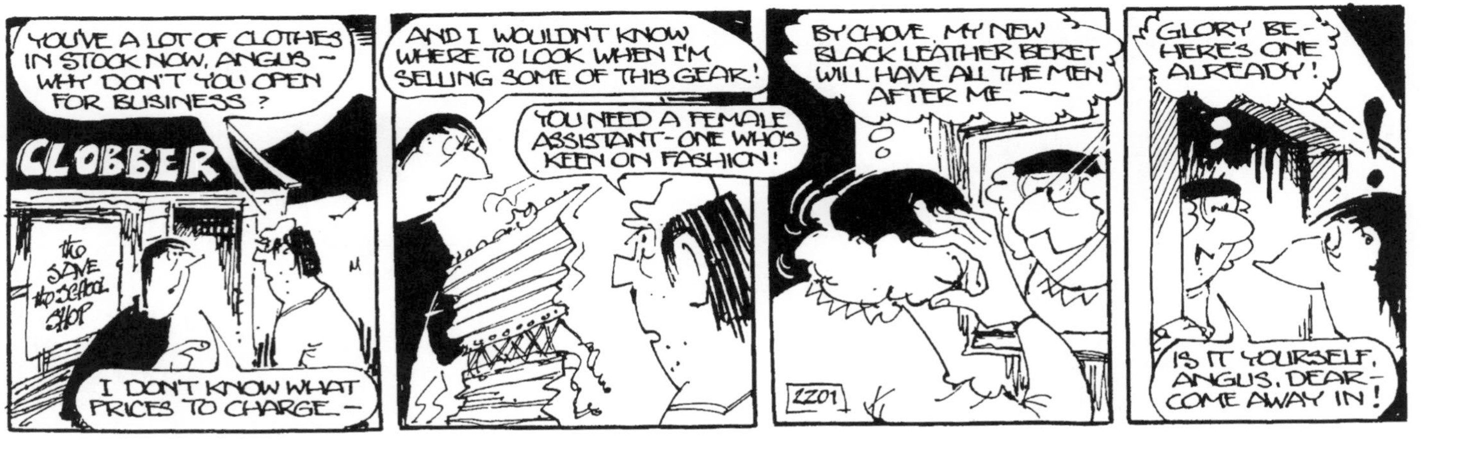
YOU'VE A LOT OF CLOTHES IN STOCK NOW, ANGUS - WHY DON'T YOU OPEN FOR BUSINESS?
CLOBBER
the SAVE the SCHOOL SHOP
I DON'T KNOW WHAT PRICES TO CHARGE -
AND I WOULDN'T KNOW WHERE TO LOOK WHEN I'M SELLING SOME OF THIS GEAR!
YOU NEED A FEMALE ASSISTANT - ONE WHO'S KEEN ON FASHION!
BY CHOVE, MY NEW BLACK LEATHER BERET WILL HAVE ALL THE MEN AFTER ME ---
2201
GLORY BE - HERE'S ONE ALREADY!
IS IT YOURSELF, ANGUS, DEAR - COME AWAY IN!

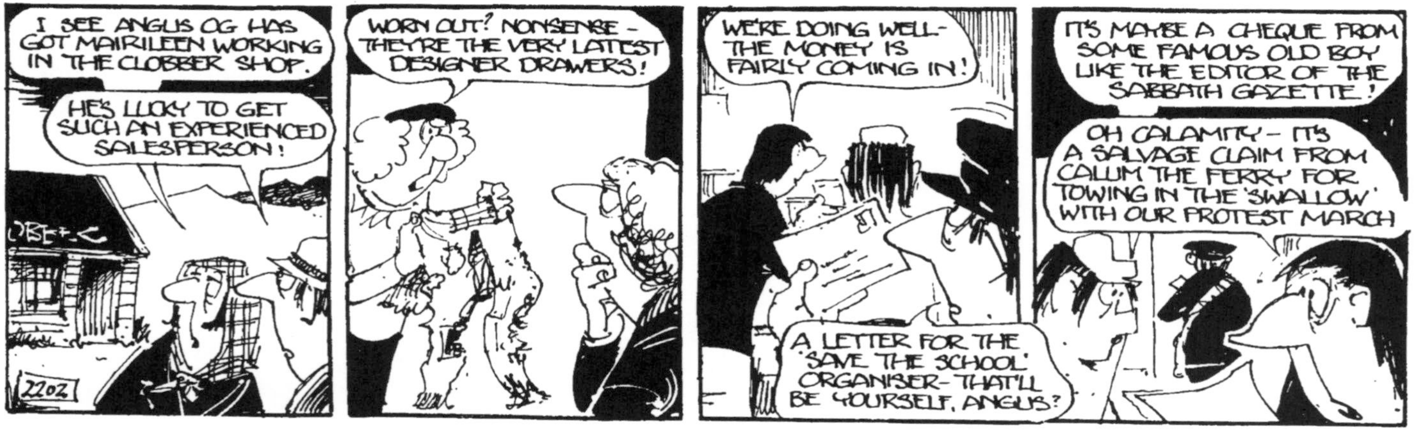
I SEE ANGUS OG HAS GOT MAIRILEEN WORKING IN THE CLOBBER SHOP.
HE'S LUCKY TO GET SUCH AN EXPERIENCED SALESPERSON!
2202
WORN OUT? NONSENSE - THEY'RE THE VERY LATEST DESIGNER DRAWERS!
WE'RE DOING WELL - THE MONEY IS FAIRLY COMING IN!
A LETTER FOR THE 'SAVE THE SCHOOL' ORGANISER - THAT'LL BE YOURSELF, ANGUS?
IT'S MAYBE A CHEQUE FROM SOME FAMOUS OLD BOY LIKE THE EDITOR OF THE SABBATH GAZETTE!
OH CALAMITY - IT'S A SALVAGE CLAIM FROM CALUM THE FERRY FOR TOWING IN THE 'SWALLOW' WITH OUR PROTEST MARCH

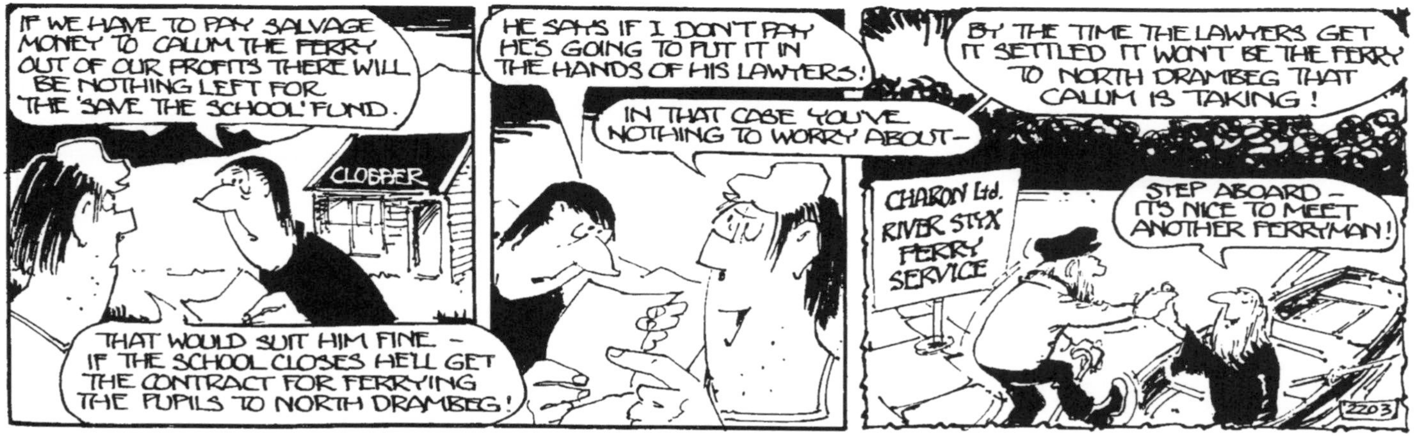
IF WE HAVE TO PAY SALVAGE MONEY TO CALUM THE FERRY OUT OF OUR PROFITS THERE WILL BE NOTHING LEFT FOR THE 'SAVE THE SCHOOL' FUND.
CLOBBER
THAT WOULD SUIT HIM FINE - IF THE SCHOOL CLOSES HE'LL GET THE CONTRACT FOR FERRYING THE PUPILS TO NORTH DRAMBEG!
HE SAYS IF I DON'T PAY HE'S GOING TO PUT IT IN THE HANDS OF HIS LAWYERS!
IN THAT CASE YOU'VE NOTHING TO WORRY ABOUT -
BY THE TIME THE LAWYERS GET IT SETTLED IT WON'T BE THE FERRY TO NORTH DRAMBEG THAT CALUM IS TAKING!
CHARON Ltd. RIVER STYX FERRY SERVICE
STEP ABOARD - IT'S NICE TO MEET ANOTHER FERRYMAN!
2203

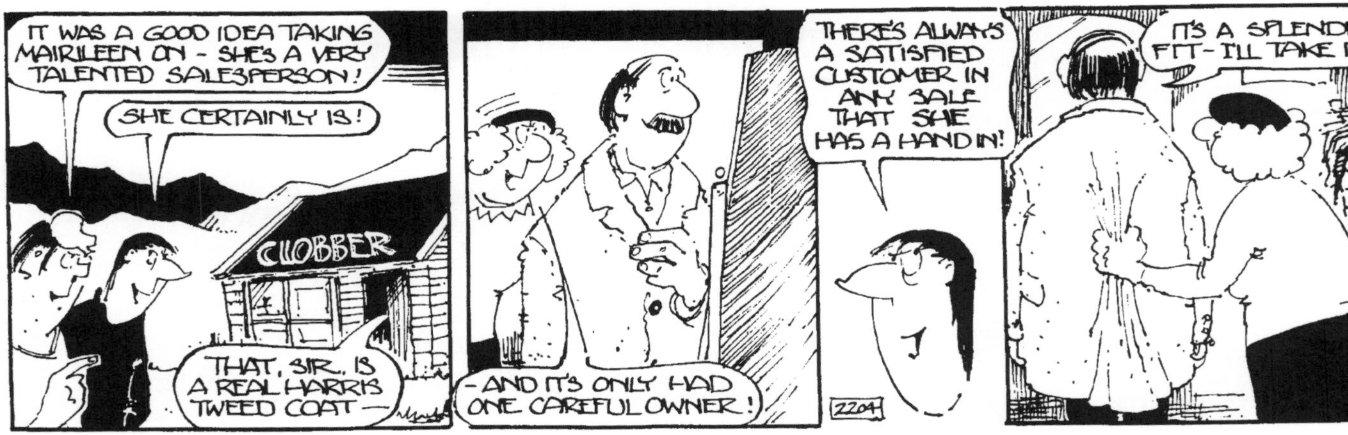
IT WAS A GOOD IDEA TAKING MAIRILEEN ON - SHE'S A VERY TALENTED SALESPERSON!
SHE CERTAINLY IS!
CLOBBER
THAT, SIR, IS A REAL HARRIS TWEED COAT —
- AND IT'S ONLY HAD ONE CAREFUL OWNER!
2204
THERE'S ALWAYS A SATISFIED CUSTOMER IN ANY SALE THAT SHE HAS A HAND IN!
IT'S A SPLENDID FIT - I'LL TAKE IT!

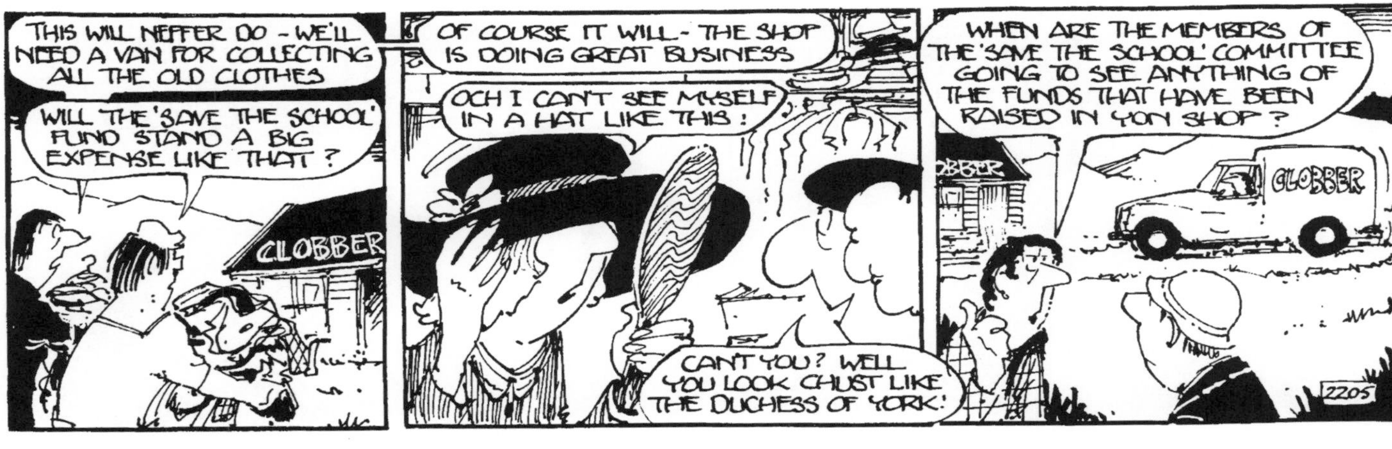
THIS WILL NEFFER DO - WE'LL NEED A VAN FOR COLLECTING ALL THE OLD CLOTHES
WILL THE 'SAVE THE SCHOOL' FUND STAND A BIG EXPENSE LIKE THAT?
CLOBBER
OF COURSE IT WILL - THE SHOP IS DOING GREAT BUSINESS
OCH I CAN'T SEE MYSELF IN A HAT LIKE THIS!
CAN'T YOU? WELL YOU LOOK CHUST LIKE THE DUCHESS OF YORK!
WHEN ARE THE MEMBERS OF THE 'SAVE THE SCHOOL' COMMITTEE GOING TO SEE ANYTHING OF THE FUNDS THAT HAVE BEEN RAISED IN YON SHOP?
CLOBBER
2205

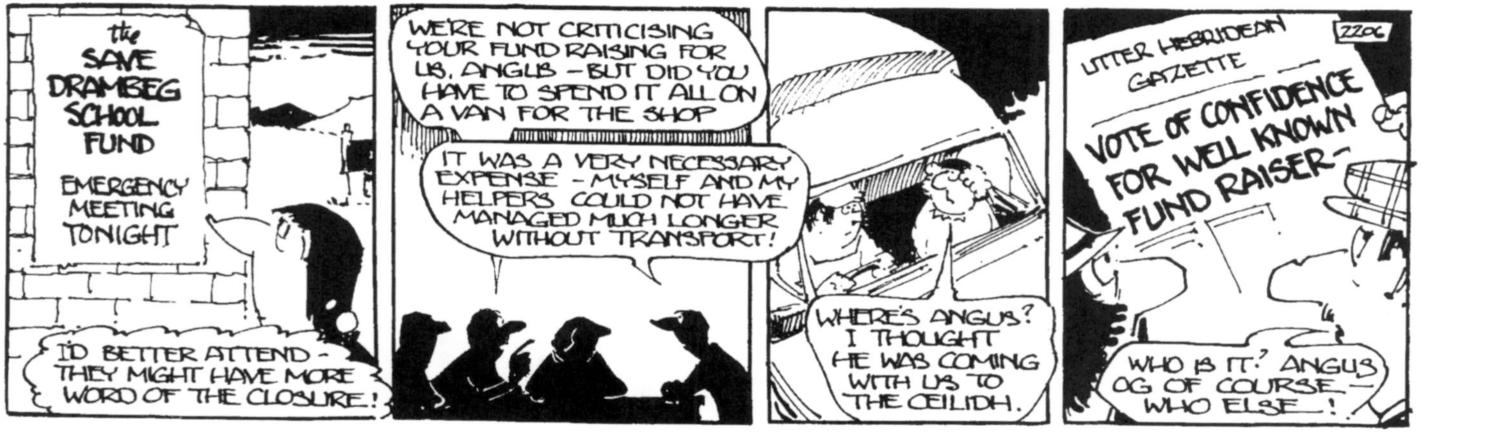
the SAVE DRAMBEG SCHOOL FUND
EMERGENCY MEETING TONIGHT
I'D BETTER ATTEND - THEY MIGHT HAVE MORE WORD OF THE CLOSURE!
WE'RE NOT CRITICISING YOUR FUND RAISING FOR US, ANGUS - BUT DID YOU HAVE TO SPEND IT ALL ON A VAN FOR THE SHOP
IT WAS A VERY NECESSARY EXPENSE - MYSELF AND MY HELPERS COULD NOT HAVE MANAGED MUCH LONGER WITHOUT TRANSPORT!
WHERE'S ANGUS? I THOUGHT HE WAS COMING WITH US TO THE CEILIDH.
2206
UTTER HEBRIDEAN GAZETTE
VOTE OF CONFIDENCE FOR WELL KNOWN FUND RAISER-
WHO IS IT? ANGUS OG OF COURSE - WHO ELSE!

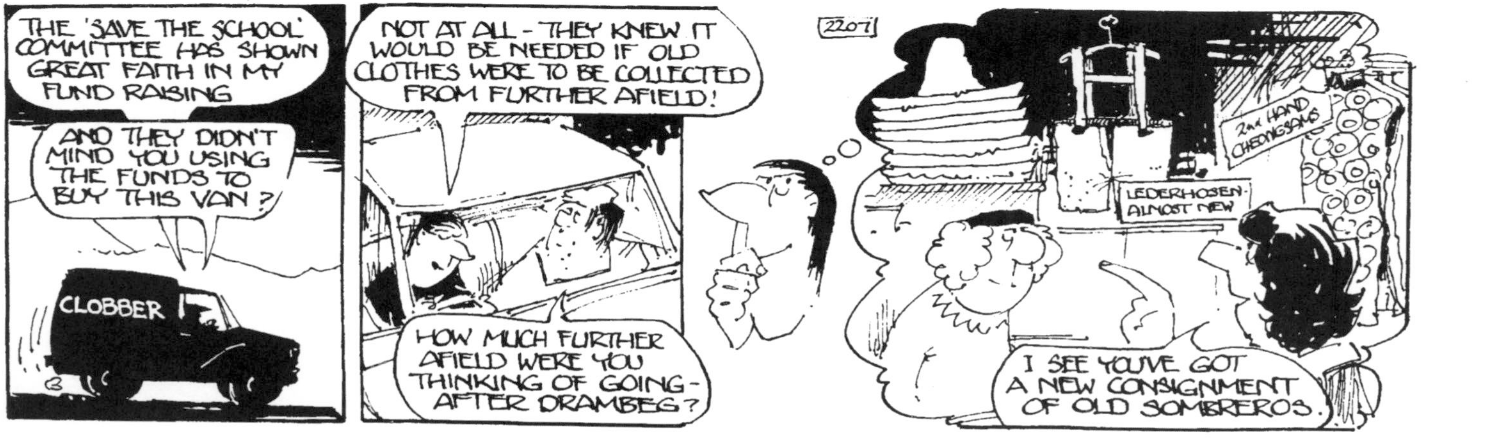
THE 'SAVE THE SCHOOL' COMMITTEE HAS SHOWN GREAT FAITH IN MY FUND RAISING
AND THEY DIDN'T MIND YOU USING THE FUNDS TO BUY THIS VAN?
CLOBBER
NOT AT ALL - THEY KNEW IT WOULD BE NEEDED IF OLD CLOTHES WERE TO BE COLLECTED FROM FURTHER AFIELD!
HOW MUCH FURTHER AFIELD WERE YOU THINKING OF GOING - AFTER DRAMBEG?
2207
2nd HAND CHEONGSAMS
LEDERHOSEN - ALMOST NEW
I SEE YOU'VE GOT A NEW CONSIGNMENT OF OLD SOMBREROS.

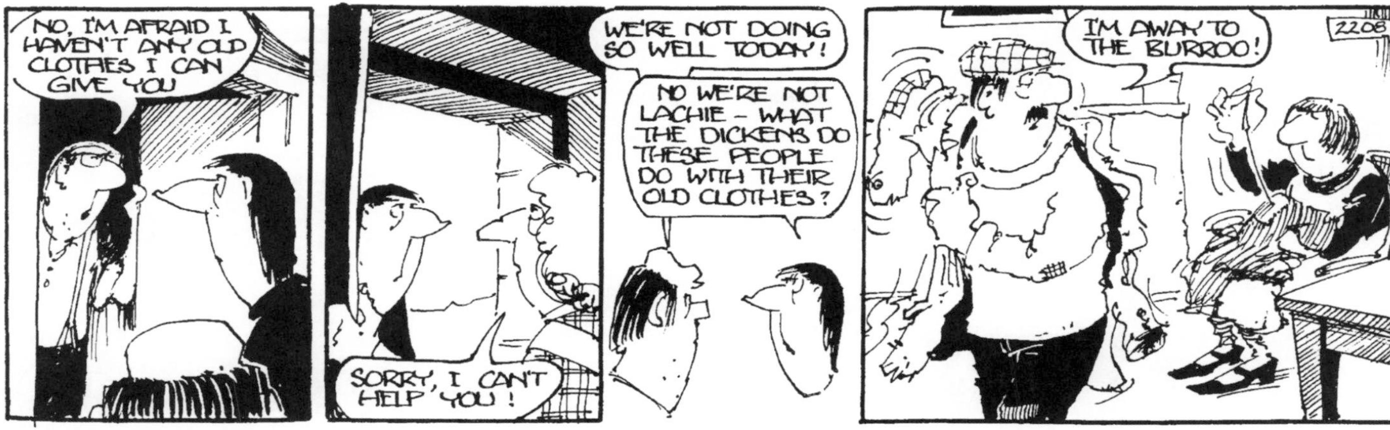
NO, I'M AFRAID I HAVEN'T ANY OLD CLOTHES I CAN GIVE YOU
SORRY, I CAN'T HELP YOU!
WE'RE NOT DOING SO WELL TODAY!
NO WE'RE NOT LACHIE - WHAT THE DICKENS DO THESE PEOPLE DO WITH THEIR OLD CLOTHES?
2208
I'M AWAY TO THE BURROO!

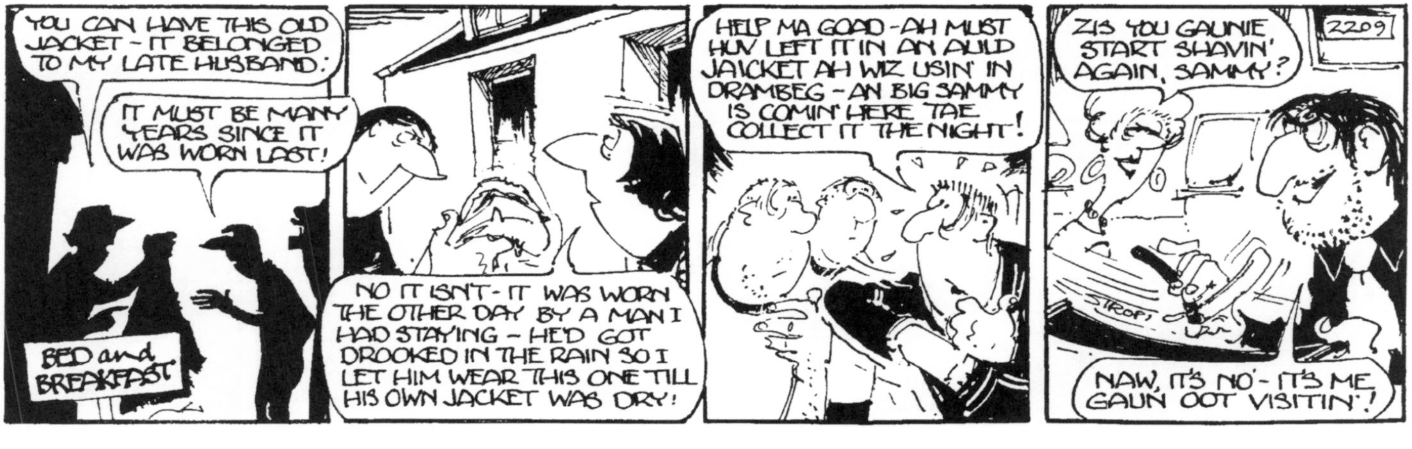
YOU CAN HAVE THIS OLD JACKET - IT BELONGED TO MY LATE HUSBAND.
IT MUST BE MANY YEARS SINCE IT WAS WORN LAST!
BED and BREAKFAST
NO IT ISN'T - IT WAS WORN THE OTHER DAY BY A MAN I HAD STAYING - HE'D GOT DROOKED IN THE RAIN SO I LET HIM WEAR THIS ONE TILL HIS OWN JACKET WAS DRY!
HELP MA GOAD - AH MUST HUV LEFT IT IN AN AULD JAICKET AH WIZ USIN' IN DRAMBEG - AN BIG SAMMY IS COMIN' HERE TAE COLLECT IT THE NIGHT!
2209
ZIS YOU GAUNIE START SHAVIN' AGAIN, SAMMY?
STROP
NAW, IT'S NO' - IT'S ME GAUN OOT VISITIN'!

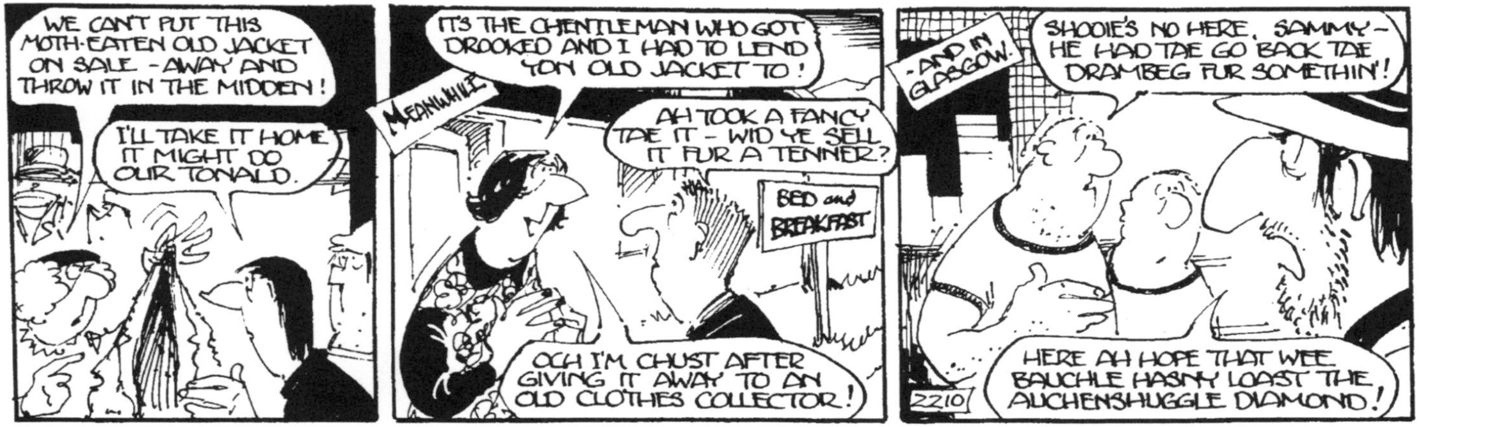
WE CAN'T PUT THIS MOTH-EATEN OLD JACKET ON SALE - AWAY AND THROW IT IN THE MIDDEN!
I'LL TAKE IT HOME IT MIGHT DO OUR TONALD.
MEANWHILE
IT'S THE CHENTLEMAN WHO GOT DROOKED AND I HAD TO LEND YON OLD JACKET TO!
AH TOOK A FANCY TAE IT - WID YE SELL IT FUR A TENNER?
BED and BREAKFAST
OCH I'M CHUST AFTER GIVING IT AWAY TO AN OLD CLOTHES COLLECTOR!
2210
-AND IN GLASGOW.
SHOOIE'S NO HERE, SAMMY - HE HAD TAE GO BACK TAE DRAMBEG FUR SOMETHIN'!
HERE AH HOPE THAT WEE BAUCHLE HASNY LOAST THE AUCHENSHUGGLE DIAMOND!

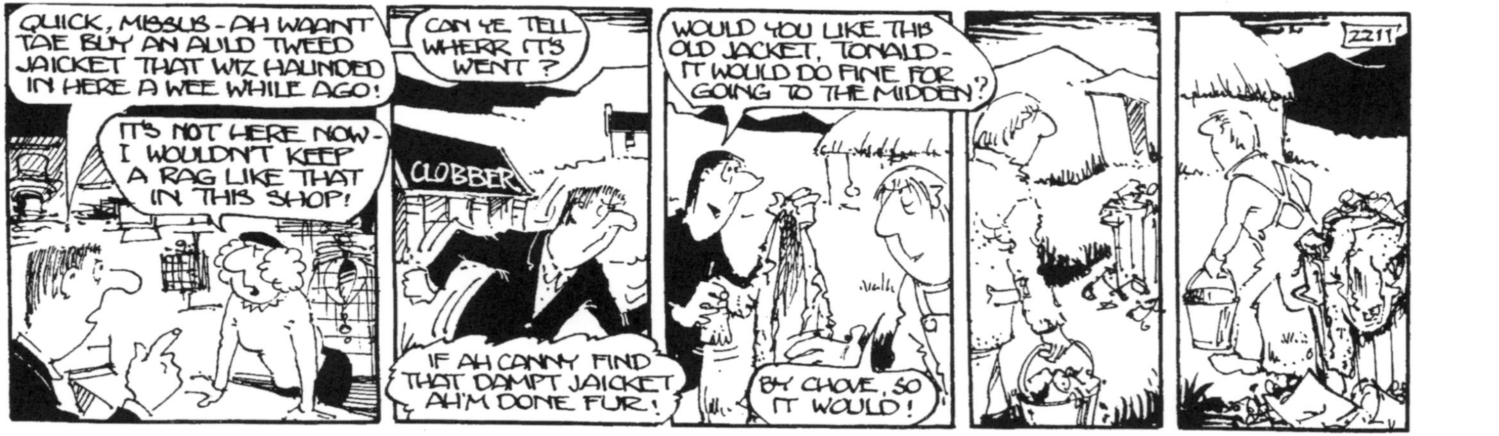
QUICK, MISSUS - AH WAANT TAE BUY AN AULD TWEED JAICKET THAT WIZ HAUNDED IN HERE A WEE WHILE AGO!
IT'S NOT HERE NOW - I WOULDN'T KEEP A RAG LIKE THAT IN THIS SHOP!
CAN YE TELL WHERR IT'S WENT?
CLOBBER
IF AH CANNY FIND THAT DAMPT JAICKET AH'M DONE FUR!
WOULD YOU LIKE THIS OLD JACKET, TONALD - IT WOULD DO FINE FOR GOING TO THE MIDDEN?
BY CHOVE, SO IT WOULD!
2211

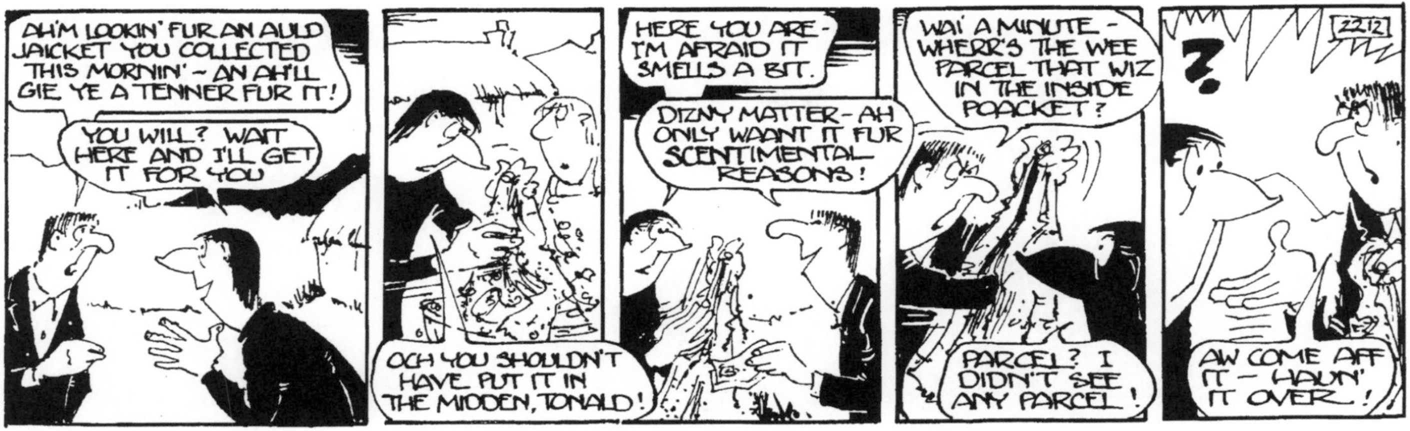
AH'M LOOKIN' FUR AN AULD JAICKET YOU COLLECTED THIS MORNIN' – AN AH'LL GIE YE A TENNER FUR IT!
YOU WILL? WAIT HERE AND I'LL GET IT FOR YOU
OCH YOU SHOULDN'T HAVE PUT IT IN THE MIDDEN, TONALD!
HERE YOU ARE– I'M AFRAID IT SMELLS A BIT.
DIZNY MATTER – AH ONLY WAANT IT FUR SCENTIMENTAL REASONS!
WAI' A MINUTE – WHERR'S THE WEE PARCEL THAT WIZ IN THE INSIDE POACKET?
PARCEL? I DIDN'T SEE ANY PARCEL!
2212
?
AW COME AFF IT – HAUN' IT OVER!

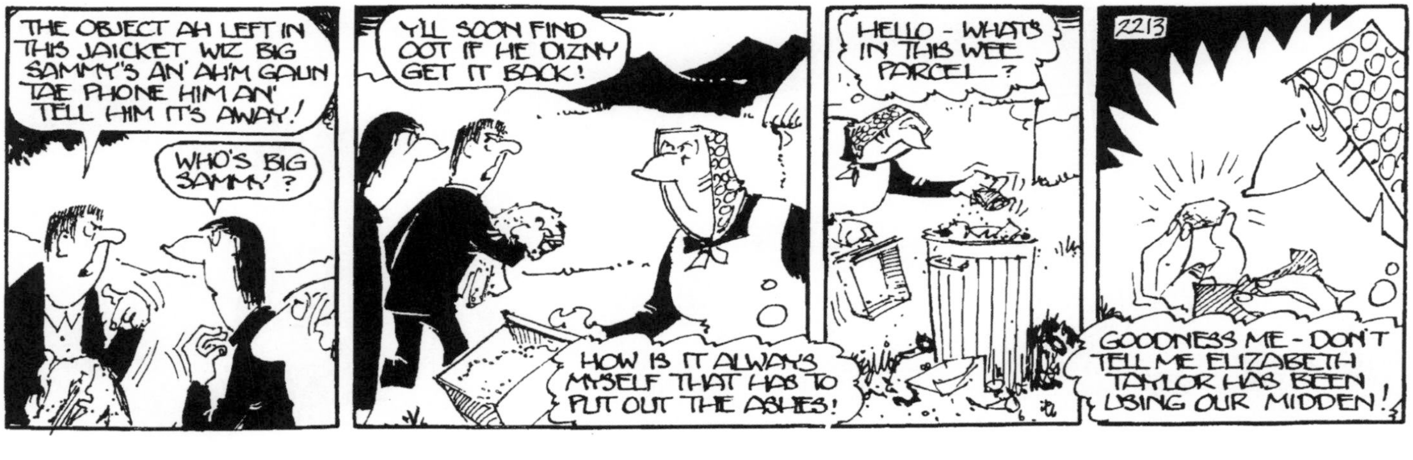
THE OBJECT AH LEFT IN THIS JAICKET WIZ BIG SAMMY'S AN' AH'M GAUN TAE PHONE HIM AN' TELL HIM IT'S AWAY!
WHO'S BIG SAMMY?
Y'LL SOON FIND OOT IF HE DIZNY GET IT BACK!
HOW IS IT ALWAYS MYSELF THAT HAS TO PUT OUT THE ASHES!
HELLO – WHAT'S IN THIS WEE PARCEL?
2213
GOODNESS ME – DON'T TELL ME ELIZABETH TAYLOR HAS BEEN USING OUR MIDDEN!

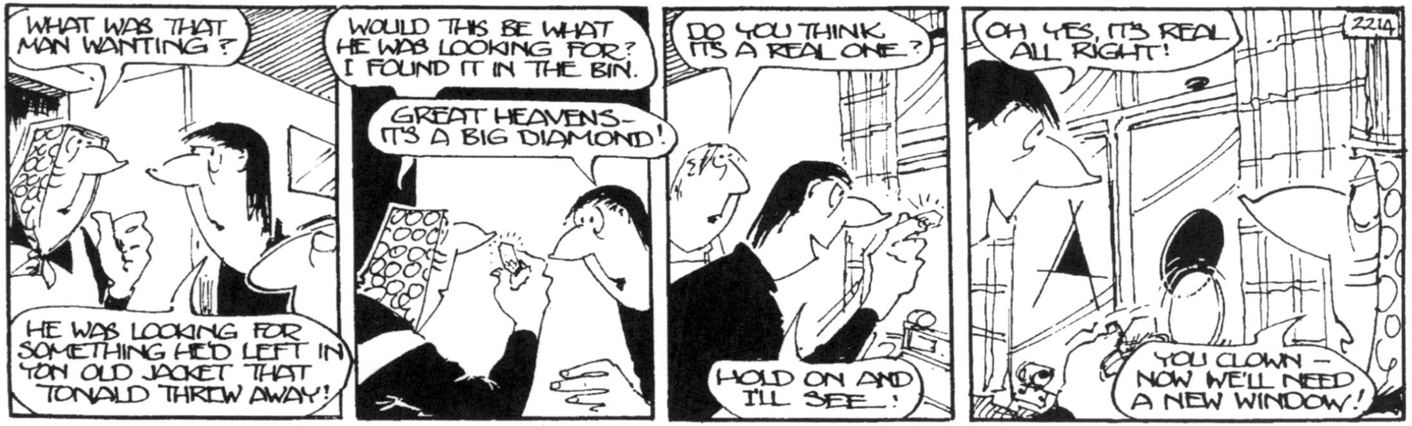
2214
WHAT WAS THAT MAN WANTING?
HE WAS LOOKING FOR SOMETHING HE'D LEFT IN YON OLD JACKET THAT TONALD THREW AWAY!
WOULD THIS BE WHAT HE WAS LOOKING FOR? I FOUND IT IN THE BIN.
GREAT HEAVENS- IT'S A BIG DIAMOND!
DO YOU THINK IT'S A REAL ONE?
HOLD ON AND I'LL SEE!
OH YES, IT'S REAL ALL RIGHT!
YOU CLOWN - NOW WE'LL NEED A NEW WINDOW!

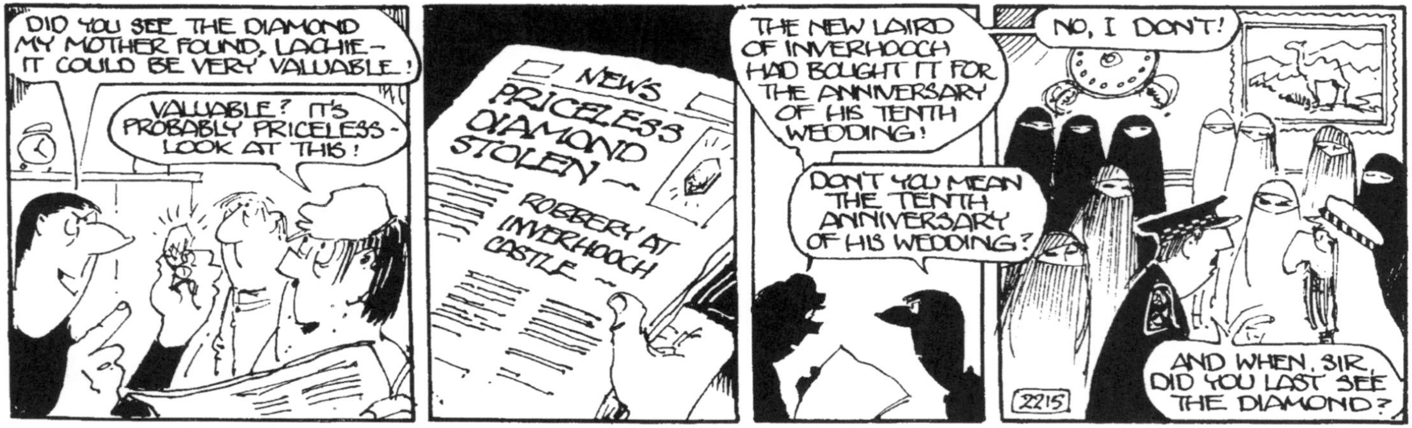
DID YOU SEE THE DIAMOND MY MOTHER FOUND, LACHIE- IT COULD BE VERY VALUABLE!
VALUABLE? IT'S PROBABLY PRICELESS- LOOK AT THIS!
NEWS
PRICELESS DIAMOND STOLEN
ROBBERY AT INVERHOOCH CASTLE
THE NEW LAIRD OF INVERHOOCH HAD BOUGHT IT FOR THE ANNIVERSARY OF HIS TENTH WEDDING!
DON'T YOU MEAN THE TENTH ANNIVERSARY OF HIS WEDDING?
NO, I DON'T!
AND WHEN, SIR, DID YOU LAST SEE THE DIAMOND?
2215

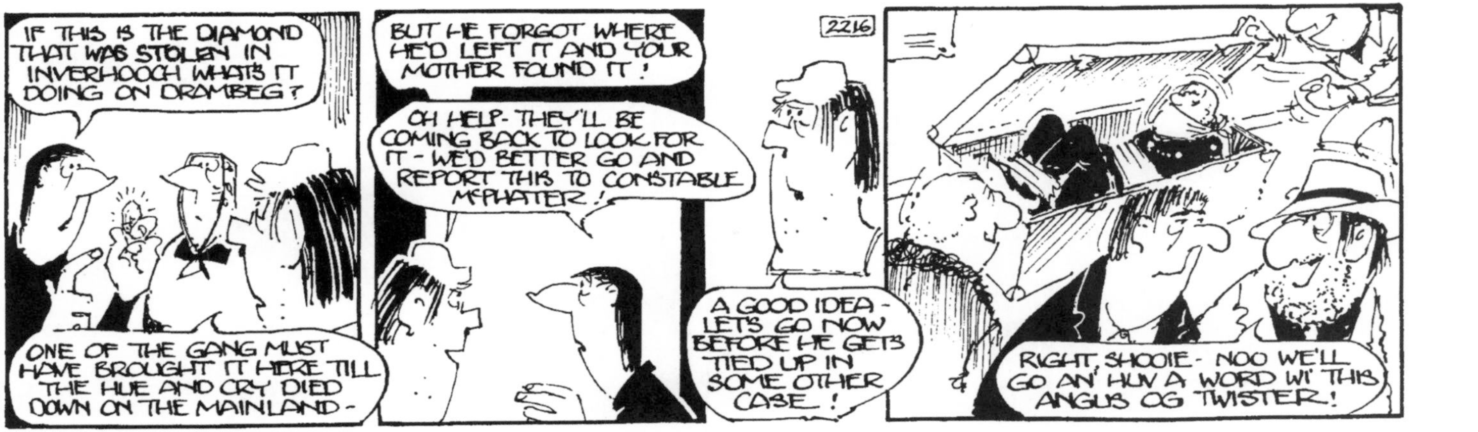
IF THIS IS THE DIAMOND THAT WAS STOLEN IN INVERHOOCH WHAT'S IT DOING ON DRAMBEG?
ONE OF THE GANG MUST HAVE BROUGHT IT HERE TILL THE HUE AND CRY DIED DOWN ON THE MAINLAND -
BUT HE FORGOT WHERE HE'D LEFT IT AND YOUR MOTHER FOUND IT!
OH HELP - THEY'LL BE COMING BACK TO LOOK FOR IT - WE'D BETTER GO AND REPORT THIS TO CONSTABLE McPHATER!
2216
A GOOD IDEA - LET'S GO NOW BEFORE HE GETS TIED UP IN SOME OTHER CASE!
RIGHT, SHOOIE - NOO WE'LL GO AN' HUV A WORD WI' THIS ANGUS OG TWISTER!

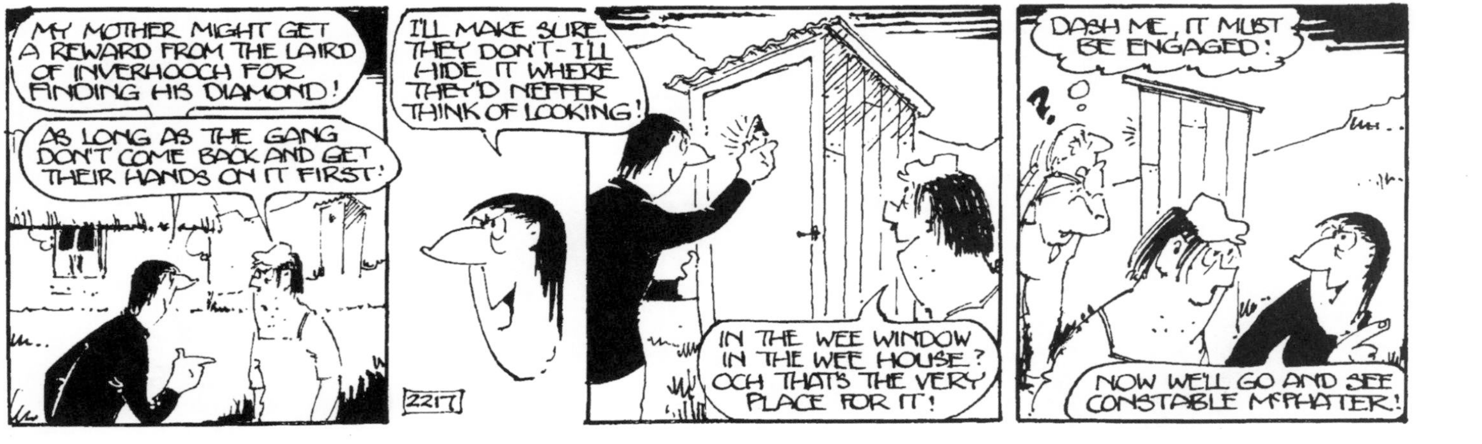
MY MOTHER MIGHT GET A REWARD FROM THE LAIRD OF INVERHOOCH FOR FINDING HIS DIAMOND!
AS LONG AS THE GANG DON'T COME BACK AND GET THEIR HANDS ON IT FIRST!
I'LL MAKE SURE THEY DON'T - I'LL HIDE IT WHERE THEY'D NEFFER THINK OF LOOKING!
2217
IN THE WEE WINDOW IN THE WEE HOUSE? OCH THAT'S THE VERY PLACE FOR IT!
DASH ME, IT MUST BE ENGAGED!
NOW WE'LL GO AND SEE CONSTABLE McPHATER!

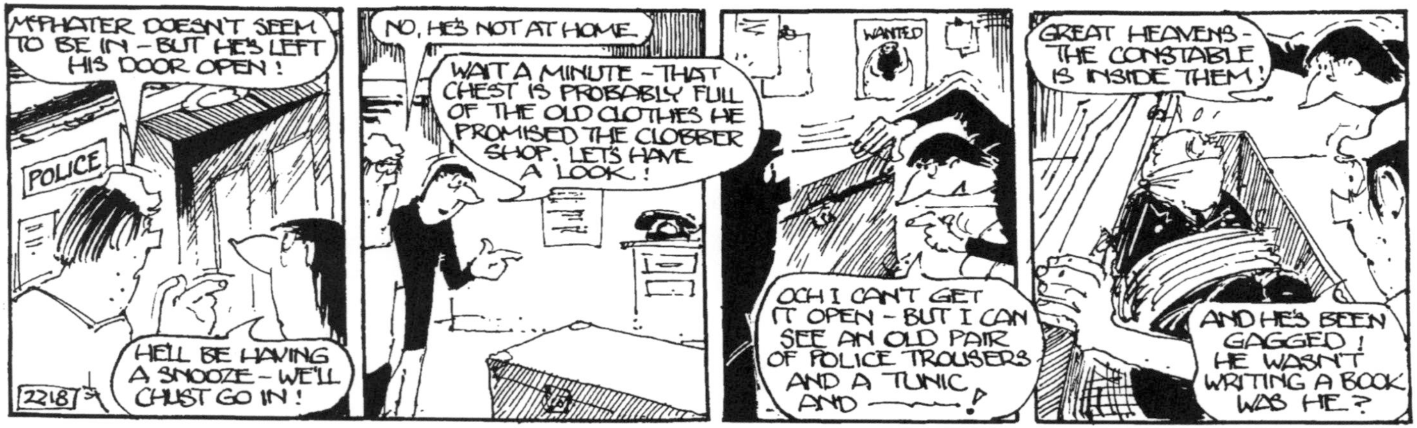
M^cPHATER DOESN'T SEEM TO BE IN – BUT HE'S LEFT HIS DOOR OPEN!
POLICE
HE'LL BE HAVING A SNOOZE – WE'LL CHUST GO IN!
2218
NO, HE'S NOT AT HOME.
WAIT A MINUTE – THAT CHEST IS PROBABLY FULL OF THE OLD CLOTHES HE PROMISED THE CLOBBER SHOP. LET'S HAVE A LOOK!
WANTED
OCH I CAN'T GET IT OPEN – BUT I CAN SEE AN OLD PAIR OF POLICE TROUSERS AND A TUNIC AND ———!
GREAT HEAVENS – THE CONSTABLE IS INSIDE THEM!
AND HE'S BEEN GAGGED! HE WASN'T WRITING A BOOK WAS HE?

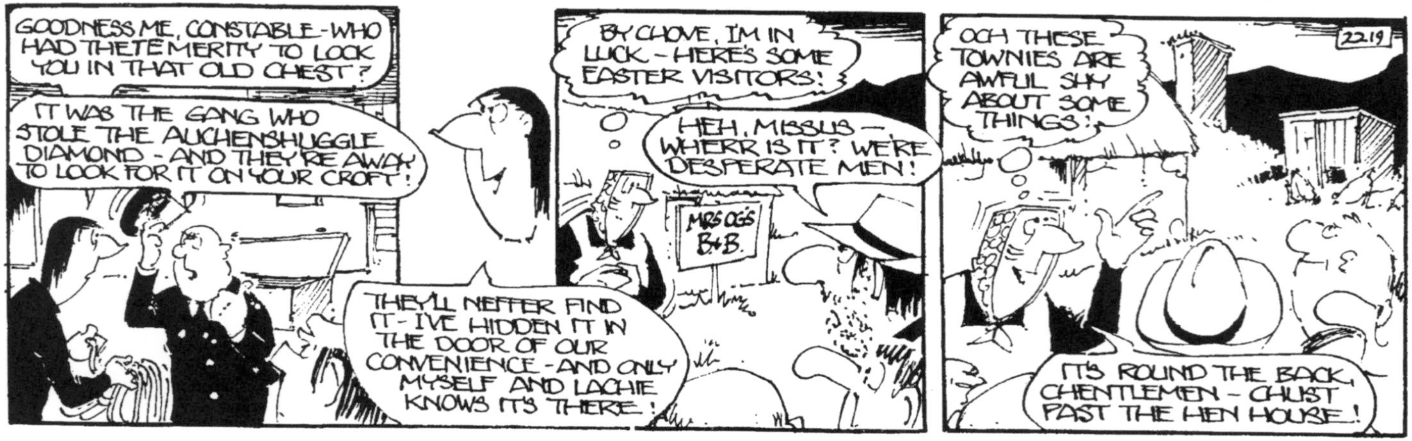
GOODNESS ME, CONSTABLE – WHO HAD THE TEMERITY TO LOCK YOU IN THAT OLD CHEST?
IT WAS THE GANG WHO STOLE THE AUCHENSHUGGLE DIAMOND – AND THEY'RE AWAY TO LOOK FOR IT ON YOUR CROFT!
THEY'LL NEFFER FIND IT – I'VE HIDDEN IT IN THE DOOR OF OUR CONVENIENCE – AND ONLY MYSELF AND LACHIE KNOWS IT'S THERE!
BY CHOVE, I'M IN LUCK – HERE'S SOME EASTER VISITORS!
HEH, MISSUS – WHERR IS IT? WE'RE DESPERATE MEN!
MRS OG'S B+B.
2219
OCH THESE TOWNIES ARE AWFUL SHY ABOUT SOME THINGS!
IT'S ROUND THE BACK, CHENTLEMEN – CHUST PAST THE HEN HOUSE!

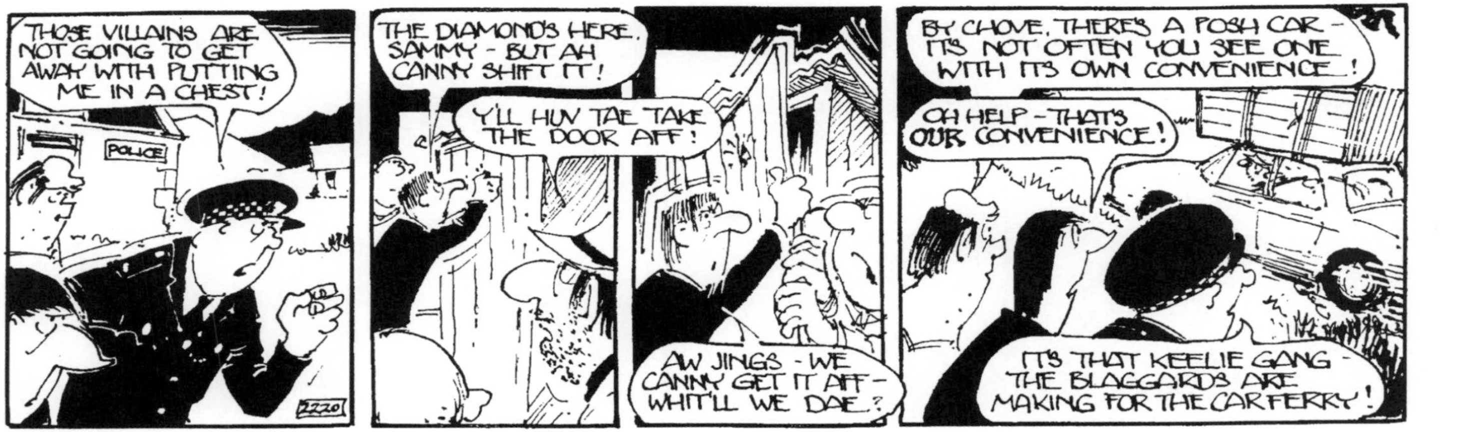
THOSE VILLAINS ARE NOT GOING TO GET AWAY WITH PUTTING ME IN A CHEST!
POLICE
2220
THE DIAMOND'S HERE, SAMMY - BUT AH CANNY SHIFT IT!
Y'LL HUV TAE TAKE THE DOOR AFF!
AW JINGS - WE CANNY GET IT AFF - WHIT'LL WE DAE?
BY CHOVE, THERE'S A POSH CAR - IT'S NOT OFTEN YOU SEE ONE WITH ITS OWN CONVENIENCE!
OH HELP - THAT'S OUR CONVENIENCE!
IT'S THAT KEELIE GANG - THE BLAGGARDS ARE MAKING FOR THE CAR FERRY!

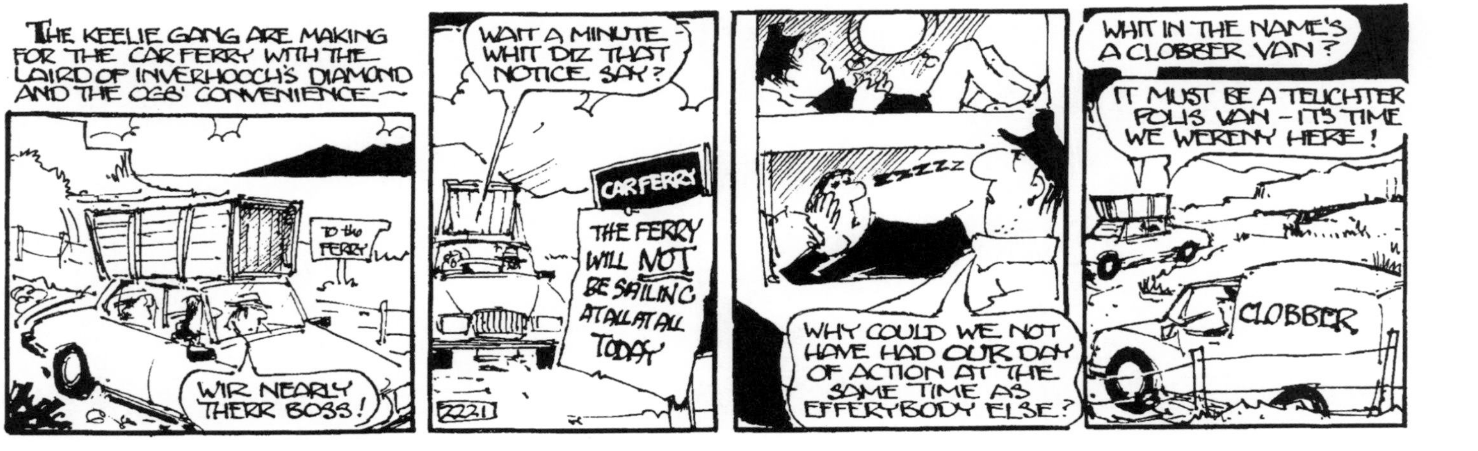
THE KEELIE GANG ARE MAKING FOR THE CAR FERRY WITH THE LAIRD OF INVERHOOCH'S DIAMOND AND THE OGS' CONVENIENCE -
TO the FERRY
WIR NEARLY THERR BOSS!
WAIT A MINUTE - WHIT DIZ THAT NOTICE SAY?
CAR FERRY
THE FERRY WILL NOT BE SAILING AT ALL AT ALL TODAY
2221
ZZZZZ
WHY COULD WE NOT HAVE HAD OUR DAY OF ACTION AT THE SAME TIME AS EFFERYBODY ELSE?
WHIT IN THE NAME'S A CLOBBER VAN?
IT MUST BE A TEUCHTER POLIS VAN - IT'S TIME WE WERENY HERE!
CLOBBER

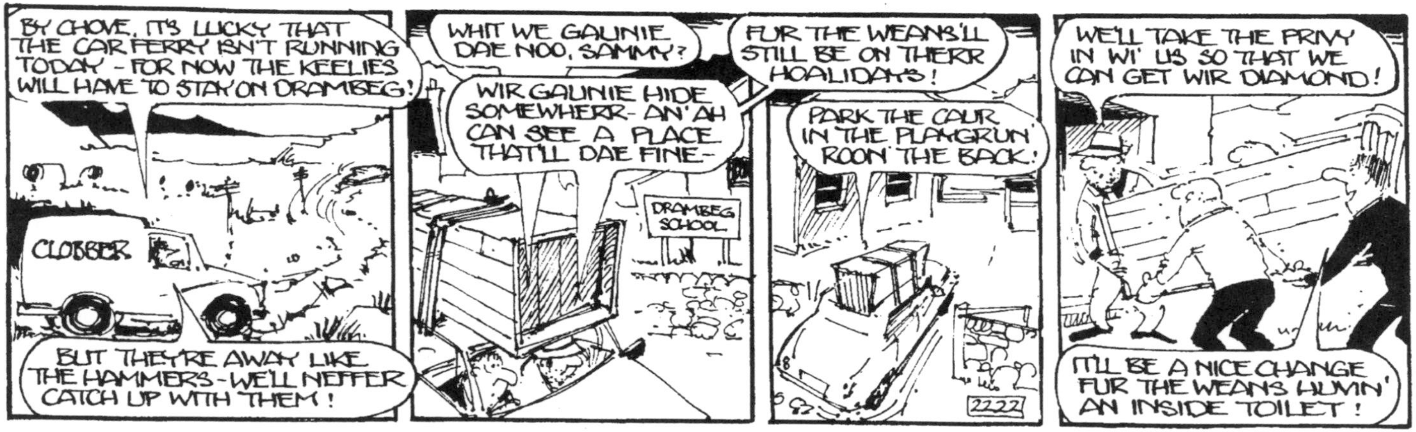
BY CHOVE, IT'S LUCKY THAT THE CAR FERRY ISN'T RUNNING TODAY - FOR NOW THE KEELIES WILL HAVE TO STAY ON DRAMBEG!
CLOBBER
BUT THEY'RE AWAY LIKE THE HAMMERS - WE'LL NEFFER CATCH UP WITH THEM!
WHIT WE GAUNIE DAE NOO, SAMMY?
WIR GAUNIE HIDE SOMEWHERR - AN' AH CAN SEE A PLACE THAT'LL DAE FINE -
DRAMBEG SCHOOL
FUR THE WEANS'LL STILL BE ON THERR HOALIDAYS!
PARK THE CAUR IN THE PLAYGRUN' ROON' THE BACK!
2222
WE'LL TAKE THE PRIVY IN WI' US SO THAT WE CAN GET WIR DIAMOND!
IT'LL BE A NICE CHANGE FUR THE WEANS HUVIN' AN INSIDE TOILET!

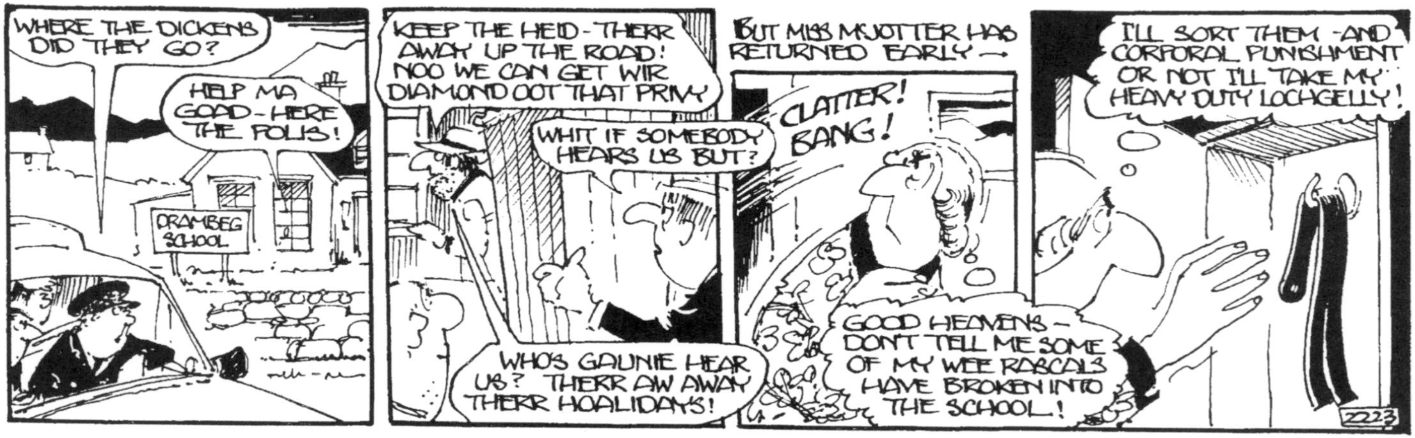
WHERE THE DICKENS DID THEY GO?
HELP MA GOAD - HERE THE POLIS!
DRAMBEG SCHOOL
KEEP THE HEID - THERR AWAY UP THE ROAD! NOO WE CAN GET WIR DIAMOND OOT THAT PRIVY
WHIT IF SOMEBODY HEARS US BUT?
WHO'S GAUNIE HEAR US? THERR AW AWAY THERR HOALIDAYS!
BUT MISS McJOTTER HAS RETURNED EARLY -
CLATTER! BANG!
GOOD HEAVENS - DON'T TELL ME SOME OF MY WEE RASCALS HAVE BROKEN INTO THE SCHOOL!
I'LL SORT THEM - AND CORPORAL PUNISHMENT OR NOT I'LL TAKE MY HEAVY DUTY LOCHGELLY!
2223

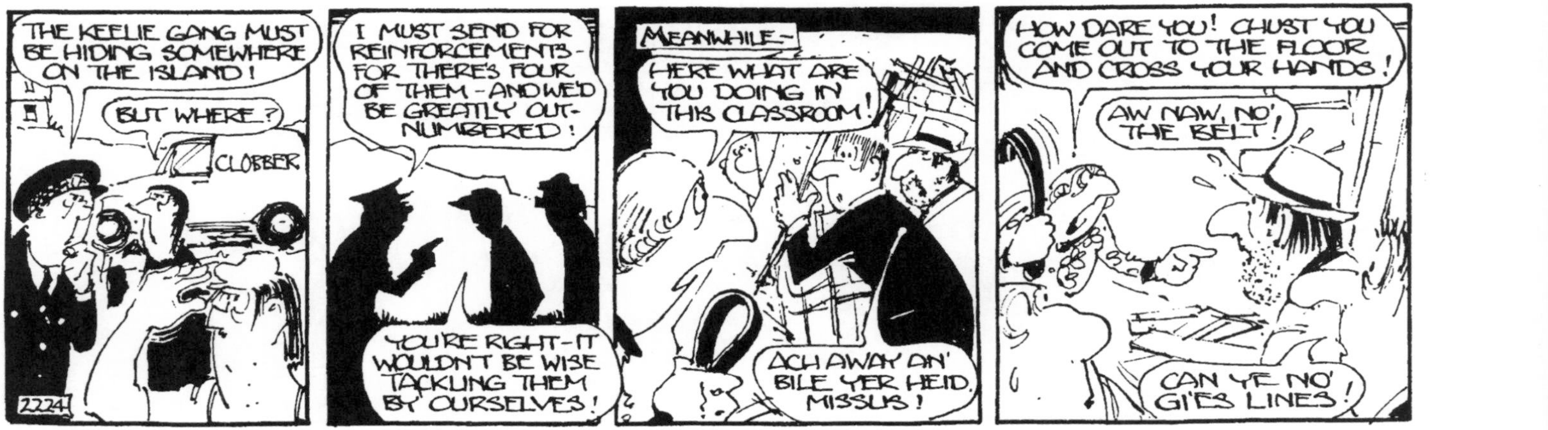
THE KEELIE GANG MUST BE HIDING SOMEWHERE ON THE ISLAND!
BUT WHERE?
CLOBBER
2224
I MUST SEND FOR REINFORCEMENTS - FOR THERE'S FOUR OF THEM - AND WE'D BE GREATLY OUT-NUMBERED!
YOU'RE RIGHT - IT WOULDN'T BE WISE TACKLING THEM BY OURSELVES!
MEANWHILE-
HERE WHAT ARE YOU DOING IN THIS CLASSROOM!
ACH AWAY AN' BILE YER HEID, MISSUS!
HOW DARE YOU! CHUST YOU COME OUT TO THE FLOOR AND CROSS YOUR HANDS!
AW NAW, NO' THE BELT!
CAN YE NO' GI'ES LINES!

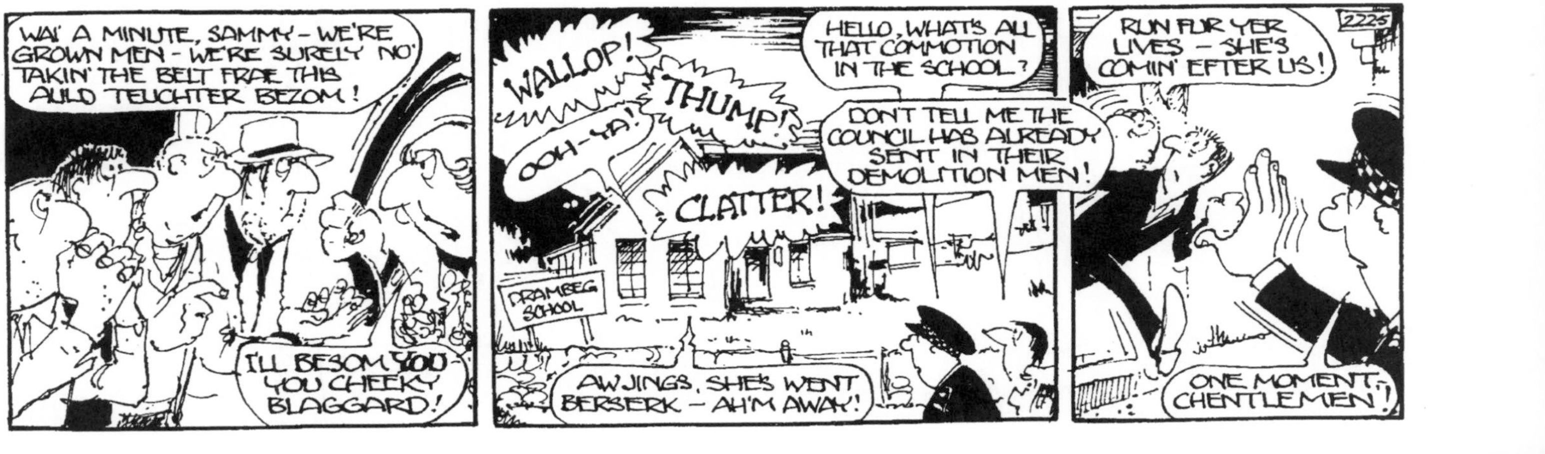
WAI' A MINUTE, SAMMY - WE'RE GROWN MEN - WE'RE SURELY NO' TAKIN' THE BELT FRAE THIS AULD TEUCHTER BEZOM!
I'LL BESOM YOU - YOU CHEEKY BLAGGARD!
WALLOP!
OOH-YA!
THUMP!
CLATTER!
DRAMBEG SCHOOL
HELLO, WHAT'S ALL THAT COMMOTION IN THE SCHOOL?
DON'T TELL ME THE COUNCIL HAS ALREADY SENT IN THEIR DEMOLITION MEN!
AWJINGS, SHE'S WENT BERSERK - AH'M AWAY!
2225
RUN FUR YER LIVES - SHE'S COMIN' EFTER US!
ONE MOMENT, CHENTLEMEN!

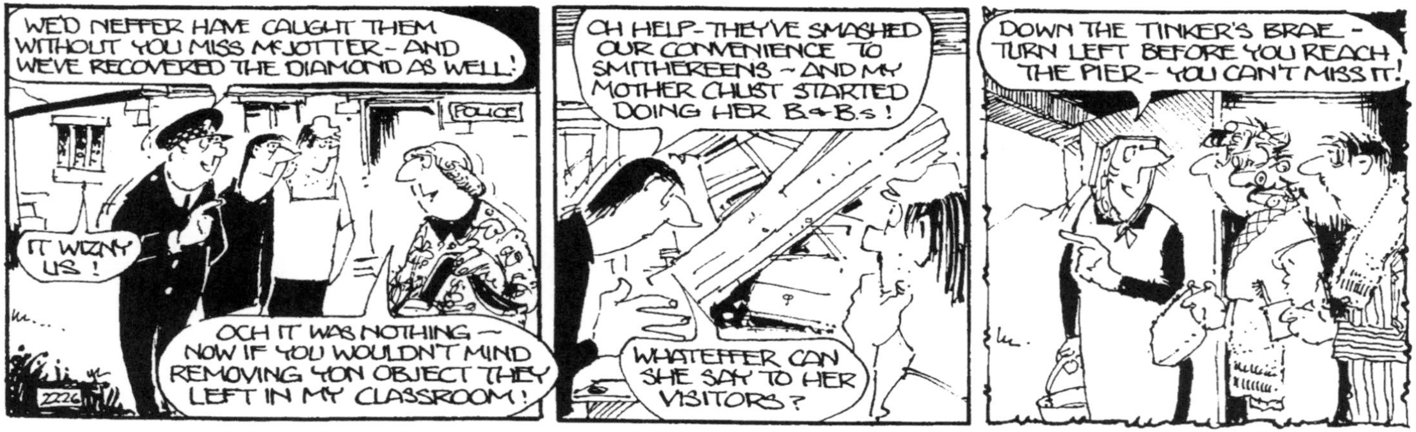
WE'D NEFFER HAVE CAUGHT THEM WITHOUT YOU MISS McJOTTER – AND WE'VE RECOVERED THE DIAMOND AS WELL!
POLICE
IT WIZNY US!
OCH IT WAS NOTHING – NOW IF YOU WOULDN'T MIND REMOVING YON OBJECT THEY LEFT IN MY CLASSROOM!
2226
OH HELP – THEY'VE SMASHED OUR CONVENIENCE TO SMITHEREENS – AND MY MOTHER CHUST STARTED DOING HER B.&B.s!
WHATEFFER CAN SHE SAY TO HER VISITORS?
DOWN THE TINKER'S BRAE – TURN LEFT BEFORE YOU REACH THE PIER – YOU CAN'T MISS IT!

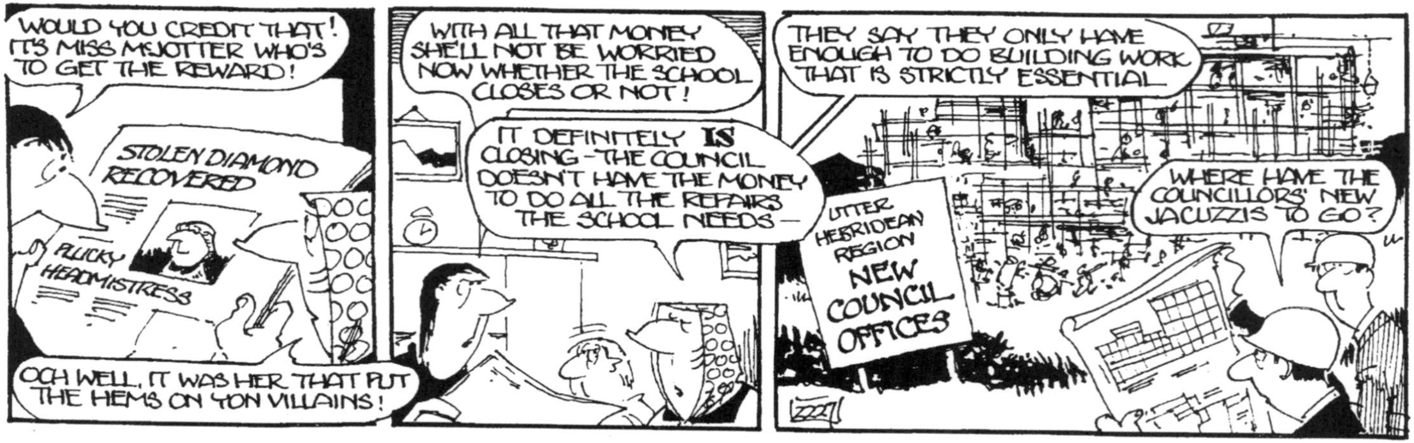
WOULD YOU CREDIT THAT! IT'S MISS McJOTTER WHO'S TO GET THE REWARD!
STOLEN DIAMOND RECOVERED
PLUCKY HEADMISTRESS
OCH WELL, IT WAS HER THAT PUT THE HEMS ON YON VILLAINS!
WITH ALL THAT MONEY SHE'LL NOT BE WORRIED NOW WHETHER THE SCHOOL CLOSES OR NOT!
IT DEFINITELY IS CLOSING – THE COUNCIL DOESN'T HAVE THE MONEY TO DO ALL THE REPAIRS THE SCHOOL NEEDS –
THEY SAY THEY ONLY HAVE ENOUGH TO DO BUILDING WORK THAT IS STRICTLY ESSENTIAL
UTTER HEBRIDEAN REGION NEW COUNCIL OFFICES
WHERE HAVE THE COUNCILLORS' NEW JACUZZIS TO GO?
2227

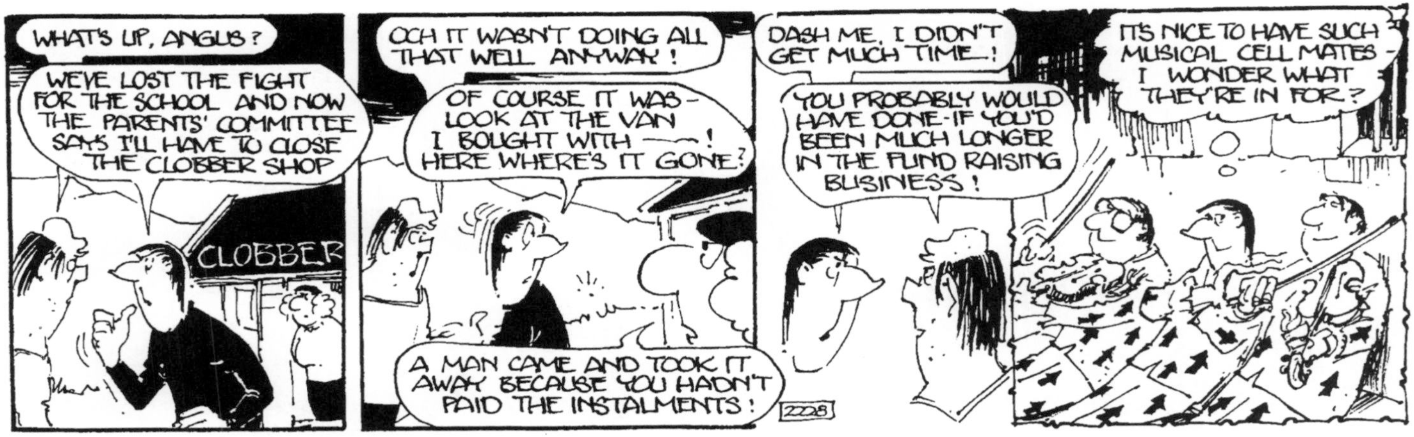
WHAT'S UP, ANGUS?
WE'VE LOST THE FIGHT FOR THE SCHOOL AND NOW THE PARENTS' COMMITTEE SAYS I'LL HAVE TO CLOSE THE CLOBBER SHOP
CLOBBER
OCH IT WASN'T DOING ALL THAT WELL ANYWAY!
OF COURSE IT WAS - LOOK AT THE VAN I BOUGHT WITH ——! HERE WHERE'S IT GONE?
A MAN CAME AND TOOK IT AWAY BECAUSE YOU HADN'T PAID THE INSTALMENTS!
2228
DASH ME, I DIDN'T GET MUCH TIME!
YOU PROBABLY WOULD HAVE DONE - IF YOU'D BEEN MUCH LONGER IN THE FUND RAISING BUSINESS!
IT'S NICE TO HAVE SUCH MUSICAL CELL MATES - I WONDER WHAT THEY'RE IN FOR?

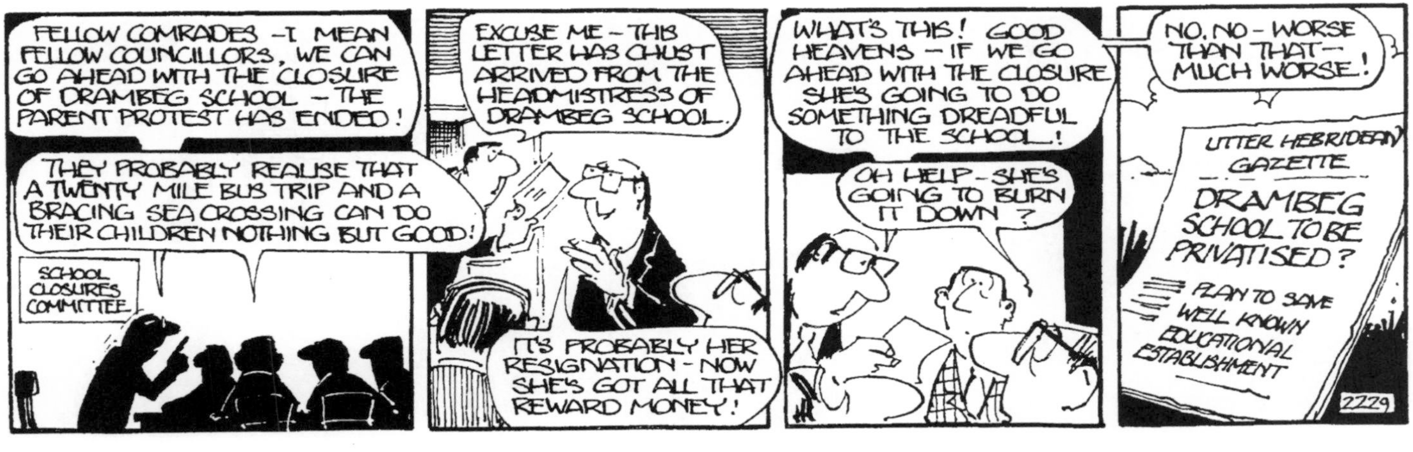
FELLOW COMRADES - I MEAN FELLOW COUNCILLORS, WE CAN GO AHEAD WITH THE CLOSURE OF DRAMBEG SCHOOL - THE PARENT PROTEST HAS ENDED!
THEY PROBABLY REALISE THAT A TWENTY MILE BUS TRIP AND A BRACING SEA CROSSING CAN DO THEIR CHILDREN NOTHING BUT GOOD!
SCHOOL CLOSURES COMMITTEE
EXCUSE ME - THIS LETTER HAS CHUST ARRIVED FROM THE HEADMISTRESS OF DRAMBEG SCHOOL.
IT'S PROBABLY HER RESIGNATION - NOW SHE'S GOT ALL THAT REWARD MONEY!
WHAT'S THIS! GOOD HEAVENS - IF WE GO AHEAD WITH THE CLOSURE SHE'S GOING TO DO SOMETHING DREADFUL TO THE SCHOOL!
OH HELP - SHE'S GOING TO BURN IT DOWN?
NO, NO - WORSE THAN THAT - MUCH WORSE!
UTTER HEBRIDEAN GAZETTE
DRAMBEG SCHOOL TO BE PRIVATISED?
PLAN TO SAVE WELL KNOWN EDUCATIONAL ESTABLISHMENT
2229

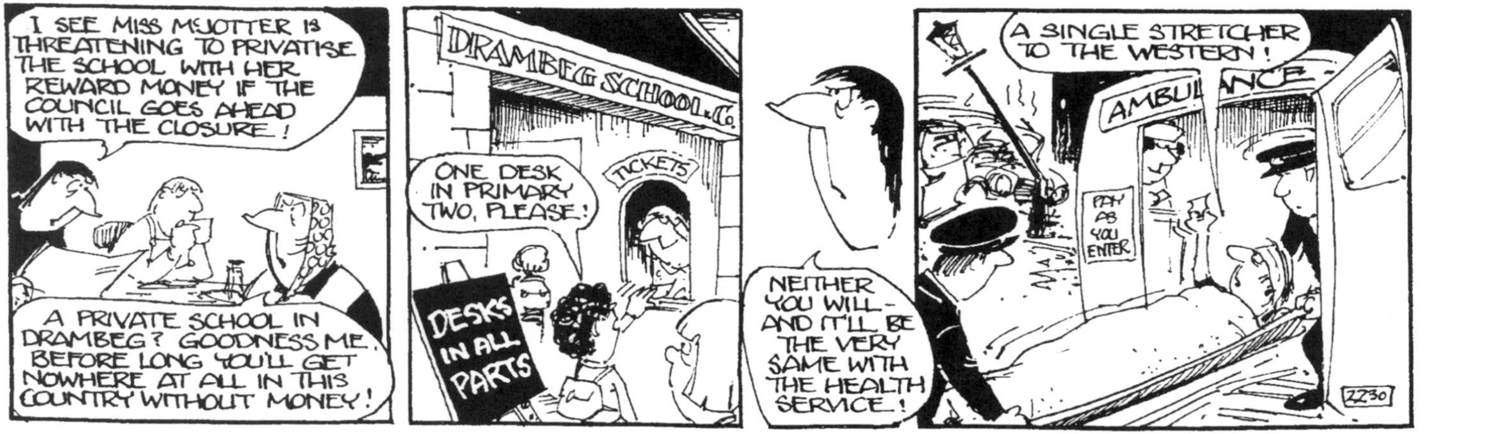
I SEE MISS McJOTTER IS THREATENING TO PRIVATISE THE SCHOOL WITH HER REWARD MONEY IF THE COUNCIL GOES AHEAD WITH THE CLOSURE!
A PRIVATE SCHOOL IN DRAMBEG? GOODNESS ME. BEFORE LONG YOU'LL GET NOWHERE AT ALL IN THIS COUNTRY WITHOUT MONEY!
DRAMBEG SCHOOL Co.
TICKETS
ONE DESK IN PRIMARY TWO, PLEASE!
DESKS IN ALL PARTS
NEITHER YOU WILL- AND IT'LL BE THE VERY SAME WITH THE HEALTH SERVICE!
A SINGLE STRETCHER TO THE WESTERN!
AMBULANCE
PAY AS YOU ENTER
2230

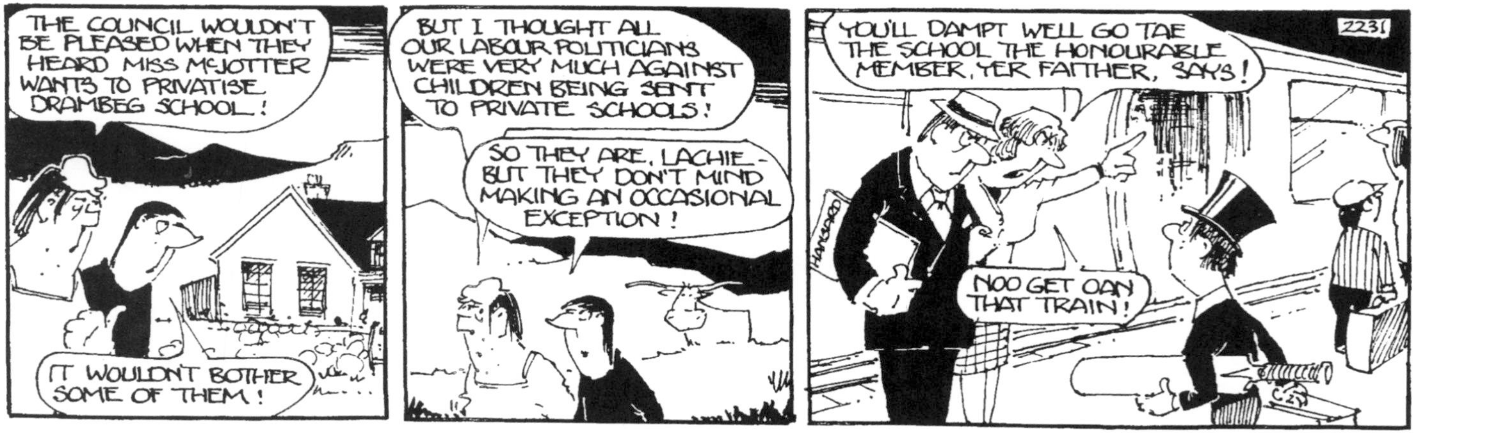
THE COUNCIL WOULDN'T BE PLEASED WHEN THEY HEARD MISS McJOTTER WANTS TO PRIVATISE DRAMBEG SCHOOL!
IT WOULDN'T BOTHER SOME OF THEM!
BUT I THOUGHT ALL OUR LABOUR POLITICIANS WERE VERY MUCH AGAINST CHILDREN BEING SENT TO PRIVATE SCHOOLS!
SO THEY ARE, LACHIE- BUT THEY DON'T MIND MAKING AN OCCASIONAL EXCEPTION!
2231
YOU'LL DAMPT WELL GO TAE THE SCHOOL THE HONOURABLE MEMBER, YER FAITHER, SAYS!
NOO GET OAN THAT TRAIN!
HANSARD

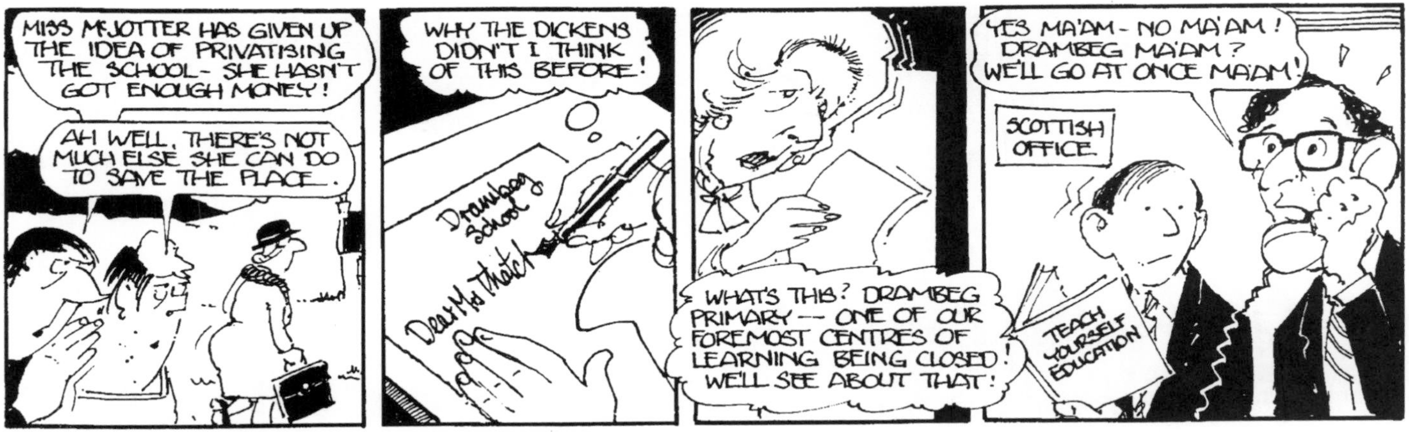
MISS McJOTTER HAS GIVEN UP THE IDEA OF PRIVATISING THE SCHOOL- SHE HASN'T GOT ENOUGH MONEY!
AH WELL, THERE'S NOT MUCH ELSE SHE CAN DO TO SAVE THE PLACE.
WHY THE DICKENS DIDN'T I THINK OF THIS BEFORE!
Drambeg School
Dear Mrs Thatch
WHAT'S THIS? DRAMBEG PRIMARY -- ONE OF OUR FOREMOST CENTRES OF LEARNING BEING CLOSED! WE'LL SEE ABOUT THAT!
YES MA'AM - NO MA'AM! DRAMBEG MA'AM? WE'LL GO AT ONCE MA'AM!
SCOTTISH OFFICE
TEACH YOURSELF EDUCATION

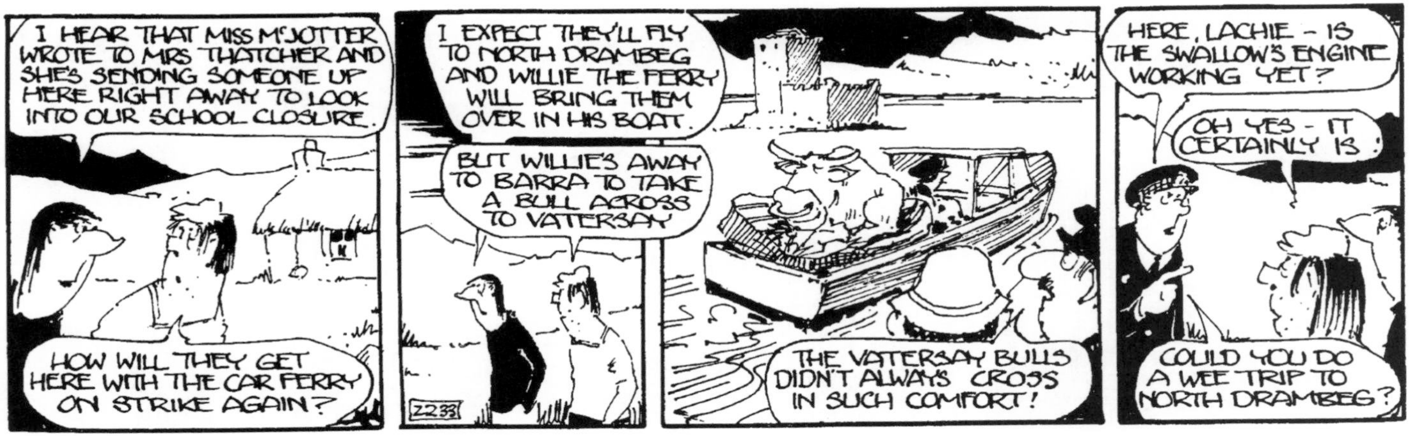
I HEAR THAT MISS McJOTTER WROTE TO MRS THATCHER AND SHE'S SENDING SOMEONE UP HERE RIGHT AWAY TO LOOK INTO OUR SCHOOL CLOSURE.
HOW WILL THEY GET HERE WITH THE CAR FERRY ON STRIKE AGAIN?
I EXPECT THEY'LL FLY TO NORTH DRAMBEG AND WILLIE THE FERRY WILL BRING THEM OVER IN HIS BOAT.
BUT WILLIE'S AWAY TO BARRA TO TAKE A BULL ACROSS TO VATERSAY
2233
THE VATERSAY BULLS DIDN'T ALWAYS CROSS IN SUCH COMFORT!
HERE, LACHIE - IS THE SWALLOW'S ENGINE WORKING YET?
OH YES - IT CERTAINLY IS!
COULD YOU DO A WEE TRIP TO NORTH DRAMBEG?

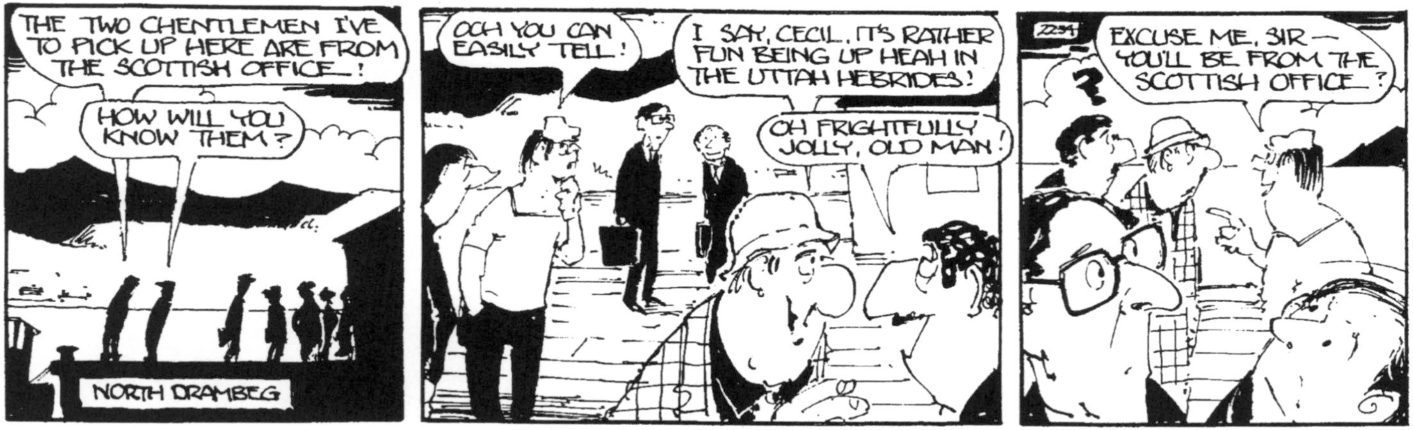
THE TWO CHENTLEMEN I'VE TO PICK UP HERE ARE FROM THE SCOTTISH OFFICE!
HOW WILL YOU KNOW THEM?
NORTH DRAMBEG
OCH YOU CAN EASILY TELL!
I SAY, CECIL, IT'S RATHER FUN BEING UP HEAH IN THE UTTAH HEBRIDES!
OH FRIGHTFULLY JOLLY, OLD MAN!
2234
?
EXCUSE ME, SIR — YOU'LL BE FROM THE SCOTTISH OFFICE?

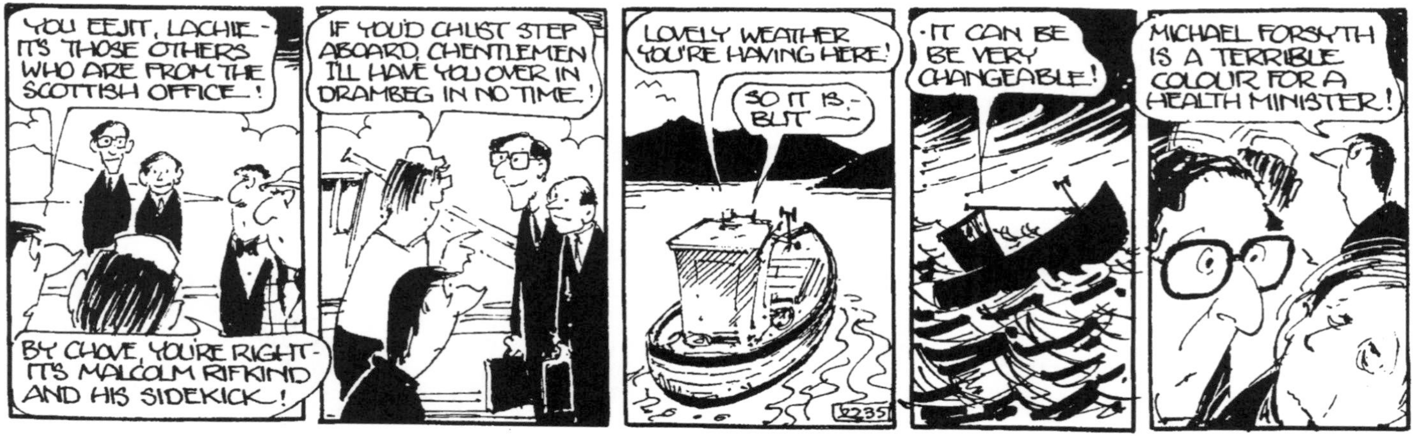
YOU EEJIT, LACHIE - IT'S THOSE OTHERS WHO ARE FROM THE SCOTTISH OFFICE!
BY CHOVE, YOU'RE RIGHT - IT'S MALCOLM RIFKIND AND HIS SIDEKICK!
IF YOU'D CHUST STEP ABOARD, CHENTLEMEN I'LL HAVE YOU OVER IN DRAMBEG IN NO TIME!
LOVELY WEATHER YOU'RE HAVING HERE!
SO IT IS - BUT —
2235
- IT CAN BE BE VERY CHANGEABLE!
MICHAEL FORSYTH IS A TERRIBLE COLOUR FOR A HEALTH MINISTER!

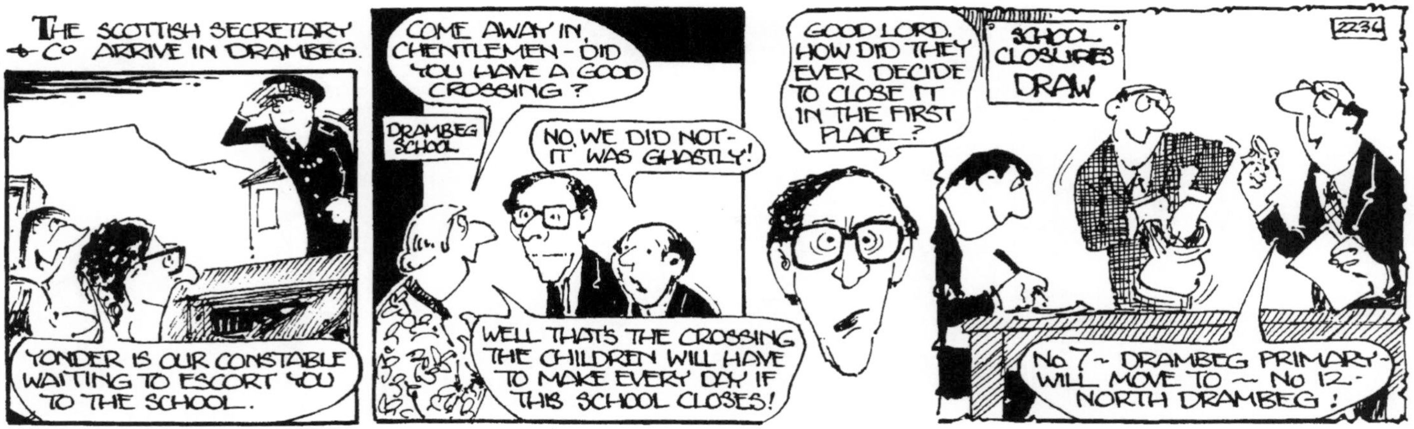
THE SCOTTISH SECRETARY & Co ARRIVE IN DRAMBEG.
YONDER IS OUR CONSTABLE WAITING TO ESCORT YOU TO THE SCHOOL.
DRAMBEG SCHOOL
COME AWAY IN, CHENTLEMEN - DID YOU HAVE A GOOD CROSSING?
NO, WE DID NOT - IT WAS GHASTLY!
WELL THAT'S THE CROSSING THE CHILDREN WILL HAVE TO MAKE EVERY DAY IF THIS SCHOOL CLOSES!
GOOD LORD, HOW DID THEY EVER DECIDE TO CLOSE IT IN THE FIRST PLACE?
SCHOOL CLOSURES DRAW
2236
No 7 ~ DRAMBEG PRIMARY - WILL MOVE TO ~ No 12 - NORTH DRAMBEG!

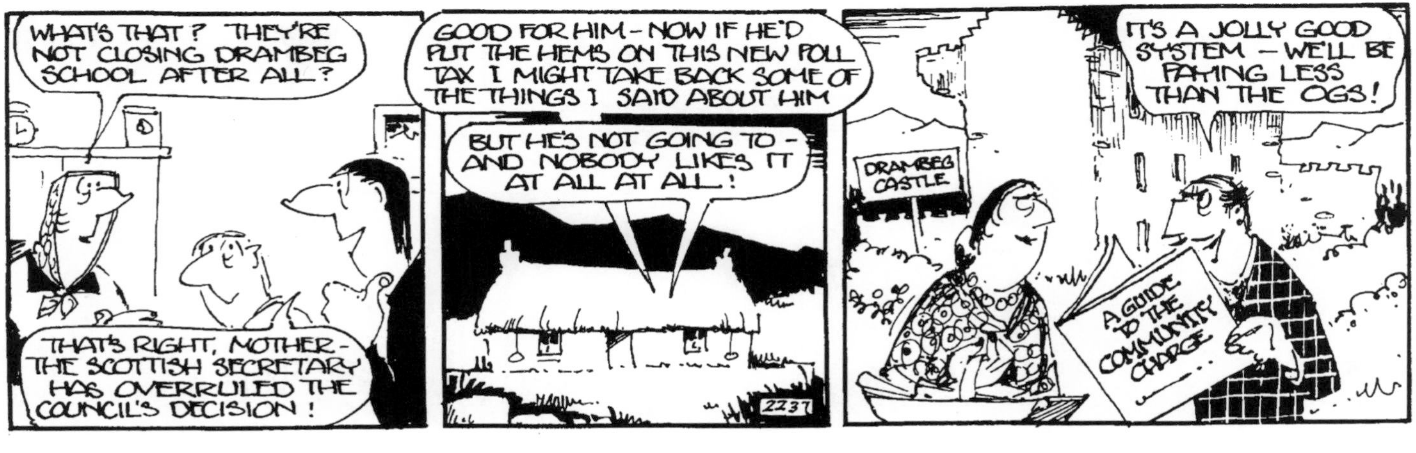
WHAT'S THAT? THEY'RE NOT CLOSING DRAMBEG SCHOOL AFTER ALL?
THAT'S RIGHT, MOTHER - THE SCOTTISH SECRETARY HAS OVERRULED THE COUNCIL'S DECISION!
GOOD FOR HIM - NOW IF HE'D PUT THE HEMS ON THIS NEW POLL TAX I MIGHT TAKE BACK SOME OF THE THINGS I SAID ABOUT HIM
BUT HE'S NOT GOING TO - AND NOBODY LIKES IT AT ALL AT ALL!
2237
DRAMBEG CASTLE
IT'S A JOLLY GOOD SYSTEM - WE'LL BE PAYING LESS THAN THE OGS!
A GUIDE TO THE COMMUNITY CHARGE...

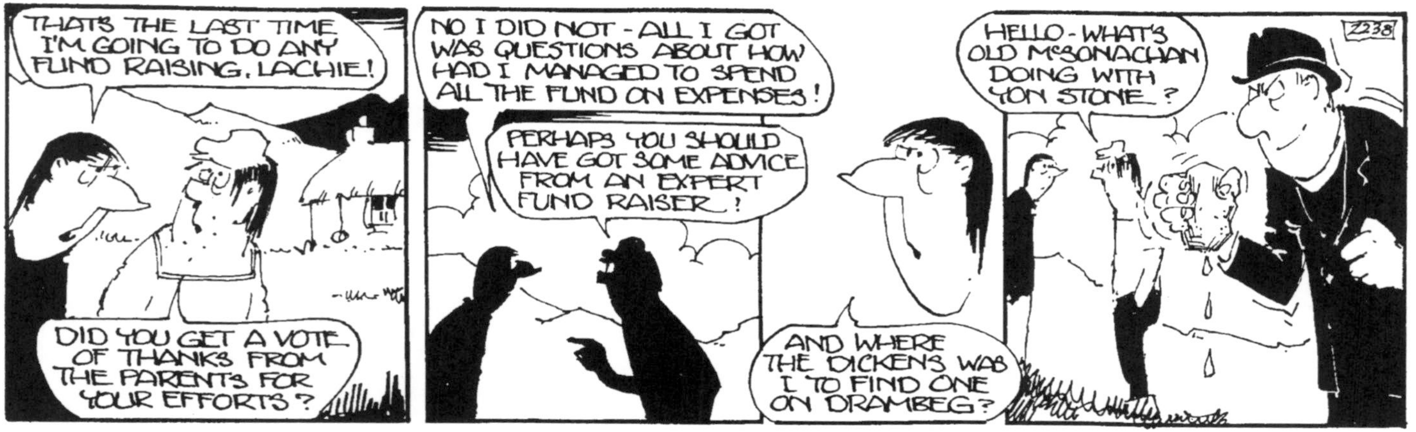
THAT'S THE LAST TIME I'M GOING TO DO ANY FUND RAISING, LACHIE!
DID YOU GET A VOTE OF THANKS FROM THE PARENTS FOR YOUR EFFORTS?
NO I DID NOT - ALL I GOT WAS QUESTIONS ABOUT HOW HAD I MANAGED TO SPEND ALL THE FUND ON EXPENSES!
PERHAPS YOU SHOULD HAVE GOT SOME ADVICE FROM AN EXPERT FUND RAISER?
AND WHERE THE DICKENS WAS I TO FIND ONE ON DRAMBEG?
2238
HELLO - WHAT'S OLD McSONACHAN DOING WITH YON STONE?

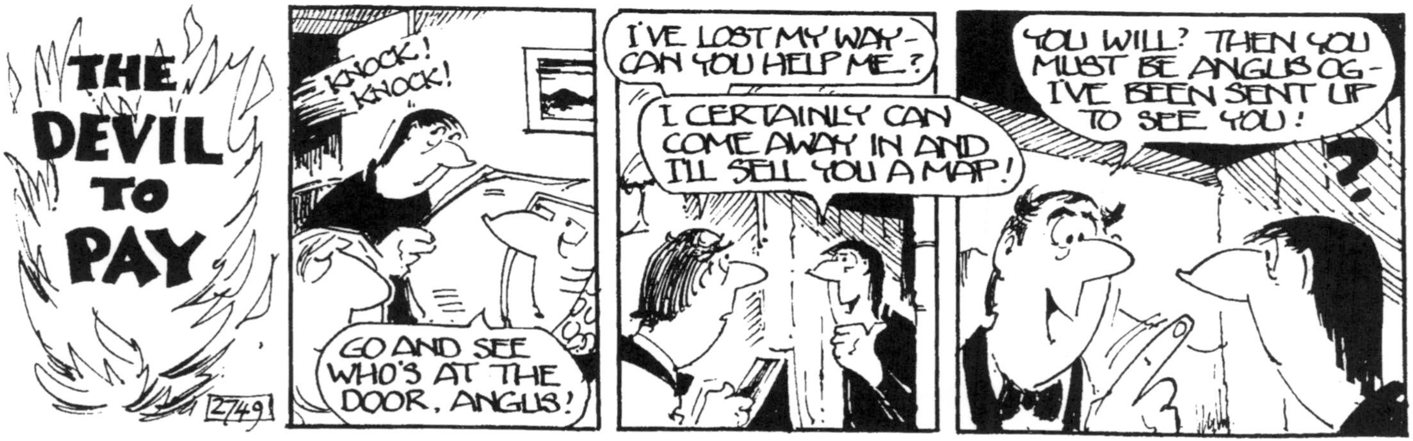
THE DEVIL TO PAY
2749
KNOCK! KNOCK!
GO AND SEE WHO'S AT THE DOOR, ANGUS!
I'VE LOST MY WAY - CAN YOU HELP ME?
I CERTAINLY CAN COME AWAY IN AND I'LL SELL YOU A MAP!
YOU WILL? THEN YOU MUST BE ANGUS OG - I'VE BEEN SENT UP TO SEE YOU!
?

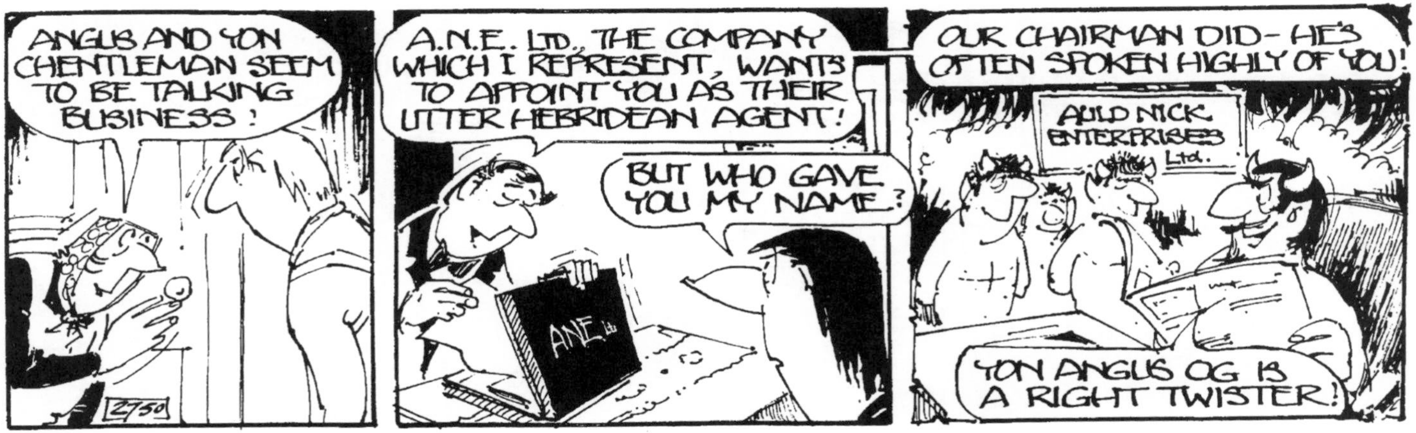
ANGUS AND YON CHENTLEMAN SEEM TO BE TALKING BUSINESS!
2750
A.N.E. LTD., THE COMPANY WHICH I REPRESENT, WANTS TO APPOINT YOU AS THEIR UTTER HEBRIDEAN AGENT!
ANE Ltd
BUT WHO GAVE YOU MY NAME?
OUR CHAIRMAN DID - HE'S OFTEN SPOKEN HIGHLY OF YOU!
AULD NICK ENTERPRISES Ltd.
YON ANGUS OG IS A RIGHT TWISTER!

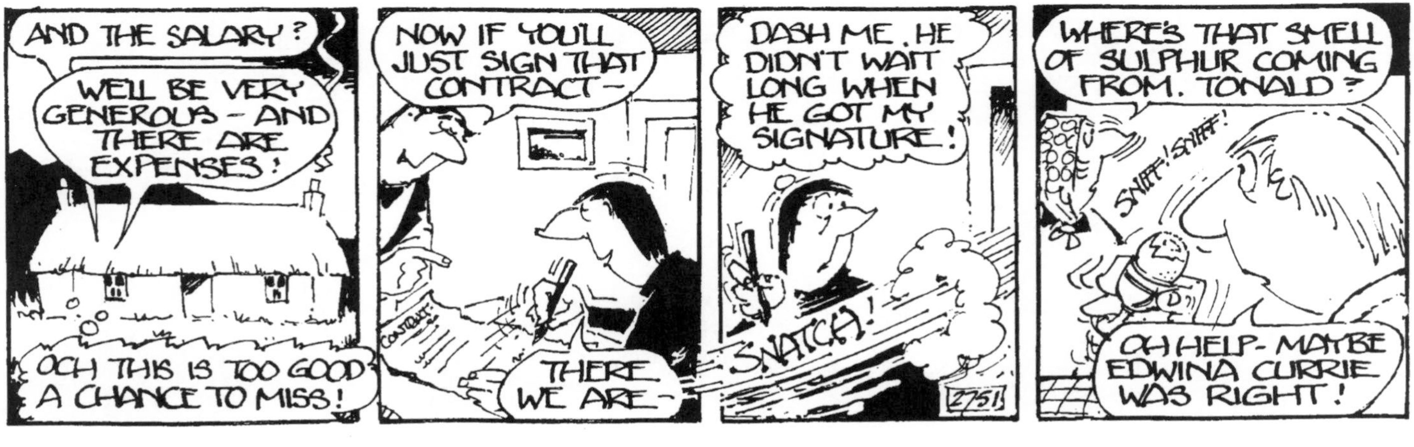
AND THE SALARY?
WE'LL BE VERY GENEROUS - AND THERE ARE EXPENSES!
OCH THIS IS TOO GOOD A CHANCE TO MISS!
NOW IF YOU'LL JUST SIGN THAT CONTRACT -
THERE WE ARE -
SNATCH!
DASH ME. HE DIDN'T WAIT LONG WHEN HE GOT MY SIGNATURE!
2751
WHERE'S THAT SMELL OF SULPHUR COMING FROM. TONALD?
SNIFF! SNIFF!
OCH HELP - MAYBE EDWINA CURRIE WAS RIGHT!

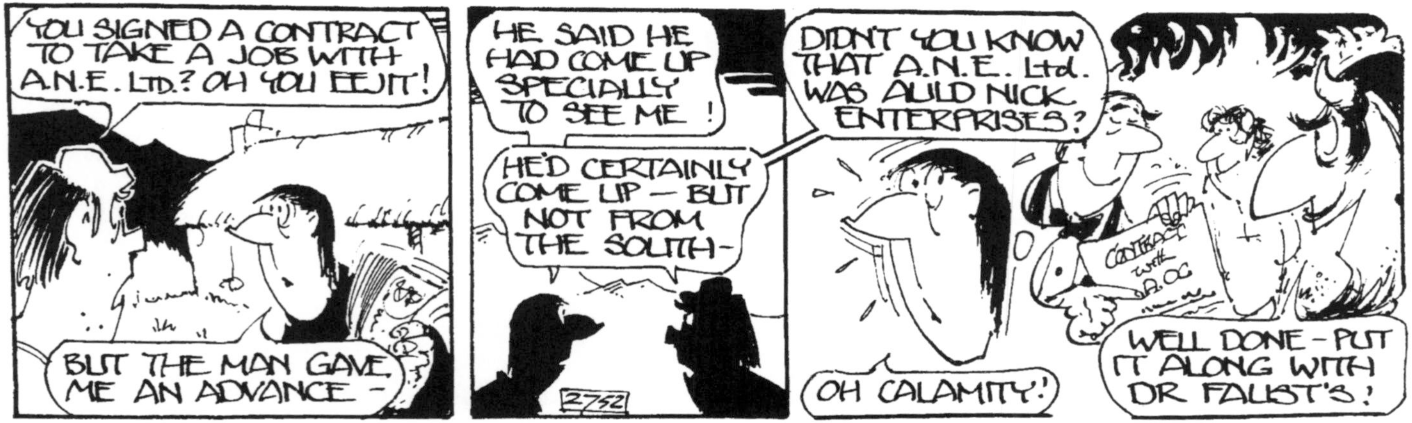
YOU SIGNED A CONTRACT TO TAKE A JOB WITH A.N.E. LTD.? OH YOU EEJIT!
BUT THE MAN GAVE ME AN ADVANCE –
HE SAID HE HAD COME UP SPECIALLY TO SEE ME!
HE'D CERTAINLY COME UP – BUT NOT FROM THE SOUTH –
2752
DIDN'T YOU KNOW THAT A.N.E. Ltd. WAS AULD NICK ENTERPRISES?
OH CALAMITY!
WELL DONE – PUT IT ALONG WITH DR FAUST'S!

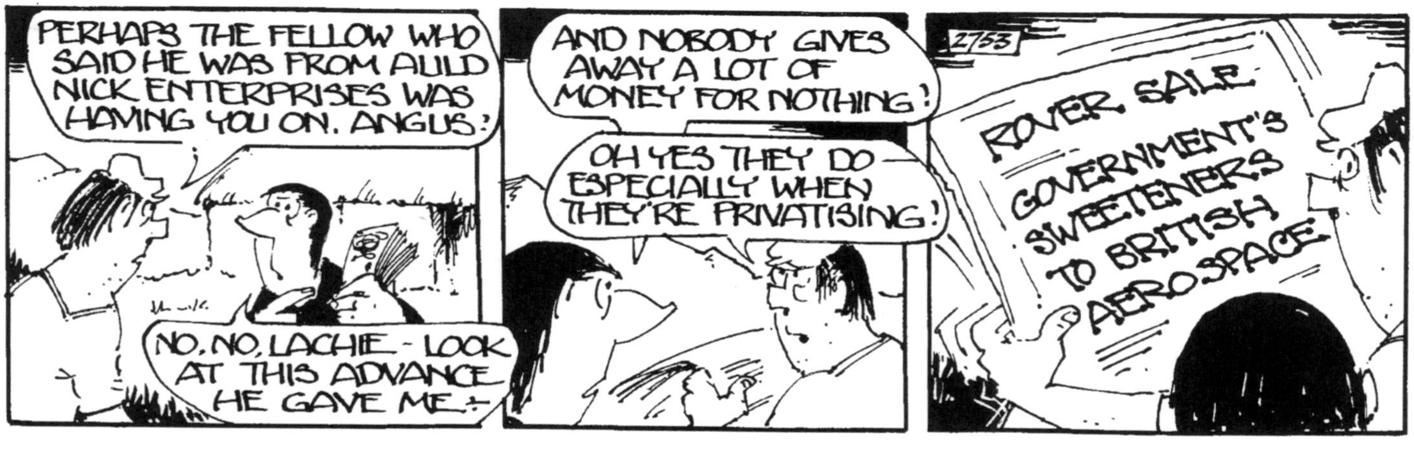
PERHAPS THE FELLOW WHO SAID HE WAS FROM AULD NICK ENTERPRISES WAS HAVING YOU ON, ANGUS!
NO, NO, LACHIE – LOOK AT THIS ADVANCE HE GAVE ME –
AND NOBODY GIVES AWAY A LOT OF MONEY FOR NOTHING!
OH YES THEY DO – ESPECIALLY WHEN THEY'RE PRIVATISING!
2753
ROVER SALE
GOVERNMENT'S SWEETENERS TO BRITISH AEROSPACE

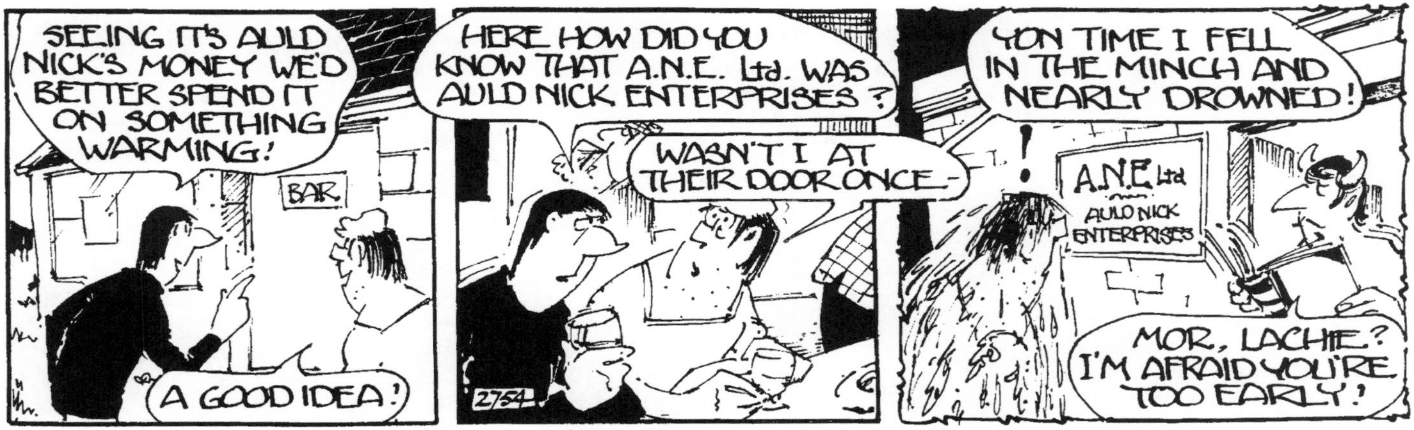
SEEING IT'S AULD NICK'S MONEY WE'D BETTER SPEND IT ON SOMETHING WARMING!
BAR
A GOOD IDEA!
HERE HOW DID YOU KNOW THAT A.N.E. Ltd. WAS AULD NICK ENTERPRISES?
WASN'T I AT THEIR DOOR ONCE -
2754
YON TIME I FELL IN THE MINCH AND NEARLY DROWNED!
A.N.E. Ltd
AULD NICK ENTERPRISES
MOR, LACHIE? I'M AFRAID YOU'RE TOO EARLY!

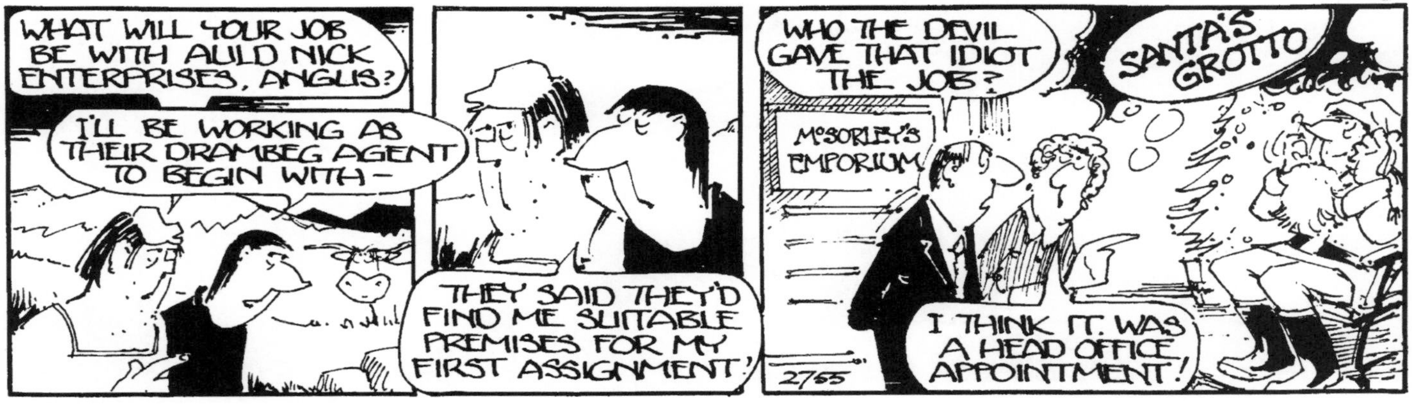
WHAT WILL YOUR JOB BE WITH AULD NICK ENTERPRISES, ANGUS?
I'LL BE WORKING AS THEIR DRAMBEG AGENT TO BEGIN WITH -
THEY SAID THEY'D FIND ME SUITABLE PREMISES FOR MY FIRST ASSIGNMENT!
WHO THE DEVIL GAVE THAT IDIOT THE JOB?
SANTA'S GROTTO
McSORLEY'S EMPORIUM
I THINK IT WAS A HEAD OFFICE APPOINTMENT!
2755

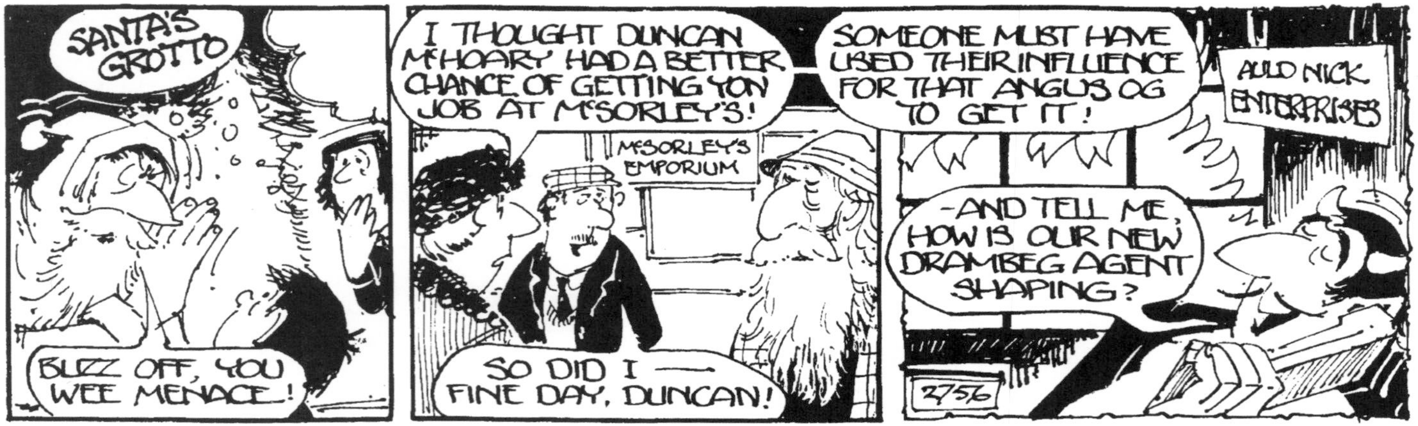
SANTA'S GROTTO
BUZZ OFF, YOU WEE MENACE!
I THOUGHT DUNCAN McHOARY HAD A BETTER CHANCE OF GETTING YON JOB AT McSORLEY'S!
McSORLEY'S EMPORIUM
SO DID I — FINE DAY, DUNCAN!
SOMEONE MUST HAVE USED THEIR INFLUENCE FOR THAT ANGUS OG TO GET IT!
AULD NICK ENTERPRISES
-AND TELL ME, HOW IS OUR NEW DRAMBEG AGENT SHAPING?
2756

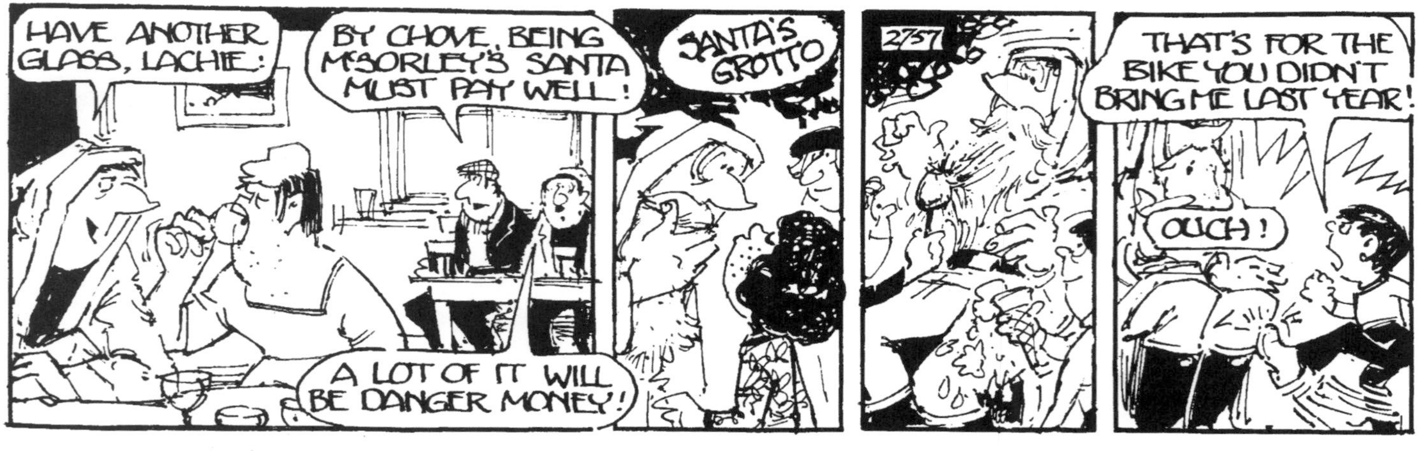
HAVE ANOTHER GLASS, LACHIE!
BY CHOVE, BEING McSORLEY'S SANTA MUST PAY WELL!
A LOT OF IT WILL BE DANGER MONEY!
SANTA'S GROTTO
2757
THAT'S FOR THE BIKE YOU DIDN'T BRING ME LAST YEAR!
OUCH!